"A sapphic delight, full of jousts, jaunts, and courtly love. *Lady's Knight* sparkles with wit and charm, and has lady knights to swoon over. Kaufman and Spooner will leave you breathless."
—**C. S. Pacat, *New York Times* bestselling author of *Dark Rise***

"Kaufman and Spooner are auto-buy authors for me, always guaranteed to get my heart pumping with their page-turning romance and high-stakes adventure." —**Susan Dennard, *New York Times* bestselling author**

"There are a lot of damsels in *Lady's Knight*, but none of them need a man to fix their problems. (Men seem to be the source of the problems, in fact.) Wholesome, heartfelt, and more fun than cheesecake on a stick, Kaufman and Spooner's latest book is all about women's work. You know, jousting, dragonslaying, and saving the kingdom—all while looking fabulous." —**Jodi Meadows, coauthor of *New York Times* bestselling novels *My Lady Jane* and *My Plain Jane***

"Clever, funny, thrilling, and romantic—*Lady's Knight* will inspire readers to take up their swords to fight dragons and the patriarchy. Perfect for fans of *A Knight's Tale* and anyone who loves a romantasy with wit, charm, and the occasional comedic fourth wall break." —**F. T. Lukens, *New York Times* bestselling author of *So This Is Ever After***

"You'll laugh, you'll cry, and you'll be ready to fight any dragon after reading this delightful tale full of swoony romance, heart-racing action, and the very best banter in the realm!" —**Beth Revis, *New York Times* bestselling coauthor of *Night of the Witch***

"Writing that is above all else marvelously warm, and at the same time witty; adventure and romance that will sweep you off your feet—a double sweep, and a triumph!" —**Sarah Rees Brennan, #1 *Sunday Times* bestselling author of *Long Live Evil***

"Sparkles with wit and romance! So many quotable lines. Not to mention the sexiest gown-lacing scene in modern literature. Like its characters, *Lady's Knight* is endlessly clever and resourceful."
—**Ellen Kushner, award-winning author of *Swordspoint***

"Move over, Lancelot: my new favorite knight is here! *Lady's Knight* is both a whimsical fantasy romp and an ode to the relationships women share with other women—in community, in friendship, and in romance. This roaring good time is perfect for fans of films like *The Princess Bride* and *A Knight's Tale*. Three cheers for *Lady's Knight*!" —**Nicole Brinkley, Oblong Books**

Also by Amie Kaufman and Meagan Spooner

The Other Side of the Sky
Beyond the End of the World

These Broken Stars
This Shattered World
Their Fractured Light

Unearthed
Undying

Also by Meagan Spooner

Hunted
Sherwood

Also by Amie Kaufman
(for children)

Ice Wolves
Scorch Dragons
Battle Born

The World Between Blinks
Rebellion of the Lost

AMIE KAUFMAN & MEAGAN SPOONER

STORYTIDE
An Imprint of HarperCollinsPublishers

Storytide is an imprint of HarperCollins Publishers.

Lady's Knight
Copyright © 2025 by Meagan Spooner and LaRoux Industries Pty Ltd.
All rights reserved. Manufactured in Harrisonburg, VA,
United States of America.
No part of this book may be used or reproduced in any manner
whatsoever without written permission except in the case of brief quotations
embodied in critical articles and reviews. For information, address
HarperCollins Children's Books, a division of HarperCollins Publishers,
195 Broadway, New York, NY 10007.
www.epicreads.com

Library of Congress Control Number: 2024952220
ISBN 978-0-06-289339-0

Typography by Julia Feingold
25 26 27 28 29 LBC 5 4 3 2 1

First Edition

For Freya.

You are never alone.

Contents

CHAPTER 1: *The sort of thing that gets a girl burned at the stake*   4

CHAPTER 2: *Ridiculously, fabulously pink*   14

CHAPTER 3: *Bring it on*   22

CHAPTER 4: *Sir Gawain's not done yet . . . just watch*   29

CHAPTER 5: *Climb down, lady, we're going out!*   36

CHAPTER 6: *I'll have a White Knight, please*   45

CHAPTER 7: *Chivalry is all well and good, but cursed inconvenient at times*   59

CHAPTER 8: *Just put her there*   64

CHAPTER 9: *Don't try to fight it, you'll only hurt yourself*   70

CHAPTER 10: *Nobody ever expects a lady to rappel off a balcony*   78

CHAPTER 11: *You are the girl who would be a knight?*   86

CHAPTER 12: *Mademoiselle le Chevalier*   95

CHAPTER 13: *Off in search of adventure*   99

CHAPTER 14: *Hast Thou Ever . . .*   107

CHAPTER 15: *Everything is context*   121

CHAPTER 16: *She was very much accustomed to people looking at her like they didn't understand what was happening and wanted it all to stop*   131

CHAPTER 17: *Damn those girls and their "tea"*   137

CHAPTER 18: *Maybe we could wash the donkeys*   140

CHAPTER 19: *A deer trying to hide in a pack of ravenous wolves*   145

CHAPTER 20: *Just don't tell the other knights I screamed*   151

CHAPTER 21: *Drop-your-cheesecake-on-a-stick-and-not-even-care spectacular*   162

CHAPTER 22: *The violence is too much for her delicate constitution*   170

Chapter 23: *No lady went in search of the privy alone when she could bring a friend* — 178

Chapter 24: *Don't bring it all the way undone . . .* — 184

Chapter 25: *What a perfectly normal conversational gambit* — 193

Chapter 26: *A wild horse of feeling and emotion* — 208

Chapter 27: *I thought we'd have more time* — 221

Chapter 28: *You are not the first to ask whether a woman could hold a sword* — 232

Chapter 29: *Do you yield?* — 242

Chapter 30: *This goes a lot more smoothly in the ballads* — 255

Chapter 31: *Did that really just happen?* — 261

Chapter 32: *Don't tell me you're scared, Sir Knight* — 267

Chapter 33: *They'll kill anyone who tries to upset the order of things* — 274

Chapter 34: *A girl who knows exactly who she is* — 278

Chapter 35: *Meditations he learned on an ancient mountaintop* — 286

Chapter 36: *Ride off into the sunset with nothing but a change of underwear* — 290

Chapter 37: *You'd be very surprised by what a fancy lady can get done* — 298

Chapter 38: *I can show you a thing or two* — 315

Chapter 39: *If I taught you to dream, then I was wrong* — 323

Chapter 40: *No better than they are* — 331

Chapter 41: *The crowd went wild* — 337

Chapter 42: *The terrible sound of a thousand people not knowing what to say* — 342

Chapter 43: *Someone get this hysterical girl out of here!* — 351

Chapter 44: *A foolish, reckless idiot with her head in the clouds* — 358

Chapter 45: *. . . Or it's tricky to put back together again* — 366

Chapter 46: *It came up from the mine* — 375

CHAPTER 47: *Like she'd ridden straight out of legend*   *388*
CHAPTER 48: *Two wounded creatures, facing each other across*   *393*
                the empty battlefield
CHAPTER 49: *You were never alone*   *402*
CHAPTER 50: *Never Sende a Manne to Do a Woman's Jobbe*   *408*
ACKNOWLEDGMENTS   *419*

IMAGINE A CASTLE.

You've probably done this before, but in case you need a bit more guidance, imagine there are towers and spires and jagged crenellations made of gray stone. Colorful pennants fly from the rooftops, bearing a vicious-looking bronze dragon against a scarlet backdrop. There's a drawbridge on thick iron chains and a moat, because so long as we're imagining a castle, we might as well imagine a cool one with a moat. Maybe there are even crocodiles in the moat—no one told you this had to be realistic, after all. If you want crocodiles, you can have them.

The castle sits on a slight hill, overlooking several acres of fields, kept clear to make sure no one can creep up on anyone inside the castle walls. At the base of the gently sloping grassy rise is a reasonably sized town spread out in a ring full of all the sorts of shops you might expect. Places to buy and sell equipment. An alchemist, tucked underneath a subtle sign bearing the mark of a hedge witch selling love potions. There's the tavern, where all the heroes go to drink mead and recount their adventures, which sports a big sign proclaiming "On Thor's Days We Have Ladyes Night."

The streets are packed earth, and the buildings are roofed with thatch, and it all looks a bit nerve-rackingly flammable. This, by the way, is what people refer to as *foreshadowing*. But more on that later.

Today, it just so happens, is Market Day. The streets, already crowded with shops, have sprouted tents and stalls and colorfully draped wagons belonging to vendors from far and wide. The lord of the castle has recently reopened the gold mine on the other side of the forest, and the influx of wealth has brought every able-bodied and able-wagoned merchant for miles around to this spot. Every inch of space on the outskirts of the market is filled with horses and donkeys, as well as a pair of extremely anachronistic llamas. Nobody is sure who they belong to, and they spit if you go too close, so we'll avoid them. Nobles and peasants alike walk down the haphazardly formed aisles of cloth and wagon wheels, while town criers offer to shout about the wares on display for a penny a word.

Market Day is always a riot of colors and sounds and the smells from baking treats and horse dung. But this time there's a particular buzz in the air, and an extra dozen or two merchants crammed in among the regulars. It's the last Market Day before the qualifiers begin for the Tournament of Dragonslayers—the first time it's ever been held in the little county known as Darkhaven—and people are pretty well psyched.

But let's real quick go back up to the castle gates, because something's happening there that will prove extremely relevant to our story. There's a commotion by the entrance to the inner castle, a flurry that builds on itself until the huge oak doors burst open with all the force and inevitability of a hurricane.

Out comes a group of girls, leaving the somewhat baffled and helpless guards to stare after them as they fall into a perfect V formation that any troop of soldiers, or flock of geese, would envy. Their leader, at the pointy end of the V, is a petite blonde wearing a fuchsia gown and an expression of absolute self-assurance, the kind of don't-*even*-with-me that the other girls in the group can only dimly imitate. She might as well have the words "Queen Bee" embroidered on her perfectly tailored pink bodice.

They breeze right past the guards on the outer gate, having built up enough momentum that nobody even tries to stop them. They appear to have a single destination in mind: the market.

Let's all take a moment to wish the market, and everyone in it, the very best of luck.

Chapter One

THE SORT OF THING THAT GETS A GIRL BURNED AT THE STAKE

Gwen ducked out the back flap of the stall, gulping a breath of fresher air and reaching for another string of horseshoes from the boxes stacked there.

She hated Market Day. It meant dealing with an endless parade of farmers, coopers, farriers, and miners, all of whom demanded to speak to her father. They assumed she couldn't possibly know what she was talking about when it came to negotiating prices, let alone when it came to the technical specifications of the tools they were looking at.

It certainly never occurred to them that every single nail, pickaxe, and barrel hoop had been made by the blacksmith's teenaged daughter.

Steeling herself, she slipped back through the flap and busied herself setting out a new row of horseshoes to replenish the few she'd managed to sell. All their customers today were regulars—not a single new face had approached her stall, though the population of potential customers had easily doubled since last month's market.

At this rate, she'd never make enough to pay the entrance fee for the jousting tournament.

It had been a mad idea, one she knew was mad even as she fashioned armor to fit her lighter frame, even as she practiced with her sword, even as she trained with her horse against trees and fences.

It was bad enough for a peasant to risk posing as a knight—impersonating nobility could deliver you to a very nasty end indeed if you were caught. Worse, in order to pose as a knight, she'd be forced to pose as a man.

And that was the sort of thing that gets a girl burned at the stake.

Somehow, though, it wasn't the thought of being arrested or roasted that felt maddest of all. The part that kept her awake at night with wanting was the idea that she thought she could be, even for a moment, *good* enough to be a knight.

So much for one day of glory, she thought, trying to swallow the lump rising in her throat.

A ragged chorus of gasps from the stall across the way made Gwen look up. The blacksmith from two counties over, in town for the pretournament Market Day, was demonstrating a flashy figure-eight slashing pattern with an ornately decorated sword. The whooshing, whistling noise of the blade cut right through the din of the crowds.

Gwen felt her brow furrowing, too annoyed to control the scowl she'd been told made her particularly unapproachable as a vendor. The only reason the sword was making such a racket—and drawing such a crowd—was because it was poorly balanced. A properly made weapon wouldn't be half so noisy.

A swirl of color at the end of the makeshift row of vendors drew Gwen's attention. A gaggle of vibrantly dressed noblewomen were sweeping their way down the aisle, people scattering back from them like frogs before a flock of colorfully plumed herons.

Gwen found herself watching them, safe in the relative anonymity of her profession—nothing at her stall would interest these girls. Their obvious leader was a girl in a blindingly pink dress—*how does one even dye fabric that color?*—with her blond hair in intricate braids coiled around her head.

She was absolutely beautiful, in that put-together fashion that waved like a big red flag to Gwen's eye. Even if she weren't a noblewoman, and entirely off-limits, her whole demeanor would've warned Gwen off flirting or even approaching her to talk. *Different worlds*, Gwen thought, continuing to watch her through her lashes. The girl's face was shapely, her skin flawless. Her nose was perfect and pert, her lips a generous pink pout, her blue eyes huge.

Of course she's got blue eyes, Gwen thought, allowing herself a bit of petty annoyance at the girl's classic beauty. And yet, for some reason, she couldn't quite make herself take her eyes off the ringleader of the ladies and go back to work.

And then the blond-haired, blue-eyed beauty turned and met Gwen's gaze.

Gwen found herself frozen with surprise—and a certain amount of panic at having been caught staring. Then she jerked her head down so fast her neck popped audibly.

"Ooh," came a clear, sweet voice, straight through the crowds to her ears. "Let's go here!"

Gwen didn't look up. *Just keep going. If I have to try to sell a pickaxe to a noblewoman, I'm going to throw myself into the lake.*

"Um," said a somewhat less sweet voice. A glance told Gwen it belonged to a square-jawed man in an impeccably tailored jacket and hose, equally as handsome as the queen of the ladies. Gwen hadn't even noticed him there—easy to miss amid the flock of jewel-toned gowns around him. He was gazing longingly at the whistling sword demonstration across the way. "Maybe this one would be better, Lady Isobelle."

Lady Isobelle frowned at him, the expression so perfect she must have practiced it in front of a glass. "Why that one?"

The young nobleman glanced between the burly, bearded blacksmith wielding the noisy sword and Gwen with her single black braid and plain gray dress. "He, uh . . . looks like he might be more experienced."

Gwen clenched her jaw. How many times had she heard that one?

Hurriedly, the young man added, "He's, um, older, you know."

The lady's frown had deepened, her eyes narrowing. She paused only for an instant before dismissing him with a toss of her pretty blond head. "You go over there if you like. The girls and I are going to *this* stall."

Dammit.

Gwen self-consciously smoothed down her skirt, rearranging the pocket hanging from her belt so it covered up the hole burned into the side of the fabric. "Good afternoon," she said, keeping her eyes down as the group of ladies swept toward her. She wanted to say, *There's nothing here for you—you've made your point, now move on.* What she said was: "How are you enjoying the market today?"

"Oh, so much!" bubbled the blond girl—Isobelle, the nobleman had called her. "It's such a gorgeous day, and I could honestly people-watch for hours. What about you?"

Gwen lifted her gaze, which turned out to be a terrible mistake. The eyes waiting for her were even bluer up close. "I, uh." She could feel the heat rising, starting somewhere in the small of her back and creeping ever upward.

The lady Isobelle waited, and when no further reply seemed

forthcoming, she cheerfully leaned forward, bracing her perfectly manicured hands on the edge of the stall. "My goodness, what a selection of . . . things." The other three noblewomen stayed clustered around Isobelle, though none were feigning the kind of interest their leader was. A fifth woman was with them, a few years older than the ringleader, but her dress was far plainer than the others.

Lady's maid, Gwen's mind decided.

A snort and a choke from behind her announced that her father, sensing the presence of customers, had woken from his doze.

"Do the thing, Gwen," he suggested in his soft, but firm, way, as he rubbed his hand over his face.

The mortified heat had reached Gwen's shoulders, and she hunched them, trying to keep the blush at bay through sheer force of will. "Dad," she protested, "these ladies have no . . . er. They're not here to buy anything."

Lady Isobelle made a noise of contradiction.

Gwen's father lifted his head and met her eyes, his eyebrows rising. "The demo," he insisted. "The new kitchen knives."

Gwen looked up at the clear blue sky, wishing a lightning bolt would magic itself down from the heavens and vaporize her. She wanted to point out to her father that these women had never set foot inside a kitchen in their lives.

Instead, she turned back to the counter and stepped over toward the end, where their array of kitchen knives was fanned out against a cheery red display cloth. Picking up the floor model, she launched into the speech that had been one of her father's few contributions to their business these past few months.

"Welcome to Amos's Armaments and Sundries," she said,

picking a puffed fold of Lady Isobelle's sleeve to address. "Allow me to demonstrate our new line of kitchen knives, stronger than Spanish steel and capable of holding a sharp edge five times longer than the leading competitor's blades. Each purchase comes with a lifetime guarantee and free sharpening, though with our innovative design, you'll almost never have to sharpen your knives again."

She could feel those intense eyes on her as she spoke. A giggle from one of the other ladies was quickly stifled—evidently, Lady Isobelle was kind enough not to let her friends laugh at the poor blacksmith's daughter running through her memorized lines.

"Gather round," Gwen went on, "and I'll show you how our knives can cut through the toughest of materials—even an old leather drinking flask." She held up the flask in question—they got them cheap from the local tavern once they'd begun to wear out to the point of leaking—and then drove the knife down into the leather. Truthfully, it required far more strength to do smoothly than any of these ladies would have, but Gwen spent her days forging iron and could make it look easy.

"See how easily the knife cuts," she said, as the bottom of the flask fell onto the counter. "See how smooth the edges are." She turned the top of the flask over to show off the even edges of the leather.

"Amazing!" exclaimed Lady Isobelle. Her tone was so genuinely lacking in patronization that Gwen glanced at her, startled. Her gaze was lowered as she ran her fingertips just beside Gwen's against the cut leather. Gwen fought the urge to jerk her hand back, for reasons she could not quite identify.

Then Isobelle looked up, the force of her stare lessened somewhat by the gentle curiosity in her expression. "Is it important that they can cut through leather?" she asked.

In all the times Gwen had run through this particular demonstration for customers, not once had anyone asked her that. She groped for a response, any response, that wasn't the truth. "Uh," she said.

"I'll take four," the lady announced, her perfectly symmetrical features alive with enthusiasm. "One for each of us. Right, girls?"

The rest of her friends had wandered off a few paces, their attention on another group of nobles strolling by. But just behind and to Isobelle's left, the lady's maid cleared her throat.

"Oh, you too?" Isobelle beamed. "Five, then!"

"Ah, no, my lady . . ." The maid's expression betrayed very little, but for the tiniest flicker of alarm. "I was going to suggest you try buying something a little less . . . lethal."

"Oh, come now, Olivia. I'm not going to cut myself." Lady Isobelle paused, lips pursing. "Not again, anyway. Oh, fine. What about these?" She took a tiny step to the side, her gaze falling upon the rows of horseshoes.

Gwen blinked at her, and then glanced again at Olivia, whose poker face was of absolutely no help. "These . . . horseshoes?"

"Oh, is that what they are?" The blue eyes flitted back up, and Gwen felt a strange sense of vertigo, as if gravity wasn't operating quite right—she couldn't tell if the lady was teasing her, or if she truly had no idea what a horseshoe was.

"I don't . . ." Gwen floundered, as the blush began rising again with a vengeance, swarming up her neck and threatening to choke her. "Surely the castle farrier would . . . I mean, you can tell him to see us if you need . . ."

Isobelle traced a fingertip along the curve of one of the

horseshoes. "I'm thinking hung on the wall, for decoration. Any decent hedge witch says iron is the thing. We could call them good luck charms. Do you have any with some decoration on them?"

"Decoration?" Gwen echoed weakly, feeling like someone had cut her legs out from under her.

"Maybe a floral pattern, or something artsy and modern and geometrical?"

Numbly, Gwen shook her head.

Isobelle pursed her lips again. "Does your father ever do anything more ornate?"

"My father?" Gwen was beginning to sound like one of the town criers, repeating what they hear over and over.

"He's the one who makes these, no? Amos himself?" Isobelle's eyes dipped, falling on the spot where Gwen's fingers curled around one of the horseshoes, her grip familiar and possessive.

Gwen let go, then immediately wished she hadn't.

The other girl's gaze, suddenly shrewd, met hers again. "Well, if your *father* ever does make any with decorations, they'll go like hotcakes the next Market Day. I guarantee this time next month, every girl will want one for her own wall."

She knew. Somehow, this airheaded noblewoman with her pink dress and perfectly sculpted hair *knew*. The people in Gwen's village pretended not to notice that Amos's daughter had taken over his smithing tasks with increasing frequency these past years—with her dad unable to work with any consistency, it was either accept Gwen or live without a blacksmith at all. *Don't ask about the blacksmith girl, and we won't tell you about the blacksmith girl.*

It wasn't technically against the law for women to be tradesmen, but men didn't find the idea particularly comfortable. A lot of female crafters tended to find themselves thrown into debtors' prison after guards confiscated their "ill-gotten" wealth by calling it stolen.

Panic interrupted the rising blush, threatening to drain all that blood away again.

Then Lady Isobelle smiled, delight radiating from her every perfect pore. "I'll take five of them," she said. "How much?"

Gwen was beginning to feel like a fence post in a raging tempest—clinging to the tiniest scrap of dry ground while the hurricane that was Lady Isobelle threatened to tear her loose and swirl her all about.

"That'll be five . . ." she began, but then stopped. Behind Isobelle, the lady's maid—Olivia—was shaking her head and signaling to catch Gwen's attention. While she watched, the other woman stuck out her thumb, turned it upward, and bounced it. "Uh, I mean, ten . . . ? Ten pen—" The thumb bounced again.

Gwen hesitated again, unwilling to raise the price more than double what it ought to be.

"Ten pennies?" Isobelle asked. "Or ten shillings?"

The bottom dropped out of Gwen's stomach.

Isobelle flashed her that radiant smile. "Ten shillings it is."

Olivia cleared her throat again. "And we'll need nails to hang them on," she reminded her lady.

Isobelle nodded vaguely. "Oh, yes. Add another five shillings onto that, would you, Liv? Thanks."

While her maid dug in a fat purse jingling with coins, Isobelle leaned forward, palms flat on the counter, and beamed at Gwen, who'd lost all ability to move or speak.

"It's been an absolute pleasure meeting you and perusing your wares," she said. "Your father's wares, I mean." The smile turned decidedly impish. One of the other ladies made an impatient sound, prompting a roll of Isobelle's eyes. "Oh, all right. Olivia will pay you, and I'm sure Sir Orson will be only too pleased to carry the horseshoes back." Then she paused, winked—actually *winked*—at Gwen, and whirled away, the storm sweeping on across the market, the other ladies following in her wake like bits of colored fabric swirling in the gale.

Gwen stayed where she was, standing utterly still, staring down at the handful of coins the lady's maid deposited into her hand.

It was enough to buy her way into the qualifying round of the tournament.

All she needed now was the courage to show up among the knights and ladies and pageantry—and enough luck that no one would notice she could never really belong in that world. To hide long enough to prove to herself, just once, that she was good enough.

Chapter Two

RIDICULOUSLY, FABULOUSLY PINK

Most of Lady Isobelle's attention was currently devoted to a particularly good slice of cheesecake on a stick. The vendor had tried to market it as being dragon-shaped and impaled on a knight's lance—everyone was merchandising around the tournament—but if it had ever resembled that legendary beast, that resemblance had ended when she'd nibbled its head off.

The others had wanted one of those potato-on-a-stick snacks, where they cut it into one enormous spiral, impaled it (quite the theme, she mused), and fried it. It was outrageous that the superior cheesecake had the shorter line, but it *did* mean she had time on her hands. Even dear old Orson, slightly puzzled to find himself weighed down by a bag holding five horseshoes, was lining up with the ladies, listening with a polite expression to Hilde's firm opinions on the proper treatment of potatoes.

Isobelle's maid, Olivia, was watching her back away into the crowd with a stern eye. Isobelle wrinkled her nose in reply, wordlessly signaling that she wouldn't go far, and ducked behind a passing wagon.

And so Lady Isobelle of Avington, jewel of her absent father's eye, setter of fashions, center of the castle's famed gossip network, and most eligible bachelorette of the king's court, vanished into the bustling crowd.

As much as she could ever vanish, anyway. The owners of the stalls and carts tended to track Isobelle's progress, recognizing instantly that she had wealth to spare. Isobelle often imagined someone would be able to follow her all throughout the hubbub of the market, just by listening for the rise and fall of voices from the merchants.

One voice penetrated the din, sweet but demanding, and Isobelle found her steps turning toward the stall even before she realized what she was doing.

The woman behind the counter was a hedge witch. Her plump cheeks creased in a smile as Isobelle approached, and stretched even wider when Isobelle stopped, frowning. It was never particularly clear how much magic a witch actually wielded, if any at all. Had Isobelle turned toward this stall because of a spell, or simply because the woman had honed her vocal instrument to such a degree that she could derail just about anyone?

"A charm for the lady," said the hedge witch, the offer far more command than question, gesturing to an array of attractive baubles made of wicker, braided wire, and polished stones.

Isobelle fished out one of her bright, cheery smiles and bobbed a respectful curtsy of greeting. It never hurt to be polite to a hedge witch . . . just in case. "Oh, they are lovely. But there's nothing I need right now." *Nothing you can help me with, anyway.*

The witch's eyes narrowed as she inspected Isobelle's face, gaze shrewd enough to make even Isobelle fight the urge to step back. "Ah," said the witch, her fingers moving to indicate a bracelet made of woven blackberry brambles. "Here, lady . . . a love charm. Not always effective unless a seed is already planted, but for you . . . yes, you will make it sing."

Isobelle felt herself stiffen. "Thank you, no." It was all she could do not to visibly recoil. The last thing she needed was for any of the knights in the tournament to do something so inconvenient as fall in love with her. She hurried away, uncomfortably aware of the hedge witch's eyes following her.

She made her way through the market, passersby bathed a dusty gold by the sunset. The merchants of the day were beginning to wind down, packing away wares and shutting stalls in preparation for the evening's celebrations. She, unfortunately, would be back up at the castle by then.

It was only as she made her way past a line of horses tethered to the old wishing tree, a town guard patiently pinning parking violations to their bridles, that she realized where she was headed.

Up ahead, the ridiculous swordsmith with the unfortunate facial hair was still swishing his noisy blade around for a new pack of admirers. Across from him, the old smith was already gone, and his daughter was packing up their stall.

Gwen. *That's what he called her.*

She had green eyes and fair skin and a generous helping of freckles. A black braid hung over one shoulder, and a streak of soot on one eyebrow lent her a sardonic appearance. During the knife demonstration, Isobelle had felt the oddest impulse to lean in and wipe that smudge away.

Then Gwen looked up and caught her staring.

Isobelle paused. She couldn't very well melt away into the crowd—not in this dress, anyway. It was ridiculously, *fabulously* pink. So, lifting her chin, she set sail toward the stall.

Gwen's eyes widened, but Isobelle had long ago concluded that she couldn't pause her daily business for people to get over their surprise and confusion, or she'd never get anything done.

"I've been thinking about the horseshoes," she said, launching herself into the conversation without much idea of where she'd take it next, but interested to find out.

Gwen drew in a quick breath, hands curling into fists and then dropping to smooth her skirts. She had the air of someone ready to do battle—longing for it, in fact—and then pulling herself back at the last minute. "If it's about the price—" she began.

Isobelle waved the words away with one hand. "Never mind the price," she said. She was well aware that, whatever a horseshoe did cost, it certainly wasn't two shillings.

Gwen blinked at her, wary. "Then what?"

Isobelle, still not sure why she'd returned, reached for a reply. "I was wondering if you'd considered a line of miniature ones," was where she landed, and she was quite pleased with it even as she said it. This felt like it might be genius, in fact.

Gwen rubbed at her brows with her finger and thumb, which explained how the soot had got there. "What would anyone want miniature horseshoes for?"

"Tiny ponies, I should think," Isobelle said brightly, just to see her face.

Gwen opened her mouth, caught her breath, and then closed it again.

"Not really," said Isobelle, taking pity on her. "I was thinking of one you could pop in your bag, or even sew into the lining of your skirt. As a lucky charm. They'd be so giftable!"

"Giftable," said Gwen, who had repeated what she'd said quite a lot the last time they'd spoken as well. Isobelle often had that effect on people, though—it wasn't the other girl's fault.

Isobelle shrugged. "They will be after *I* gift one or two."

"I'll . . . I'll mention it to my father," Gwen managed.

"Mm-hmm," Isobelle agreed, with a twitch of a smile. She could see the caution in the other girl's eyes—she could tell Isobelle had guessed who did the work at the stall, but she wasn't sure what she was going to do about it. That was the world, though, wasn't it—you always had to wonder who you could trust.

Isobelle ran her eye over the remaining wares. There were the knives and the sliced leather bag from poor Gwen's performance—though she *had* looked fearsome as she dragged the knife through the wineskin—a collection of horse-related bits and bobs, and a few repaired pots and pans. She considered asking, wide-eyed, what the frying pan was for, but was faintly concerned that might drive Gwen over the edge.

At the far end was—oh, interesting! A sword leaned against the table. It wasn't really on display, though. Perhaps the smith—or his daughter—had brought it along and then decided not to show it off.

Isobelle squashed her skirts with both hands and slipped through the gap between the counter and the edge of the tent, popping out the other side like a champagne cork as Gwen made a startled sound. It was usually better to ask forgiveness than permission, Isobelle found.

She reached for the sword. The hilt was beautifully made—the grip wrapped neatly, the pommel carved with intricate knotwork designs.

"Now, this," she said, even as Gwen raised her hands in protest. "Look at the—is it engraving, on the end bit here? If you could do this kind of thing on a horseshoe, you'd—whoops, maybe I won't try and lift it, these are surprisingly heavy."

Gwen had lurched forward in case Isobelle planned on dropping the sword, but (though it strained the biceps more than she'd like to admit) she managed to hold on to it until she could hand it over to the other girl.

"Whoops," Gwen echoed, and Isobelle thought she saw her lips twitch. Without any sign of effort at all, the blacksmith's daughter wrapped her own hand around the grip, swinging the sword up to horizontal and taking the scabbard with her other hand, so she could pull the weapon a few inches clear of it. She looked ... dashing, really.

"Oh, now look at that," Isobelle murmured, stepping closer to inspect the engraving that wound its way down the blade of the sword itself. She only realized how close she'd stepped when Gwen swallowed and spoke.

"You have good taste." And then, after a pause: "I'll tell my father you admired it."

Isobelle looked up to meet her green eyes—they were part wariness, part curiosity, and a touch of pride. They were the color of the forest: a mossy green with hints of oak.

"I—" For once, when Isobelle launched herself, the rest of her words didn't show up. To cover, she took a smart step back and spun away toward the goods on the counter. "It's such a pity you don't have anything else with that sort of engraving," she said, listening to herself babble with a kind of fascination as she reached for a roll of linen she assumed was for wrapping purchases.

Feeling a lump, she twitched a fold of fabric aside, revealing a tiny figurine worked in iron, as far removed from the great horseshoes and buckles as Isobelle herself was from the lout across the way, still waving his noisy sword around.

The figure was that of a tiny iron knight, his lance raised, pennant frozen mid-billow. The horse he rode was elegantly and quite realistically depicted, one leg raised to take a spritely step. The armor itself was a thing of beauty, so detailed there were even tiny etched rivets at the joints.

"Oh, I love him!" Isobelle squealed, folding her hands behind her back in the universal sign for I-won't-touch-this-fragile-thing and bending over to take a closer look. "Look at this handsome fellow! What is that on his pennant, a lavender blossom?"

"No!" Gwen gasped, darting around her to grab for the fabric, trying to whisk the figurine out of sight. "That isn't meant to be—" She caught at one edge of the fabric, and as she snatched it up, the little knight tumbled to the ground, landing on the muddied grass at their feet.

"Oh, I'm sorry," Isobelle began, trying to sweep her dress out of the way as Gwen dropped to her knees to retrieve the little knight. "He's beautiful. How much is he? I quite fancy the idea of a knight who'd do what he was told, for once."

"Sir Gawain isn't for sale," Gwen said firmly, closing her hand over the figurine. She looked about to say more when Sir Orson's voice rang out, startlingly close.

"Lady Isobelle, please tell me you're not buying more horseshoes. I've already run out of hooves." There he was on the other side of the counter, with a lopsided smile at finding her where she shouldn't be. "I assume they're for me," he continued. "Given I'm playing the packhorse today." And indeed he was—the girls had added another couple of bags to his load since she'd slipped away.

"I'll be good," Isobelle replied, producing her dimples on cue. "Sir Orson, this is . . . ?" Though she'd heard the blacksmith address his daughter by name, it only seemed polite to offer a proper introduction.

"Gwen," said Gwen, glancing between the lady and the knight with a neutral expression. "Of Ellsdale."

If Orson was confused as to why Isobelle was introducing him to a random vendor at the market, he hid it beautifully. That was the nice thing about him—he could be friendly toward anyone. "Pleased to meet you, Gwen."

Gwen blinked at him—no doubt as stunned by his square jaw and princely good looks as every other girl on the planet. "Uh . . . you too, Sir . . . Awesome?"

Isobelle managed not to giggle. It wasn't the first time someone had misheard Orson's name, and it certainly wouldn't be the last. "Orson," she enunciated carefully. "With an 'R.' But don't worry, he responds to both."

Sir Orson laughed good-naturedly, throwing his head back and looking just like a legendary hero who had stepped straight out of an illuminated manuscript of chivalric romantic poetry. Even his hair seemed to glow—outrageous, since Isobelle knew he didn't use any product in it.

He offered Isobelle his arm. "It's getting late, my lady—shall we?"

Isobelle glanced back at the blacksmith's daughter, searching for some reason to linger at the stall, without having any idea why she wanted to stay.

Their eyes met again—and again, there was that strange sensation. But there was nothing more to say, especially with her friends catching up.

She let Orson lead her away. But when she looked back over her shoulder, Gwen was watching her go.

Chapter Three

BRING IT ON

All Darkhaven was buzzing about the tournament. Lord Whimsitt had hosted jousts before, but never on such a scale as this—where in the past there'd be maybe six knights in competition, now there were dozens upon dozens, drawn by the prestige and pageantry of the Tournament of Dragonslayers.

There were so many knights angling to compete, in fact, that the first week of matches didn't even count toward the final tournament brackets, instead serving only to separate the wheat from the chaff. If an up-and-coming young knight wanted to compete against the established favorites, he had to first qualify for the opening round by jousting his way into it.

Which meant week one was an absolute bloodbath. Sometimes literally. Young, untested knights getting knocked flat in one charge, while the favorites of the tournament barely broke a sweat—with only the occasional surprise upset. Still, the crowds flocked to the lists, because what better way to pass a beautiful late summer's day than by watching unspeakable violence unfolding before you for your entertainment? Plus, there were snacks.

Gwen stood in the changing tent, willing herself to move. The hum of the spectators was like nothing she'd ever heard before, vibrating in every fiber of her being. The crowd was like a living creature—like one of the ancient dragons, demanding blood sacrifices to be kept at bay.

She'd snuck into the changing tent an hour ahead of time, making a few trips to carry her armor and her sword.

It had taken her months to get each piece exactly right, requiring her to work between commissions, when her father was asleep. Countless hours in the heat of the smithy, sleepless nights spent designing and planning, a whole host of new calluses and burns covering her hands and arms. The hardest she'd ever worked in her life for anything, and Gwen had begun running her father's smithy when she was thirteen.

But now that it came time to don the armor and emerge in public as a knight, she found herself rooted to the spot.

Something happening in the lists made the crowd erupt into a roar, quickly tapering off into a groan. Someone must have been badly injured to elicit such a universal visceral response.

Outside the tent, Achilles whickered a comment on the crowd. The sound unfroze Gwen enough for her to turn her head and call out to him where he waited, already wearing his armor, just behind her tent. "Hang in there," she murmured to him—or to herself. "We can do this."

Not for the first time, a snide voice in her head demanded to know *why* she was doing this. Sneaking into the qualifying round for one ride, only to vanish again afterward, win or lose, would gain her nothing. And it risked *everything*—disgrace, imprisonment, even terrible injury or death. Or, worse, her *father* finding out.

And yet, the only thought that had lingered in her mind when the pink-garbed Lady Isobelle had tossed fifteen shillings her way was that it would buy her entry into the qualifiers.

She could ride, just *once*, and prove to herself that she was made of something as strong as any of them. That if only the world were different, she could've been a knight.

But all that would require her to actually *put on her damned armor.*

Gwen swallowed, shutting her eyes.

"Oh daaaang," came a slightly muffled voice from the next tent over. "Did you see Darby? He's got splinters sticking out of his leg as thick as a dick."

Gwen froze, listening.

"Um, that's a massive nope from me," came a second voice, sounding slightly ill.

Laughter, and the reply: "Dude, what kind of knight feels faint at even the mention of blood? You're a hundred percent in the wrong place."

"He does have a point, you know," came a third voice.

There were three of them, young knights gathered in one of the nearby changing tents, discussing the events taking place out in the lists. Despite her increasing sense of urgency, Gwen found herself tilting her head, leaning closer to the fabric wall of her own tent in order to listen.

"I'm only here because my dad would totally murder me if I backed out." The ill-sounding knight gave a drawn-out sigh. "To be honest I'm hoping I can just, like, fall off my horse or something before the other guy's lance hits. Sell it like I got knocked out honorably, you know?"

One of the other men laughed, though the sound of it was rueful. "I can't believe you don't want to try to win. It's the *Tournament of Dragonslayers*, it's a once-in-a-lifetime kind of thing." His enthusiasm was puppy-dog-like. If puppies were also bloodthirsty and talked about dick splinters.

"Technically," the third guy interjected, "it's a once-every-four-years opportunity if you're willing to travel. It's just never been here in Darkhaven before." He had a somewhat nasal tone that gave everything he said a rather pedantic air—like he knew everything, and wanted to make sure all those around him *knew* he knew everything.

"Not if you get split open and murdered by splinters your first ride," countered the one with the puppy-dog enthusiasm.

"Uhhh," said Sir Sickly.

"Put your head between your legs," suggested Sir Puppydog, his tone somewhat callous. "Seriously, though. You've got to at least try."

"Easy for you to say, already through to the tournament proper." Sir Know-It-All sounded tense. "Harder to admit you care when you might not even get to compete."

"Yeah, but the *Dragonslayer* tournament. Set aside the prestige, the glory, the prize treasure at the end. Have you seen the girl they've got as the sacrifice this year?"

A pause, and then Sir Know-It-All said slowly, "That good?"

"Unbel*ieee*vable," Sir Puppydog replied fervently. "She may well be the hottest girl I've ever seen. What I wouldn't give to have a crack at her."

"So all that bullshit about honor and glory was just that, huh?" Sir Sickly had recovered enough to snap at his companion. "You're just in it for dibs on the hot girl?"

"Why not both?" Sir Puppydog retorted cheerfully.

Gwen was torn between being put off by their conversation and being fascinated by this glimpse into the way they talked when they thought there weren't any women in earshot.

She'd half forgotten that one of the many favors bestowed upon the winner of the tournament was the opportunity to marry one of the land's most sought-after bachelorettes, chosen by some arcane process behind the scenes. Symbolically, she was the dragon sacrifice being offered up to appease one of the ancient beasts. A few hundred years ago, she'd have been handed over to a dragon to be gobbled up in a ritual believed to keep the dragons from attacking the countryside.

Now, she was being offered to whichever knight won the tournament, one object among many in the prize pot, her whole life determined by the flick of a wrist in a bloody sporting event.

Gwen wasn't sure the poor girl wouldn't have been better off with the dragon.

"I think I know the one you're talking about," Sir Know-It-all was saying. "Isn't she a bit . . . forgive me for saying so, but a bit *stupid?*"

Laughter. "That seems like a good thing to me," replied Sir Puppydog.

Gwen felt the muscles in her jaw contract, something stirring deep inside her body.

"Seriously, though." Sir Puppydog wasn't done. "So. Fucking. Hot. Tournament or no, I've got to take a swing at hitting that."

"You and every other guy here," drawled Sir Know-It-All.

"They can have her, just so long as I get there first." Sir Puppydog's tone was tense.

There was a roaring sound rising in Gwen's ears—she longed for something to hold on to, to lean against, something for support. Bad enough the poor girl was being married off to whoever won the tournament—but to be treated like this, ogled and hunted and slobbered over like a piece of meat?

Gwen wasn't used to letting anger win. She ignored it most of the time, shoving it away into some dark, distant recess of her mind, because anger didn't *matter*. It didn't solve anything. It didn't let her change anything about herself, her life, the world around her.

But just now, the anger wouldn't let her push it away.

"What's her name again?" Sir Sickly asked, his voice sounding dim and muffled through the rushing in Gwen's ears.

"She's a fixture here—Isobelle, I think. The super-hot blonde. Lady Isobelle, yeah."

Gwen went still, her mind filling with the image of that blue-eyed girl with the impish smile from the market a few days ago. Her interest as she inspected the horseshoes. The knowing glint in her gaze as she talked about Gwen's *father's* wares. Her laugh. Her . . . her *momentum* as she just sailed in, doing exactly as she pleased, taking charge of everyone around her.

Gwen didn't hear anything else the knights next door said. Something red-hot had filled her, rising up from her very bones to inhabit her muscles and her skin and animate her at last. This time, she didn't hesitate, strapping on each piece of armor in turn, letting that red-hot fury soak through the cold metal as it warmed to her body.

The next thing she heard, as she threw back the tent flap and reached for Achilles's reins with one armored hand, was the herald standing on his platform by the lists.

"Next to compete in the qualifying round of the jousting tournament is newcomer Sir Gawain of Toussaint, against Darkhaven's own Sir Evonwald!"

Gwen barely registered the cheers of the crowd—Evonwald was a local favorite, for all he was starting to get up there in years.

Her field of vision through the slit in her visor was limited, but she swung her head around until she could see the raised platform where Lord Whimsitt presided over the tournament—and where the symbolic dragon sacrifice would sit, watching helplessly as her fate unfolded.

She was there. Blond hair perfectly styled, a dress this time of peacock blue to match her eyes, coolly watching proceedings. Holding a snack of some kind, surrounded by her noblewomen friends, and managing not to look like all this was building up to the absolute end of her life.

Gwen had expected to be so consumed by nerves that she'd barely be able to ride. Instead, she swung up into Achilles's saddle as if her armor weighed nothing at all and accepted a lance from one of the tournament lance boys. She barely noticed riding up to the start of the lists, barely noticed fitting the end of the lance into the platform on her stirrup.

All her life she'd waited for this moment—and now all she could feel was a fury that had built into a white-hot torrent.

At the other end of the lists was Sir Evonwald on his horse, raising his hand to gesture to the crowd, accompanied by a resounding—if a bit stale—cheer in response. Then he turned toward Gwen.

"Sir Evonwald, ready?" the herald cried.

Evonwald slammed his visor down and wheeled his horse around with a flourish.

"Sir Gawain, ready?"

Yes. Bring it on.

Chapter Four

SIR GAWAIN'S NOT DONE YET ... JUST WATCH

Lord Whimsitt had hired some local girls to rouse the crowds in these early qualifiers, putting them in skimpy clothes and giving them bundles of streamers to wave, in the green and red and gold colors of the dragons. For the most part, these poor cheerleaders swept the streamers overhead in perfunctory arcs, about as interested in proceedings as the rest of the crowd—but just now, the tournament favorite, Sir Ralph, was riding around the lists in a lap of victory. He had dispatched his opponent so easily and thoroughly that they were forced to drag the unconscious boy off on a stretcher. The crowd, bloodthirsty as ever and coming to life for their favorite, loved it.

The man had finished his lap and reined in his horse before Lord Whimsitt's raised box. Sir Ralph saluted with his sword, and Whimsitt simpered at him in return. Darkhaven's lord was a portly man of medium height, with an infamous collection of very fine hats that hid his thinning hair. Today he wore a brilliant emerald chaperon-style turban in velvet—the wrong choice, given his temples were now trickling with sweat.

Isobelle, sitting in the box beside and below his, contemplated her guardian with a faint scowl. She'd realized recently she didn't know all that much about him, beyond the hat collection. Her parents had entrusted her to his care three years earlier, but Olivia had been far more parent and guardian to her than Whimsitt had. He didn't believe in educating women, and Isobelle didn't believe in dealing with boring men, so they'd avoided each other by mutual agreement. Until he'd taken advantage of her parents' absence and put Isobelle and her dowry up for grabs in his tournament. Now, she deeply regretted her failure to pay attention.

Isobelle shivered and looked away from her guardian. *Smirk all you want*, she thought, lifting her chin. *I'll find a way out of this yet, you'll see.*

Sir Ralph had not left. Instead, he'd walked his horse over to stand before Isobelle's box. He raised his visor, revealing a pair of predatory hazel eyes that swept over her, hair, dress, and all, and then fixed back on her face with an unnerving intensity.

Lord Whimsitt had informed Isobelle that she must show herself at each stage of the tournament, even the qualifiers. Now she wished she'd bothered to defy him, because she would've rather not seen just how easily Sir Ralph had won.

"My lady," said Sir Ralph—and though the words were a standard greeting, Isobelle could not help but hear the slight emphasis he placed on the word "my."

He already believed he'd won her.

Isobelle did not even notice her own reply, though she must have said something, for Sir Ralph inclined his head in a bow, gracious and courtly in front of his fans, and slammed the visor back down before turning his horse to ride for the exit to the lists.

One of Isobelle's companions, Sylvie, laid her fingertips on her friend's arm. "Are you all right?" she murmured, too low for anyone else to hear.

Isobelle forced air into lungs that were trying to shrivel away from the cold seizing her body. "You never know, he might get knocked out before the finals," she said brightly. "Or fall into the moat and find himself eaten by one of those lizard moat monsters the servants claim live there. The possibilities are endless."

Sylvie squeezed her arm but correctly interpreted Isobelle's desire to avoid speaking about the man who would almost certainly claim her as a prize in a few weeks' time.

Meanwhile, the next two knights had ridden out into the lists. One was Sir Evonwald, somewhat older than the other knights but formidable in experience. The other was a knight Isobelle didn't recognize, mounted on a gorgeous bay stallion, immaculate save for a tuft of mane that stuck up insistently at the front. Isobelle was familiar with the challenges of styling stubborn hair, and so was rather taken with him.

The horse and his rider were readying themselves for their first charge as the cheer girls fanned out into a half circle, creating...

"Is that supposed to be a dragon's flame?" Hilde was on Isobelle's other side and hadn't heard the exchange between Isobelle and Sylvie. She was too busy leaning forward and frowning sweetly with the effort of artistic interpretation.

"Wait for it," said Sylvie, leaning back in her chair, as cynical as the other girl was soft.

The girl at the center of the formation flipped a new layer down over her skirts and was suddenly clad in the bright pink that was Isobelle's signature shade. As she marched about triumphantly, the others scattered to all corners of the list, clearing the way for the joust, and—presumably—demonstrating the power of the sacrifice to safeguard Darkhaven from draconic influences.

Isobelle kept her features smooth as a halfhearted smattering of applause started up around them, then died away.

Whatever she was forced to give them—and there was almost no limit to that—she would not let them have her composure.

The flag dropped, and Sir Evonwald and Sir Gawain—as the announcer had introduced him—prodded their horses to a rolling trot, gathering momentum as they charged toward each other from opposite ends of the lists. Their lances wavered and then firmed, and the two men braced themselves in their saddles, as they—

"I've got snacks!" a cheery voice announced from behind them. "Oh, someone open the gate, my hands are full!"

Isobelle leaned backward to open the little gate and let in Jane, who was accompanied by an unholy amount of food. The perfect distraction from the unpleasantness of Whimsitt's machinations and Ralph's cool possessiveness.

"Did I miss anything?" Jane asked brightly, squeezing herself in beside Sylvie. Isobelle turned back to find the two knights had passed each other and were slowing once more.

"Nothing," Sylvie drawled. "Or rather, *they* missed something. Each other."

"It's their first run at it," said Hilde, ever-forgiving. "They're just warming up."

The pair were wheeling around once more to face each other, and Isobelle popped a toffee into her mouth and studied Sir Gawain. His opponent was familiar enough, but the younger knight—for he certainly moved more nimbly than old Sir Evonwald, and his build was slimmer—was a new name to her.

Once more the two horses began to accelerate, and when Sir

Evonwald's lance banged off Sir Gawain's shield, sending the young challenger reeling back in his saddle, a ragged cheer went up from the crowd.

"Are they against Sir Gawain?" Jane asked, still handing out her snack haul.

"I think they're *for* any kind of action," Sylvie replied.

Isobelle said nothing, still leaning forward and studying Sir Gawain as he shook his arm out, trying to ease the pain of the collision. She wasn't sure why her attention had fixed on him, but if there was one thing her maid, Olivia, had taught her—and Olivia's advice was always to be heeded—it was to pay attention to whatever caught your eye. Especially if you didn't know why.

"Where is Toussaint, anyway?" Hilde asked, thoughtful. "It sounds French, I think?"

"I don't think it's going to matter much longer," Jane replied. "Pity, he at least looks younger than Evonwald. He could've been good for some fun! Then again, he's about to have some spare time on his hands, so . . ."

"You can make anything dirty," drawled Sylvie.

"I don't think he's finished." Isobelle hadn't realized she was going to speak until she'd done it.

"What?" Jane asked, doubtful.

"Sir Gawain's not done yet," Isobelle murmured. "Just watch."

On the other side of the lists, a halfhearted attempt to start a wave began, then petered out before any of the girls were required to pretend enthusiasm, though Hilde was already setting her drink down in readiness.

The two knights turned toward each other a third and final time. Sir Evonwald had scored points on Sir Gawain, so it was almost impossible for the younger knight to win now. If he could at least connect with the other man's shield, then perhaps he could force the fight on to a tiebreaker on foot, with swords.

Sir Gawain's shield sagged as his horse pushed into a canter, and his body leaned back as though he might slide from his horse.

"I think that hit was harder than—" Jane began.

And then, just as the two came together—as Sir Evonwald raised himself in his stirrups to dispatch his opponent—Sir Gawain straightened and shifted his grip on his lance.

Then the two were clashing—there was a deafening ring of lance on shield, then a sound like a dozen saucepans being dropped out a window onto the ground below as Sir Evonwald was swept backward off his horse and onto the dusty ground behind it.

Silence blanketed the stands. No one had expected Sir Evonwald to win the tournament, but it was just as unlikely for him to get knocked out in the preliminaries.

The herald raised his large metal cone to his lips. "Sir, uh . . ." There was a pause as he frantically hunted through his notes. "Sir Gawain of Toussaint progresses to the first round of the tournament proper!"

"Huh," Sylvie murmured, turning a sidelong glance on Isobelle. "We should get you making predictions more often, we might make some money."

But Isobelle wasn't listening. Sir Gawain might have been momentarily interesting, but there wasn't any prediction about this tournament that ended the way she wanted, no matter how hard she looked.

A couple of stewards were helping a limping Sir Evonwald to his feet. He pulled off his helmet to get some air, and even at this distance one could see how red-faced he was, blustering like a very cross walrus. The winning knight had barely moved at all, probably as shocked by his unexpected victory as the crowd.

Then Sir Gawain wheeled his handsome stallion around. He approached the platform, drew his sword, and lifted it in a chivalrous salute to Isobelle.

Automatically she leaned forward and waved her acceptance, showing her dimples, laughing as Jane waved back far too enthusiastically beside her. But there was something tickling at the back of her mind—like gazing at one of those patterns they made in Italy, unfocusing her eyes until the picture emerged from the noise.

Why are you so familiar?

Her gaze ran over Sir Gawain and lingered for a moment on his sword and the beautiful, delicate engravings adorning the base of the blade.

And then her eyes widened as the truth leapt out at her.

Oh.

Chapter Five

CLIMB DOWN, LADY, WE'RE GOING OUT!

Gwen's blood was still singing by the time Achilles's hooves struck the hard-packed earth of her village streets. She barely remembered taking her armor off and completing the transformation back into herself. She did remember one moment when she led Achilles out of the jousting arena and overheard two of the spectators talking.

Who the hell is Sir Gawain? one of them had asked.

Never heard of him, the second one replied. *I tell you, though, no one's going to forget his name after that.*

Everything before that was a blur of isolated images and sensations. The sweat trickling down the small of her back to collect in the padding she wore beneath her armor. The thud of Achilles's hooves beneath her, reverberating through her body like a war drum. The singing of the fury in her blood as the world narrowed to a single spot on her opponent's shoulder. The infinite stretch of stunned silence after the final blow and crash of an armored man hitting the ground—the collective sound of at least a hundred spectators forgetting to breathe.

Even now, Gwen was only half present. Part of her knew she had arrived at the stable at the edge of the pasture her neighbors let her use—the rest of her was still on her horse, in that arena, floating on a cloud of glory.

She wasn't the only one buzzing. Achilles was practically dancing as she tried to get his saddle off him and brush out the spots where his own armor had rested. He tossed his head and pranced, snorting his desire to do whatever they'd just done *again*. Gwen ran a hand down his nose, as steadily as she could for all that her own hands were still shaking.

"That was it, love, we're done," she murmured to him, trying not to let her own heartbreak at those words come through in her voice or her touch. "You did beautifully."

The forge outside the house was cool—unsurprising, though Gwen had entertained the tiniest of hopes that maybe she'd come home to find her father working. Inside, though, there was a cheery fire burning in the hearth, and a stew bubbling away in the cast-iron pot.

She gave herself a bracing mental shake and prayed her father would not see how utterly everything had changed for his daughter.

"Hey, Dad," she called, hanging her cloak on the iron hook her father had made for her when she was a kid—it was fashioned to look like a knight's lance, and the blunted end of it was shiny and worn from the touch of her fingers over the years. "Dad?"

"I was weeding the garden," came his voice from the back door. He walked in, wiping his hands on a rag. "Well?"

Gwen blinked at him. "Well what?"

"You're going to make me ask? The interview for the internship, girl! Tell me how it went." Her father gestured her over toward the fire and sank down into his chair. He was a large man, not tall or fat, but barrel-chested, the epitome of a village blacksmith. He'd never worn a big bushy beard like the man in the market—*Don't give sparks an extra place to rest*, he'd always said, *especially when that spot is an inch from your nose.*

Gwen dropped into her own chair by the fire. "The internship, right. It was fine. I don't think I got it, though." Sitting down drained away all the fire that had been keeping her upright, and exhaustion reached up and grabbed her.

Her father frowned. "What do you mean, you didn't get it? You've been working on those armor pieces for months. Years, if you count all your drawing and daydreaming. They're flawless, ingenious. Who the hell saw those and didn't snap you up?"

Gwen kept her eyes on the fire, uncertain whether she could keep up her facade of indifference if she actually saw the indignation she could hear in his voice. "It's fine, Dad. I wouldn't have done it anyway, I just . . . I just wanted to see if I was good enough. If I *could* do it."

Her father was quiet, so Gwen risked a glance his way through her lashes. He was staring down at his knees, his longtime habit when he was thinking. His sandy brown hair was in disarray and his face was tired, as it usually was, but there was a spark in it she hadn't seen in some time.

"You know I'd be fine, right?" His eyes lifted and met hers. "If you wanted to . . . to go grab something, something like that internship, I'd be okay."

Gwen dropped her eyes. "Yeah, I know, Dad."

"I mean it." His voice sharpened, the barest edge needed to make Gwen look at him and listen. It was the voice he'd used when she was a child, teaching her about safety in the forge—the voice that told her when to stop running, when to put her hands behind her back, when to pay attention.

"I know I've come to rely on you too much these past years," he went on, his face showing signs of that old ache, as fresh as the day her mother died. "But I don't want you shutting yourself down to anything because you think you've got to stay here and take care of me. If there was something you wanted, something that would take you away for a while . . ." He didn't finish the sentence, but his eyes were penetrating, too keen for comfort.

Gwen shifted in her chair, unwilling to admit even to herself that his words were cutting too close. "I told you, Dad. I don't think I got it." She paused, and then added, "If nothing else, I'm a girl. They wouldn't let a woman prove she could do a man's job as well as he can." She could still see the stunned faces of the spectators all around her when a completely unknown knight had knocked Sir Evonwald off his horse—could imagine how quickly that shock would have turned to horror if she'd pulled off her helmet and shown them who'd really beaten their local favorite.

Her father didn't bother to hide his chuckle. "True. But you've never let anyone tell you what you can and can't do with your life. Where you belong, and what you deserve." He held out his hand, and Gwen leaned forward so he could take hers and give it a squeeze. "Don't start now."

Gwen's throat tightened, trying to stop the words welling up inside her from coming out. How could she tell her father that, as much as she liked smithing, it wasn't what she really longed for? That out there today, on the lists, weighed down by the armor she'd made and listening to the roar of the crowd, she'd been more alive than she'd ever felt holding a hammer and tongs. That the one thing she truly wanted—had *always* wanted, since her mother told her that first story of knights and dragons and chivalry and protecting the helpless—was the one thing she could never have for herself, not in a million years, not in a world that was, and ever would be, run by men.

There was a line. She'd already crossed it by taking up her father's craft, but that was the sort of infraction people could ignore.

But to masquerade as a knight?

That would leave the line so far behind her she might never find her way back.

Gwen squeezed her father's hand in return. "Thanks, Dad," she whispered, and tried not to let him see how much her heart ached.

Later, as she lay in bed while the moon rose and the village slumbered, her head was spinning so much she could scarcely keep her eyes closed and her body still. Logistics kept pouring through her mind. Technically, Sir Gawain was through the qualifiers and could ride in the first round of the tournament proper in a couple of weeks. But to have any hope of competing, she'd need far more than the sheer fury and luck that had carried her through today. She'd need training. She'd need a place to stay; though the castle was only a few miles away, Achilles was distinctive, and someone would be bound to spot her riding between the tournament and her poor, non-noble village. She'd need money, because if she was riding in a tournament, she couldn't be making pickaxes, and how would her father live?

She turned onto her side, pillowing her hands beneath her cheek. It was impossible. Even if she could sort out the details, what right did she have to try to be a knight? Just because she could fight, and ride, and hold a lance—she wasn't *one of them*.

A hint of a memory threaded through her thoughts, insidious, like a snake creeping in under her blankets. *So. Fucking. Hot*, one of the knights had said of Lady Isobelle, helpless sacrifice to the honor and symbolism of the tournament. *I've got to take a swing at hitting that.*

Gwen's rage had probably made all the difference when it came to beating Sir Evonwald. She should probably feel grateful that she'd overheard them. And yet, now, thinking back . . . she felt the tiniest bit more heartbroken.

Even the knights aren't knights.

The thatch rustled overhead, and Gwen stifled a groan, rolling once more onto her back. If they were getting rats in the straw again, she was going to scream. A few years back there'd been an epidemic of them in the village, until this absolute weirdo with a flute had turned up and driven them out. He'd stuck around afterward for an embarrassing amount of time, eyeing the village young people in the creepiest way. Eventually the local hedge witch came and stared him down until he moved on to the next town.

If only Gwen had had any aptitude for magic and herbalism, maybe she could've studied with the hedge witch. It wouldn't be holding a sword, but she'd be able to protect her village in some way against creeps like that.

The rustle came again—and then, a half second later, a *thunk* against her window's shutters.

Gwen sat up in bed, clutching at her blanket. Rats didn't clunk against shutters.

When the noise came again, she got out of bed and crept to the window, holding on to the knife she used for trimming her candles. After a breath, she flipped the latch and threw open the shutters.

A figure stood on the ground below, wearing a long, hooded cloak. As Gwen watched, a hand emerged from the cloak and pushed the hood down to display a wealth of long blond hair that gleamed like white gold in the moonlight.

Lady Isobelle beamed up at her and called in a carrying whisper-shout: "Climb down, lady, we're going out!"

Gwen stood frozen, staring down at *Lady Isobelle*—apparently the most eligible noblewoman in the entire county—standing under her window.

Isobelle waited patiently for a few heartbeats, as if used to eliciting this kind of paralyzing shock from the people she encountered. Then, raising her voice, she called, "Get dressed! Haven't you ever snuck out before?"

"Hush, you'll wake my father!" Gwen hissed back. She turned her head, listening for any sounds within the house. Her room was a loft over the main house, one of the few buildings in the village to have a second story, thanks to her father's cleverness with engineering. "What . . . what are you *doing* here? *How* are you here?"

The lady flashed her a positively impish smile. "I have my resources. I'm here to take you out, let's go."

Gwen felt her mouth open and then close again. She couldn't even be curious about why Lady Isobelle had bothered to track her down in a village all this way from the castle—she was too busy being frantic to get rid of her before her neighbors noticed, before her father woke, before someone could see them together and somehow blame Gwen for absconding with a noblewoman in the middle of the night.

Isobelle's smile shifted, the change so subtle Gwen would've missed it if the moon overhead weren't half full and bright. "Fine, then," she said airily. "If you won't come out, why don't you send down *Sir Gawain?*"

Oh shit.

A familiar roaring rose in Gwen's ears, only this time the rush of feeling wasn't anger or fury. She could feel the blood draining from her face as fear finally unfroze her. She moved away from the window long enough to grab her dress from the foot of the bed and throw it on over her night shift. She tried to banish the million questions flooding her brain—*How does she know? Has she told anyone? Are there guards waiting just out of sight to arrest me? Why on earth does she still look like a fairy-tale princess while sneaking out in the middle of the night?*—and carefully swung a leg over the windowsill.

As soon as she began climbing down, a lance of pain shot up through her arm. Her shoulder was still aching from that first clash with Sir Evonwald. She hadn't noticed it much on the ride home, but it had stiffened up as she lay in bed, and now . . . god, now it was agony. But if there was any chance of rolling back Isobelle's revelation, convincing her that she didn't know what she thought she knew, Gwen would have to pretend she was fine.

She made it to the ground and then whirled to face the other girl, pain and fear combining to create a pretty decent semblance of anger indeed. "You can't be here!" she snapped. "I don't know what you're talking about, or why you've come, but you've got to let me get you home before someone sees us."

"Oh, you don't know, do you? Gwen, Gawain . . . it's all really very clever, isn't it?" The force of Lady Isobelle's smile was like the heat radiating from an active forge—Gwen had to fight not to take a step back. "I'm here for Ladies' Night. It's Thor's Day, they have Ladies' Night every week at one of the taverns at the edge of town, and you're coming with me."

"Ladies' Night," Gwen echoed weakly.

"Or, you know, a lady knight." Isobelle's smile was decidedly smug. Gwen got the sense the other girl was used to getting her way, and that she was fighting a losing battle trying to resist.

"Look," Gwen managed, "if you won't come with me back to where you belong, I'll fetch someone who'll make you go."

Isobelle bit her lip to smother a laugh. "If you're going to threaten me," she replied breezily, "I think you ought to do it over a drink while hearing me out. Come on, I'm buying."

Gwen was experiencing the oddest sensation, as though she were no longer inside her own skin, watching the absurdity of this interaction from somewhere above and to the left of herself. She could see the blacksmith girl fighting and losing the battle, while the lady just stood there, totally at ease, waiting for her to capitulate.

"Five minutes," Gwen said slowly. "Five minutes and then you go home, understood?"

The lady grinned at her. "Whatever you say, Sir Knight."

Chapter Six

I'LL HAVE A WHITE KNIGHT, PLEASE

Isobelle hadn't been sure about what she'd seen at the tournament qualifiers—not until she'd seen Gwen respond to the name "Sir Gawain," looking like she was going to throw up right out the window and ruin Isobelle's shoes.

The question had been chasing itself in circles around her head all day, like a dog determined to catch its own tail. *Could it be . . . ? But no, it really seemed . . . But maybe?*

It was impossible for a girl to ride in the qualifiers. Where would she get the armor? The horse? The training? The *nerve*?

But perhaps, if she were a blacksmith . . . if she'd already proven to herself that a girl could do a man's work, then . . .

Somehow, Isobelle had found herself here in the village Gwen had mentioned when introducing herself, wondering if the pressure of the tournament had finally caused her to crack.

But she *hadn't* cracked. She wasn't wrong. And if it was true—if Gwen really was Sir Gawain—then anything was possible.

The tavern was situated at the edge of the town clustered around Darkhaven Castle, and it had been a long walk from Gwen's village. Isobelle had tried once or twice along the way to strike up conversation, but Gwen's grim, thundercloud expression warned her not to push her luck before she'd made her case. It gave Isobelle time to mentally work on her pitch, and she was so absorbed in the task, she nearly ran into Gwen's back when the other girl halted.

Above them hung the sign for the Siren's Sting, complete with a lovingly painted depiction of a plump, cheerful sea nymph holding an improbably foaming mug of ale.

Isobelle caught Gwen's eye and beamed at her, noting that the other girl's only response to her trademark killer smile was a tightening of her already-worried features, like someone preparing for a blow. Isobelle softened her smile, winked, and murmured, "Brace yourself."

She pushed the door open.

They stepped into an ocean of raucous sound, women packed in tightly with drinks in hand, everyone raising their voices to be heard over everyone else. The fiddler (a woman, of course) had the dance floor hopping, and Isobelle recognized a few noblewomen in town for the tournament who had snuck away from the castle to join the fun.

Isobelle squared her shoulders and pushed her way through the crowd, letting it half carry her and Gwen toward the bar.

They reached the bar together, where the tavern owner herself was taking orders. Isobelle braced herself with her forearms to hold her space, squeaking as she was jostled against the wooden counter. Without speaking, Gwen put an arm behind her to fend off the crowd—she used her left arm, which made sense. The right one would be smarting after that hit she took from the second round with Sir Evonwald.

Isobelle glanced up to make a joke about that, but her gaze snagged on the other girl's, and she forgot what she'd planned to say. There was a challenge in those moss-green eyes, a kind of barricade that Gwen had shut herself behind.

This was, Isobelle reflected, the first time she'd heard of a lady needing to storm the castle to reach a knight.

"Good evening, ladies, how can— Oh, Lady Isobelle!" The tavernkeeper had turned toward them, her face splitting into a grin. She was a middle-aged woman with sleek dark hair and black eyes and a nigh-uncanny talent for remembering the names of everyone who walked into her tavern. "But where are your friends? Surely you didn't come alone?"

"Hi, Jinna! I'm here with my new friend Gwen." Isobelle turned slightly so the woman could see Gwen standing behind her, face still frozen in confusion at the hubbub.

"Well, then your first round is on the house." Jinna gestured to the board on the wall behind her, where a dozen handwritten drinks had been listed. "Gwen, since you're new here, I do things a little differently in my place, and I mix my own drinks for my customers. Each coquetel is handcrafted, each guaranteed to conjure exactly what its name promises."

Isobelle scanned the list, noting such tempting options as "Midnight Rendezvous" and "Twinkle-Toe Toddy," until her eyes lit on the final drink on the menu. She found herself grinning. "I'll have a White Knight, please."

"An excellent choice. And you, Gwen?" The tavern owner's gaze flicked across to Gwen, and Isobelle's did, too.

Gwen blinked and tried to respond naturally, though even Isobelle could see the faint indicators of panic around her eyes and lips. "Oh. I, uh . . . do you have ale?"

Jinna raised her impeccably arched eyebrows, and Isobelle half expected her to push back and insist Gwen try something more adventurous. But, displaying that uncanny knack she had of anticipating her patrons' needs, she simply nodded, letting Gwen stick to the familiar. "Coming right up, ladies."

Isobelle realized she was staring at Gwen too, watching her even more intently than Jinna had, and wrenched her gaze away toward something, anything, else. "Oooh, there's a table opening up against the wall. Grab it, quick!"

Looking mildly relieved to have a reason to run away, Gwen ducked through the crowd, dodging a cluster of dancers moving toward the fiddler, then making a lunge for the table, getting a hand on it just before a trio of well-dressed women reached it. One of them opened her mouth to argue, but then they all took a look at Gwen's *you would not believe the night I am having* expression, and silently but unanimously took a step back.

As Isobelle slid into her chair opposite Gwen, she braced herself, trying to remember how her rehearsed pitch began.

But Gwen's eyes slid from her face, fixing instead on the tavern owner bustling away behind the bar. "She said this was her place," she murmured, just loud enough to be heard over the din. "She owns it?"

Isobelle nodded. "My friend Sylvie told me about this place a few months ago. Jinna's a widow, and her husband didn't have much when he died. But she bought this place from the previous owner after working her way up, and now . . . well, you can see what it is now."

She glanced out toward the dance floor stuffed full of women dancing and talking and gesturing wildly, laughing at bawdy jokes and shouting over the music. There were men in the crowd here and there, but they were decidedly in the minority.

"It's a little like something... magic," Gwen murmured, a slight wistfulness slipping past the defenses in her expression. "I never knew a place like this existed."

Isobelle watched Gwen's profile as she gazed out at the spectacle. She was aware of a strange tugging in her chest, a need to speak or act, though she hadn't the faintest idea what to say.

And then Jinna was there, shattering that moment of tension. She set down Gwen's ale, and then Isobelle's drink, a white concoction topped with a sprig of mint and several blackberries speared through with a miniature wooden lance.

Gwen stared at it as Isobelle thanked Jinna. "What on earth is *that?*" she murmured finally. "She said... cocktail?"

Isobelle grinned. "She did. It's all the rage on the continent, and Jinna imported the idea. I would've ordinarily gone for the Midnight Rendezvous, but I couldn't quite resist trying the White Knight. It seemed... thematically appropriate." She raised the lance to her lips and popped one of the berries into her mouth, her eyes never leaving Gwen's face.

Gwen's barricades snapped back into place, so firmly that a faint frown line appeared between her eyebrows and her rosy lips flattened into a line.

"There's no need to be so cross." Isobelle lobbed her opening salvo across the net with a flash of her dimples. "I came to congratulate you on your victory."

The frown line did not go away.

"No need?" Gwen echoed. "You wake me in the middle of the night, drag me out of my house, make me come to this... this... mad place, and accuse me of being..." She trailed off, then lifted her hands to scrub at her face, her voice muffled. "You're like something out of a ballad," she muttered, more to herself than to Isobelle. "And not one of the more believable ones."

"Well, firstly, literally none of the fun ballads are about anything believable," Isobelle pointed out. "And secondly"—and here she lowered her voice, leaning in for a deliciously dramatic effect—"you think *I'm* the one out of a ballad, *Sir Gawain*?"

Gwen's eyes closed, and she allowed herself a long breath. "My lady," she said, addressing her ale, rather than risking looking up at Isobelle. "Before you turn me in, you should know that's as far as this was ever going to go. I wasn't going to compete in the tourney proper. I just . . . I wanted to know that I *could*."

She did glance up then, and for a moment, her fear and her frustration were supplanted by a sort of wistfulness that made Isobelle catch her breath. Then it was gone, Gwen's expression closed and shuttered again, that hope locked away.

"I'm finished," Gwen said quietly. "No one will ever see Sir Gawain again."

"What?" Isobelle was glad a round of screaming from the dance floor drowned out what could charitably be described as a squawk. "No, no, you can't! You can't stop now! You knocked Sir Evonwald right off his horse, it was magnificent!"

Gwen tried to stifle a laugh, then shook her head, making herself serious again. "Doesn't matter. I'm not a noble. I'm a woman. I have an actual job to do." She ticked the reasons off on her fingers one by one, and without thinking, Isobelle let herself reach out, closing her hand gently over Gwen's and folding her fingers back down again.

For some reason, Gwen held still and let her do it.

"You *do* have a job to do," Isobelle agreed. She knew she needed to infect Gwen with some of the wild hope that had lit up inside her own chest when she'd realized what she was watching in the jousting lists. That hope made something flutter behind her ribs, gave her prickles between her shoulder blades—made even Isobelle, for whom boldness was a way of life, sound uneven. The noise of the tavern probably covered that, too.

She had an inkling Gwen might be susceptible to that kind of hope. She might play at practicality, but no woman would masquerade as a knight in shining armor without a spark of romance and imagination in her soul.

"Your job is to keep knocking them flat." Isobelle injected her voice with confidence. "With your helmet on and visor down, who's ever going to guess you're a woman? It won't even occur to them. Sir Evonwald wasn't a nobody, that was a proper win. And wasn't it glorious?"

"You saw through me," Gwen protested. "And when they do find out—I don't even know what they'll do to me, there's no precedent. I know it'll be bad." But even as Isobelle searched for a reply, the corners of Gwen's mouth flicked up, trying and failing to hide her smile. "It was pretty good, though, wasn't it?"

"He landed square on his butt," Isobelle crowed. "He'll be waddling for weeks, and the ladies of the court thank you. He's an absolute lech, anything that slows him down is a gift. But truly—unless you showed all the members of the court the engraving on your sword, then why would they notice?"

"I didn't show it to *you*," Gwen protested. "You grabbed it. And they won't need that kind of clue, not once they're paying attention. Barely anyone was watching this time."

"Even when people do watch, they don't *see*. Not if they aren't expecting what's there in front of their eyes."

Gwen picked up her ale, cheeks pink, but then put it down again. "Why are you doing this?" she asked finally. Isobelle thought she saw a glimmer of something—a hint of that hope?—hidden behind her scowl. "Are you just *bored* being a lady, and want some kind of adventure?"

"No," Isobelle replied firmly. Staring down the approach of her own doom was a lot of things, but she could honestly say that boring wasn't one of them. "I just think it's wonderful. Don't you want to see how far you could go?"

Gwen didn't answer. The urge to fill the silence tugged at Isobelle, and she made herself take a breath, let it out. She let her gaze trace the other girl's features, breaking them down, centering herself as she made a list: the constellations of freckles across her strong nose and cheekbones. The line of her jaw. The strand of black hair that had escaped her braid and was curling in toward her lips like a beckoning finger.

"You're the dragon sacrifice this year," Gwen said eventually. "I heard the knights talking about it."

Isobelle felt like a cold grip was squeezing her stomach. "Yes," she said simply. "My dowry guarantees that whoever wins will most certainly claim my hand in marriage."

"That's such bullshit," Gwen retorted, her good hand tightening into a fist. There was a cold fury in that gaze now, not nearly so shielded as before. "What if he's an asshole?"

"That, unfortunately, is not a hypothetical," Isobelle replied, swallowing down a wave of revulsion at the memory of Sir Ralph's direct gaze after his effortless win. "Almost all the favorites are. So, can't blame a girl for trying a wild scheme, can you?"

Gwen's eyes were narrowed, but she seemed thoughtful, rather than dismissive. "What about the guy you were with at the market? Sir Awesome?"

"Orson's not so bad," Isobelle admitted with a rueful smile. "But we grew up together, and . . . he's not interested in me. Or women in general. Or anyone, really. He'd still marry me, I suspect, for the dowry—his estate is pretty badly in debt, thanks to his late unlamented father's unwise decisions." She steadied herself with a breath. "The best of my bad options is a man who doesn't want to marry me at all. And the most likely is a horrible excuse for a human, who can't wait for the wedding night. Either way, whoever it is won't love me in the least."

Gwen was still watching her, her expression scarcely changing except for the barest flicker.

Isobelle thought it might be understanding, and she added quietly, "Is it such a reprehensible thing to want something *more* than the least terrible option? To choose my own fate instead of being parceled off to someone like property?"

She took a sip of her cocktail for good measure, then grimaced and set it down. "Can I try a sip of your ale? Maybe ordering on name alone was a bad idea."

Gwen pushed her mug across, but her gaze was on Isobelle's drink.

"Oh," she said simply, a subtle shift taking over her features. Realization. "A white knight."

Isobelle held her breath, barely daring to hope. Trying, with everything she had, not to let Gwen see the fear gripping her at the mere mention of the fate awaiting her if she didn't find some way out of it.

"Like something out of a ballad," she agreed softly. "Someone who could win—who could take the treasure, the glory—but *not* trap me in a marriage that's loveless at best, and ... worse, at worst." She tried for a smile, though it felt watery. "I thought perhaps on Ladies' Night I could find a lady's knight, if you'll forgive the terrible pun."

"We're *not* talking about this." Gwen dragged her gaze away from the cocktail, fixing it on Isobelle. "We're not talking about it, we're not considering it, we're not even— It's madness."

"Is it?" Isobelle asked lightly.

"Of course it is!"

"If you say so."

"I do! I mean . . . isn't it? Even if I competed—even if I could avoid being discovered—how would I win? I don't know what I'm doing. I got extremely, ridiculously lucky today. I need training, but anyone we went to for help would turn me in in a heartbeat."

"A man might, true." Isobelle grinned at her, pushing the cocktail forward to offer it to Gwen.

Gwen was staring at Isobelle like she was waiting for her to grow an extra head, or explode into a puff of pink glitter. "You know a woman who can joust? I mean, there *is* a woman who can joust? And *you* know her?"

"Yes and yes."

"Simple as that?"

"What else is there? You already have a very nice horse. Where did you get him?"

"He's mine," Gwen replied, so fast it was almost a snap, curling her hands around the cocktail glass as if she could use it as a shield.

Huh. Interesting.

"No doubt," Isobelle agreed, though to be honest, the stallion Gwen had been riding earlier that day looked far too well-bred to have a history pulling a plough.

"Achilles was a foal from my mother's mare," Gwen said, stiffer than she'd been before, holding herself upright. "And she—she brought her horse with her when she left home to marry my father."

"Well, he's very handsome," Isobelle replied, letting the other girl off the hook and focusing her attention on the aesthetic. "Bays are really in fashion this season."

Gwen's shoulders dropped a little. "I'd need to hire someone to help my father in the smithy on the days I'm away," she murmured.

It took everything Isobelle had not to tip her head back and let out an unladylike hoot of victory. Until this moment, even Isobelle wasn't sure this plan would work.

"I can help with that."

Gwen bit her lip, clearly in the throes of mental calculation, tracing the edge of her glass with one finger. "Stop looking at me like that," she muttered, eyes flicking up, glittering with a combination of bemusement and terror. Isobelle was used to inspiring both. "I haven't decided."

"I like looking at you," Isobelle replied. Sometimes, honesty really was the best policy. Gwen had a charming, unique style of loveliness that was all her own. "Did you want to try that cocktail, Sir Knight?"

Absently, Gwen lifted the glass for a sip. Then she blinked, a tiny flush of pleasure rising behind her freckles, and she took another, longer sip. "It's all right," she muttered, as if her delight at the frivolous drink weren't adorably plain to read on her face.

She was quiet after that, her eyes distant. Longing and fear warred in her expression, the battle as easy to see as her pleasure had been.

"I think," said Isobelle with great care, "that it must have been an enormous amount of work for you. Making the armor. Learning how to make the armor in the first place! Teaching yourself to joust—making the lances, finding the time."

A grudging nod from Gwen conceded that all this was true.

"And I think," Isobelle continued, treading even more cautiously now, "there's only one reason someone would do all that."

"And what do you suppose that reason is, my lady?" Gwen asked as she took another heartfelt sip from the cocktail.

"I think she must truly want to be a knight," Isobelle said simply. "I think, unlike most of the oafs wandering around the castle right now, she must have found something noble in the idea."

Gwen was silent, but her expression was eloquent—the yearning was there in her eyes, and the hubbub of the tavern seemed to fade away into nothingness around them, everything falling quiet, the dancers and drinkers blurring at the edge of Isobelle's vision.

"I think," Isobelle said, her eyes intent on the girl across from her, "it would be a great loss indeed if she were to give it up."

For a time they were quiet, and Isobelle waited. Her heart was fluttering so strangely, beating against the inside of her ribs like a bird against the bars of a cage. She didn't want Gwen to agree just because Isobelle couldn't think of any other way to escape her fate. She wanted the world to be bigger than that.

"None of them were what I expected at all," Gwen said, so softly Isobelle had to lean toward her to make out the words. "The other knights."

"*You* could be," she countered. "You could be what they aren't. Someone should."

"I'll need to be up at the castle to train," Gwen said, and Isobelle bit her lip against her smile. "But I can't be Sir Gawain all the time, I'd never pass as a man without my armor on. I'll have to stay somewhere as myself."

"You can stay with me," said Isobelle brightly, somewhat surprising herself. "I have a spare room."

Gwen looked surprised too, and took another sip of the White Knight. "How will I explain why I'm there? You can't just import a blacksmith's daughter and install her in your apartments."

"Well, I probably can't explain a blacksmith's daughter," Isobelle admitted, feeling a wave of genius wash over her and grinning. "Actually, I've had a thought—"

"No," said Gwen firmly. "Whatever it is, no. I've already learned not to trust those dimples."

"We could make you Sir Gawain's sister. That'll help prop up the illusion that he's real."

Gwen nearly choked on the drink. "We want people to believe Sir Gawain is a noble," she pointed out. "You don't think we'll tip people off when his sister is a backward village girl with the manners of a peasant?"

Isobelle was so delighted by the idea—and by the way Gwen was now talking about the plan as though the decision had been made—that she couldn't pack away the dimples, even to appear more dependable. "As it happens, I like his sister's manners very much."

Gwen propped her chin on one hand, abandoning the drink, which was mostly finished now anyway. "This is madness," she said. "Tell me you know it's madness to even talk about this. I need to know you understand that."

Perhaps it was. No, scratch that—it most certainly was. But with all the resources at Isobelle's command, with the training she knew Madame Dupont could offer, with Gwen's determination, the steel in her gaze . . . that didn't mean it couldn't work.

"Does it being madness," Isobelle asked carefully, "preclude us from doing it?"

Gwen stared at her, and the moment drew out as their gazes locked. Isobelle wished she were the sort of person who prayed. She'd always found it best to make her own luck, though.

"I think," said Gwen slowly, braced like a girl about to put her hand in a fire, "that I don't mind a little madness."

Chapter Seven

CHIVALRY IS ALL WELL AND GOOD, BUT CURSED INCONVENIENT AT TIMES

The girl from the castle was absolutely, breathtakingly mesmerizing. Gwen, head spinning and thoughts whirling, found herself clutching her drink and trying not to stare. She was beautiful, sure, but it was Isobelle's sheer force of will that kept robbing Gwen of her good sense. Every time Gwen thought of an objection to her lunatic plan, Isobelle had an answer. Every time Gwen thought she'd gotten her feet steady again, Isobelle swept the rug out from under her.

And, worst of all, Gwen's heart was swelling with that same dangerous, euphoric feeling of hope that had surged through her when she'd knocked Sir Evonwald off his horse. She thought she'd stamped it out after she'd gotten home.

Gwen swallowed hard and finished the cocktail Isobelle had ordered. "So if—*if*—I agree to this . . . what happens next?"

Isobelle's eyes lit with delight, glowing like miniature sapphire stars. "Oh, Gwen—"

"I said *if*!" Gwen interrupted, trying desperately not to smile like some spell-charmed idiot in response to the other girl's giddy relief. "Wipe that grin off your face."

Isobelle made a token effort to sheathe her dimples. "Well, you come to the castle in the morning, and we'll get you settled in, and then—"

The door of the tavern banged open with a loud, shuddering crash. Gwen started to her feet, but she couldn't see what was happening through the crowds of people on the dance floor. The fiddle music petered out, the dancers halted, conversation and laughter and cheers evaporated into tense, frightened silence. The crowds began to shrink back from the door, revealing a posse of half a dozen intruders.

Men in matching armor bearing the red-and-bronze emblem of Darkhaven, their swords drawn.

The castle guard.

Their leader, a short but burly man with a large, bushy blond mustache, addressed the crowd. "Break it up, girls—go home quietly. We're not here for you."

No one moved.

The man scowled slightly and glanced around at the now-silent crowd. "What a circus." He strode a few more steps into the room. "We're here for the woman claiming to own this place. Where is she?"

Isobelle started to rise, her body tensing. Gwen, her heart shriveling at the phrasing of the guard's demand, put a hand over Isobelle's. One of the waitstaff who'd been helping to deliver drinks stepped forward, her chin lifting. "She ain't here, mister."

The mustachioed guard snorted, eyeing the girl with disdain. "Here or not, we're shutting this place down. Unlicensed hedge witchery on the premises."

This was too much for Isobelle, who lurched to her feet despite Gwen's warning. "Hedge witchery?" she sputtered. "On whose say-so?"

The guard's gaze traveled toward Isobelle and his eyes widened as he realized he was speaking to a noblewoman. "That's confidential, my lady. But it's obviously true. Here, look at that list of potions there." He jerked his chin toward the board bearing the list of cocktails.

"Those aren't potions!" Isobelle objected, her eyes blazing. "They're drinks!"

The guard seemed to find Isobelle's gaze nearly as difficult to withstand as Gwen, but he managed, gritting his teeth. "If the woman called Jinna is not here, we'll take this one in her place to speak for her," he said, reaching out to take the arm of the waiter who'd spoken earlier.

"Enough!" Jinna made her way through the crowd, her eyes flat, her lips set. "Enough, let her go. I'm the one you're after."

The guard looked her up and down, matching her up to some mental description. "You're to come with us."

"This isn't about my license or lack thereof," said Jinna, folding her arms as she came to a stop between the guard and her waiter. "I know who your informant was—my dear brother-in-law, isn't it?"

The mustachioed guard stepped forward, shifting his grip on his sword menacingly. "It's up to Lord Whimsitt to arbitrate his claim of inheritance on your late husband's property. Come with us peacefully now. No one needs to get hurt."

Gwen could see Isobelle vibrating with fury, could feel the echo of that fury in her own breast—mingling with the awful dread she'd lived with ever since she began taking over her father's smithy.

This was what happened to women who did men's work. Jinna had earned her place owning and running this tavern by herself, but what did that matter to the men who ran this world? All they saw was a woman who dared set foot in their territory. Who dared dream for herself.

Jinna was standing there, her face serene, but her eyes as flat and hard as obsidian. Then, lifting her head, she said, "All right. I surrender."

The words had barely left her lips when a cry rippled through the gathered crowd. The waiter on whose behalf Jinna had intervened surged forward, shouting, "Here, now, you can take her over my cold, dead—"

The head guard let out an oath as she flew at him, and with one sweep of his arm, he knocked her down.

The smattering of outrage turned into a deluge. The crowd surged forward, engulfing the guards, tables and chairs overturning. Gwen lurched to her feet and caught hold of Isobelle's hand, desperate not to lose her in the melee. The other girl met her gaze, her eyes wide with shared fear and anger and shock.

And then someone grabbed her and pulled her out of Gwen's grip.

The crowd buffeted Gwen away, and it took her several long, heart-stopping breaths to find Isobelle again. She was being held by the arms firmly, but respectfully, by a familiar-looking man not in the livery of the castle guard, but a simple, well-made doublet and hose. A flash of memory provided Gwen with a name: Orson, the handsome young knight who'd accompanied Isobelle at the market. The one who didn't want to marry her, but would anyway.

"How *dare* you become involved with this," Isobelle was shouting at him, trying to free herself. "She's an innocent woman, all of this is—"

"I know!" Sir Orson cut her off, his face grim, brows drawn in with concern. "Isobelle, come on, I know that. We can look for a way to help her later, but I need to make sure you're okay first. I only came along because I knew you'd be here—I've got to get you back to the castle before anyone realizes you were here."

Isobelle stopped struggling and stood panting, body still rigid with fury. "I can see myself back," she snapped.

Orson groaned. "Izzie, *please*. I have to see you back safely. For my sake, allow me to escort you, so I know you're okay."

Gwen bit her lip. Chivalry was all well and good, but cursed inconvenient at times.

She'd been tense, ready to launch herself at Isobelle's captor—but now there was nowhere for her fighting instinct to go. The guards had Jinna in irons and had gotten her to the door of the tavern, and the riot of her patrons had been very neatly quelled.

Gwen felt Isobelle's eyes before she saw them—lifting her head, she saw the other girl craning her neck as Orson walked her toward the door, one arm protectively around her shoulders. For an instant, Isobelle's eyes met Gwen's.

In that moment, Gwen would've wrested a sword from one of the guards and gone after her, if Isobelle's eyes had demanded it of her. Instead, in Isobelle's face there was a single desperate question.

Will you still come?

Gwen shifted her weight, feeling the crunch of the shattered cocktail glass under her boot.

She nodded, and Isobelle vanished into the night.

Chapter Eight

JUST PUT HER THERE

Isobelle buried Orson in icy silence the entire way back to the castle. She let him lead her, too busy with her own whirl of thoughts, the absolute injustice of Jinna's fate jostling side by side with that last, burning look she'd exchanged with Gwen.

So busy, in fact, that she didn't realize where they were headed until they were a few paces from the door.

She stiffened. "I thought you wanted to get me back before he found out I was gone."

Orson reached for the latch on the door. "He knows. I had to get you back before anyone *else* noticed and he couldn't pretend ignorance. Izzie, we're not kids anymore. You . . ." Orson's handsome features were uncharacteristically solemn and grim. "You've got to start taking these things more seriously. There are consequences."

And with that, he opened the door and led her through.

Lord Whimsitt stood at the window, silhouetted by the light of the broad fireplace behind him. He looked up as they entered and nodded. "Thank you, Sir Orson. Just put her there—you may go."

Isobelle fought a flash of indignation as Orson deposited her in a chair, bowed, and left. "I'm not some bag of laundry you can just have placed somewhere," she protested.

Whimsitt had returned his gaze to the window, but his hands, folded behind his back, whitened at the knuckles. "Explain yourself," he said, ignoring her protest. "Why did you sneak out of the castle tonight?"

"To go out." Isobelle swallowed and lifted her chin. "To meet some friends. Why should that matter to you?"

"Because you are my responsibility!" snapped Whimsitt, finally turning from the window, his face reddening with irritation. "Because you continue to act as though your conduct has no impact on those around you. I thought time would mellow your childish disobedience, or your parents would return to manage your discipline, but as I am still your guardian, I am still the one to decide what you do and where you go."

Isobelle hadn't had a moment to relocate her equilibrium since the guards had burst into the Siren's Sting. Now she searched for that easy, charming veneer of calm she'd learned to cultivate. "I know, my lord." She lowered her chin and gazed up at him through her eyelashes. "I was only—"

"Isobelle, you will be wed in a few months' time to the winner of the tournament." The words hit Isobelle like a body blow, cutting her off and leaving her without breath to reply. Whimsitt continued, "I thought you would understand how your situation has changed when I informed you of my decision to announce you as the dragon sacrifice—clearly, I must spell it out for you."

"My lord—"

He moved toward her, half a step too far into her space, eyes boring into hers. "Your conduct must be above reproach. Your virtue without question. Your obedience . . ." He sucked in a breath through his nose. "Your obedience immediate. Whichever man is to be your husband, I guarantee he will not be so lenient nor negligent as I. Nor as forgiving in his method of discipline."

Isobelle felt her veneer of charming calm drift away in tatters, an icy chill sliding slowly down her spine. "My lord, if my conduct is so objectionable to you, perhaps I'm not the right choice as the prize for this tournament. Maybe the treasure alone, even if it came from my own dowry, would be—"

"Enough!" Whimsitt ran a hand over his head, sans hat for once. "Enough, Isobelle. The decision is made, your name announced. And as of tonight, you will not leave the castle grounds unaccompanied, and then only to show your face at the tournament as expected. Do I make myself clear?"

Isobelle stared at him, feeling the floor drop out from under her. "You're—you're *grounding* me?"

His face was thunderous, her protest budging him not an inch. "I have let you run wild and indulged your girlish whims for far too long—this is the answer for us both. I will do whatever I must to keep you safe until the tournament is won, and you are wed. You *will* learn obedience—and I will have discharged my duties as your guardian."

And I'll be someone else's problem, thought Isobelle. That was what he really meant.

"My lord," she said, trying one last time to dull the edge of his outrage. "I'm sorry for angering you—I never meant to show you any disrespect. I'm grateful for all you've done for me."

Whimsitt's face softened a touch. "I know, child. Go, get some rest. Let us put all this foolishness behind us and look ahead to the delights of the tournament."

Isobelle understood the dismissal for what it was—and noted

he had not rescinded his ultimatum. She felt herself drop into a curtsy, seemed to watch from a distance as she left his quarters and made her way back toward her own.

She should have known better than to try again to talk him out of his decision to give her away to whichever knight managed to stay on his horse the longest. He was a petty, ineffectual man, but unreasonably attached to his declarations once they were made.

She needed a different sort of plan.

In her mind's eye she replayed that last, glorious instant when Gwen's eyes had met hers across the chaos unfolding in the tavern. Isobelle hadn't spoken or called out, but somehow Gwen had seen her, heard her. Had Isobelle only imagined the resolve in the other girl's face as she nodded?

She'll come, she told herself firmly. *She has to.*

BY NOW, DEAR READER, YOU'VE probably decided that Lord Whimsitt is our villain. But let's not be so hasty to judgment. He has, after all, rather a lot on his mind, and you've been swept up in the charisma and charm of his ward and her champion.

Perfectly understandable. She's *very* charming.

The Tournament of Dragonslayers takes place once every four years, but for generations, the tiny county of Darkhaven never had a chance at successfully bidding to host. Wealthy counties could always double or even triple the amount of Darkhaven's bid, not to mention the absolute fortunes spent on bribing the TODS executive committee.

Darkhaven's only real source of wealth is a gold mine that hadn't been used in centuries for the superstitious fear of waking that which ought to be left alone. Until a great man named Whimsitt had a dream.

The lord of Darkhaven is, in fact, ahead of his time. Doing away with silly old superstitions and campaigning tirelessly to bring fame and fortune into his land, even devising a way to offer the largest prize pot in tournament history by tapping into his ward's dowry.

Even now, the whole world is descending on Darkhaven. And Whimsitt would much rather be rushing around, muttering about infrastructure, than dealing with a spoiled, willful teenaged girl with more money than sense.

He never asked to be her guardian. He was, in actuality, a saint for agreeing with the king's order to watch over Avington's only child.

Someday they will write about him in the history texts as a great leader, daring to defy custom and usher in a modern, enlightened age. A man universally loved by the little people and admired by his peers.

Respected by all.

I ought to pause here and ask you, reader: Are you familiar with the term "unreliable narrator"?

Chapter Nine

DON'T TRY TO FIGHT IT, YOU'LL ONLY HURT YOURSELF

By the time the sun cleared the horizon the next day, Gwen was waiting in the shade of an oak tree outside the castle walls, holding Achilles's reins somewhat more tightly than she needed to. The stallion was far more at ease than she felt—he stood calmly, head swinging occasionally to track a passerby, whereas Gwen was fighting the urge to fidget wildly. She needed to vent the buildup of nervous energy buzzing through her body, but she was all too aware she had to avoid drawing attention.

There were so many risks and logic holes in Isobelle's plan that Gwen couldn't bear to look at them all head on for fear she'd talk herself out of the whole thing, so she'd settled for focusing on the challenges directly in front of her. Today, she had to slip into the castle unnoticed so Isobelle could transform her into Sir Gawain's sister without anyone making the connection between that fictitious lady and the somewhat hollow-eyed and hungover blacksmith's daughter standing outside the gate.

Somewhere ahead of her lay challenges like "somehow look like a lady" and "don't fall off my horse while men twice my size try to knock me off with sticks," but she decided not to think about that.

Gwen was good at not thinking about things.

She'd very nearly not come at all this morning, trying to

convince herself that the night before had been a dream. Or some drunken fantasy. That Isobelle herself, flighty and flirty and so expert at hiding what was going on behind her smile that it often seemed *nothing* was going on there, would forget the scheme she'd proposed. Or that she'd rethink the wisdom of the idea after seeing what had happened to Jinna.

The woman's arrest had certainly shaken Gwen. Fear and anger both had kept her tossing and turning most of the night. But something had made her dress and saddle Achilles and ride out into the still morning air. Gwen had spent every step of the journey to the castle trying not to think about the sheer insanity of what she was doing.

Too late to turn back, now she was here.

Or was it?

A trio of young men, attired like vendors or performers here for the festival, emerged from the castle gates and began making their way down toward the chaos of the festival grounds. One of them, a curly-haired, dark-eyed beauty, glanced at Gwen and flashed her a charming smile.

She stared at him blankly, her mind so preoccupied with planning for contingencies that she couldn't so much as nod.

The charming smile faltered, then vanished as the guy hurried his steps. No doubt counting his blessings that he hadn't struck up a conversation with the weird girl clutching a horse's reins like she might fall down without them.

Somewhere to her left, someone cleared their throat.

Gwen jumped, glancing back to find a young woman standing there watching her with one eyebrow slightly raised. Gwen recognized her as the lady's maid who had accompanied Isobelle the first day they met—the one who had not so subtly encouraged Gwen to inflate her prices because her lady could afford it.

Though she hadn't exactly been warm and friendly that day, her demeanor had been positively genial compared to the icy stare directed at Gwen now.

"What the— You came out of nowhere," Gwen blurted, shifting her grip on Achilles's reins. The horse dropped his head over her shoulder, eyeing the new arrival that his mistress found so terrifying.

The lady's maid didn't so much as smile. "I get that a lot." Her gaze swiveled over toward the horse. "He's a massive one, isn't he?"

"What?" Gwen's heart was still hammering. She glanced at her horse, who was tossing his head coquettishly, showing off the stubborn cowlick that gave his mane the look of a crested Greek helmet. "Oh—yeah, this is Achilles. He, uh, comes from good stock."

"Well, that's something, I suppose." The woman's tone made it effortlessly clear Gwen's own stock was rather wanting.

"You're Olivia, right?" Gwen reached for something friendly, uncertain as to the source of the maid's clear animosity.

"And you're the girl my lady's decided to play with for the next month. She is confined to the castle after last night's fiasco, so she sent me to fetch you. Come along, I've found a place to stable your horse that won't attract attention from the other knights."

Olivia turned back toward the castle without bothering to check that Gwen was following her. Gwen glanced at Achilles, who gazed back at her out of one eye, rolling it slightly in an equine shrug. With an inaudible sigh, Gwen turned and followed the maid up into the castle grounds.

Olivia had identified a nobleman who was overseas for the

season, leaving his section of the stables—and his stableman—idle. Gwen took an instant liking to the stableman, who without hesitation reached into his pocket for a slightly withered apple and offered it to Achilles. Jeffers had little attention to spare for Olivia or Gwen, his attention immediately and wholeheartedly captured by the stallion.

Gwen left them, Jeffers murmuring a steady, unintelligible stream of sweet nothings to the massive bay horse, Achilles rolling his eyes and looking like the coyest of ladies batting her eyelashes and fanning herself.

Ruefully, Gwen couldn't help but think she was the only one of the lot of them feeling rather sick as she walked away from the stables again, leaving behind the one friend she had in this massive, imposing place.

"My lady asked me to bring you to her quarters after finding a place for your horse," said Olivia as she led Gwen up a winding set of stone steps. She'd brought Gwen in through a side entrance for servants, far less grand than the main doors at the front. "Then we'll decide what to do about clothes." Her head turned slightly, flashing her a sidelong glance. "And the rest of it."

Gwen felt the tension lacing her shoulders tighten the tiniest bit more. "Believe me, I'm no more enthused about this than you are. Is— Lady Isobelle is the one who thinks it'll be no problem passing me off as a noblewoman."

They reached the top of the staircase, which opened out into a long corridor. The space was narrow, but the floor was adorned by long, fine carpets, and the torches lighting the way guttered and smoked far less than the ones downstairs.

Olivia paused for another look at Gwen. Grudgingly, she

murmured, "I guess you've got good hair, at least. You're not planning on chopping it off for this ridiculous charade as Sir Gawain, are you?"

Gwen closed her fingers protectively around the braid hanging over her shoulder. "Of course not," she replied hastily. She was all too aware that her long, thick black hair was one of her only feminine beauties. "It fits under my helmet."

Olivia nodded, still watching Gwen with a measured gaze. "As far as my lady is concerned, she doesn't always think through her schemes. With any luck, she'll lose interest in this one quickly and we can all go back to our normal lives."

A portion of the air in Gwen's lungs whooshed out, like she'd been slammed with another of those blows from Sir Evonwald's lance. Instinct planted her feet, balled her fists, went coursing through her system, telling her it was time to fight.

Except Olivia wasn't wrong. It probably *would* be better if they could all go back to their lives.

But then there was Isobelle herself. Even after Gwen had snuck back into her bedroom last night, she lay awake, unable to shake the torrent of thoughts and images invading her mind every time she closed her eyes. Isobelle had a face designed for openness and vulnerability, with delight and frivolity shining from every pore. Gwen had no doubt that the vast majority of people in Isobelle's life dismissed her as a vapid, fashion-obsessed idiot—as Gwen herself had nearly done at the market, until the whirlwind that was Isobelle had swept down on top of her.

Isobelle was no idiot. She'd seen through Gwen's masquerade in a heartbeat when no one else even questioned Sir Gawain's existence. She'd come up with this entire plan, which was brilliant.

Mad, but brilliant. Gwen couldn't help but think that open, honest, charming face of Isobelle's that seemed to show her every thought and whim might be a far better mask than any of Gwen's scowls had ever been.

Her mind could not stop replaying one specific moment from that night, when Isobelle's mask had slipped. A flicker of something deeper, gripping, consuming, had shown through when Gwen realized what Isobelle was proposing.

A white knight, Gwen had breathed.

Isobelle's eyes had met hers. *Like something out of a ballad.*

Gwen blinked, swallowed, and lifted her head to meet Olivia's gaze. "I don't think this is one of those schemes," she said slowly. "I don't think she'll lose interest."

Olivia's eyes narrowed. "I know my lady a little better than you do, Gwen of Ellsdale."

"But you don't know me." That tension in her shoulders that had been gathering since she left the village that morning snapped free.

"I suppose it's a once-in-a-lifetime chance to play at being something more than you are," said Olivia coolly. Suddenly, her animosity made sense.

"She asked me to help her," Gwen replied simply. "I intend to do so."

Olivia held her gaze, letting the silence draw out, her own eyes clearly scrutinizing the shabby, plain girl in front of her. Then, after an agony of waiting, the corner of her mouth lifted and a spark in her eyes hinted at the thawing of that icy attitude.

"That's good," she murmured. "You're going to need to hold on to that. Your reason."

She tipped her head, beckoning, and together they continued down the corridor. Gwen had only enough time to process that Olivia, too, excelled at the donning of masks, before they came to a halt in front of one of the doors.

"Last chance to say no." The lady's maid laid one hand on the latch and turned to look at Gwen, her eyebrows raised. "I can handle her, if you want to change your mind."

Gwen shook her head, smiling a little to match that faint thawing of Olivia's expression. "I think I was always going to end up here, after she decided to track me down."

Olivia's eyes gleamed again. "She does have that effect on people. My advice, if your mind is made up, is just . . . ride the whirlwind. Don't try to fight it, you'll only hurt yourself."

Gwen huffed a faint laugh, amused but unsurprised that Olivia had chosen the very same word Gwen had thought of when facing the sheer force of will that was Isobelle. Then Olivia was lifting the latch and pulling the door open.

Outside, the hall was a dreary dark gray, lit at intervals by the dull orange of torchlight, barely warmed by the worn maroon of the carpeting. Inside . . .

Inside was a riot of colors and textures and light. Fabrics everywhere, tapestries on the walls, mirrors, sunlight, ornaments on tables—an absolute explosion of luxury, stunning Gwen where she stood. Pinks and turquoises and golds, more color than she'd ever seen in one place. It was like Olivia had opened the door to an entirely different world. For a moment, she could scarcely breathe.

And then there was Isobelle's face, shining and full of that excitement and enthusiasm that had to be seen to be believed. She bounced up to the doorway, throwing out her arms to take hold of Gwen's unresisting hands and draw her inside.

"Oh, splendid!" she exclaimed, managing to sound delighted without allowing an ounce of surprise or relief to enter her voice. As if she'd never doubted, not for a single second, that Gwen would show. "You're here."

Chapter Ten

NOBODY EVER EXPECTS A LADY TO RAPPEL OFF A BALCONY

Isobelle had only been half sure—at best—that Gwen was going to show up. Even now she couldn't quite let go of the other girl's hands, wanting to anchor her here, lest she float away like smoke on the breeze. But already the distress of last night—the whitening of his lordship's knuckles, the sneers of the guards—was fading away into the background.

Isobelle decided to leave it all there. It was far less interesting than the girl before her.

"What *is* this place?" Gwen asked weakly, allowing herself to be drawn into the room.

"This?" Isobelle twisted around to get a better look at her surroundings. "This is my suite of rooms. Now, how is your horse? All settled?"

She'd been raised to ask about someone's family as a matter of courtesy, and she could immediately see she'd won herself some credit with the girl from the village for thinking of him.

"Achilles is very well settled, and already snacking," Gwen replied, but she was distracted. She pulled her hands away and drifted into the center of the room, leaving Isobelle flexing her fingers on empty space.

"I've never seen anything like this," she murmured, her gaze jumping from the chandelier to the silk pillows on the window seat to the racks of dresses Olivia had pulled out when choosing which to alter for Gwen.

"It's one of a kind," Isobelle agreed cheerfully. "I decorated it myself." Then, at a faint noise from Olivia: "Well, I had lots of ideas about how to make it lovely, anyway, and Olivia executed them flawlessly. Olivia excels at flawless execution."

Gwen's eyes flicked across to Isobelle, and then to Olivia, her mouth covertly twitching at that revision. Isobelle had a sneaking suspicion Gwen was amused by her, those forest-green eyes mirthful behind her ever-present shields. She found she didn't particularly mind.

Isobelle tried to take in the apartments through a newcomer's eyes as Gwen turned away to walk over to a wall of small portraits, each no larger than her palm. There must have been two dozen of them, quick studies of Isobelle, Sylvie, Jane, and Hilde undertaking various pursuits—they'd been daubed by a painter Jane had fancied, and Isobelle had tacked them up as reminders of her friends.

Isobelle had never much noticed the richness of the fabrics, the thick braiding along the edge of the sofas, the lush velvet of the curtains, the gold thread running through the tapestries.

This must be so very different from what Gwen was used to. But even as the girl from the village kept staring about her with a sort of appalled wonder, she stood her ground.

That was what Gwen did—she stood her ground. Whether she was running her father's smithy, ignored by everyone around her even as she did the work they all needed, or she was strapping on her armor to venture into the realm of knights and chivalry, a place where she was far from welcome. This much, Isobelle had already learned about her. Gwen simply lifted her chin, set her mouth, and—

Olivia poked her in the small of the back, and Isobelle blinked out of her daydream. What *was* it about Gwen that kept making her do that? The same thing that kept drawing her gaze back to her, she supposed—she was one of a kind. That was all.

Gwen had torn herself away from her inspection, and she was looking at Isobelle expectantly. It was very possible she'd said something and was waiting for an answer.

"Olivia's at work on your dresses," Isobelle said, setting off in a conversational direction of her choosing rather than requesting a recap of what she'd missed. "We can stay here this morning while she fits you."

"Already?" Gwen blinked. "But how do you know—"

"I noted your size at the market," Olivia replied, as though it was perfectly normal to mentally measure up everyone you met.

"I can do it myself," Gwen offered. "I'm no seamstress, but I can do alterations. I don't want to put you to any trouble."

Olivia snorted.

"I'm the one putting *you* to trouble," Isobelle said gracefully. "Anyway, we have the time. It's not like I need more dresses—apart from the way in which one always needs more dresses—and Olivia's the best there is. Now, breakfast will be here in a moment. I think we should eat out on the balcony."

"Breakfast?" Gwen glanced toward the window and the sun high in the sky. "But it's nearly noon. I ate when I rose."

"Well, lunch, if you like," Isobelle allowed generously. "Or whatever you call something that comes between the two. Brunch, how about that?"

"Brunch," Gwen murmured, absorbing the concept. She had this habit of echoing things Isobelle said in a way that didn't agree or object, but commented, as if to some third party who might find Isobelle's pronouncements as odd as she did.

"Then later we can practice curtsies and courtesies, so you can move around the castle with me as one of the ladies here for the tournament. And then this afternoon, your combat instructor."

"Absolutely nobody is going to believe I'm a noblewoman," Gwen countered, a line appearing between her brows.

"You'll be fine," Isobelle promised, resisting an inexplicable urge to smooth that frown line away. "We'll tell everyone you're terribly shy, which should excuse you from plenty of missteps."

"I *am* terribly shy," Gwen replied.

"Well, there you go, then." Isobelle accepted this news as evidence of her genius without missing a beat. "I think that has to be the plan, Olivia. Sir Gawain's sister ventures out into the world only when she must. Just as well—the absolute last thing we need right now is suitors."

"Suitors?" Gwen squeaked, half reaching for a sword that wasn't at her belt.

"A problem with which I am intimately acquainted," Isobelle replied regretfully. "Though not as intimately as some of them would prefer. At tourney time, it's something of a marriage market around here. You're a newcomer of the appropriate age, so you'll draw some interest. We can put them off by implying you have no money, but Olivia's dressmaking is exquisite, so she'll have to hold herself back if we don't want them to decide they simply don't care you're poor."

"I'm pretty good at discouraging men," Gwen said, with a shrug and a wry smile. "I don't think we need to worry too much."

Isobelle raised one brow. "I find it hard to believe you don't have admirers."

"They find me intimidatingly competent," Gwen replied with another shrug, Isobelle's compliment rolling off the other girl's back unnoticed. "And that's when I'm not even trying to put them off."

The clock on Isobelle's mantel chimed the hour, drawing Gwen's attention away. Shaped like a darling little chalet, its doors opened to emit a huntsman brandishing an axe—or they had done, before Isobelle replaced him with a sparkly little cat. Gwen turned to inspect it, her movements easy with a very different kind of grace than Isobelle had been taught all her life. Gwen was so unlike anyone Isobelle had ever known, and for the first time she could recall, Isobelle found herself restlessly self-conscious in her own domain.

"You find it hard to believe," Olivia murmured by Isobelle's side, "that she doesn't have admirers?"

Isobelle folded her arms. "What?" Then she unfolded them immediately, so as not to appear defensive. Her mind told her she had nothing to be defensive *about*, and yet there was the urge to step back from Olivia's inspection of her face, like her maid was some kind of inquisitor accusing her of a crime.

Olivia twitched a half smile.

"You'll play the game just fine, my lady," she said firmly.

For a moment, Isobelle thought Olivia was talking to her. The words were aimed at Gwen, though, who turned and blinked at her.

"We'll get you dressed like a lady," Olivia continued, "and you'll be of no particular note quickly enough."

"Think of the dresses like a new kind of armor," Isobelle agreed, her mind still trying to sort out what Olivia had been implying with that aside, while also being somewhat reluctant to examine it too closely. Isobelle had a lot of practice at not examining her thoughts too closely, and she clambered back aboard the moving carriage of the conversation without missing more than one or two beats.

"Indeed," Olivia said. "I'll see about your meal, if you'd like to take your places on the balcony, my ladies."

Gwen, with the expression of one who was abandoning herself to her fate, allowed Isobelle to lead her through the double doors and out onto the balcony, which ran the length of Isobelle's quarters. On one end a door led directly to Isobelle's bedroom, and on the other end another door led to the spare room where Gwen would be staying. Here, in the middle, stood a table and a pair of chairs.

Isobelle took her place at the table and busied herself straightening the silverware, while Gwen drifted over to lean on the balustrade, studying the hills rolling out to meet the forest and the mountain that housed the newly reopened mine in the distance.

"Isobelle," she said after a little while, her gaze having drifted downward toward the moat below. "I know I'm asking a lot of questions about this place, but . . ."

"Go on," said Isobelle, suspicion dawning.

"Has someone hammered iron rings into the outside of your balcony?"

"Oh yes," Isobelle replied. "That was Olivia."

"Olivia."

"There's a rope in that wicker box over there. Olivia says you should always have at least one emergency exit, and nobody ever expects a lady to rappel off a balcony."

Gwen turned to regard her—to make sure Isobelle wasn't mocking her—and then turned back to study the rings once more. "I certainly wouldn't expect you to," she said eventually.

"It's not easy with the skirts," Isobelle agreed. "Oh, here's brunch."

Olivia appeared with a tray holding a quartet of croissants, a dish of butter, and a pot of Isobelle's favorite apricot jam. She set the plates down on the table as Gwen took her place, and then unloaded a teapot before disappearing once more.

"Olivia's not sure about me," said Gwen, once she'd craned her neck to be sure Olivia was gone. Olivia probably wasn't gone, but Isobelle didn't point that out.

"I'm sure she has every confidence," Isobelle replied breezily.

"She thinks we're playing a dangerous game, and it'll end in disaster," Gwen shot back. "You're already facing backlash—she told me you've been confined to the castle." Her tone softened, eyes apologetic, as if it were Gwen's fault Isobelle had snuck out in the middle of the night.

"Nonsense," Isobelle said firmly, with a confidence she trusted to become real if she believed in it hard enough. "Whimsitt will forget about his decree in a day or two. And Olivia wouldn't go along with our plan if she didn't think we were onto something. She's just sulking because she thought the best solution to my current predicament was an assassination or two."

"What?" Gwen blinked at her, startled, and Isobelle thought she heard a faint throat-clearing from just inside the door.

"Try a croissant?" Isobelle handed her the plate of pastries. "They're rich enough to eat plain, but I like them best with piles of butter and jam."

"I've never tried . . ." That was as far as Gwen got before she popped the first piece into her mouth. Her breath caught, her lashes lowered in sheer, naked bliss, and she made a sound of pleasure that brought a flush of answering pleasure to Isobelle's cheeks.

Isobelle watched the other girl's enjoyment through her lashes, declining to ask herself why she couldn't stop *staring* at Gwen.

The next little while, they were both silent, each contemplating their own novel experiences. After a minute, Isobelle pushed the rest of the croissants across to Gwen.

"I think it's the butter," she ventured, when they were mostly gone. "Olivia taught one of the girls in the kitchen to make them, and . . . well. They're very nice."

Gwen visibly tried to get herself under control. She reached for the teapot, but paused after pouring the first few drops, setting it down and lifting the cup to give it a curious sniff. "What's this?"

"It's called cocoa. It's a sort of bean, added to hot milk. I'll have some too."

Gwen filled her cup and handed it across to Isobelle, then claimed Isobelle's to pour her own. "I've never had . . . cocoa, you said? It smells good."

Isobelle braced herself as Gwen lifted the cup for a cautious sip.

Gwen's eyes went wide, fixing briefly on Isobelle's before they fluttered closed again. "Holy . . ." she managed, when she'd swallowed and could breathe again, her voice full of satisfaction. "I should've started impersonating nobility years ago."

Isobelle, rarely lost for words, scrabbled for something to say. "Well, wait until you taste the next course. There are plenty of good things to come."

Gwen paused, the cup halfway to her lips again. "The *next* course?"

"It'll just be something simple. Sausages, eggs, things of that nature."

Gwen stared down at the wreckage of four croissants. "Oh," she said, before looking up once more to meet Isobelle's gaze. "I've made a terrible, delicious miscalculation."

Chapter Eleven

YOU ARE THE GIRL WHO WOULD BE A KNIGHT?

Remember how we decided at the beginning that this castle could be whatever we wanted it to be, with crocodiles in the moat and high, impractical turrets scraping the sky? Well, while most castles tend to be pretty spartan and concerned primarily with defense, let's say this one is more palatial in its design. The following scene will be more fun if it takes place in a grand ballroom rather than in some cramped, dark hallway with defensible slits for windows.

Gwen probably would've preferred the dark hallway, but we can't always get what we want.

Isobelle's quarters were located in the upper floors of the castle, requiring them to traverse long, winding staircases and slip through room after ornate room as they made their way toward their destination. The ballroom occupied its own wing of the castle and lay at the end of a long corridor lined with portraits—past lords of Darkhaven, Isobelle explained to Gwen, who drew half a step closer under the cold, haughty stares of noblemen past. Toward the end of the parade of old men was one particularly surrounded by wealth and luxury.

"The first Lord Whimsitt," Isobelle explained, with a look on her face that told Gwen she found him as unfriendly looking as she did. "Ancestor of the current lord. He's the one who built this castle, with all the income from the gold mines. I suppose that wealth will start flowing again, now the current Lord Whimsitt has reopened them."

"It's a miracle they waited as long as they did," Gwen replied. "Just goes to show how rumors of dragons liking caves and mineshafts can make even the greediest of men a bit nervous."

"Not nervous enough to stop him, alas." Isobelle sighed. "The tourney will cement his place among the who's who of the king's court, and he needed the mining profits to successfully bid to host it this round."

"It's not his neck he risks by going up against superstition," Gwen muttered. "Do you spend much time with him?"

"Thankfully no, but technically he's my guardian," Isobelle replied, with a small but heartfelt shudder. "My parents are diplomats, abroad in the service of the king. And *that's* how I ended up the sacrifice this year. He didn't have to ask anyone for permission, and when you put me together with my dowry, we're quite the prize."

Gwen felt herself tense, that old ache of helpless anger making it difficult for her to speak—she found herself gazing mutely at Isobelle, hoping at least the other girl would see the outrage and sympathy she didn't know how to express.

Isobelle caught her eye for a long moment, then gave herself a little shake. "I should have been paying more attention and seen it coming."

"You shouldn't have to . . ." But Gwen left her sentence unfinished, because they both knew better.

They'd reached the ballroom, and Isobelle lay a hand on the

latch to one of the double-tall doors, flashing Gwen a sidelong look. "We're a bit early, but we can sneak in and watch the end of the dance lessons."

Gwen's steps halted, diverted from her anger, blinking slowly. "Dance lessons? I thought we were going to meet your combat instruct— Wait—"

But Isobelle had already pushed the door open, cheerfully ignoring Gwen's protests.

That's beginning to turn into an annoying habit, Gwen thought, though she was too full of pastries and sausages to work up a really good sulk.

She slipped through the crack in the door after Isobelle.

The grand ballroom was a massive space of cream and gold and intricately patterned details. Broad windows with sheer curtains lined either side of the space, allowing diffuse golden light to spill across the inlaid marble floor. The high buttressed ceiling arced up toward the center, from which hung a massive, ornately worked chandelier.

Antique weapons hung at intervals along the walls, decorative and menacing—above the fireplace at one end of the hall was a huge, ancient dragon-slaying spear. A reminder of days gone by, when knights rode out in glorious combat against the now-extinct monsters who threatened their loved ones.

If only that was the challenge ahead of me, thought Gwen rather desperately, hovering on the edge of this room that was the epitome of Isobelle's world, and so decidedly not Gwen's. A wave of dread swept through Gwen at the prospect of having to live in this place for the duration of the tournament and keep up the pretense that she belonged here.

Assuming she didn't lose in round one. Which, if Gwen let herself think about it at all, seemed all too likely.

Isobelle took her hand and sat her down along the edge of the room as Gwen became aware of a voice shouting, slightly distorted by the echoes of the vast space.

"They will step on your toes!" the voice snapped in a noticeably French accent. "They will bumble about, sweaty-palmed, too close, with the grace and elegance of newborn foals."

The owner of the voice was a wiry woman whose obvious athleticism and angular features made it impossible to place her age any more accurately than somewhere between forty and sixty. Her brown skin was barely lined, but her hair was a luminous silver. She was stomping up and down between two rows of twelve girls, carrying a cane she used to thump on the marble floor to accentuate her words.

"You must be ready!" she shouted, paying no attention to the two new arrivals now perched at the edge of the room, watching. "You must guide them without seeming to guide, for they must believe they are in control. You must protect your precious feet without appearing to wince. You must be ever prepared!"

"Yes, Madame Dupont!" the two dozen girls chanted in unison, each staring straight ahead like military recruits.

"Sophie!" Madame Dupont whirled and pointed her stick toward a younger girl with auburn hair and liquid eyes. "What do you do if his sweaty hand starts to slide down your back, inexorably lower?"

The girl went even straighter, barking her reply instantly. "I giggle! 'Oh, sir, we will be seen,' I say breathily! I blush and look distressed!"

Madame Dupont turned again, choosing a new target among her charges. "Arabella," she snapped, "what do you do if you encounter a toe-stomper?"

"I am nimble, madame!" Arabella replied, folding her hands behind her back and lifting her chin. "If he cannot be stopped, I pretend I am faint!"

Madame Dupont reached the end of the formation and turned once more, resting the cane against the floor and folding her hands across the stone at its top. She gazed at them, twenty-four girls all holding their breath at once.

Then Madame Dupont shook her head. "You are not ready yet. But you will be. Clarissa, Joriana, I will know if you haven't practiced your footwork next week. Now, filez! Off with you all!" She thumped the cane against the floor. "And you, Mistress Hobbes, merci."

An elderly woman with a stoop in her shoulders materialized at the edge of the room, rising from the bench of an organ where she'd evidently been accompanying the lesson at some point. The girls scattered, eager to be done with their schooling and to flee their instructor's obvious intensity—Gwen could feel the force of the woman from here. Madame Dupont followed them to the door, allowing Mistress Hobbes only a little more leeway to make her exit, and then shut and locked the door with a sigh.

Then she turned, and her dark eyes fixed on Isobelle and Gwen. Evidently she hadn't missed their arrival at all.

"Well," she said, tucking her cane under her arm and striding toward them. "Is this she? Let's have a look."

Isobelle beamed at her and then leaned toward Gwen to whisper, "Don't worry. She adores me. It's just everyone else who's terrified of her." Then, more loudly, she said, "Be nice, madame. This is Gwen, and she's doing me a great service."

Madame Dupont snorted and came to a halt in front of them.

Gwen rose to her feet without fully registering the impulse to do so. Madame Dupont was a head shorter than she was, but somehow she seemed to loom as she inspected the new girl she was to teach. The silence stretched, giving Gwen an opportunity to inspect her in return.

Her broad face and angular features were dusted with black freckles against a dark brown backdrop, and she had her hair bound up, woven through with a colorful scarf of French-designed silk. Her eyes were shrewd and penetrating, and Gwen found herself longing to look away—but feared doing so would give Madame Dupont some kind of ammunition to use against her.

"So," Dupont said eventually, "you are the girl who would be a knight, with our Isobelle's favor pinned to your breast?"

"I am, madame." Gwen found herself straightening, lifting her chin, feeling like one of the girls who had gone scurrying from the room. She'd assumed that stiff attention was something Dupont had taught them, but apparently that was just how one stood while being inspected by Madame Dupont. "And you are . . . a dancing instructor?"

She couldn't quite hide the confusion in her voice. What could a dancer teach her about something as brutal as jousting?

Madame Dupont's eyes were severe, but the corner of her mouth twitched. "Oui, Mademoiselle le Chevalier. You think I have nothing to teach you?"

"Um," said Gwen, glancing over at Isobelle, who had no help to offer but a grin. If there'd been popcorn available, Isobelle would be leaning back in her chair and munching it while she watched. "I didn't say that," Gwen said, floundering.

"But you are thinking it. I can see it in those pretty green eyes. Come." She turned away, walking toward the organ and gesturing for Isobelle to follow her. Gwen was somewhat gratified to see Isobelle scramble to her feet with alacrity.

Gwen trailed along in their wake. "But—how are we to practice jousting in a ballroom?"

Madame Dupont let out a sharp laugh. "Do you see any horses, girl? No, we shall begin on foot, with a sword. I wish to see what I am dealing with."

Next to the organ was a long bench whose lid flipped up to reveal a cavernous storage space below. Dupont stooped to rummage through it, removing items here and there to make room to search more deeply. There were batons with ribbons attached, a pair of shoes with metal soles, a long, seemingly never-ending garland of multicolored silk flowers, the top half of a man-shaped dummy with faded paint in the pattern of a jester . . .

Gwen snuck an incredulous glance at Isobelle, but the other girl was settling at the organ. The sun streaming in through the long windows fell on Isobelle like a caressing hand, coaxing white-gold highlights from her hair and limning her form in a halo of light. She positioned her hands over the keys, each finger arched gracefully, and then looked back expectantly at Gwen.

Gwen swallowed, distantly aware she was staring, but just as distant from her ability to control herself. It wasn't until a sharp crack a few feet away broke the spell that she was able to jerk her gaze back to where it belonged.

Dupont had rapped her cane against the floor, a hint of

disapproval in her gaze, as well as a knowing glint that warned Gwen she would need to be much, much more careful about who she stared at and for how long. "Pay attention, mademoiselle," Dupont snapped, before tossing a dull-tipped practice blade, hilt first, to Gwen.

Gwen managed to catch it and tried not to look so surprised by having done so that she ruined any semblance of cool she'd managed to reclaim.

"We will move on to jousting in time," Madame Dupont said, letting the storage bin lid fall closed as she turned to face Gwen, a second sword in her own hand. "Today I wish to see how you move, how well you anticipate the movements of your opponent."

"I know how to handle a sword," Gwen said, gaze flicking from the sword in her hand to the Frenchwoman standing before her.

"I should hope so," replied Madame Dupont. "We shall begin with the gavotte."

She swept her blade to the side in some sort of signal or salute to Isobelle, who straightened and began to play. The music was stately, each set of four beats easy to notice and follow. Madame Dupont gestured to Gwen and took up a position opposite her.

Gwen felt the bottom dropping out of her stomach, her eyes darting between the organ and the dancing instructor. "Wait—you want me to dance?" She couldn't help but notice her voice had risen in pitch. "I thought you wanted to see if I could fight."

Madame Dupont raised an eyebrow. "You told me you could handle a sword. Should I not take your word that this is so?"

"No. I mean yes. I mean—" Gwen took a breath, wishing for once that Isobelle weren't there. "I . . . I don't know how to dance. Not to something like this." She gestured with her free hand toward the organ, where Isobelle kept circling back around to the introductory phrases of the music, like a carriage driver waiting for her charges to hop on.

Gwen was not accustomed to being taken at her word as far as her abilities were concerned. Handling a sword was one of the things she *knew*, and in this world of chandeliers and croissants and curtsies, she'd been telling herself all she had to do was make it far enough to prove there was a reason Isobelle had brought her here.

Madame Dupont was watching her with an even expression, her black eyes giving nothing away.

"I don't even know what a gavotte is," Gwen murmured.

"That is why I have chosen it," said Madame Dupont. "I trust that you know how to hold a sword. What I must teach you is how to use it while someone else is trying to stab you through the weak points in your armor. To do this, you must learn to see what they will do an instant before they do it. That is why we will begin with a dance you do not know—you will learn by watching me and predicting how I will move next."

Gwen looked down at the practice blade she held, shifting her grip until it felt balanced in her hand and giving it a few experimental swings. It was noticeably lighter than her own sword, but it wasn't a bad one—she could work with it. "All right," she told Madame Dupont. "I'll try."

Madame Dupont tilted her head, something very nearly like a smile changing the set of her mouth. "Good. Let us begin."

Chapter Twelve

MADEMOISELLE LE CHEVALIER

Isobelle let her fingers dance across the keys, a lifetime of lessons taking care of the music while she addressed her attention to the two figures on the dance floor.

This was her great gamble, and she knew it. If Gwen couldn't learn—or worse, couldn't understand why Madame Dupont was the perfect teacher—then all Isobelle's plans would begin to dissolve like a spun-sugar castle left out in the rain.

Madame Dupont began the first steps of the gavotte, offering no compromise in terms of speed or technique, moving in toward Gwen and then back again. She was light on her feet, elegant and controlled. Playing the organ was automatic for Isobelle, but these steps were a *part* of Madame Dupont.

At first Gwen didn't move at all, her eyes on her instructor's feet. She blinked and drew breath, and Isobelle's heart skipped a beat as she waited for her would-be champion to protest. Then Gwen let the breath back out again and lifted her gaze to watch Madame Dupont move as a whole, rather than just staring at her shoes.

Slowly, she began to mirror her. At first, it was simply Dupont's movements. And then, after a few bars, Gwen started to match her footwork.

"One may learn the correct grip for a sword," rapped out

Madame Dupont, gesturing with her own sword as the two women bobbed in toward each other, and then gracefully back. "One may build the strength for a swing, make the weapon an extension of one's very arm. The question is, can one do so when a large and odorous knight is lunging in for the kill?"

Gwen moved differently with a sword in her hand. She was more sure of herself, even though she'd never seen this dance before. She flowed, light on her feet, her skirts swirling around her legs as she took her cues from Madame Dupont.

"You must see the way they shift their weight," Madame Dupont continued. "Watch their chest as they announce which way their arm will go. Note the turn of a foot, the preparation for a lunge."

And Gwen was. She was doing it! Isobelle felt like cheering, but she kept her hands firmly on the keys, contenting herself with throwing in a merry little flourish. Gwen held her space confidently, her full attention locked on Madame Dupont as the older woman led her back to the beginning of the dance once more.

"Yes, good," her teacher said, and Isobelle glanced up in surprise, nearly fumbling the next phrase of the music. *Praise*, from Madame Dupont?

Gwen seemed to sense it was unusual as well, and blinked.

"Watch your step," the Frenchwoman said, with what could be described as at least a moderately evil grin. And then she swung her sword at Gwen's head.

Isobelle hit a wrong key, the discordant note ringing out and echoing around the ballroom. Gwen's sword hand snapped up, blocking the attempted blow with seeming ease, though she did miss a single step before she resumed her footwork.

There was a gleam in her eye to match Madame Dupont's now, though.

"Next!" cried Madame Dupont, snapping the fingers on her free hand in Isobelle's direction.

She scrambled to shift to a new tune on the organ, and with it, a new set of steps for Gwen to learn.

Gwen moved like she'd been born with a sword in her hand. Isobelle could imagine her practicing on her own behind the smithy, picture her working with her sword—a sword she had made herself, how many knights could say *that?*—for hours.

Isobelle shifted tunes each time Gwen had mastered the latest steps, but whatever challenge she and Madame Dupont threw at the girl from the village, she was ready.

"Now!" cried Madame Dupont. "It is time for our friend to learn the woman's part."

"What do I need that for?" Gwen panted.

"For the tournament's grand ball," Isobelle called out. "The night before the final joust, everyone who's anyone will be there!"

"Because the woman must be able to do everything the man does," Madame Dupont corrected her, a gleam in her eyes. "Only she must do it backward."

Isobelle circled back to the gavotte once more, and for a song or two, Gwen slowed down—her blocks and parries just in time, her footwork not quite as rhythmic. But it didn't take her long to recover her newfound ease with the steps.

And then, as she came out of one of the twirls, Gwen shifted her weight, improvising her own footwork, and launched her attack—a clever half strike, half parry with a flick of the wrist that sought to disarm her opponent.

Madame Dupont swung up her own weapon with visible surprise, just managing to parry the blow. "Good, good!" she crowed as Isobelle tried to slow her racing heart. Knightly training was quite the exertion, she was concluding, and she was only observing.

Madame Dupont grinned as she and Gwen fell into step once more. "We will make something of you, Mademoiselle le Chevalier. Oh, indeed we will."

Chapter Thirteen

OFF IN SEARCH OF ADVENTURE

Earlier that day, when Isobelle had shown her where she would be sleeping during her time at the castle, Gwen had floomphed backward onto the spacious bed, spreadeagled and shivering with the luxury of it.

Now, she sank gingerly onto its edge, stifling a groan.

Madame Dupont had kept her at her lessons for over four hours. Whenever she managed to glance up and catch the older woman's eye, Gwen was certain she could see a glint of mischief in them—Dupont had been *trying* to break her.

Gwen would've sooner died than given her that satisfaction. If a woman more than twice her age could do it, so could she.

In the end, Madame Dupont had finally stepped back, raised her voice, and called: "Finissons!" Isobelle had trailed off in the middle of a musical phrase, blinking owlishly over at them as Gwen nearly stumbled, having forgotten how to walk if she wasn't following a prescribed set of dance steps.

Dupont had barely broken a sweat.

Gwen was used to manning the forge for an entire day, for there was no sense spending the fuel to heat it only to work an hour or two. And her arms and shoulders were fine—wielding a blade for hours was far less strenuous than swinging her hammer.

But Oh. My. God. Her *feet*.

Gwen let herself fall back onto the mattress, the soles of her feet pulsing with her heartbeat. When she closed her eyes, she could almost feel the bed swaying to the beat of an imaginary waltz. She dipped her hand into the pocket of her skirts and drew out the tiny iron knight—Sir Gawain—and closed her fingers around it.

Remember why you're doing this.

When a tapping came at the door, her mind dismissed it as a phantom rap of Madame Dupont's cane. It came again, though, and Gwen sat up with some effort, half dreading whatever fresh horror awaited her.

The door opened, and Isobelle's face appeared at the crack. "Can I come in?" she asked brightly.

Gwen drew herself up to sit cross-legged. "Of course."

Isobelle had changed her clothes, discarding the aquamarine layer cake of a dress she'd worn that afternoon in favor of a slimmer dress of soft, gleaming gold. Gwen swallowed, all too aware she was still wearing the sweaty—and now rather clammy—dress in which she'd faced off with Madame Dupont.

When Isobelle drew closer, Gwen saw draped over her arm a couple of damp, steaming towels. Isobelle had a wry smile on her face as she plopped herself down on the bed beside Gwen, effortlessly tucking that silky, shiny skirt beneath one bent knee.

"If I'd known Dupont would keep you at it that long on the first day, I would have warned you." Isobelle wrinkled her nose. "Believe it or not, that's a compliment from her. She wouldn't have run you into the ground if she didn't think you could go the distance. Here, give me your feet."

Isobelle gestured toward Gwen's crossed legs, and though Gwen wasn't quite sure what she intended, she leaned back and nudged her aching feet out from under the edge of her skirt.

Isobelle bent her head and began carefully wrapping one of Gwen's feet in the hot towel. Fighting every instinct to flinch away and protect her battered limbs, Gwen waited—and a few seconds later, the half-scalding flash of heat dissolved into a warm, soothing cloud of relief.

"Oh my god, thank you." Gwen slumped, propping her forehead against her hands. "How did you know?"

Isobelle laughed, though somehow she managed to make it a kind sound. "Oh, please. We have to do this after every ball. Nobody can dance for four hours straight without suffering for it." She paused thoughtfully. "Well, except maybe for Dupont."

Isobelle began tucking the towel in, pressing against the bottoms of Gwen's feet and making her flinch. The other girl grimaced and laid her hand across Gwen's ankle, a gesture of apology that made Gwen instantly forget the pain. She glanced up and met Isobelle's eyes, her insides giving an odd lurch before she pulled her gaze away, reminding herself of Dupont's admonition to stay focused.

"Oh, I have news about Jinna," Isobelle said, carefully shifting her grip. "His lordship controls my finances—that's how my dowry's ended up as the tourney prize—but I'm not the only one who's snuck off to one of her ladies' nights in the past. I've gathered enough contributions for her to hire an advocate to contest ownership of the tavern. At least she won't be alone."

A flash of anger pushed through Gwen's tiredness at the memory of Jinna being bundled out of her own tavern in chains, but she watched Isobelle thoughtfully. "I'm glad you thought of doing that. I'm not sure I would have."

"Madame Dupont's donation was generous," Isobelle confided with a smile. "Apparently Jinna imports French wine just for her."

Gwen couldn't help a smile. "What's Dupont's deal, anyway? How is she such a . . ." But words failed Gwen at that point, and the sentence ended in a helpless gesture.

Isobelle snickered, lifting one shoulder in a shrug as she reached for the second towel and Gwen's other foot. "Such a force of nature? No one knows. She's been around since before my parents first dumped me here three years ago. Obviously, she's from France, but no one knows much more than that." She leaned in, ducking her head to catch Gwen's eye again, her own sparkling. "They say she was raised by dragons, or sorcerers, or maybe the fae, and that's how she knows everything and never gets tired or sore."

Gwen laughed, because the rumor was clearly a joke—and yet she couldn't deny there was something superhuman about the wiry old dance instructor. She kept her eyes on the graceful, perfectly manicured hands wrapping her foot. What had it been like for Isobelle, left behind by her own parents? Isobelle's smiles and laughs never told the whole story, that much she knew. She couldn't imagine being separated from her own father—or knowing he'd let it happen.

Gwen felt a twinge in her chest, a sharp and unexpected longing for home. She'd left her father in good hands, recruiting the apprentice blacksmith from a neighboring village to help him while she was gone, but she knew it would be a massive change for him not to have her there. She ran her thumb over the figurine still clutched in her fist, finally distracted from Isobelle's well-meaning and entirely too engrossing ministrations.

Isobelle was tucking in the last edge of the second towel. "There, now. Ooh!" She had spotted the model knight Gwen held. "May I?"

Gwen handed Sir Gawain over, still half distracted watching Isobelle's face. The dimples had vanished in favor of a softer smile.

"He really is spectacular. Did you . . . ?" The long, fair lashes lifted as Isobelle glanced up at Gwen.

"Hell no." Gwen leaned back, watching Isobelle turn the knight over in her hands. "I'm not that talented. My dad made it. For my mother. Lavender was her favorite flower." Gwen touched the sculpted pennant bearing its etching of the lavender sprig that now marked Gwen's own pennant in the tournament.

Isobelle's eyebrows shot up, her hands pausing on the knight. "Your dad made this?"

Gwen's throat tightened, as it always did whenever the subject of her father came up among the villagers. "He's not what you think," she said softly. "He's actually quite brilliant."

Isobelle's head tilted to one side. "I promise I didn't think anything, just that your work was what I saw on display at the market."

Gwen bit her lip, briefly meeting Isobelle's eyes. "He's just . . . had a tough time since my mother died. It's harder for him to work, especially since he'd rather make things like this, things the village has no use for. And I can make nails and horseshoes well enough to keep us fed."

Isobelle gently set the little knight down, nestling him among the rumples of the bedspread between them. "When did your mother die?"

"About five years ago. I was twelve." Gwen was grateful for the safe, neutral place to rest her eyes—it looked like Sir Gawain was galloping on his horse through snow-covered hills. *Off in search of adventure*, she thought.

"I'm sorry," Isobelle said softly. A sympathetic gaze was no doubt waiting for Gwen if she lifted her head, but she didn't.

"She was always obsessed with knights and chivalry," Gwen said, reaching out to nudge the knight more firmly into the fold holding him upright. "She would tell me stories about Sir Gawain, and I'd imagine I was living those stories."

"And now you *are* living them."

Gwen looked up and found Isobelle regarding her with a tiny smile—somehow a much warmer one than the bright, dimpled things she tended to flash about. The cozy warmth enveloping her battered feet was spreading, as if the rest of her body had still been stuck in combat, but had now received the message to stand down.

"I suppose I am," Gwen managed, the tightness in her chest easing.

Isobelle's keen eyes saw that tension shifting, and her smile widened. "Well, tomorrow we're going to have to do an etiquette crash course. Then I'll introduce you to the girls—I think we should probably keep all this secret from them. I trust them, but the more people who know a thing, the more chances there are for someone to slip up. We'll need a name for Sir Gawain's sister. Maybe something flowery and nonthreatening, like Rose or Lily?" She turned and slid off the edge of the bed.

Gwen glanced down at the tiny iron knight galloping across the bedspread. "How about . . . Céline?"

Isobelle's smile flashed with delight. "Ooh, beautiful. Where'd that come from?"

Gwen closed her fingers around Sir Gawain, drawing him back into the safety of her pocket. "It was my mother's name."

IT'S PROBABLY FOR THE BEST, dear reader, if we draw a veil over what comes next. If only to spare poor Gwen her dignity.

The crash course in etiquette that takes place the next day involves all the usual parts of such a thing—from curtsies to laps of the room with a book on one's head to flash cards featuring sketches of the court's most notable personalities. None of this is Gwen's strong suit. But if Isobelle has any doubts . . . well, she's an expert at ignoring those and focusing on the joys at hand.

If you'd really like to know more about what Isobelle has Gwen learning, then please direct your attention to one of the myriad texts on the subject, such as *Ladye Hostlethwaite's Primer on Graciously Goode Manneres* or *On Being of Noble Stocke* by Lord Rollin Moisey of Dalmerlington. They should only take a day or two to read and commit to memory—each is but a few hundred thousand words.

Go on, take your time.

We'll wait.

Chapter Fourteen

HAST THOU EVER...

The tea party at which Lady Isobelle planned to introduce "Lady Céline" to her friends took place the following afternoon, in the solarium in the south wing of the castle. Olivia was still finishing up the gowns she was altering for Gwen, but she'd located one that needed minimal alterations to fit. Isobelle was a good bit shorter than Gwen, so Olivia must've gotten the gowns from somewhere else, though neither girl asked her where.

"Just be yourself," Isobelle was saying firmly as she all but bodily dragged Gwen down the corridor leading to the south wing. "Avoid any mentions of the smithy or your village, and you'll be fine."

Gwen opened her mouth to point out that they'd spent the entire day teaching Gwen how *not* to be herself, but Isobelle had stopped in front of a door and turned to give her one of those wide, dimpled smiles she employed to cover her true feelings.

She's nervous. At least that's something.

After a morning of etiquette lessons during which Isobelle acted as though none of Gwen's slipups or mistakes mattered—as though selling Gwen as a knight's sister was the easiest thing in the world, with no life-and-death consequences for Gwen should she fail—any sign that Isobelle understood the stakes was a relief.

"Here we are!" she announced, and then pushed the door open.

The solarium was a round room situated above Isobelle's quarters in one of those inappropriately designed turrets of the castle, with windows at regular intervals all around. Sunlight streamed in through clouded glass, falling upon the soft, rich fabrics covering the floors and the divans and daybeds strewn in a rough circle.

In the center of the room was a low, round table on which sat a gleaming silver tea service and several platters containing tiny cakes and some kind of unidentifiable pastry. A trio of young women were sprawled on three of the divans, with a fourth empty one embroidered with pink roses clearly left for Isobelle. Gwen recognized the trio from the day she met Isobelle at the market, each of them wearing a different jewel tone, each of them with perfectly coiffed hair and gleaming jewelry.

And each of them turning in perfect unison to stare at the girl who'd entered with their ringleader. When Gwen had first donned the dress Olivia had provided, it had been the most beautiful dress she'd ever worn—now, she felt plainer than the drabbest sparrow.

Oh god. Give me a dozen armored men on horseback over this.

"Girls, this is Céline," Isobelle announced, sweeping into the room as Gwen paused to stare. "Her brother is Sir Gawain, that dashing young knight who unseated Sir Evonwald in the qualifiers. She's in town for the duration of the tournament."

An indistinct wave of protest rolled across the other girls, and they lifted their teacups to drink and wash away the taste of that pronouncement.

"You said the 'T' word!" cried one of the girls, a honey blonde with shining braids and pink cheeks.

Gwen glanced between them and Isobelle. "What's wrong with

mentioning the tournament?" she managed.

"It makes half of us furious and the other half start swooning," drawled a dark-haired, dark-eyed beauty in a maroon gown that perfectly set off the warm brown of her skin. She lounged against a navy-blue divan with utter self-assurance. "Welcome, Céline—I'm Sylvie. My, what lovely freckles you have." The dark eyes narrowed, putting Gwen in mind of a tiger about to pounce.

Gwen had a sneaking suspicion that the girl's comment was more a shrewd observation than a compliment—a noble-born lady was expected to avoid the sun and preserve her complexion. But was she merely nitpicking a new arrival to the circle, or was that tiger-sighting-prey look a warning that Gwen's masquerade was already under fire?

Gwen swallowed, smiled as best she could, and eased her way into the room.

The round-faced girl with a coronet of buckwheat-blond braids who'd protested Gwen's mention of the tournament got up to wrestle a fifth divan into the circle. "Yes, welcome! I am Hilde—and you must tell us whether you are a romantic or not, ja?" Her pink cheeks brightened with a smile.

Gwen sank down on the extra divan as Isobelle claimed her spot on the rose-embroidered one. "Um . . . a romantic?" she echoed, in confusion.

"Ja! Perhaps you can decide whether we are glad about the tournament or not." Hilde's Germanic accent gave her voice a rolling, rhythmic quality full of dips and high points, expressive and cheerful.

Gwen glanced at Isobelle, who was accepting a cup of tea from the third girl with a murmured, "Thanks, Jane."

"I suppose I'm not much of a romantic," Gwen said finally, smiling her thanks as another cup was pressed into her hand. "My brother is the romantic in the family."

Hilde clasped her hands together with a sigh—her teacup and saucer, perched precariously on one thigh, tilted at an alarming angle. "A young knight who's a romantic? Ach, if only I were not promised to my Arnau, I would seek him out to know him better."

"Gawain is, um, rather shy," Gwen said, curling her fingers around the handle of the teacup. "You probably won't see him much. Who's Arnau?" Desperately, she tried to change the subject.

Sylvie opened her mouth, but Isobelle swooped into the conversation first. "Arnau is Hilde's beau, and a very charming man by all accounts."

"He is away in France," Hilde said with a sigh, gazing down into her teacup. "We miss each other so."

"Yes, they wrote each other constantly," commented Sylvie, tilting her head back so she could settle a stray hair into place with one perfectly manicured hand. "For the first year or two. How long has it been now? Six years?"

"Oh, but he is so very busy there," exclaimed Hilde, though Gwen could see her fingers tightening on the handle of her cup. "He would write more often if he could."

"So," interrupted the third girl—Jane, Isobelle had called her—in an obvious attempt to change the subject before Sylvie could needle poor Hilde any further. "You say your brother is a romantic? Perhaps we will see him at the ball at the tournament's end, then. You must tell him to save his first dance for me."

Jane leveled her gaze at Gwen. She had a round, luscious figure, gleaming auburn hair and full lips, with eyelashes so long they swept her cheeks. Just now, her eyes were fixed on Gwen, one corner of her mouth lifted in a smile that made her throat tighten. *Talk about a tiger sighting prey*, Gwen thought, privately relieved Jane's interest was in her fictitious alter ego and not herself.

"None of that, Jane," Isobelle cut in swiftly before taking a prim sip of her tea. "Sir Gawain is mine, you keep your hands off him. His first dance belongs to me."

Gwen barely had any time for her relief at the rescue to register before the rest of Isobelle's words sank in. "Uh," she said, trying to catch her eye. "I doubt Sir Gawain will be attending any ball. He is more comfortable in his *armor*, after all."

But Isobelle just laughed, her eyes gleaming.

Jane's eyebrows had shot up, her teacup settling against her saucer loudly enough to cut through Hilde's giggle. "Hang on," she said. "You're into Sir Gawain? Has someone managed to displace Tristan of Cambridge? Are you telling me that his dark eyes—"

"Dreamy eyes," Hilde corrected her. "She said they were *dreamy*—"

"That the poet's *dreamy* eyes," Jane graciously corrected herself, "have lost their hold on you?"

"He is a very talented poet," Hilde informed Gwen, raising her cup to the absent man in a toast. "When he came through on tour, Isobelle made us attend all three of his performances."

"I never spoke a word to him!" Isobelle finally managed to break in, her gaze threatening to set the two of them on fire.

"More's the pity," Jane replied. "The man's diction was beautiful. No doubt just as beautiful as his—"

"Jane!" Finally Isobelle managed to quell her friend. "Honestly, if a girl can't admire a traveling poet, what's left in the world?"

"Sir Gawain, apparently," Jane replied, unrepentant.

Sylvie's eyes were swinging between Isobelle and Gwen, taking in everything and revealing very little. "Perhaps he is merely the least of all the evils awaiting this year's dragon sacrifice."

"Anyone's better than Sir Ralph," Jane agreed, wrinkling her nose.

"Sir Orson is a good man, is he not?" Hilde chipped in, with the air of one reviving an old argument. "Isobelle has known him since she was small, and there is something to be said for familiarity."

Isobelle shrugged noncommittally. "I wouldn't mind being married off to Sir Gawain," she said airily, before letting her gaze slide toward Gwen's, merriment making it sparkle. "He's a dreamboat."

Gwen ducked her head to study the contents of her cup, doing her best to look merely demure instead of utterly rattled. She was used to the twinge of disappointment she felt whenever a pretty girl started talking about the boys she fancied, but the compounded confusion in this situation made her body tense.

Is it still jealousy if the girls are swooning over my alter ego? she wondered, raising her cup for a sip to cover her uncertainty. In her haste, she accidentally took a somewhat larger swallow than she intended to and braced herself for a burned tongue—only to choke, gasping, "Oh, fuck!"

The liquid in the cup was *not* tea.

At least, not only tea.

The drink burned all the way down her throat to settle, tingling, in her belly. She covered her mouth with her hand, but the epithet she'd blurted hung there in the air, like a big signpost proclaiming her lowborn nature.

Until Hilde burst into giggles, breaking the silence and

triggering a cascade of laughter from the other girls. "Mein Gott," she gasped when she could, "did you actually think we drank tea at our tea parties? How dull you must think we are!"

Gwen was still fighting valiantly not to cough at the strength of the stuff—while simultaneously feeling an increasing urge to taste it again. "What is it?"

"My parents got it from an Irish merchant—they call it uisce beatha. It packs a powerful punch, no?"

Gwen sniffed at the contents of her cup, not quite game to take another taste yet. One sip—albeit more of a gulp than a sip—and she could feel it buzzing in her legs, like she'd just pounded an entire flask of wine. "It's, uh. That's something, all right."

She snuck a glance at Isobelle and found the other girl watching her with obvious delight. Annoyance flickered at Gwen, nearly as unsettling as the uisce. Didn't Isobelle understand how important it was that these girls accepted Gwen as a noblewoman, as one of *them*? If Gwen could fade into the background as one of Isobelle's flock of ladies, no one would pay her much attention. She could throw herself into her role as Sir Gawain, focus on the actual battles she had to fight, instead of wasting her energy trying to pretend to be something she *really* wasn't.

She felt eyes—other eyes—on her, and turned to find Sylvie watching her. The lazy, disaffected air she gave off didn't quite conceal the keen edge to her stare, and Gwen found herself jerking her gaze away.

"So . . . do all of you live here in the castle?" Gwen asked, hoping to shift the focus off herself.

Hilde laughed. "Heavens, no! We are here for the tournament, staying in the castle guest quarters."

"But we visit Isobelle a lot even when there isn't a tournament," Jane said with a languid gesture around the suite with its lush decor. "She's so much more fun than sitting by a window embroidering cushions. Plus, a girl tends to run out of options fairly quickly in a small county like mine."

"By options, she means boys," explained Hilde helpfully. Jane fluttered her long eyelashes at Hilde in an over-the-top impression of coy flirtation.

"I think," said Sylvie slowly, tracing a finger around the edge of her teacup, "that we should play a game." She hadn't taken her eyes off Gwen's face.

"Oh yes!" cried Hilde, all delight and cheer. "How about—"

"I think we should play Hast Thou Ever," Sylvie said over her without skipping a beat, and still watching Gwen. "Can you think of a better way to get to know each other, Céline?"

Gwen's instincts told her to brace, to find firmer footing than plush carpeting and a sagging divan that threatened to swallow her, and get her hands on some sort of weapon. "Hast Thou Ever?" she echoed, uncertain.

Sylvie's eyes widened. "Oh, have you never played before? We take turns asking questions, like—I'll go first—hast thou ever been alone in a room with a man who wasn't related to you? And if you have, then you take a drink, like so." She lifted her cup for a demure sip, then glanced over at Jane expectantly.

"It's only one sip," said Jane with a wink, lifting her cup. Her rounded cheeks were already pink. "Even if you could justify the whole bottle."

Gwen could feel icy fingers of dread starting to creep up her spine. It was one thing to have memorized the rules of who she was supposed to be in this situation. It was another thing entirely to figure out which rules she was meant to have *broken* in order to fit in with these ladies.

Sylvie could not have picked a worse game for Gwen.

Gwen snuck a glance at Isobelle, hoping to take some kind of cue there. Gwen had been alone with men—they came every day to the forge to make orders and pick up mended equipment. But that wasn't the sort of "alone" Sylvie was talking about.

Hilde had set her cup down on her saucer, making Jane snort into her uisce and pat her hand sympathetically. Isobelle made a show of setting her cup down, only to wink at the girls and lift her cup at the last minute.

Gwen found herself staring at the cup, distracted from the puzzle she was meant to be solving for herself in favor of a far more compelling one. *She's been alone with men?*

Isobelle's face betrayed nothing but cheerful enthusiasm for the game, as if she hadn't realized yet how dangerous this sort of conversation was for Gwen, living as she was a double life.

No, a triple life. Gwen the blacksmith's daughter, Sir Gawain the knight, and Céline, his naive sister. Good god, this was a terrible idea.

But Isobelle's dimples were rigidly on display. Whatever she was feeling—whatever concerns she might have about the game they were playing—she wasn't showing it.

"Not you either, Céline?" asked Hilde mournfully.

Gwen blinked, then looked down at her cup. She hadn't taken a drink. "My . . . my brother never would have let me hear the end of it if I had," she said finally.

"I nominate Isobelle to ask the next question," Sylvie said lightly.

"Hast thou ever . . ." Isobelle began, drawing out the words as she thought. "Left off your underskirts on a hot day, and hoped no one would notice?"

The questions continued in that vein, giving Gwen the opportunity to get to know the other girls in the group.

Hilde, the hopeless romantic, dreaming of the beau she'd been waiting on for years, deeply invested in finding happy endings for all those around her.

Jane, beautiful, easygoing, and quick to love—and more than willing to share that love, by the sound of it. Daring and kind all at once.

And Sylvie. Reserved, guarded, with no interest in courting suitors or chasing marriage. Revealing little of herself. Observing much.

It was Sylvie's turn to ask the next question. Jane had slid to the floor with a piteous cry of "Braid my hair, Hilde!" and Hilde was giggling as she tried and failed to do something complicated involving ribbons.

Sylvie was smiling at Gwen as she suggested her next question. "Hast thou ever worn another lady's gown?"

For a split second, Gwen didn't understand the sudden interest from Sylvie, why *that* question had made her watch for Gwen's reaction.

Then her stomach clenched. Whose dress *was* she wearing? She'd assumed Olivia was altering Isobelle's dresses for her, but she was closer to Sylvie's size than Isobelle's. Was this Sylvie's castoff? Gwen's mind went blank, sheer panic taking hold.

"Oh, come now, Sylvie, don't torture poor Céline by making her drink every time." Isobelle's smile was honey sweet. "Her trunks were delayed en route and should get here in a few days. I asked Olivia to alter a few of last season's dresses to tide her over. Besides, we'll all have to drink to this one—remember when Hilde spilled mead all over us a few years back?"

Gwen carefully lifted her cup for a sip, not meeting Sylvie's eyes. Instead, she caught Isobelle sneaking a peek her way. A tiny reminder that Gwen wasn't out here on the battlefield alone. Isobelle may have been acting like she hadn't a care in the world, but she was monitoring the conversation like a hawk.

The questions went round and round after that, with the girls taking a special—if laughing, friendly—delight in following suit with Sylvie. One of the questions that made Gwen drink was *Have you ever had black hair?* and another was *Have you ever had a brother named Gawain?* Soon enough she was in a haze, and if she hadn't had such secrets to keep, the haze—the *hazing*, she decided— would have been fun.

The temptation to let down her guard and give in to the game was strong. Gwen's head was positively spinning after a few more cups of "tea," and she was beginning to envy Jane's spot on the floor by Hilde's divan.

Isobelle was clearly feeling the effects of the beverage, too. Her cheeks were flushed, her eyes sparkled, and her voice spilled out in laughing, burbling quips. Gwen tried to keep her eyes on each of the girls in equal measure, but it was hard not to watch the queen of this court, presiding over her ladies with the perfect mix of tipsy whimsy and graceful composure.

The next question from Jane, *Hast thou ever been from France?*, made Gwen choke and take the tiniest sip she could manage from her cup.

"Please, I beg of you," she pleaded, laughing. "Any more and I will lose the ability to speech. Speech." She paused, then tried one more time. "*Speak.*"

Isobelle snorted, the sound rather startling Gwen—she usually kept herself in better check than that. Gwen wasn't the only one who'd had too much of the uisce.

Hilde let out a long, lusty sigh. "Hast thou ever kissed a boy?" she asked, though no one had nominated her to ask the next question.

Jane slumped down into a supine position, moaned something about being personally victimized by this game, then downed the rest of her cup in one swig. Gwen watched Isobelle out of the corner of her eye, her own heartbeat sounding very loud in her ears. The queen bee of the group reached for the handle of her cup—but only to turn it on its saucer, adjusting its position.

"At least when I do," Isobelle said cheerfully, "I'll be ready for it."

"There is that," agreed Hilde with a giggle. "Practice makes perfect."

Gwen was missing something, she felt sure—but before her fuzzy brain could quite grasp what it was, Sylvie was leaning forward, gazing at her with interest. "Hast thou ever kissed *anyone?*" she asked pointedly.

Everyone—except Gwen—drank.

Gwen watched Isobelle's cup rise to her lips and lower again, her mind churning as it tried to understand, through her haze, the significance of that.

Hilde noticed Gwen's cup still on its saucer and lurched upward. "Ach, but, Céline, how will you be ready? Surely you have had friends to practice with, back in Toussaint? Come now, we will teach you. Maybe not Jane, unless you wish to lie down on the floor." She took Jane's cup from her, receiving a mild protest—or possibly a thank-you—from the supine girl.

Gwen's heartbeat was surely loud enough now to be heard. This time she very carefully did *not* look at Isobelle. The pleasant warmth in which the uisce had wrapped her suddenly felt heavy and cloying, an anxious knot twisting inside her. "Um . . . you all kiss each other? To practice for men?"

"It is a skill to be perfected to attract a rich husband, like any other." Sylvie's smile was wide and languid.

"And it's fun," Jane supplied from the floor.

"I would offer," Sylvie continued, "but I'm so comfortable. Besides, I think it should be your friend, no? Perhaps we've been playing the wrong game all along. Izzie, I *dare* you to kiss our new friend here. And make it a good one."

Isobelle was rolling her eyes at Sylvie, though Gwen noticed she rather hastily put down her cup and saucer. Eager, or trying to hide an unsteady hand? She glanced back over at Gwen, blue eyes dancing and the tiniest bit unfocused. "It's just for practice," she assured her, her already pink cheeks going a little pinker. "And only if you want to."

Gwen's lungs constricted, her mind summoning up memories of girls in her village who would play at flirtation, never realizing Gwen felt something different, something deeper; never noticing her heartache when they ran off back to their beaus.

Gwen was frozen, gazing at Isobelle as she rose from the embroidered divan and came to drop down next to her, mirroring her pose with one leg folded under her—knee to knee, shin to shin. The dimples were there, but trembling slightly as she gazed beseechingly into Gwen's face.

Of all the things that should've been running, screaming really, through Gwen's mind—that this was risky when Isobelle was meant to be courting Céline's brother, that this whole party was like something out of a nightmare, that they were both drunk and silly and maybe it didn't matter—the only thought Gwen could think stood out like a fiery beacon amid warring feelings of longing and confusion.

Not like this.

Isobelle was actually leaning toward her when Gwen jerked back, sliding off the divan and getting unsteadily to her feet. "Um, sorry," she managed, over the pounding of her heart. "I . . . I think I've had too much to drink. Forgive me."

And without waiting to figure out if that was a ladylike, *appropriate* way to excuse herself, she turned tail and fled.

Chapter Fifteen

EVERYTHING IS CONTEXT

Isobelle scrambled to her feet, windmilled her arms for balance, and kept herself vertical mostly by sheer will.

Down at the tournament grounds there was an inflatable knight, held upright by the warm air of a fire beneath him that was constantly tended. He swayed gently in the breeze, and his arms flailed around unpredictably as the wind and updraughts caught them. Isobelle and the girls liked to joke about him: *Full of hot air, just like the real thing.*

Isobelle had an unpleasant suspicion she might have resembled him just now.

"Gw—Céline!" she called, hoping the slip sounded like a hiccup, and took off after Gwen.

Usually, after tea parties, Isobelle reclined in a languid fashion upon her daybed until her head was in good working order. Now, she was in the worst possible shape to be discovering a drawback to recruiting a fit, strong blacksmith as your partner-in-crime: they're *fast*. By the time Isobelle completed her barely controlled descent of the stairs, both hands grabbing at the wall, she caught only a flash of Gwen's skirts as she disappeared around the corner at the end of the hallway.

Isobelle hurried after her, but when she rounded the corner, there was no sign of which way Gwen had gone next. A particularly stern-looking portrait squinted down at her in disapproval, and Isobelle rested one hand on the wall to catch her breath and return his glare. "You know," she muttered, "I don't recall asking your opinion."

She had very little brain available for thinking through what had just happened as she commenced her search for her friend. Almost all of it was taken up with the combined tasks of guessing where Gwen might have run to and keeping herself upright.

There was no sign of her errant blacksmith down in the stables—though Achilles was very pleased to see her. She had no apples in her pockets to feed him, so she gave him a caress on his velvety nose.

She crossed into the wing of the castle that housed the ballroom, venturing into Madame Dupont's territory, hovering at the door to see if she could spot Gwen hiding among the rows of young children currently learning their first carole.

And eventually, having managed a full lap of the castle, she was forced to drift back up to her own quarters. *How could I have miscalculated so very badly?*

She was about to drop onto the edge of her bed, defeat and confusion dragging her downward, when she saw a silhouette against the sheer curtains of the window overlooking the balcony stretching from her room to Gwen's. Isobelle's blood thundered in her ears as she eased the heavy door to the balcony open enough to peek through.

Gwen had her head bowed, both her hands braced against the stone railing, and she was taking long, steadying breaths. It wasn't quite sunset yet, but the sun was low in the sky, bathing Gwen in a golden light. She seemed almost to glow.

Isobelle, having given up on the pursuit completely, pulled up short at the sight of her quarry, simply gazing at her. Gwen looked like a painting, a goddess or queen whose every detail had been lingered over by a master's delicate brush. Suddenly, Isobelle felt something very close to . . . shyness? This was a new experience for her.

"Gwen?" she ventured, hovering at the open door. "May I join you?"

Gwen turned her head to blink at her, and the familiar frown line between her brows broke the spell. "I don't think I've ever heard you ask permission for anything before," she murmured. Which wasn't technically an invitation—but as she said it, she moved along the balcony, making a space beside her.

"First time for everything?" Isobelle suggested, easing up beside Gwen as though she were a spooked horse, keeping her movements small and slow. She curled her hands around the balcony railing beside Gwen's and gazed down at them.

Gwen's hands were not those of a lady, and even Olivia's best manicure couldn't hide the calluses. A few freckles dotted the backs of her hands, matching the ones that Isobelle so admired across her nose and cheeks. There were a few tiny white spots that must be old burn marks, long since healed.

As Isobelle absorbed all these small details, she realized that although she'd trotted all over the castle, she hadn't taken any of that time to come up with proper opening remarks. "I'm sorry, Gwen. I didn't mean to upset you."

Gwen shook her head, then clearly thought better of it, grimacing. "You didn't," she replied, and then amended the statement. "I mean, not really. It just caught me off guard, and . . . and it didn't occur to me that you'd all have . . ." She too gazed down at their hands where they rested side by side. "Just for practice," she concluded, with a note of bitterness in her voice that Isobelle couldn't identify.

Isobelle made a genuine effort to parse this. "It—it bothers you to think of kissing another girl?" she asked carefully, doing her damnedest not to examine the tangle of confusion that accompanied that particular question. It was, she decided, simply that she couldn't imagine Gwen, of all people, being so easily shocked by a harmless game.

Gwen huffed a breath that was almost a laugh. "Of course not."

"So . . . what exactly *is* the problem, then?"

Isobelle felt Gwen's eyes on her and made herself lift her head. There they were, the forest-green eyes with those hints of oak, waiting to catch her as firmly as any snare. This time, though, they were unguarded. And in their slow blink, in the tilt of the strong brows framing them, they showed her something . . . something worryingly close to hurt.

Gwen's lips parted. "All these things you've been teaching me about how to be a lady—it all keeps coming back to context. The same gesture at a feast might mean something completely different at a picnic. The promise of a dance at the midsummer ball is worlds away from an impromptu waltz when someone plays the harp after dinner—even though they're both just meals, both just dances. That's what you keep saying—everything is context."

"Everything *is* context," Isobelle agreed, distantly aware that she'd adopted Gwen's trick of echoing words when she wasn't sure what was happening.

"Yes!" Gwen's voice grew louder. "Are you really trying to tell me that you, of all people, don't see why I might object to kissing someone in front of all her friends, on a dare, to practice for whatever nobleman eventually wins her hand in marriage?"

Isobelle couldn't seem to disengage—couldn't break her gaze away from Gwen's. "I . . ." she began. "Well, I . . ." Heavens above, was she *stammering*? What had Hilde *put* in that tea?

Some of the heat drained from Gwen's gaze, her defenses lowering a touch at the sight of Isobelle scrambling for words. "I suppose I just don't kiss people for practice."

"I thought . . ." Isobelle heard herself say, as though someone else—someone particularly insipid—was speaking. "I thought it might be quite nice."

Gwen's lashes dipped into a slow blink, and she spoke so softly that Isobelle had to lean in to hear her. "If someone kisses me," she whispered, "I want it to be because they want to. Because they *need* to."

Isobelle couldn't remember how to breathe.

Gwen was gazing at her lips now, and she didn't bother to conceal the fact. "I want it to be because they can't take another second wondering, *dreaming* about what it would be like."

Isobelle was watching Gwen's mouth too—watching the way her lips shaped the words—and she was mesmerized as they curved into a hint of a smile.

Gwen's voice was soft. "*Quite nice* isn't quite enough for me."

"No," Isobelle agreed, breathing the word. She was pinned in place now. There was something magnificent about Gwen, gilded by the sunset, seeming to glow from the inside out.

Gwen stepped back. "And given what we're trying to protect

you from—how little choice you'll have if we fail—I don't think it should be enough for you, either."

Without another word she turned and strode back inside. Isobelle could hear her footsteps, softened by the rug, until the door of her room closed behind her.

Slowly, Isobelle turned and leaned back against the edge of the balustrade. Then she gave up and let her legs fold, slithering down and pulling her knees in against her chest.

She felt she was on the edge of understanding something truly important, but her head was still spinning when she turned it too fast.

What had Gwen said? *You, of all people, don't see why I might object to kissing someone in front of all her friends, on a dare, to practice for whatever nobleman eventually wins her hand in marriage?*

Perhaps that was it, and Gwen was hurt because Isobelle had made her think that she expected one of the men to win the tournament. That she should make herself ready for him.

A small part of her mind raised its hand for her attention, attempting to lodge an inquiry as to whether the relevant part of that sentence was definitely the bit pertaining to the nobleman.

Could it have been the dare that was the problem? The game? The audience?

But it had been a very long day, and pushing her way through the fog of that question felt like trying to locate a landmark without any idea of the direction in which it lay, or even what it looked like.

And so, instead, she stayed where she was as the sun sank below the horizon and velvety darkness fell all around her.

She was still sitting there, gazing at Gwen's door, when Olivia came to find her.

Isobelle took one look at her maid's face and sat up straighter. "Oh dear," she said. "What's happened?"

Olivia walked over, leaning down to offer her a hand. Isobelle took hold, and Olivia's strong grip pulled her up.

"Last rounds of the qualifiers tomorrow," Olivia said. "And then comes the dragon bonfire, and then the start of the tournament proper."

"I know, I'm looking forward to it," Isobelle replied, enunciating her words as carefully as she could and resting one hand casually on the balustrade to make sure she didn't wobble. "What's the problem?"

"It's Lord Whimsitt," Olivia replied grimly.

"What's he done now?"

"He's worried about interlopers in the tournament, that the wrong sort of people might weasel their way in for the money. The head steward has announced that every entrant will be required to provide formal patents of nobility, with seals attached."

Isobelle felt all the heat draining from her face, leaving something very cold in its wake. "But we don't have those for Gwen."

"No," Olivia agreed. "We don't."

When the sunlight crept across Isobelle's face in the morning, slowly dragging her toward wakefulness, the patents of nobility weren't the first thing she thought of.

The first thing she wondered was why the inside of her mouth felt and tasted like a hessian sack. The second thought—much slower, trickling into the cracks in her consciousness until it had flooded her entire mind—was of Gwen.

She had tossed and turned until shortly before dawn, rehearsing conversations with Gwen, trying to plan out every way their next encounter might turn.

She owed Gwen an apology, of that much she was sure.

She just wished she were entirely clear on what the apology was *for*. She felt a strange sense of loss—the uncomfortable feeling that something between them had gone, and she couldn't see how to get it back when she wasn't even sure what it had been.

In the bright light of the morning, Isobelle wasn't sure what she needed, except to talk to Gwen. Whatever had happened the night before, now their heads were clear, and she would fix it. Isobelle's greatest strength had always been her ability to select a course of action and then simply *believe* her way to success, and that was what she would do now. She would fix this hiccup with Gwen, and things would go back as they were.

So she rolled out of bed and set about strapping on her own armor.

The right clothes always fortified one against difficult situations. She chose the deep purple dress with yellow trim that reminded her of an iris, and, wondering vaguely where Olivia had gotten to, wriggled into it on her own.

Leaning into the botanical theme, she bound up her hair with green ribbon, pinched her cheeks to make them pink, and headed for the door to the living room—only to find the world had begun its morning without her.

Olivia had a map spread out on the table and was leaning over it with Gwen and Madame Dupont, their three heads bowed together as Olivia traced out a route with her finger. Saddlebags were sitting in a heap in the middle of the floor, and a pile of bread and cheese presumably constituted breakfast.

Gwen glanced up as Isobelle emerged. Her gaze lingered briefly, then dropped to the map again.

You can hide behind cartography for now, Sir Gwen, Isobelle told her silently, trying not to examine too closely the stab of disappointment she felt at Gwen's unwillingness to meet her gaze. *But we have a conversation waiting for us.*

"Good, you're up," Olivia said. "The three of you can get on your way."

"To?" Isobelle asked, heading for the bread and cheese. Mental and emotional confusion was no reason to skip breakfast. In fact, Isobelle had discovered that breakfast often helped sort out such things. Or at least provided a helpful distraction.

"I'm sending you to an old friend of mine," Olivia replied, stepping in behind her to tighten the laces on her dress. "He may be reluctant to assist you—if he objects, give him this." She pressed a small round token into Isobelle's hand. It bore a worn depiction of an owl in flight, each feather individually engraved into the metal.

Isobelle eyed Olivia askance. "I don't suppose there's any point in my asking what this is about?"

Olivia shrugged. "He's an old friend. This will remind him of a debt he owes me. It should take you half a day's ride to reach him—Madame Dupont will escort you."

"What about Whimsitt?" Isobelle asked, hearing the words and hating herself for caring. Ordinarily she would have cheerfully risked his wrath, but there had been a different, darker edge to his anger the night she'd snuck out to meet Gwen. An edge that made Isobelle, for once, hesitate.

"If he asks, I'll cover for you. Easy to say you're indisposed with a monthly condition of some delicacy." Olivia's lips quirked. "I can guarantee he won't ask any further questions."

Olivia always had an answer ready. It was Isobelle's experience that Olivia could sort out almost anything, though it was often better if you didn't ask for details.

She wasn't particularly surprised to find the wheels of their salvation already in motion this morning, and from that point on, she devoted her attentions to gathering up more of the bread and cheese, in case there wasn't a nice place to stop for morning tea along the way.

Half an hour later, they were on the road.

Chapter Sixteen

SHE WAS VERY MUCH ACCUSTOMED TO PEOPLE LOOKING AT HER LIKE THEY DIDN'T UNDERSTAND WHAT WAS HAPPENING AND WANTED IT ALL TO STOP

The movement of Achilles's haunches was hypnotic, if you watched it long enough. Isobelle had been gazing at the back of Gwen's horse—and, if she was honest, the back of Gwen—for hours. Achilles wasn't the sort of horse you saw down in the village, but Gwen rode him as if she'd been born to it, swaying slightly to match his movements, her touch light. Isobelle herself was mounted on a friendly silver mare with whom she was getting along passably. She'd tied one of her green ribbons around her bridle to give them a little cohesion in their look.

They rode along the top of a ridgeline. To their left, the land dropped away to open farmland, fields neatly laid out and combed into rows. With summer nearing its end, the wheat and barley fields were a bright, coppery gold, and they swayed in the breeze, whispering secrets.

To their right lay the real secrets—there, the open grass gave way to the tangled dark of the great forest, which in turn gave way to the craggy base of the mountains that housed Whimsitt's mine.

There had *not* been a nice place to stop for morning tea, and Isobelle was now certain there would not be a nice spot to stop for a bite of lunch, either. There had been a hurried snack under a tree during their one break, which Isobelle suspected they only took so they could water the horses.

There had also not been a single moment alone with Gwen.

Up ahead, Madame Dupont was still talking about jousting.

"The qualifiers have cut the number of challengers down to sixteen," she was saying, "but though the path to victory is shorter now, the greatest difficulties still lie ahead." None of them were willing to name those difficulties—the old hands who'd done this for years, the veterans Gwen would have to make her way through before she ran up against the favorites, like Sir Ralph.

"You will need to win four more times," Madame continued. "And a loss in any match will mean the end of your tournament."

"And the rules are the same?" Gwen asked.

"Oui. Zero points if you do not connect with your opponent. One point if you hit his shield. Three points if you unhorse him. An instant win if your opponent is . . . ah . . . unable to continue. If you are both still upright and equal in points at the end of three rounds—possible, if you each score once, or you each unhorse the other, or you miss every time—then we move on to the sword. Now, let me explain a few of the jousting styles you will encounter . . ."

Isobelle's attention drifted. The only time she remembered watching a tournament was more than a decade earlier—a patchwork quilt of memories, a piece snipped from each and all sewn together. The bright, fluttering flags. Her fingers sticky from the iced currant bun her father had bought her. The thunder of the horses' hooves. The warmth of her parents sitting on either side of her to protect her from the breeze blowing through the grandstands. She could barely remember the knights themselves at all.

She returned to the present as Dupont guided them off the main road and up toward a farmhouse on a hill. It was a small, humble home, flanked by a pair of larger outbuildings, but it had a commanding lookout over the approach. Fruit trees lined the path as they grew closer, and a flock of geese came waddling up, honking a loud commentary on the newcomers. Isobelle suspected it was not complimentary. She saw Gwen turn her head as if to exchange a glance with her, and then check the movement.

Curses.

As they drew closer, more details emerged. There were wide beds planted with neat rows of vegetables, and pens holding pigs and chickens. A pair of soft-eyed cows chewed moodily at them from behind a fence.

"One could live entirely off this farm," Isobelle marveled as they reached the yard in front of the stone building to find lines strung with bunches of drying herbs.

"That's the point," growled a voice from behind them, and the trio wheeled their horses around to find a short, wiry old man stomping out to meet them. He had a grizzled gray beard that reached halfway down his chest and wore an eyepatch to great effect. His skin was the same light brown as the thatched roof behind him, and almost as covered in ridges and wrinkles.

"When you've seen what I've seen," he continued, looking them over, "you're always prepared. Might be the day comes, you can only rely on yourself. Now, who are you?"

"I'm Lady Isobelle of Avington." Isobelle slid down from her saddle, biting her lip against a yelp as her thighs and . . . upper thighs screamed a protest after the long ride. "These are my companions, Madame Dupont and Lady Céline. May I say, sir, your farm is a delight—very well prepared for the fall of civilization."

The man squinted at her, but Isobelle was on solid ground and waited with a bright smile. She was very much accustomed to people looking at her like they didn't understand what was happening and wanted it all to stop.

"What is it you wanted?" he asked eventually.

"We were told you might be able to assist us in the creation of some documents," Isobelle said, with her best dimples yet.

His expression cleared. "Me? No. I can't even read, much less write. Who told you that nonsense?"

Isobelle dug in the purse at her belt, pulling out the small metal token Olivia had given her. "My maid, Olivia," she said.

The man took it from her, inspecting its owl engraving and turning it over in his callused fingers. He barked a laugh. "So she's calling herself Olivia now?" he asked, glancing up.

"Indeed," Isobelle agreed, intrigued by the news that Olivia hadn't always been Olivia.

"All right then," he said, handing back the coin. "You'd better come in."

The inside of the house was crammed tighter than Isobelle's wardrobe. Bales of cloth were tied with string, crates were stacked to the rafters, barrels jammed into corners. A series of large cupboards ran down one side of the room, their doors ajar, probably because they couldn't be closed. Oddities and canvases and jars and boxes and scrolls covered every surface, including the floor. A couple were marked with stamps or seals bearing the mark of the owl that had been on Olivia's token. Madame Dupont took one look and announced that she'd go tend to the horses, and made a hasty retreat from the chaos.

The man, who introduced himself as Archer, peppered Gwen with questions, taking notes in some kind of shorthand that didn't resemble any language Isobelle knew. Gwen scrambled to keep up, explaining the need for patents of nobility for her "brother," showing him the pennant on the Sir Gawain figurine, and then—so easily and quickly that Isobelle could only stare—rattling off an entire imagined lineage for Archer to note down on the patents.

Was that what Gwen had been doing on the ride here? Inventing Gawain's backstory, while Isobelle was mentally composing and discarding whole speeches that sought to explain what had happened between them, and apologize for it?

Archer continued to interview Gwen, and Isobelle found her attention drawn to the taxidermied head of a black-and-white-striped horse above a little hand-scrawled label that read "Hippotigris." Isobelle had been taught Latin from an early age, and her mind supplied the translation: horse-tiger.

She'd just begun to lose herself in a glorious fantasy of making a grand entrance mounted on such a creature—she'd be in black and white, too, with a red lip and feathers in her hair—when, abruptly, reality came crashing back in as her ears caught up to her.

"That should be enough for me to get to work," Archer was saying. "The papers should be ready in three or four hours."

Isobelle stopped in her tracks, and finally, *finally*, Gwen glanced across at her, eyes wide.

"Hours?" Gwen echoed. "We'd never make it back to the castle before dark."

"You'll stay here," Archer replied. "E—er—Olivia can cover for you, I have no doubt."

"But . . ." Gwen's eyes were still on Isobelle, unwilling to mention that Isobelle was meant to be confined to the castle, and every moment they spent away increased the odds that her absence would be discovered.

Archer sighed and dismissed their doubts with a wave of his hand. "It'll take the time it takes, kids. Go outside and play, and let me do my thing."

Gwen gave a little shrug, finally dropping her gaze from Isobelle's, and they emerged once more from Archer's house into the afternoon sunlight.

Dupont was just coming out of the stable, and though her lips tightened at the news that the papers would take hours, she nodded. "We must not waste the time—this is the perfect place to practice the joust, away from the prying eyes of the castle. Come!"

Isobelle opened her mouth to protest—it had been a long day, they were tired, Gwen needed rest—but Gwen was already striding after Dupont. And none of those excuses were the real reason Isobelle wanted just a moment's pause.

She sighed and turned to trail along in their wake, trying not to think about how desperately she needed to talk to Gwen and make things right between them.

Lucky Gwen, able to drown out her feelings by hitting things.

Chapter Seventeen

DAMN THOSE GIRLS AND THEIR "TEA"

Gwen was feeling rather lucky that she was able to drown out her feelings by hitting things.

All day, every time she looked around, she'd found Isobelle staring at her, eyes full of questions, lips half parted, ready to throw herself into some kind of speech at the first opportunity.

Last night, Gwen had been utterly certain she was saying the right thing—setting the boundary she needed Isobelle to respect, protecting her own heart as she had learned to do.

This morning, she couldn't shake the sinking realization that she had said too much. That maybe Isobelle had realized what took Gwen a night's tossing and turning to figure out herself: that what had bothered Gwen the most was just how badly she'd wanted to throw those boundaries of hers to the winds.

Damn those girls and their "tea."

Gwen had tried to spend the day being as aloof as she could, hoping that if Isobelle *had* realized how pointed Gwen's remarks had been the night before, today's distance would shake her understanding.

And through it all, Isobelle's gaze had stuck to her like some cornflower-blue curse from a hedge witch, and Gwen was desperate to figure out the terms of her release.

"Where is your head at, girl?" shouted Madame Dupont, chasing away the mental image of being haunted by wide blue eyes and replacing it with the tree bearing the tiny dangling target—a dragonseye, she had called it. "Ride, damn you! We do not have much time to practice!"

Drowning one's feelings by hitting things only worked if one, you know, actually hit things.

Stop thinking about Isobelle, she commanded herself, and let Achilles burst into a gallop as she lowered the makeshift lance—a pole from Archer's barn—into place. She tried to force the world to narrow down to that dragonseye, but her heart kept jerking bits of her attention this way and that. Achilles's hoofbeats thudded against the ground, traveling all the way up her spine, her arm beginning to shake with the fatigue of having held the lance so many times in a row. She tried to focus on those sensations, if not that fury.

What it must be like to be Isobelle right now, watching her fail over and over to hit this mark, *knowing* her fate depended on Gwen being able to do this impossible thing? That thought opened a floodgate in Gwen's mind, which surged with a thousand different questions, each of them triggering a pinprick of emotion, until she felt like she was bleeding from countless tiny wounds.

The dangling target whizzed by, untouched.

Dupont made a noise somewhere between a cluck and a hiss and stalked a few steps away before turning back around. "Again," she snapped.

Stuffing her misgivings down was becoming harder and harder with every passing moment—but the alternative was whirling round and unleashing them on Isobelle, telling her there was no way Gwen could pull this off, and consigning her to her fate of being married off to someone who didn't love her. Hiding her fears was hard—but hurting Isobelle was impossible.

Gwen swallowed, gathered up Achilles's reins to turn him, and pointedly did not look at Isobelle.

Chapter Eighteen

MAYBE WE COULD WASH THE DONKEYS

"A hayloft!" Isobelle squealed. "Just like in an adventure story!"

Below in the barn, the horses and a couple of sweet, but rather fragrant, donkeys occupied the stalls. Isobelle sat with her feet dangling over empty space, basking in the narrative glory of it all and nibbling on a piece of straw. She felt delightfully rural, and she thought the straw probably made her look quite like a philosopher.

"What?" Gwen looked up from where she was trying to kick a bunch of hay into something shaped like a mattress.

"That's where they always sleep in tales," Isobelle replied. "The hero out to seek his fortune, forced to seek refuge in a humble hayloft."

Archer had a single spare bed in his cottage, and—aware there were also stories hinging entirely on the predicament of there being only one bed, for she had read many of them with great relish—Isobelle had insisted Madame Dupont take it. The last thing she wanted was for Gwen to think she was being flippant again about being close to each other. Still, something in her had wilted just a touch when Gwen agreed quickly and firmly. Isobelle wondered if by chance she had read the same stories.

Beneath her dangling feet, one of the donkeys shifted its weight and let out a little rumbling sigh. Isobelle wrinkled her nose. "I wonder if we should fetch some of the dried herbs," she mused. "To scent the hay."

"I think we might be beyond the help of herbs," Gwen said, dumping another armful of hay on the pile and then spreading her cloak on top of it.

"Maybe we could wash the donkeys," Isobelle suggested brightly, abandoning her perch to see about her own hay bed.

Gwen gave an explosive huff of badly restrained laughter. "I'd kind of love to see you try." She sighed, eyeing their nest. "Dress it up how you like, a hayloft is smelly and itchy and uncomfortable."

"You wouldn't say that if you were in a ballad," said Isobelle, spreading her own cloak and then dramatically collapsing onto her makeshift mattress, flinging out her arms.

Gwen was silent as she blew out the lantern, and Isobelle's senses magnified every small sound and movement in the dark. She heard the soft pad of Gwen's footsteps, the rustle of the straw and the soft rasp of the cloak as she found her spot to lie down. She felt the way the two cloaks shifted against each other every time Gwen moved.

Here was the chance Isobelle had been waiting for all day—to *talk* to Gwen. She drew a deep breath and then immediately sneezed violently, her whole body curling around itself.

"Are you all right?" Gwen asked cautiously once she'd subsided.

"I think I might be allergic to straw," Isobelle admitted.

There was a muffled sound suspiciously akin to a snort.

"They might have left a few details out of the ballads." Isobelle sighed. "I should have known."

"Well," said Gwen, and Isobelle realized her eyes had adjusted—now she could see Gwen's silhouette illuminated by the faint moonlight filtering in through the cracks in the walls. "Perhaps they got a few things right, too. This does feel a little like an adventure."

Isobelle bit her lip, on the verge of blurting out something quite embarrassing indeed—that if Gwen could have only seen herself this afternoon as she practiced her jousting, she would have known what Isobelle herself knew. That whatever they were doing, it was better than any adventure story Isobelle had ever read. She could tell how frustrated Gwen was, missing more often than she struck the target at first, but Isobelle had the advantage of knowing how often knights missed the shields of their opponents entirely. She'd watched Orson practice enough times to know he probably wouldn't have hit Dupont's tiny swinging target even once.

And with Orson, she'd never found herself watching with such breathless focus, needing the sight of the form astride the horse more than she needed air.

They were both quiet again—thinking, Isobelle was certain, very different thoughts—until Gwen broke the silence. "Well, good night, I suppose. We should get some rest."

It was the forced cheerfulness in Gwen's voice that made something inside Isobelle snap. All the half-formed speeches she'd been rehearsing fractured into pieces, falling around her feet like the shards of a mirror. She'd given herself all day to find the right words, and none had come. Her only course was to launch into the conversation before she lost her moment, and hope she found her destination without too many detours.

"Look, Gwen. About yesterday. I owe you an apology, but I also want to say—"

"There's no need to apologize," Gwen cut in, the words tumbling out.

What Isobelle really wanted was to get to the next part, the *I also want to say* part, not least because she was interested to find out what, precisely, she also wanted to say. But she made herself deal with the apology first. "No, I must. I made you feel pressured to do something you didn't want to do, and—"

"Truly, it's fine, Isobelle. We'd both had too much tea, and you didn't know I— Well, I overreacted."

"But what I want to say is—"

"Isobelle, *please*."

She stopped. It felt like a fist had wrapped itself around her stomach and begun to squeeze.

"Let's just forget any of it ever happened," Gwen said gently.

Isobelle wanted to reply, but she couldn't seem to get a proper breath.

"We can get back to being partners in crime," Gwen continued. "We have to stick together if we're going to succeed, right?"

Isobelle said nothing. She felt as though one of the donkeys was sitting on her chest, pressing her down into the hay.

"Isobelle?"

"Yes," she managed weakly, turning her head to see Gwen's silhouette once more. She saw the way she shifted, saw the starlight picking out a stray lock of her hair. Saw her close her eyes.

"We are partners, aren't we?" Gwen asked, uncharacteristically hesitant.

"Of course we are!" Isobelle rolled onto her side to face her, surprised at how normal her voice sounded. "Of course we are." She made herself stop before she could say it a third time. Olivia always said that repeating something a third time undermined one's credibility. "Back to normal."

"Oh, good," Gwen said, the words a rush of relief. "I didn't mean to make things awkward."

"Don't be ridiculous," Isobelle batted back. "I didn't mean to cause all this drama. I'll warn you about the tea next time."

Gwen laughed her near-silent laugh, and Isobelle tried with all her might to make herself believe that the feeling coursing through her veins was relief. Gwen had shown her all day long what she thought of the not-quite-a-kiss. She was lucky to have found Gwen on her balcony at all—lucky she hadn't run all the way back to the village, never to be seen again. She was lucky Gwen was still here to fight on her behalf.

Lucky, she told herself. *Lucky, lucky, lucky.*

But watching that encounter on the balcony slip through her fingers and allowing time to carry her away from it, she couldn't make herself feel it was true. Gwen was only a few inches from her, every movement making her skin prickle, but Isobelle felt as though some vast and uncrossable chasm had opened up between them.

She felt as though she'd held something precious in her hand, just for a moment, and then she'd dropped it. And now she'd never have a chance to get it back.

Chapter Nineteen

A DEER TRYING TO HIDE IN A PACK OF RAVENOUS WOLVES

Archer provided them with Gwen's papers at sunrise, and he gruffly waved away the purse of coins Isobelle tried to press into his hand. "El—Olivia would skin me alive if she found out I'd taken your money."

They saddled the horses and set off as soon as it was light enough. The ride was quiet, uncomfortably so—Gwen never thought she would miss feeling the constant tingle of Isobelle's eyes on her, but, as it turned out, she felt far worse when the other girl wouldn't look at her at all.

As they approached the castle gates, Madame Dupont drew her gelding off the road and into a copse of trees, signaling her need for a conference before they got too near the castle.

Isobelle looked as poised and well rested as ever, only the dust dulling the vibrant purple and goldenrod of her dress to tell of their journey. They'd clothed her in a heavy cloak when they left, to make sure no one saw Isobelle sneaking away from the castle—now, reluctantly, Isobelle slung the heavy cloak back on.

"Écoutez, girls," said Madame Dupont as merchants and townsfolk passed by on the road beyond the concealing row of trees. "We are entering a most dangerous phase of our deception."

"But we have the proof of Sir Gawain's nobility now," protested

Isobelle. "We can hand it in tomorrow, before the first round of the matchups are announced—she'll be safe."

Madame Dupont raised an eyebrow at Isobelle. "Leaving aside that she is about to engage in a very dangerous sport indeed, that is not what I meant. Just now, no one knows who Sir Gawain is. When she wins the first round of the tournament, however, the entire county will wish to solve the mystery of this new young knight."

"*If* I win," Gwen muttered. "We don't even know who I'll be fighting."

"Hush," retorted Isobelle, though she was looking at Madame Dupont. "None of that. She'll be fine, right? Odds are she won't be up against anyone really tough straight out of the gate."

"You are getting ahead of yourselves," replied Madame Dupont reprovingly. "Tonight is the key."

"Tonight?" echoed Gwen, feeling her mouth go dry. "What happens tonight?"

"You must go to the dragon bonfire celebration tonight as Lady Céline," Madame Dupont told her. "You must show yourself to many people, so they will tell their friends, who will tell their friends, about the sister of this most intriguing new competitor on the scene. There must be no doubt that Céline is a person in her own right, because this will help sell the illusion that Sir Gawain is real, too."

Gwen stifled a groan. She'd been hoping to slip away to the village tonight to see her father and join in their own version of the yearly bonfire. It would be far less of a to-do than the one held just outside the castle gates, attended by all the nobles in the land, but it was the one she'd grown up with. Her relationship with the other villagers might not be the easiest or most secure, but it was a far sight better than posing as nobility all night.

At home she might be a deer trying to hide among goats, but here she was a deer trying to hide in a pack of ravenous wolves.

Isobelle, however, failed to notice Gwen's lack of enthusiasm. Or, if she had, she was trying to make up for it with a surfeit of excitement all on her own. "Oooh, Gwen, we'll have such a blast!" She still wasn't quite meeting her eyes, addressing Gwen's collarbone instead. "It's a great party every year, but this year they're pulling out all the stops because the tournament is here. You'll love it, I promise. The food, if nothing else. Oh, and the dancers—you'll see."

Gwen summoned up a weak smile. "Sounds great, then. Maybe we ought to slip off for some more jousting practice, though, Madame—"

"Non," the older woman interjected. "You must rest. The truth is . . ." She paused, clearly struggling with whatever she was about to say. She too seemed to be having trouble looking directly at Gwen.

Gwen looked over at Isobelle to find the other girl finally willing to meet her gaze, if only to signal her own confusion at Madame Dupont's uncharacteristic hesitation.

Dupont glared down at the reins she had clenched in one hand, still wrestling with whatever she wanted to say. Finally, she let her breath out in a quick, sharp sigh, and looked back up at Gwen, her gaze frank. "The truth is, you are a natural on horseback. It is hard to believe you have not been fighting this way all your life. I envy how easily it comes to you."

Gwen could not move or think, distantly grateful for Achilles's solid body holding her up. Dupont was sparing with praise—Gwen usually had to find validation in between the lines of her critiques, and in the way she'd ramped up the difficulty of her training exercises so quickly. She glanced at Isobelle, only to find the other girl staring at Madame Dupont with her mouth open.

Dupont's eyebrows lowered and drew together in one of the most fearsome scowls Gwen had ever seen from her. "Don't gawk at me! Elles me regardent comme si c'était *moi* la folle!" She wheeled her horse around and went cantering up the road and through the gate, muttering to herself in French as she moved out of earshot.

For a long moment, there was only silence. Then Isobelle gave a soft laugh. "Gosh," she said, turning her horse to watch the Frenchwoman depart. "That was unexpected."

"Tell me about it," murmured Gwen. Beneath her, Achilles stamped his foot impatiently. He could see the stables where he'd be allowed to take off this ridiculous side saddle—and, more important, get hand-fed last year's carrots and apples by his new best friend, the stableman—and Gwen was sitting here doing nothing as far as he was concerned.

Isobelle waited for her to hand Achilles off to Jeffers, who was already rummaging in his pockets for treats and gazing at Achilles with his heart in his eyes. Together, the girls made their way toward Isobelle's suite of rooms. Was this an awkward silence between them, or an ordinary one?

Gwen was so distracted by her own thoughts, as turbulent and chaotic as a summer storm, that she scarcely looked at the girl seated in one of the chairs by the hearth, waiting for them.

It was Isobelle who stopped short in surprise. "Sylvie? What're you doing here?"

Gwen blinked and refocused on the figure she'd first taken to be Olivia.

Sylvie rose gracefully to her feet, inclining her head and smiling a small, spare smile. Her eyes, however, glowed with a keen, curious satisfaction. "When Olivia told us you were unwell last night and not accepting company, I assumed you would still be feeling poorly this morning. But I see you've been out riding with Céline—has Lord Whimsitt rescinded his restriction on your movements?" Her gaze took in their rumpled riding frocks and flushed faces.

Gwen fought an instinct to reach for a nonexistent sword at her belt. Though Sylvie's tone was faultlessly polite and solicitous, the sharp interest in her eyes told Gwen to be wary.

Isobelle gave a sigh and cast an unconcerned smile at Gwen. "Well, Céline pointed out this morning that some fresh air and gentle exercise might help me feel better. And she was right, the clever thing! We never left the sight of the guards, so I wasn't technically breaking Whimsitt's orders."

Gwen wished she could lie so easily.

Sylvie's measuring gaze swung over toward Gwen and stayed. "Clever indeed," she murmured. "Is fresh air and riding a common remedy for such ailments where you come from? Toussaint . . . that is in France, isn't it?"

Gwen nodded, forcing a slight smile to curve her lips, trying to relax her shoulders. "Yes, northern France."

Sylvie's smile widened, and Gwen had only time to brace herself before the other girl murmured, "Ne vous sentez-vous pas seule, loin de chez vous? Quelle chance qu'Isobelle vous ait prise sous son aile."

Gwen could sense Isobelle stiffening at her side. This was, at least as far as Isobelle was concerned, the one flaw in their masquerade. Gwen was not French, and a peasant girl certainly would have no reason to be taught the French language the way a well-bred noblewoman would.

Gwen had been right about Sylvie—she *had* been suspicious of Céline, and now . . . now she was testing her in the most direct way she knew how.

Gwen swallowed. She'd scarcely spoken a word of French since her mother died. But when she opened her mouth, the words came to her as if she'd been conversing with her mother just yesterday. "Il m'arrive parfois d'avoir le mal du pays, c'est vrai. Mais comme vous le dites, j'ai de la chance d'avoir Isobelle." Gwen hesitated. She wasn't sure why Sylvie was so suspicious, unless she thought Gwen herself was taking advantage of her friend. "Je reconnais la valeur de son amitié."

I know the value of her friendship.

Gwen dared not look over at Isobelle, the other girl's stunned silence already too much to bear. Sylvie was frowning slightly at her own failure to discover what untruths Gwen was hiding from her.

Gwen gave her a watery smile, and said in English, "Forgive me, but I'm quite tired—I will see you all tonight, at the bonfire." She inclined her head and then made her way as quickly as she could toward her room.

She could feel Isobelle's eyes, wide and staring, following her the entire way.

Chapter Twenty

JUST DON'T TELL THE OTHER KNIGHTS I SCREAMED

It seemed all Darkhaven had turned out for the dragon bonfire. The grassy slopes around the castle were a riot of sounds and colors, with commoners and nobility alike mingling to enjoy the spectacle. Dotting the grounds were piles of wood and brush waiting to be lit, and directly down the hill from the castle gate was a vast open area and a platform where the speeches and main entertainments would take place.

From the moment Olivia had popped into Gwen's room with a pile of fabric over one arm and a box of cosmetics in the other, Gwen had been dreading the entire affair. Dealing with Isobelle was a challenge at the best of times, when Gwen was wearing armor or riding her horse or holding a sword, and all was as it should be between them. But thus far, every effort to face her down on her home turf—the land of fabrics and cosmetics and social niceties—had been disastrous.

She'd tried a halfhearted protest, but Olivia had taken a step back and looked at Gwen, chin lowered, eyes intent, and said evenly, "The only way you are escaping this room is wearing this dress, these cosmetics, and these hair ribbons. Do I make myself clear?"

Now, as Gwen stood on the edge of the bonfire grounds, waiting for Isobelle to finish rounding up the girls, her heart was doing a flip-flop in her chest. She'd never been one for pretty garments, or rouges to make her lips redder, or herbal rinses to make her hair shine. Hazily, she remembered her mother occasionally doing her hair or prettying up a dress with a spare bit of ribbon, but by the time she was old enough to learn those strange and arcane rituals of femininity for herself, her mother was too ill to teach her the proper magic.

For the most part, trying to look "pretty" made Gwen uncomfortable. Far more uncomfortable than she felt roasting on a summer's day in a suit of armor, facing down an opponent over a sharpened bit of stick. At least the worst thing that could happen to her in that situation was gruesome and painful death.

But this dress . . . this dress was doing something to her.

It was a deep, dark green that looked inky in the twilight, except for the way its velvety fibers caught the light and flashed whenever she moved, like verdant lightning. Olivia had cut the neckline low and square, revealing freckles on Gwen's pale shoulders that she hadn't even noticed herself before. Despite the veritable army of potions and pots and paints Olivia had brought with her, she'd done very little to Gwen's face except to darken the lines of her eyelashes and add a deep, dusky rose to her lips. And through her hair she'd tied a ribbon of the same material as the dress, pulling the strands back on one side into a twist and left to fall in heavy waves on the other.

Olivia had shown her a mirror right before she left. Gwen looked like some kind of sorceress, emerging from the forest with magic crackling around her ankles and smoky, sultry promises in her eyes.

As she stood waiting, Gwen could feel eyes on her, though when she turned in a slow circle, she could see no one staring. She tried to dismiss the sensation, and yet something was sending a shiver down her spine—a not altogether unpleasant sensation.

"Céline!"

Isobelle appeared from behind a group of ladies who looked somewhat surprised to find her popping up in their midst. Isobelle's dress was a brilliant violet blue, cut in her signature style and done up in flounces and layers. Her hair was absolute perfection, eyes sparkling, lips a bright pink and shining softly in the light from the torches. Gwen swallowed, trying to find some other detail to stare at.

Isobelle's cheeks were pink, much pinker than Olivia ought to have painted them. Closer to her now, Isobelle lowered her voice and murmured, "Gwen, you look so beautiful!"

Gwen shrugged, glancing away to watch the crowd. "Olivia is talented."

Isobelle's fair eyebrows drew in. "Why do you always do that?" she asked, a flicker of genuine distress in her face. "If I compliment you on your riding or your smithing, you're fine. But god forbid I should say you look nice, or you start scowling and rolling your eyes at me."

Gwen blinked at her. Moments ago she'd been standing there, reflecting on how uncomfortable all the finery made her feel, and Isobelle had seen through her in a heartbeat. "I . . . I don't know," she managed, fighting the inexplicable urge to tell Isobelle absolutely everything about herself, her past, her heart. "But you're right, I do do that. I'm sorry."

The scowl smoothed away, and the gleaming lips curved a touch. "Why do I get the feeling you're telling me what you think

I want to hear? Never mind. Just say 'thank you, Isobelle, you look gorgeous, too.'"

"Thank you, Isobelle." Gwen let her breath out as Isobelle came up beside her to link arms and steer her over toward the festivities. A shiver ran up Gwen's arm from the point where Isobelle's hand rested against her sleeve, and Gwen ruthlessly halted the rather foolish smile threatening to spread across her features. "You look gorgeous, too."

"Good girl," said Isobelle, her tones velvety with smugness. "Now, we can either catch up with the girls—they've got a spot not too far from where the speeches will take place—or we can explore." Isobelle's eyes swung up and to the side, watching Gwen through her lashes.

Had Gwen imagined the slight, barely perceptible trailing off, a sign of reluctance, when Isobelle mentioned joining the other girls? Or did she just *want* Isobelle to be reluctant, want her to wish for Gwen's company over that of the others? She'd never had a close female friend before—was it normal to want to keep her all to herself?

"Gwen?" The blue eyes widened a touch in concern as Isobelle turned toward her more fully. "You okay?"

"Uh." Gwen cleared her throat. "I've never seen this version of the dragon bonfire before—it's different in the village. Let's explore."

The concern evaporated, and Isobelle flashed her a look of pure delight. "Excellent, that's what I was hoping you'd say."

Isobelle led her through the makeshift festival streets, with tents set up in rows along the hillside selling food, drinks, and knickknacks. One stall owner was painting faces with a most spectacular level of skill—Isobelle proposed Gwen get a knight's visor painted on her face, and then burst into silvery laughter at Gwen's expression. Musicians were stationed at regular intervals, all playing their own music, so the tunes shifted as they walked—spritely fiddle morphed into soulful flute into a drum circle into a quartet playing a waltz.

"We could dance?" Isobelle's offer was a touch hesitant. The only couples moving around the quartet were composed of men and women. In the village, no one would care too much to see two women or two men dancing together, even in a partnered dance such as this one. But perhaps the rules of high society were stricter about this—they certainly were about far more trivial matters, like which fork to use and how deep to drop into a curtsy.

"I don't know how much more dancing I can take after Madame Dupont's endless drills," Gwen admitted ruefully, giving Isobelle's hand a squeeze in the crook of her elbow. "Though, between you and me, I actually rather enjoy it."

"Anyone who doesn't enjoy Dupont isn't paying attention," Isobelle replied airily, moving along from the quartet. "That woman could defeat a dragon all on her own."

"Gosh, how marvelous would it be to see that?" Gwen's mind had filled with the most fantastic image of the stately middle-aged woman in armor, astride a war horse, javelin tucked under her arm as she faced down an enormous, craggy bronze dragon. "It'd almost be worth having dragons around just to witness it."

Isobelle laughed, evidently not nearly so captivated by the image as Gwen, and led them on through the festival.

Scents of grilling meat and frying dough filled the air, along with wafts here and there of spices and caramelizing sugars. Music continued to float by, tugging Gwen's attention this way and that. Though the big bonfires had yet to be lit, smaller fires had been laid, sending their sparks shooting skyward like ephemeral fireflies trying to court the stars.

Suddenly, the only thing Gwen could think of was the night before, in the hayloft, when she'd interrupted Isobelle.

But what I want to say is—

Isobelle, please.

As Gwen kept her eyes resolutely on a floating ember until it vanished against the indigo velvet above them, she could have kicked herself black and blue for not letting Isobelle finish that sentence.

Then a gust of flame shot out inches from Gwen's face, close enough that the heat struck her before she knew what she was witnessing. A lithe young dancer, his chest bare and his leggings leaving little to the imagination, bounced around in front of them, sipped from a flask, and then shot another jet of fire up into the sky.

Belatedly, Gwen realized she was clutching at Isobelle, and her throat was raw from some sort of shriek. Isobelle, for her part, seemed rather more collected, and was doing her damnedest to hide the way the corners of her mouth wanted to dance.

Gwen carefully loosened her grip on Isobelle's arm. "Whoops."

Isobelle raised an eyebrow, her grin positively lascivious. "Hold on to me all you want, young lady," she said in a low voice. "I'm sturdy, I can take it."

Gwen snorted, rolling her eyes a fraction. "Just don't tell the other knights I screamed."

Isobelle mimed locking her lips shut before throwing away the imaginary key, then pulled Gwen on to look at another stall.

Gwen looked down at the spot where Isobelle's hand rested on her arm. "Er—Isobelle," she started, not completely certain where she wished to steer the sentence. "Last night, you started to say something and I cut you off. Did you—"

"Ooh!" exclaimed Isobelle, her head lifted and turned to one side. She'd evidently been listening for something going on elsewhere in the festival. She began tugging at Gwen's arm, dragging her off in the direction she was looking. "I think we're just in time! Come, I've been so wanting you to see this."

The emotion tangling Gwen's response into a wordless murmur of assent was rather difficult to pinpoint. Frustration, certainly. But also a heavy dose of relief.

Just be glad everything is as it was, she told herself sternly. *And enjoy what connection you have as co-conspirators.*

Isobelle led her to a space that had been cleared on the slope of the hill above, dominated at the far end by a group of musicians. To judge from the crowd gathering around the area, some favorite event of the festival was about to take place.

The drummer had begun a low, pulsing beat. The crowd rather melted in front of Isobelle to let her and Gwen up to the front, either recognizing the tournament's sacrifice and her reputation, or else assuming that the size and number of layers and frills on her dress meant she should be allowed to do as she wished.

Gwen had a flash of insight—was *that* why Isobelle wore such insanely over-the-top dresses?

The drummer added a second, lesser, syncopated beat that made Gwen's blood sing strangely, until she recognized it for what it was: a heartbeat. Slow, decorous, far more languorous than any human heartbeat, but a heartbeat nonetheless.

An *ancient* heartbeat.

The hairs had begun to lift all along the back of Gwen's neck before the first dancers emerged from the crowd. Their costumes were a riot of color—some in brightest red, orange, and yellow, and others in more muted shades of green, brown, burnished gold, and maroon. Something deep and primal and instinctual was signaling Gwen at the sight of those colors, though she could not have explained why.

The dancers began to move, in seeming chaos at first. Then the rest of the musicians began to play, adding to the pulsing heartbeat the *screel* of a reeded woodwind, the low bleat of a deep horn, and several layers of strings weaving the sounds together. As if the music were the start of a spell, the chaotic movements of the dancers coalesced into one single, fluid shape that undulated in the firelit night with eerie realism.

A dragon.

The creature roared out of three dozen throats at once, and out of its mouth spilled the dancers costumed in the colors of flame. The slope of the hill they moved on was nearly invisible in the darkness, and the illusion of a three-dimensional dragon taking form before their audience's eyes was stunningly complete. The movements of the dancers were so perfectly synchronized that it was impossible to see them as separate people instead of one massive, deadly beast. So much so that when the dancers scattered and coalesced again, in a new place, as if the dragon had taken wing and flown to the opposite edge of the cleared space, the audience members closest to them screamed and leapt back.

Gwen's heart was pounding, her muscles demanding action. Some instinct from deep within her wanted to reach for a weapon, even as the rest of her mind tried frantically to remind her that what she was witnessing was a dance, a celebration, a mere echo of ages long past. That there were no dragons, not anymore.

The dragon veered sharply toward them, and the flame dancers shot out in a riot of reds and yellows. Isobelle, laughing, leapt back, but Gwen couldn't move. One of the dancers caught her eye and grinned knowingly—then she tugged lightly at the edge of Gwen's skirt, as if to say, *See? Now you're dead.* And then she skipped off to rejoin the rest of the dragon.

A new instrument joined the musicians at the high end of the hill: the bright, brassy glare of a trumpet. From the side of the square came a lone dancer, not a part of the living, breathing creature the others had become. This one wore a suit of armor—or, at least, silver-threaded leggings and flowing drapes that suggested the overlapping panels of a suit of armor—and a helmet.

The knight.

He came wearing a sword at his belt and with a long, gleaming lance tucked under one arm. He charged the dragon, which scattered and coalesced again on the other side of the clearing. The dragon roared at the knight, spitting flames that reached out toward him with grasping arms—but he leapt and dodged, landing and rolling easily back to his feet.

For a long stretch of heartbeats, they were perfectly matched. The knight could not charge fast enough to strike the dragon before it fled, and the dragon could not get an angle good enough on the knight to roast him alive.

Gwen's head spun. Distantly, she realized she'd forgotten to breathe.

Then the dragon twisted the other way during one of the knight's charges, and it caught the lance in a sweeping blow with one of its arms. The sound it made as it shattered was a screech of strings and the deep thump of an ominous drum.

The knight went sprawling, landing inches from where Gwen and Isobelle stood. With a start, Gwen realized that the body wearing the knight's armor was quite obviously female, and not even a young, boyish female at that—the dancer moved with such overt masculinity that Gwen would never have known had the woman not landed literally right before her eyes.

With a scream of rage to match the roar of the dragon, the knight lurched to his feet and drew his sword. Without his lance, he seemed tiny, one man facing down dozens—one man facing the most massive creature ever to walk these lands.

The fight was quick and brutal. Without his lance the knight was doomed. The dragon closed in, swarming around the knight so thickly his gleaming silver armor became invisible. The knight leapt back, but then lost his balance—for a horrible moment he stood there, as if on the edge of a cliff, about to fall. At Gwen's side, Isobelle cried a wordless shout of warning, as wrapped up in the spectacle as Gwen was.

The dragon saw its chance and charged.

The knight moved with deliberate grace. He had never been off-balance at all. Before the dragon could stop its charge, the knight had raised his sword and driven it deep into the eye of the beast.

The dozen-throated dragon howled in rage and pain, and flames spilled out of its mouth to lie, smoldering, against the hillside. Its wings flapped futilely—its arms tried to grab for the knight, who held on grimly to the sword long enough to twist it once—and the beast collapsed into a hundred pieces, scattered on the grass.

Dimly, Gwen was aware of the crowd screaming, thundering applause, but she could not take her eyes off the dancer who had been a knight. The silver-clad figure was still gazing down at her sword, embedded between arm and rib cage of the dancer whose costume had born the eye of the dragon. She pulled the sword out, very much the way someone would pull a blade from a beast they had killed. Gwen half expected her to clean it of the creature's blood. The dancer gave a shake, stepped back, and replaced the sword in the sheath at her belt. Slowly, slowly, she became herself again.

It was Isobelle pulling her hand from Gwen's arm that shook her from her trance. The dancers who had been the dragonsfire were skipping around the perimeter of the clearing and weaving through the throngs of watchers, holding open jingling velvet bags that were beginning to sag under the weight of the coins the viewers tossed in. Isobelle had let go of Gwen in order to fumble in the pocket of her skirt, pulling out a fistful of coins and shoving them into the nearest bag.

Gwen swallowed and forced herself to take a deeper breath. She felt almost as though she had been that knight, as though she had not simply witnessed the epic battle, but fought it herself. The fire that had coursed through her veins and held her riveted to the spectacle was beginning to recede, and as Isobelle turned to her, face shining with excitement and pleasure, Gwen had to bury her hands in the folds of her skirt to hide how they were beginning to shake.

Isobelle's gaze followed the movement, and a fraction of her joy dimmed. She folded her own arms across her chest rather than reach for Gwen's arm again. Still, she was smiling as she tilted her head. "Come on. There's one more thing I want to show you."

Chapter Twenty-One

DROP-YOUR-CHEESECAKE-ON-A-STICK-AND-NOT-EVEN-*CARE* SPECTACULAR

When Isobelle had seen Gwen arrive for the bonfire, her first thought had been *oh no*.

Gwen looked spectacular—dizzyingly, heart-stoppingly, drop-your-cheesecake-on-a-stick-and-not-even-*care* spectacular—and it was only luck that she hadn't seen Isobelle gawking. What was going to happen come the tournament ball, when she finally saw Gwen in full finery? Would she simply pass out? *Why* couldn't she stop staring?

She had been forced to be quite stern as she reminded herself that this was not a sensible time to start asking herself questions about why she couldn't take her eyes off Gwen.

Or perhaps, said the small part of her mind that sometimes led to her doing things like climbing down from her balcony and recruiting herself a new champion, *this is* exactly *the time*. There was a kind of pressure building inside her, and she knew she couldn't hold it at bay forever.

She'd pulled herself firmly together and had been doing quite well. Up until now, at any rate, when Gwen had hidden her hands swiftly in her skirts before Isobelle could take her arm again.

The two of them wove through the crowd, Isobelle leading and Gwen following in her wake, until they could duck behind the tents to which the dancers had retreated. There, Isobelle paused to fish down her cleavage—the frills really could hide a multitude—producing the small packet she had stowed there.

Before Gwen could ask, for she did not wish to spoil her surprise, she continued on until she found the member of the company who was standing guard at the tent flap.

"Dobry wieczór!" she chirped, with a curtsy that made him grin. "We have come with a gift for your lady knight."

He bowed in return, pulling aside the tent flap and indicating with a tilt of his head that they should continue on to the right. The dancers inside were laughing and talking and jostling for space, the air hot and their good mood infectious. As Isobelle ducked under a wildly gesturing arm and pushed through to the next section of the tent, she was grinning herself.

"Astreta!" she squealed, and the dancer—still shedding her shimmering silver knight's costume—turned to greet her with a laugh and seized her to plant a kiss on each cheek, then returned for a third where she'd begun.

"Isobelle, moja droga!"

Isobelle turned to see Gwen's expression melting from one of wariness to a shy pleasure at seeing their reunion. Her cheeks were flushed with the heat of the tent, a smile slowly curving her lips.

"Gwen, this is my friend Astreta—her troupe just arrived from Poland. I thought you'd like to meet a woman who can do a man's job as well as he can. Astreta, this is Gwen, who is a blacksmith of great skill."

"As well as he can?" Astreta asked with mock outrage and a strong Polish accent. "Please, no man can leap as I do."

"Of course not," Isobelle agreed, some part of her mind concentrating on Gwen, who'd gone quiet. "We have brought you sweets."

She handed over the little bag, and Astreta held up a hand in a gesture that informed them they would have her attention again very soon, then pulled it open to inspect what was inside.

"They're from a place in Paris she likes," Isobelle told Gwen as Astreta nibbled on one and made extremely happy noises in the background.

"How do you know each other?" There was a carefulness in the way Gwen asked the question, setting the words out like she was laying a table with particularly fine porcelain and didn't want to break anything.

"I bluffed my way backstage last time the troupe was in town," Isobelle confessed, tilting her head as she tried to parse that caution. What was Gwen really wondering?

Again, that pressure inside Isobelle that demanded an answer—that demanded she look at its questions directly and understand what they were—pushed to be released.

"Hard to believe you'd do something like that," Gwen replied with her customary wry sarcasm, but again, there was that layer of... something. Could Gwen be...? Isobelle hardly dared whisper the word to herself. But if she didn't know better, it would almost seem as if Gwen was *jealous*.

"I wanted to talk to the costume designers," Isobelle pressed on, like one who had been traipsing through the woods, then heard a concerning noise, and was now proceeding with considerably more thoughtfulness. "But then I met Astreta, and we got to talking about dessert..." She gestured to the sweets, which the dancer had already half devoured, but was now packing away. "I promised I'd come back this time with her favorite."

"And so you did," Astreta replied with a grin. "I must save a few for my husband, or he will be, what do you say? Cranky. He is already not pleased he had to dance the part of the dragon's behind."

At that, everybody dissolved into laughter, and the strangeness was gone, vanished like smoke on the breeze.

"Well, it was a remarkable performance by *all* parts of the dragon," Gwen told her. "Though *you* excelled."

"I knew she would inspire you," Isobelle replied, and Gwen shot her a quelling look, which was, in fairness, well earned.

"It made me wish I could dance like that," Gwen agreed. "Truly, to move that way, each of you different but all in unison—you must practice from sunup to sundown."

"Tak, yes, we rehearse until our bodies know their purpose," Astreta agreed, resuming her undressing until she was down to the sleek black suit she wore beneath her armor, and fanning herself. "Until the steps are a part of the body, one must practice. One cannot be thinking of the steps—put my foot here, twist like so—and also of the emotion required."

Gwen wasn't bothering to hide that she was listening far more intently than the average noblewoman might. "And I imagine you can't put your foot just so, or twist like so, if your emotions are caught up where they shouldn't be, either."

"The mind must be one with the dance," Astreta agreed, delighted to have found a willing audience. "There are so many of us, and moving so quickly. We cannot simply learn the steps and then produce them like windup toys. We must become this great creature together."

"And how do you do that?" Gwen leaned forward. "How do you clear your mind? I find mine spins on and on—as if I'm on a badly trained horse, and the harder I try to control it, the more it rebels."

Astreta's smile changed to one of understanding. "Ah, I do

not clear my mind," she replied. "I am part of a dance company, my friend. I am full of fire. There is always drama here—always someone coming, someone going, someone falling in love, someone crying out in grief. I cannot stop all the horses that wish to gallop through my mind. I simply guide them. I create a valley, with steep walls on each side, and tell them 'You may run as fast as you wish, but run this way!' Then I take all the power of their galloping, and I make it my performance."

Gwen's lips parted a little, as though she'd seen something she wanted but couldn't have. Isobelle nibbled her lip, watching her. Had Gwen been worrying about her jousts, about knighting without panicking? She'd always seemed so calm, so determined. So natural at it, as Madame Dupont had told her.

"I wish I knew how to do as you do," Gwen said simply.

"I am not sure how to teach it to someone," Astreta replied thoughtfully. "But I will say this. The horses listen better if you are not afraid of them."

That caught Gwen off guard—enough to make her eyes widen—and then her solemn expression cracked into a smile. "Are you sure you're not a mind reader?"

Astreta laughed merrily. "I dance alongside a dozen others every night. We leap over, under, through. Of course I am a mind reader."

Gwen echoed that laugh with a quiet one of her own, and Astreta drew a deep breath before continuing briskly, "I must see to the company, and make sure nobody plans to make any foolish decisions tonight. Isobelle, I shall write to you next month, from Spain."

Isobelle had been so absorbed in the exchange that she startled at hearing her own name. "It was good to see you again, Astreta."

Astreta flashed a smile at them, then poked her head into the other half of the tent to check the way was clear. "Matthew, put away your naked body!" she shouted. "There are ladies present."

Isobelle made what felt like the obligatory disappointed sound, and led the way back out, turning her face up to the cool night air as she and Gwen left the tent.

"She was extraordinary," Gwen breathed. "I've never met anyone like that in my life."

"I suppose not," Isobelle agreed, finding rather uncomfortably that now *she* might be the one experiencing a twinge of jealousy. "I've been trying to learn some Polish, to be polite, but it's awfully difficult. Do you speak any?"

"Me? No." Gwen sounded surprised at the idea. "Why would I?"

"You spoke lovely French," Isobelle replied with a shrug. She didn't want to make any assumptions about Gwen's education—the French had been a surprise, and had reminded her that she didn't know what commoners were taught. Maybe it wasn't strange at all for Gwen to burst into another language as easily as she spoke English.

"French? Oh, yes." Gwen sounded uncomfortable, then pressed on, letting Isobelle guide her through the crowd. "I think she's right. Astreta, I mean. That's what I have to learn, to fight in this thing. When I'm smithing, I can do it. It's like being somewhere else, present but utterly focused. I don't know how to do that with a sword in my hand, or a lance against my shoulder."

"Perhaps," Isobelle said slowly, "it's not so different. When you're smithing, you're creating. Whether it's something for yourself, or for someone else, you're repairing, you're bringing into being. It's an act of . . . of love." For some reason, Isobelle found her cheeks heating, and she kept her eyes on the ground.

She could feel Gwen's eyes on her. "And you think that's not so different from jousting? I wouldn't call it especially loving to knock a guy off his horse with a big stick."

Isobelle fought back a laugh. "What I mean is, when you're smithing, your heart is open. But when I watched you practicing with Madame Dupont . . . I could see your racing thoughts from the other side of the orchard. It wasn't about feeling, you were trying to think your way through it."

Gwen made a soft sound, half exhalation, half *hmmmm*. "Men speak of mastering their emotions," she replied. "They say women are too emotional to fight, even if we were strong enough to wield a blade."

"But Astreta can't do what she does without her emotion," Isobelle pointed out. "I don't think you can beat the other knights by trying to be like them—your strength comes from a different place than theirs. Maybe all you need to do is stop trying to block it out, and . . . let it come."

An answering silence made Isobelle lift her head finally, to find Gwen's eyes on her, the green glinting with gold in the light of the torches. Gwen's fair cheeks were flushed, her gaze intent in a way Isobelle had never seen before.

"I have to just let the horses run," Gwen murmured. "And not corral them."

Isobelle's heart was leaping as quickly as it had been when the dragon dancers first coalesced into that mighty, ancient beast. For a wild moment, she wanted to grab Gwen by the hand and race with her back to the stables, to find Achilles, to ride out under the moon and watch her champion joust *her* way, their way. To see what

Gwen could do when she let herself go.

Then a group of children tore by, shrieking with laughter and making them both jump. Gwen blinked and shuddered a breath, and Isobelle looked up with some surprise to realize they were in the middle of a crowd, not on a moonlit field of battle—and, worst of all, they were not far from where the other girls had set up a picnic on the lawn.

For a moment, Gwen looked as though she might say something. But then Hilde spotted them and called out—"Isobelle! Céline!"—and the moment was lost.

Chapter Twenty-Two

THE VIOLENCE IS TOO MUCH FOR HER DELICATE CONSTITUTION

It wasn't until they'd reached the edge of the picnic blanket that Gwen remembered the uncomfortable truth. The last time she'd seen the rest of Isobelle's friends, she'd been fleeing the room at the prospect of kissing Isobelle in front of them. Her steps flagged, but Isobelle had sped up, and she stood surveying the food the girls had collected in the center of the blanket like a trio of dragons hoarding their treasure.

Too late to run away now.

She pasted on her best imitation of Isobelle's flighty smile and joined the other girls. They all looked spectacular—Sylvie was in a saffron gown that contrasted with her hair and her complexion like the yellow and brown petals of a pansy. Jane too drew the eye in a dress that loved her curves—Hilde was teasing her about her cleavage as Gwen approached.

Once she sat, the aromas of fried dough and grilled meat hit her nose, and she half forgot her qualms. Hilde gave her arm a kindly pat and then handed her a metal cup.

"Dragonsblood punch," the German girl said with a wink. "Nowhere near as strong as the tea, ich verspreche."

Jane gave a cheerful laugh and downed her cup, and all was normal again. Well, all except for Sylvie, who regarded Gwen with a flat, expressionless stare as she sipped her punch.

Though that, Gwen supposed, was becoming normal, too. She wished she could tell whether it was just that the other girl didn't like her, or that she could tell something wasn't quite right about "Céline" and her cover story.

Gwen took a cautious sip of her drink—it was sweet and dark, mulled wine mixed with berry juices, liable to stain her whole mouth a charming maroon—and surveyed the food as the other girls regaled Isobelle with bits of gossip they'd picked up from around the festival.

The main bonfire, some distance down the hill from where they sat, was being lit. Workers carried bundles of sticks and straw to the giant pile of wood, where a torchbearer set them ablaze before they were thrown, streaming sparks, onto the heap. The whole thing leapt to life, changing the colors of the night from violet and azure to smoldering orange and gold.

Isobelle had seated herself beside Gwen. "I'm excited for you to see the ceremony," she said, leaning back with a grin. "Even if most of it is boring speeches about the days when the villages hit by dragon attacks would send representatives to the castle seeking aid and shelter."

Sylvie cocked her head in their direction, one eyebrow rising. "Do they not have dragon relief ceremonies where you come from, Céline?"

"Hmm?" Gwen blinked at her, pretending she hadn't heard to buy herself time to think. "Not in Toussaint, no. The dragons tended to stay farther north, and at any rate we are a small enough province that the—the peasants"—Gwen choked the word out—"were dealt with one on one."

A fanfare erupted down by the bonfire, and the girls turned toward the action, sparing Gwen any further interrogation about the homeland she'd never been to. Lord Whimsitt had arrived to a smattering of halfhearted applause, and was starting to give a rather predictable speech about the trials of ages past, when dragons roamed the land. Rolling her eyes, Hilde began quizzing Jane on the latter's newest boyfriend, a lowly squire to one of the visiting knights—*But he's so strong, girls, if you could see him without his shirt, my goodness.*

Whimsitt's speech wrapped up, and a visiting nobleman took his place to give his own speech. Others began to circulate among the clusters of society scattered along the hillside. Whenever they stopped at Isobelle's miniature court, she would introduce Gwen as Céline and mention her fictional brother—doing exactly as Madame Dupont had instructed her. Fortunately, Gwen was not required to contribute much at all to these conversations. It seemed perfectly acceptable for her to smile shyly and say nothing.

A familiar form passing some distance away caught her eye, and Gwen had to stifle a laugh. When Isobelle glanced at her, Gwen leaned in and whispered, "There is Sir Evonwald. He's still limping."

"How tragic for him," Isobelle whispered back, her lips close enough to Gwen's ear to stir the hair there, and making Gwen lose track of her amusement altogether.

"Don't look now, Isobelle," said Sylvie sharply, her tone for once devoid of the knowing languor that so often marked it, her eyes fixed on someone amid the crowd.

Isobelle's gaze snapped over, and she gave a swift gasp, her face paling. "Oh, crap. Hide me, girls. Quick—"

There was a flutter of activity and a hissed, "No, no, it's too late, he's seen you," and then all was serene again, as a middle-aged man in a rust-colored doublet approached the blanket.

"Ah, Lady Isobelle," he said slowly, coming to a halt a step closer to their blanket than was strictly necessary.

His proximity made Isobelle crane her neck a touch to look up at him—which she did, with a brittle, fully dimpled smile.

"Sir Ralph," she replied. "How nice to see you."

Gwen froze, unable to stop staring at the man towering over them. So *this* was the Sir Ralph who was favored to win the tournament—and thus, win Isobelle? This was the man she would have to face in the lists in order to win Isobelle's freedom.

He must be three times Isobelle's age, but where other men might have put on some fat and lost some muscle, he looked solidly built. His face was angular, and it would have even been handsome but for an undefinable miserly quality to his expression. The eyes were a pale hazel, narrowed, piercing, like those of a bird of prey.

Or a dragon, thought Gwen.

"Enjoying the informality of the festival, I see," he said, gaze sweeping across their rumpled blanket, the remains of their feast, and the semi-reclined forms of Isobelle's friends. His voice had an uncomfortable thickness to it, like something—phlegm, perhaps—was permanently lodged in his throat. "How fortunate Lord Whimsitt decided to permit you to attend."

"Indeed," said Isobelle, allowing her smile to fade now the greeting was over. "What is tonight for, if not for relaxing the restrictions of conventional society?"

"I heard," said Sylvie brightly, "that in Spain, their dragon bonfire ceremonies are masked, and it leads to all sorts of bad behavior.

Though I'm not entirely sure I know what they mean by that." That last was with an innocent, puzzled flutter of her lashes. Sir Ralph's gaze slid toward her, allowing Isobelle a moment to breathe.

Sylvie was taking the heat off her friend, if only for a few heartbeats.

Gwen could have hugged her just then.

Sir Ralph's piercing, raptor-like gaze swiveled back toward his intended prey. "I have brought you a gift, Lady Isobelle."

Isobelle was a beat too late in responding. Gwen could feel the other girl's flare of panic. A gift, from someone like Sir Ralph, was little more than a transactional loan.

Isobelle would be expected, eventually, to pay him back in whatever way he demanded.

"How kind of you," she said finally.

"I seem to recall you being fond of dragonscale sweets," said the man, reaching for a pouch hanging from his belt and unhooking it. "I thought I would bring you a bag, so you wouldn't have to knock anyone down to get them this year."

"Knock anyone . . ." Isobelle looked blank for a moment, until a wave of realization swept through her, and she pressed her lips together as though she might be sick. "I was seven years old when that happened, Sir Ralph."

The man smiled, though it did little to dispel the predatory set of his eyes. "Yes, I distinctly remember remarking on it to my wife, may she rest in peace. *Seven years old and already such a beauty.*" He inclined his torso in as courtly a bow as any girl could wish from a suitor and placed the bag of sweets in front of Isobelle on the blanket. "Enjoy your evening, Lady Isobelle." A glance toward Sylvie, even the slight pretense at a smile vanishing. "Ladies." This, uttered in the same tone one might say "boils" or "fungus." And then he was turning to move on toward a group of dignitaries.

Nobody spoke until he was out of earshot.

Hilde broke the silence with a vocalized shudder, extending one leg so she could kick at the bag of sweets and knock it off the blanket. Then she looked over at Isobelle, who was sitting stock-still, her hands folded neatly in her lap, her eyes distant. "He will not win, Isobelle," said Hilde softly. "I know it in my heart."

Gwen couldn't take her eyes off Isobelle's face. For a stretch of heartbeats, she didn't move, didn't respond, didn't so much as acknowledge Hilde had spoken.

Then Isobelle blinked, as if hearing a voice across a long, long distance and waking from a dream. "Hmm?" Her head turned, and she laughed, a high, sweet sound that wiped away the memory of Sir Ralph's low, rattly tones. "Don't worry. If he does win, I'll just have Olivia assassinate him after all."

That elicited a laugh, however strained, from the other girls. Slowly, they began to claw themselves back toward some kind of normal—weaving around them that soft, careful magic of camaraderie that kept the world, and men like Sir Ralph, at bay.

But Gwen's whole body still felt chilled. It was one thing to know Isobelle would be married off to whoever won the tournament, or even to imagine someone harmless like Sir Orson at her side. It was another to *see* the man everyone expected to win her as a prize.

Gwen had never quite let herself imagine truly winning, for what good could possibly come from it? Isobelle would hardly be allowed to marry a fictional knight—even if the deception held through the inevitable ceremonies and awards to follow a victory.

But now, in this moment, she realized she could not bear to lose.

As the other girls turned their attention back toward the bonfire, Gwen took a slow, steadying breath and leaned toward Isobelle.

"I won't let him win," she whispered.

Isobelle met her gaze for the first time since Sir Ralph had approached their blanket. She said nothing, but that remoteness in her eyes faded, and, hidden between their bodies on the blanket, her pinky slid over and curled around Gwen's.

"I cannot wait until tomorrow," Hilde's voice cut in, and Isobelle jerked her hand away from Gwen's. "Have you a favorite, Céline? Someone other than your brother, who you intend to give your favor to?"

Gwen scrambled for an excuse as to why she wouldn't be watching the joust, but her mind was on the way her hand was still tingling against the blanket. "A favorite?" she echoed.

"Céline neither hands out favors, nor attends jousts," Isobelle broke in smoothly and firmly. "The violence is too much for her delicate constitution."

Gwen burst into a round of coughing and wished she had some food or drink in her hand on which to blame the sudden fit.

"She is more civilized than the rest of us," Isobelle went on, raising her voice over the spluttering. "If only I could beg off, too. But I have to put on a smile and sit front and center through the whole thing."

Gwen, managing to get herself under control again, glanced askance at Isobelle. "Maybe you'll enjoy it this year," she murmured. "I may not care to watch my brother in the lists, but he has a rather unique style of combat. He may surprise you."

"I look forward to marrying him, then," Isobelle said wryly. On another night, it would be one of Isobelle's flighty flirtations. Just now, Gwen could hear the edge in her voice.

Sir Ralph had rattled her. Because even if it wasn't him, and wasn't now, it would be *someone* eventually. Even the best-case scenario in their deception would not spare Isobelle forever.

It was one of those rare moments when Isobelle seemed fully aware that her wild plan to enlist her own champion was full of holes.

Gwen curled her fingertips into the blanket beneath her hand. "Correct me if I'm wrong," she said slowly, "but the tradition states that the winner of the tournament may ask for the hand of the dragon sacrifice. *May*, not must." Isobelle's gaze swung over to meet Gwen's. "Perhaps he will surprise you there, too. Maybe if he won, he would ask you what *you* wanted."

Isobelle's smile was wistful, as if she were regarding something lovely, but very far away. "If any knight ever thought to ask that, then I would surely wish to say yes."

Chapter Twenty-Three

NO LADY WENT IN SEARCH OF THE PRIVY ALONE WHEN SHE COULD BRING A FRIEND

As the speeches continued, covering the many fine qualities of men past and present, Isobelle let her mind drift. She carefully steered it away from the tangled maze of knights who asked her what she wanted, and knights who didn't, and contemplated instead whether it was worth taking another turn around the stalls, to see if there were any sweets the girls had missed.

She was going to think about dessert, and nothing else.

"Are they doing some sort of play to commemorate the occasion?" Gwen asked, her voice summoning Isobelle back from her daydreams. A ripple of agitation was spreading outward from the base of the hill as a ragged group of women pushed their way toward the speechmakers.

"If it is a play, the lighting leaves something to be desired," Jane murmured, squinting.

"Please!" The rough cry came from one of the new arrivals. "Let me through! I must speak with Lord Whimsitt! We seek protection!" The woman broke past those trying to hold her back, dodging her way up the hill toward the dignitaries. "It is your *duty* to protect us!"

Every line of the woman's body spoke of desperation, her clothes ragged, her face filthy. With a well-placed kick that made one of the castle guards double over, she sprinted toward Lord Whimsitt, her hair streaming free from its braids.

"This is the dragon bonfire—we seek your aid!" she screamed as another pair of guards grabbed her, pulling her away from his lordship. "If you won't help us, then at least know you were warned—the dragons are alive. Remember us when they come for you, too."

A gasp spread through the crowd like wildfire, and Jane tilted her head like a spaniel. "Isobelle, *is* this meant to be a reenactment?"

"It is a little violent for a play," Hilde chimed in as the woman kicked at the guards again, her companions downhill fighting for their own freedom. "Though excellent dramatic timing, and I do not mind the interruption to the speeches."

"She doesn't look like she's acting to me," Gwen said slowly.

"I don't think she is," Isobelle replied, a feeling like a stone inside her chest. "I think she believes it. Poor thing. The bonfires must have set her off. I wish they'd let go of her friends so they could come and fetch her. Someone should be taking care of her. She needs a hedge witch."

All around them, debates were breaking out about whether the woman was a paid actor, but their little rug was an island of quiet. They watched as the woman and her companions were corralled away by the guard, and as one, the girls winced as a cry of pain arose from one who struggled too hard.

After a hesitant glance at Lord Whimsitt, the herald climbed up onto the stage once more. "And now," he shouted, "a word from our sponsor, Freya's Fashion Emporium, featuring the brightest designs from the continent!"

Gwen reached across to take Isobelle's cup and refill it, and when their eyes met, she tilted her head toward the shadows to indicate a desire to speak privately.

"Do excuse me, ladies," Isobelle said, popping up to her feet like the sparkly little cat that sprang out of her clock on the hour. "Nature calls." She held out her hand to Gwen—everybody knew that no lady went in search of the privy alone when she could bring a friend—and Gwen rose to her feet with barely a hint of pressure on her fingers, as though she'd been fighting the urge to stand.

As soon as Gwen reached the shadows, her steps lengthened, and Isobelle muttered imprecations against her impractical shoes as she skipped along to keep up.

"Gw—Céline," she hissed, as they made their way past the picnickers who'd chosen more remote spots, half hidden by darkness, ignoring their meals in favor of each other. "I think the people here might like some privacy!"

She kept her eyes firmly on the other girl's back, feeling her cheeks heat and fighting the urge to take an educational peek at what they were passing. It was one thing to drink tea and practice, but a girl needed practical information at some point.

Gwen pulled her in near the trunk of an oak tree, her green eyes flashing with a hint of bonfire light as she turned back toward her. For one dizzying heartbeat, Isobelle's imagination provided her with a startling image—she saw herself step in closer to Gwen, letting the momentum of that tug on her hand bring them together. She saw herself lean in, and tilt her face toward Gwen's, and . . .

"Isobelle, are you listening?" Gwen's voice broke through her thoughts, low and intense.

"Um, what?" Isobelle dropped Gwen's hand like it had scorched her. Her heart was beating like a wild thing trapped within the cage of her ribs. She hid her hands in the folds of her skirts, hoping Gwen hadn't noticed they'd begun to shake.

She'd daydreamed about kissing people before, even if she'd never done it when it counted. But those dreams hadn't forced their way into her mind like this, pushing through the doorway and taking over, insisting they be heard.

And those people . . . they hadn't been girls. Why was that? Had nobody before Gwen been the *right* girl, or was it just that everybody expected her crushes to be boys, so she'd never looked at anyone else?

If someone kisses me, Gwen had whispered, *I want it to be because they* need *to.*

"Isobelle," Gwen said again, and a bolt of sheer panic went through Isobelle, zipping down her spine and nearly sending her legs buckling.

"Yes," gasped Isobelle. And then, steadying her breath and lifting her chin, she made her voice sound normal through sheer effort of will. "Yes, Gwen. What is it?"

Gwen paused, studying her carefully. For a moment, Isobelle was certain Gwen had seen the same imagined embrace she had. That she could read in Isobelle's eyes that something had just shifted, irrevocably, undeniably. Then, with a shake of her head, Gwen continued. "I don't think we should just dismiss that woman."

"Nobody's going to dismiss her," Isobelle said, marshalling her attention toward the conversation at hand. "Someone will make sure she's taken care of."

"No," said Gwen, her jaw twitching. "I mean, I think we should *listen* to her."

Isobelle blinked. "You're saying you think that woman saw

a dragon?" she asked. Then, feeling she had to clarify: "A real dragon?"

Gwen produced one of her charming scowls, eyebrows drawing together. "I don't know what she saw," she said. "But that's the whole point. How terrified must she have been to do something like this? Did you see them hauling her away? You can be killed for assaulting someone of noble blood. Why would she ever risk something like that, unless she already had nothing to lose?"

Isobelle forced herself to dismiss her electrifying fantasy and properly bring her mind to bear on the problem. "I'll grant something distressed her," she said eventually. "But I struggle to believe she saw a dragon. The reason all you knights are forced to charge at one another is that there *are* no dragons anymore, and haven't been for over a century. But—" She held up a hand to forestall Gwen's reply. "Olivia will find out what's happening. I can guarantee she's already on her way to see what that woman has to say. She loves a mystery."

Gwen was quiet, brooding on that. Isobelle did not reach up to deal with the curl that kept falling across the other girl's brow. She was quite proud of her restraint.

"You're sure?" Gwen said eventually.

"I am," she promised. "We should wait until we hear from her. Then, if you feel we need to do something, we'll try to think what that might be. It will take her some time, though. Even Olivia can't walk through walls. I don't think."

Across by the stage, a group of musicians had started up, trying to get the festival back on track.

Gwen nodded. "We'll wait for Olivia. Thank you for not laughing at me."

"I would never," Isobelle replied, mildly outraged. Then, fairness compelled her to continue: "Well, not over anything that really meant something to you. For now, everything that can be done is being done."

Gwen nodded slowly, nibbling her lip. Isobelle made herself look away, out at the bonfires, and so she was taken by surprise when Gwen reached out, sliding her fingers down Isobelle's arm to find her wrist in the dark, and then her hand, giving it a squeeze.

Sparks ran all the way from Isobelle's fingertips, up her arm, and straight to her heart, as best she could tell. It was intensely distracting.

"Would Lord Whimsitt notice if you and I didn't come back right away?" Gwen asked. "There's something I want to show you, if you're up for a walk."

Isobelle considered the question. Then she considered the sheer impossibility of taking herself back to the picnic rug to pretend everything was normal, when everything had changed.

She considered letting go of Gwen's hand.

She did not.

"If he does, the girls will cover for us," she said, squeezing Gwen's fingers in return. "Show me something."

Chapter Twenty-four

DON'T BRING IT ALL THE WAY UNDONE...

Gwen had had to drop Isobelle's hand to sidle single file past a cart making its way late to the festival. Her impulse had been to reach for Isobelle again, but she'd hesitated. Taking her hand in the first place had been a gesture to tell Isobelle to trust her. Keeping gentle custody of it afterward could easily be dismissed as absent-mindedness.

To take it again now would be to reveal that Gwen simply *wanted* to hold her hand.

For the last hour, as they made their way down from the castle, Gwen had tormented herself in a limbo between reaching out and turning away. Her palm burned where it had rested against Isobelle's. Inexplicable tension sang between them like a taut wire, and knowing she was the only one feeling it made it all the more terrible for Gwen to bear. The few miles separating her home from the castle had never felt so vast. By the time the glow of the village bonfire shone through the branches bowing low over the road, she was ready to scream.

Rather than head toward the village center, Gwen turned and led Isobelle around toward the smithy via the garden path. The scent of the lavender filling the garden beds was ghostly on the evening air, the aromatic oils heated by the afternoon sun almost gone now. Isobelle, unfamiliar with the terrain, took a step off the packed path and into the softer soil, releasing a waft of perfume as her skirts brushed a cluster of dusky purple blooms.

For the love of god, Gwen, FOCUS. You are here on a mission.

Gwen eased the latch of the back door open. Light spilled onto the path, and when Gwen glanced back, she could see it falling on Isobelle's face. After so long walking together in utter darkness, interpreting every step and breath, to see her expression so clearly felt like being blinded by a sudden glare of sunlight. Gwen just blinked at her, dazzled.

"Are we sneaking in?" Isobelle whispered, her eyebrows rising.

Gwen *commanded* herself to get a grip. Isobelle's manner was easy and calm, and utterly oblivious to the tension that had seized Gwen the entire walk here from the castle. "If we can. Come on, up the back steps."

The steps were more ladder than staircase, and while Gwen had been climbing them in full skirts all her life, Isobelle wouldn't be used to them. She was trying to figure out which would be easier—to have Isobelle climb first, so Gwen could follow and break her fall should she slip, or to go up herself and offer a hand down to assist—when a voice shattered the quiet.

"Gwen, is that you?"

Her father's voice was slow and rough, suggesting that he'd been dozing before the hearth. Her heart ached guiltily—she'd been longing to find the time to sneak back to Ellsdale and catch up with her father, but this was certainly not that time.

"Dad, hi," she called, glancing at Isobelle and putting a finger to her lips before gesturing to the steps up to the loft. "I'm just changing my clothes and then I'm going to catch the rest of the bonfire."

"How's the internship?" His chair creaked as he shifted, but it didn't groan as it did when he stood up.

"Fine so far. I'll come back for a proper visit in a few days and tell you all about it. I don't want to miss old Bertin tonight."

There was a pause from the next room as Gwen held her breath. Somehow, the silence had an unnervingly knowing quality to it, as if her father had heard more than one set of footsteps creep into the house.

When he replied, however, all he said was, "Have a good time at the bonfire, Gwen."

Gwen followed Isobelle up the steps and into the loft, pausing at the threshold to her room and listening intently for sounds from below, but all was quiet. She eased into her room and slid the makeshift door closed.

"You told him you have an internship at the castle?" Isobelle said softly, amusement in her tone.

"Well, what was I supposed to tell him?" Gwen replied tartly, going to the window to open her shutters and let in the light from the bonfire in the village square. "Hey, Dad, I'm using a mysteriously acquired amount of wealth to hire an apprentice from the next town over to help you while I prance around in armor, pretending to be a knight?"

Isobelle let out a soft laugh and drifted closer to the wall. It was covered in sketches Gwen had made—some more recent, detailing her plans for the armor she'd made, and others older, less designs and more imaginings.

Gwen had brought her here so they could change out of their fancy clothes and draw less attention from the villagers. She hadn't considered that bringing Isobelle into this tiny corner Gwen called her own would allow the other girl to inspect each detail of her life with such naked curiosity. Covering her confusion, Gwen went to the chest at the foot of the bed and began rummaging through it.

"Here," she said finally, pulling out an old charcoal-gray dress. "This will do. It's a bit small on me anyway."

Isobelle had obviously figured out why Gwen had brought her here, coming to the same conclusion that she probably shouldn't waltz into Gwen's village center wearing a multilayered dress of violet-blue silk. She startled when Gwen spoke—she'd been gazing rather intently at the wall of sketches, though Gwen couldn't tell which one had captured her attention—and turned.

Gwen laid the charcoal dress on the bed and turned her gaze down again, the only privacy she could offer the other girl in her tiny, cramped room. She'd already located the dress she intended to change into herself, but she pretended to be searching for it as Isobelle turned away and began fiddling with the laces at her back.

"I suppose an internship is as good a story as any," Isobelle mused with a sigh, returning to their earlier conversation with ease, not the slightest hint of concern at getting undressed in Gwen's room. Gwen wished she knew whether that was because of Isobelle's absolute mastery of body language and vocal control, or because it simply didn't occur to her to be flustered.

"The stories never talk about what to do regarding your commitments at home while you're off slaying dragons and rescuing damsels," Gwen managed, keeping her tone dry.

A soft huff of frustration made Gwen look up, in spite of her resolution to stare at the gloom inside the chest while Isobelle changed. The laces behind Isobelle's back were getting tangled, and the other girl was struggling to contort her arms enough to deal with them.

"Do you . . ." Gwen began. "Uh . . . you normally have Olivia, don't you? Do you need . . . ?" Gwen could only hope that Isobelle could fill in the gaps. For some reason, the sentence *"Would you like me to help you undress?"* couldn't make it past Gwen's lips.

Isobelle laughed, unbothered by this display of helplessness, and turned to grin at Gwen over her shoulder. "I do normally have Olivia. Both to help me with my dress, and to handle my responsibilities when I run off on an adventure." She stepped closer to Gwen and then turned to present her back, the violet fabric tinged with the peaches and reds of the bonfire outside, like an inky sunset.

Gwen abandoned the clothes chest and stood inspecting the tangled ruin of laces before her with some chagrin. At least there was a problem to focus on, instead of the curve of Isobelle's neck or that the fabric, as she touched it, was warm from her skin.

Gwen put a hand on Isobelle's arm to reposition her slightly and have better light to see the laces, and Isobelle moved swiftly and easily under her hand.

Isobelle swallowed, cleared her throat, and sighed. "You know why the stories never talk about how to handle your home when you're off to, I don't know, find a missing thing hid high atop the mountain, that sort of business?"

Gwen's fingers began to work the lacings free, even as she struggled to keep her mind on the task. The conversation was a welcome distraction. "Well, of course. But I don't have a wife to leave at home to take care of everything while I go adventuring."

"The more I think on it, the more questions I have about that system." Isobelle's head bowed—in amusement, perhaps, or perhaps to give Gwen more room to work as she pulled free a trailing end that Isobelle had somehow jammed inside her neckline. "Don't bring it all the way undone, or it's tricky to put back together again."

"The system, or the laces?" Gwen huffed a tiny laugh as she finished untangling the ends.

"Both, I guess." Isobelle shivered, a light, tiny movement, and swallowed audibly again.

Gwen ought to have continued their casual conversation, but that little shiver of Isobelle's had captured her attention as singularly as a stray spark flying from a hot forge toward a pile of hay. Scarcely daring to acknowledge the experiment to herself, she breathed out again, a soft laugh, stirring the curls of escaped hair at the nape of Isobelle's neck.

Isobelle shivered again, a light ripple of movement that made her sway, just the tiniest bit, into Gwen's hands.

Gwen's thoughts, which had been crowding round her like customers all jostling to be served first, fled. She started where the lacings were already loose at Isobelle's shoulder blades, and began to pull them out, one at a time, until just the ends were still tucked through the eyelets. Each shift and tug elicited a response from Isobelle's body, a swaying rhythm that began to feel like a dance as the firelight outside flickered a slow, accompanying tempo.

Gwen laid a hand against Isobelle's rib cage, and the other girl leaned into her, instantly recognizing the support for what it was. Gwen slipped her fingers beneath the crisscrossing laces, and bit her lip as she registered the warmth of Isobelle's skin, the thin chemise she wore beneath the dress no more substantial than a cobweb.

The hand at Isobelle's ribs slid to her waist as Gwen's fingers—moving entirely without direction from her mind—worked down into the dip at the small of Isobelle's back.

Isobelle made a soft sound, like a gulp for air, and then said in a nearly inaudible rush, "I, uh, I like your quilt."

Gwen's awareness flickered toward the bed in the room, but she refocused her attention on her task before the rush of desperate thoughts could overwhelm her again. Or ask herself why Isobelle might be staring at her bed. "My mother made it for me," she said, noting with a kind of strange wonder the way Isobelle's head turned a fraction at the sound of her voice, like a flower seeking the light. "It's one of my most treasured possessions. I'm glad you like it."

"I wish I could have met your mother," Isobelle said softly.

"She would have loved you." She'd reached the end of the lacings where they sat at the base of Isobelle's spine. The temptation to let her fingers continue their work was so overwhelming that Gwen had to bite her lip, hard. Instead, she ran her fingertips lightly over the edges of the dress back up to the shoulders, to tug at the fabric and test whether it was loose enough to let Isobelle slip free.

Had she leaned back into Gwen's fingertips? Gwen could not make her touch any less of a caress than it was—the most she could hope for was that it had not occurred to Isobelle that behind Gwen's careful movements was a tempest begging to be set loose. That every gentle touch was a deeper impulse restrained and packed carefully away.

"My own mother would be mortified by me, I feel sure," Isobelle said dryly, with a sigh that made her shoulders rise into Gwen's hands and fall again.

"Sometimes I think most mortification is just envy in disguise." Gwen's voice was low, intimate. "We're embarrassed by those who are more free than we are because secretly we wish we could be so free, too."

Gwen's hand moved again, this time to trail across the back of Isobelle's shoulder to rest against the ties at the top of Isobelle's chemise. The firelight outside limned the edges of everything in rose gold, including the curve of her neck, the fine velvet hairs on her skin, each shift and movement of the delicate muscles in her throat as she swallowed.

Isobelle's head turned a little, her features lit in profile, giving her skin a flushed, heated quality. If only Gwen dared to touch that cheek, the parted lips, and discover how much of that fire was hers, and how much came from the light filtering in through the open shutters.

"Gwen," Isobelle said, her voice low, a strange note in it cutting straight to Gwen's core and making her pulse quicken. "I . . ."

A sudden burst of raucous laughter from outside interrupted her and made them both startle and leap apart, like lovers caught embracing. Distantly, Gwen recognized the voice of Lambton, the potter and farmer who lived on the north edge of the village. He'd be telling one of his raunchy jokes, full of double meanings that the little kids never got but the older ones did.

Gwen turned away, too scattered by the shattering of that moment, the loss of that sight of Isobelle all lit by firelight, dress falling off one shoulder, lips parting to say her name . . . Gwen cleared her throat roughly, trying to bring herself back to reality.

Don't do this, Gwen. But the admonishment she'd intended for herself sounded weak, more like a desperate plea than a command.

Don't risk what you have with her. Too much is at stake for you to be so foolish.

"You should be good from there," she said aloud in a brisk tone, turning back toward the chest to retrieve her own dress.

Isobelle hadn't moved, and she stood clutching the loosened dress to herself like Aphrodite gathering seafoam around her naked form. "Will you need help with yours?" she asked, her voice carrying a quiver that gave it an uncharacteristically nervous quality.

Gwen grinned a cheerful grin. She might not be getting better at most ladylike endeavors, but she was certainly learning how to copy Isobelle's public smile. "Olivia was clever and knew I might be needing to make quick changes of clothing, given my many identities in our deception. She's put the lacings down the side on all my dresses, so I can do it easily by myself."

Isobelle made a soft "ah" and turned away. Though Gwen kept her eyes averted, she could hear the rustle of fabric as Isobelle pulled the beautiful violet dress off over her head and began wriggling into the plainer, coarser fabric of Gwen's old gray one.

Gwen ducked her head and got to work on her own cleverly designed laces that she could undo all by herself.

Damn you, Olivia.

Chapter Twenty-Five

WHAT A PERFECTLY NORMAL CONVERSATIONAL GAMBIT

The village bonfire was in the middle of the square, with a few dozen villagers ranged around it. The golden flames must have been more powerful than the castle bonfires, though, because Isobelle could feel the heat on her skin long before they reached it.

She matched her pace with Gwen's as they approached, and found herself twisting her hands around her borrowed skirts. She released her grip and tried to smooth out the wrinkles with sweaty palms.

Just now, above the smithy, Gwen's fingers had struck a spark, and Isobelle had been the waiting kindling. She had stood there as the flames started to creep along her limbs and embers tingled beneath her skin, and if those louts outside hadn't broken into laughter, hadn't thrown a bucket of cold water over the pair of them . . .

With a wrench of effort, she directed her attention to her surroundings, though all she wanted to do was linger in the moment when Gwen had slowly unlaced her dress.

Rapidly calculating all the variables in a new social situation was one of Isobelle's strong suits, and she distractedly took in the dancers, the musicians, the families eating and drinking, before noticing the two people at the center of the crowd's attention.

One was a man playing a handheld drum, his fingers rapping out a rhythm so fast the firelight rendered them a blur. He shifted the beat and tempo without warning—and his eyes were on the other figure, a young woman who was circling the fire, dancing.

The girl was uncommonly lovely, with long dark auburn hair down her back, left to sway unbound around her hips, her skin gleaming with a faint sheen of perspiration. Every time the rhythm shifted, so too did her steps—she was matching him, challenging him. It was a sort of duel, she realized. The drum beat fast then slow in compelling syncopation, and Isobelle felt her own heartbeat drumming in time with it.

She jumped when Gwen laid a hand on her arm, startling her free of her trance. Gwen guided her in to join the crowd at the edges of the firelight.

"You have dancers too, I see," Isobelle murmured as the girl executed a spin. *There*, she congratulated herself. *What a perfectly normal conversational gambit. Well done.*

"I was hoping we wouldn't miss her," Gwen admitted, and there was a note in her voice that prompted Isobelle to wrench her eyes from the dancer to study her champion. It was hard to tell whether it was the firelight or whether Gwen's cheeks were also pinker than usual. "I, uh—" She paused, hesitating.

Isobelle's heart threw in an extra beat, sensing something important was happening. "Yes?"

"I used to have such a crush on her," Gwen murmured, eyes locked on the dancer. She most determinedly did *not* look at Isobelle to check on her reaction.

Isobelle's breath caught, and for a moment she couldn't remember how to make herself draw it in, so the pressure built behind her ribs as her heart tried to push its way out. She was pinned in place, gazing at Gwen's silhouette and blinking slowly as the silence drew out between them.

As if reflecting the way Isobelle's mind was unravelling this evening, the shifting beat began to lose its cohesion, the dancer to miss a step here or a spin there—and the duel fell apart to the sound of cheers and applause, and with no indication who had won.

The drummer shook out his aching hand, and the dancer let herself fall against the crowd, laughing, and Isobelle made herself lift her hands to clap alongside everybody else. Gwen applauded enthusiastically, still determinedly not looking at her companion.

Isobelle knew she had to say something. Gwen had just shown her a secret piece of herself, and . . . had she been asking if Isobelle shared that secret, too?

Surely not.

"Gwen," she found herself saying, stumbling into the conversation before she was ready—before the door Gwen had nudged open between them slammed shut.

"Gwen!" The voice belonged to a large, broad-shouldered young man who came hurrying up to Gwen and Isobelle, and the spell was broken.

In that moment, Isobelle could quite cheerfully have fed that huge boy to a dragon, and offered the beast his hat for dessert.

The newcomer was not bad looking to her practiced eye, with the potential for handsome one day. He had the sort of broad, earnest face that suggested he was still growing into his size and strength. "I wasn't sure if you'd be back for the bonfire."

"Oh, hi, Theo," Gwen said, employing what Isobelle immediately recognized as a Maintaining the Gap voice. There was a distance between these two that Theo wished to close, and Gwen was maintaining by shuffling away. She took a step back now, angling her body to include Isobelle in the conversation. *Good move, Gwen. Strength in numbers, when fending them off.*

"Is-zie. Izzie." Gwen recovered from the stumble quite well. "This is Theo. He's helping out my father while I'm completing my internship. Theo, Izzie's a maid from the castle."

"Pleasure," said Isobelle, carefully moderating her smile and unleashing about a seven out of ten on him, just to see what would happen. It distracted him for a moment, but then he blinked free of her and turned his attention back to Gwen, sending a flash of irritation through Isobelle.

Why had she done that? Gwen clearly didn't want him, so why was she trying to show Gwen he wasn't worthy of her?

Isobelle did not believe in lying unless it was *strictly* necessary, and she tried above all to be honest with herself. And so there was only one conclusion: despite Gwen's clear lack of interest in Theo's charms, Isobelle was nonetheless jealous of him. She probed this realization in the same way one probes a loose tooth, poking and prodding for a reaction.

"The dancing's almost done," Theo was saying. "But I'm sure we could squeeze one more song out of them."

Gwen tensed. "I have my friend here, and . . ."

Theo's face fell, and Isobelle had to give him credit—his earnest features were perfectly suited to looking utterly crestfallen. "I could give you an update on how things are going at the forge," he offered. "Tell you how your father's getting on."

Isobelle eyed the boy, grudgingly awarding him a point on her mental scoreboard.

Gwen muttered something under her breath and stepped forward. "Two minutes," she promised Isobelle.

"By all means, dance!" said Isobelle cheerily, and clamped her jaw shut before she managed to say something like *Dance all night, you make a lovely couple!* Or, even worse: *No—stay, and dance with me instead.*

Fortunately, before any of those words could escape, Gwen and Theo were gone.

"Poor lad," drawled a dry, amused voice behind Isobelle.

She desperately wanted to pretend the voice wasn't talking about Theo, and wasn't talking to her. She needed space to steady herself, to try to calm her whirling head, which was reeling like a punch-drunk boxer from a succession of blows.

"Though hardly his fault," the voice continued. Slowly, Isobelle turned.

The woman standing in the shadows was older than her, but not old enough to have earned the gray and white streaks through her sable hair. They gave her the air of a striped tabby cat, and the slow blink of her eyes as she took Isobelle in did nothing to dispel that image. Her dress was plain, well mended and cared for, and she wore a wide belt holding up several pockets and pouches.

If everything about her didn't scream *hedge witch!*, possibly while waving some of those streamers the cheerleaders at the tournament were using, then the wicker charm dangling from the leather thong around her neck certainly would have gotten the job done.

Isobelle reacted on instinct, bobbing a polite curtsy—not too deep, but flawless in execution. On the upper end of the I-very-much-respect-hedge-witches spectrum. She threw in a smile and a dimple for good measure. *Sweet, harmless maid from the castle. That's me!*

The woman's brows rose—Isobelle had a feeling she'd just been thoroughly examined and completely understood—but when she laughed, the sound wasn't unkind. "Well, aren't you charming? And you're new." She inclined her head in a hint of a bow, an oddly formal response to the curtsy.

"Izzie," Isobelle offered. "I'm from the castle. Gwen told me she'd show me what a real celebration looked like."

"Delia," the woman offered. "And the *real* celebration won't start until later this evening. The circle will take place by the river—there's an old oak. You'll find it if you follow the creek out past the fields."

"The circle?" Isobelle blinked at her foolishly before understanding arrived. "Oh! I'm—I'm afraid I'm no witch."

Delia studied her for a moment that went on a beat too long, her lips curving into a faint smile. "Are you not?"

"I'm—" Why was Isobelle even hesitating? It wasn't the sort of thing you missed about yourself, any more than you missed that you were seven feet tall, or a knight in shining armor, or that you were attracted to . . . "No," she said, her tone somewhere between apologetic and confused.

"Mmm," Delia said eventually. "Forgive my mistake, in that case. How are you enjoying the tournament?" the hedge witch asked, and Isobelle suddenly knew what it felt like to be a mouse played with by a cat. Did Delia *know things*, or did she just cultivate an air that made it feel as though she did?

"It's very loud when the knights crash together," she replied. "None of it makes much sense to me."

"You should ask our Gwen about it," Delia replied. Bat, bat, went her paws. Isobelle-mouse squeaked somewhere inside. "She could explain it to you. And here she comes."

Isobelle was sure she whipped around far too fast, and sure enough, there was Gwen bearing down on them. Without thinking, she extended her hand, and Gwen simply took hold of it, curling her warm fingers around Isobelle's as she reached her side.

"I see Delia found you," she said, but with a warmth that suggested she was quite pleased to see the hedge witch. "I got away from Theo by pointing out that old Bertin is setting up over on his crate. It's dragon bonfire night. I wanted Izzie to hear a real story. She's only ever heard the nobility's versions."

Isobelle blinked. "Your stories are different from those told up at the castle?"

"Ours are true," Delia replied. "Go, listen. Learn. I have my own business to attend to this evening." She inclined her head again in one of those almost-bows, and Isobelle couldn't help feeling that it was directed at her. "Gwen, it is good to see you are well. Izzie, I feel certain our paths will cross again."

There was a great deal for Isobelle to consider as they walked away from the hedge witch, but one look at Gwen's expression distracted her from her own issues. Though her tone had been easy enough, there was a hint of a line between her brows that Isobelle immediately wished to smooth away.

"Did he step on your toes?" she asked, giving Gwen's hand a daring squeeze.

"Mmm?" Gwen glanced across at her, and then let out a slow breath. Isobelle tried to ignore the little leap her heart gave, realizing that squeeze had eased Gwen's tense expression. "Not the way you mean, no. There's nothing wrong with Theo."

"Oh my. Nothing wrong with him? Now there's some high praise."

Gwen led her through the crowd before she replied, and found them a place together on a log that had been rolled up to the edge of the circle around the fire. Isobelle made a brief and fruitless attempt to dust the log off enough to keep her borrowed skirts clean, then conceded.

Once they were seated side by side, Gwen turned her head to speak quietly to Isobelle once more. "It's true. There's nothing wrong with Theo. He's from a family a couple of villages over. His father's the blacksmith in Nether Foxholm. His older brother will inherit the business."

"Ah," said Isobelle slowly, feeling many feelings at once. "And perhaps Theo will work for his brother. But perhaps he might also marry the daughter of a blacksmith who lacks a male heir."

Gwen grimaced in reply. "He's a nice boy. I think he'd be kind to me."

"That's almost as bad as *nothing wrong with him*," Isobelle observed. "Oh, Gwen. I'm not Hilde, not swept up in the romance of finding a perfect match. I know nobody gets a fairy-tale ending. But are we really meant to . . ." She trailed off, for what else was there to say?

Gwen was doing everything she could to save her from the Sir Ralphs of the world, who'd treat her like a prize without a voice of her own. To save her even from the Orsons, who would, like Theo, be *kind*.

Gwen was putting everything on the line to protect Isobelle from those fates, so she could write her own happy ending one day—whatever it might be.

But what would become of Gwen's ending?

Before Isobelle could begin to answer that question, a ripple went through the crowd. Like flowers toward the sun, everybody turned toward an old man who was rising to take his place by the fire. He was ancient, with the sort of wiry build that looked like he could live forever, and a face made craggy by wrinkles.

He walked all the way up to the fire, studying it in silence as his audience watched. It was only when he turned to make his way back that Isobelle saw one side of his face was a mass of scars.

"The thing about your stories up at the castle," Gwen whispered in Isobelle's ear, setting her skin prickling, "is that they're all about knights fighting the big dragons. The ones who were foolish enough—or enormous enough—to attack the castles. Our stories are about what happened after. Who had to deal with the rest of dragonkind in the generations that followed."

Her words were enough to yank Isobelle out of her contemplation of the sensitivity of her earlobes. "The *rest* of them?"

A young man carried over a crate for Bertin—for this must be he—and the old man eased down to sit on it with a groan. He made a great show of reluctance, but when he spoke, his tone and cadence were those of a seasoned storyteller.

"I suppose, what with it being dragon bonfire night, you'll be wanting to hear about the night I got this," he began, tapping gently on the scarring that knotted its way down the side of his face.

Around them the crowd gasped and whispered, and Isobelle gasped too, willingly letting him draw her into the tale and away from her own thoughts and questions and complications.

"This was, oh, so many years ago my hair was still a glossy black, my limbs as straight and strong as tall pines," the old man began, straightening as he spoke, recalling that younger version of himself. "It was harvest time, and the world was golden. But all was not well, for when we went to fetch the woodsman and his family for the harvest feast, we found their house burned away to cinders and all of them gone."

Isobelle let herself join in on the ripple passing through the crowd with a delightful shiver, and silently resolved that if she ever came into possession of a dreadful scar, she'd make up an equally thrilling story to go with it.

She let Bertin carry her along as he told of gathering a dozen of the village's menfolk, the great-grandfathers of those there tonight. "And me the youngest," he said, "a lad of seventeen. Together, we set out into the forest to track the beast."

His gaze drifted beyond the circle of listeners to the trees that came up to the edge of the village, and Isobelle couldn't help twisting in her seat to look, too. To picture the band setting out together, dwarfed by the trees looming above them.

"Now, dragons are the only creatures in the world that never stop growing," he continued. "The older they are, the bigger they get. The knights of old took out the biggest, the cruelest, the ones who knocked down castles for fun. But the wee ones, well. They could hide among the trees or deep in their caves and wait 'til they grew before venturing out to pick us off, one by one."

Isobelle's mind gave a funny little shiver as an army of *but what ifs* and *how do you explains* tried to make themselves heard, and then sank beneath the tide of Bertin's mesmerizing voice.

"It was just such a beast we were hunting," he said. "About the size of a wagon, to have enough flame to burn down the woodsman's place and feast on all his family. The first track we followed ended at a cave, all right—full of bears, settling down for their winter sleep. The second, we were sure we had it, but a fox hunt came through, two dozen nobles on horses, with dogs, trampling every sign of it. The third trail led to what we used to call the witch's cave, though if there was ever a witch there, the dragon must've eaten her long ago. There were jagged rocks all around the opening, so it looked like a dragon's toothy maw, waiting to close on us with a *snap*."

The audience jumped at his *snap*, and a couple of cries went up around the circle, whispers adding to the soft crackling of the fire.

"But before we could decide which one of us would have to brave it," Bertin continued softly, "the dragon dropped from the sky, crashing down into the clearing, and lunging for Ranulf Turner. He hadn't even time to cry out before his head was halfway down its gullet."

The twinkle in his eye was gone now, and his voice lower, his gaze set somewhere long ago.

Isobelle lost all sense of where she was as the flames crackled before him, painting him the same hue as the great corroded bronze beast of his story, a dragon with foul, acrid breath and fire dripping from its mouth. She cried out and recoiled with everyone else as one by one, the man's companions fell, crushed by a whip of its tail or torn apart by its great jaws.

Isobelle dragged her gaze away, glancing at Gwen beside her with a flash of a question, lips parting, though she hardly knew what she wanted to ask.

Gwen caught her eye, her own face grave—but she squeezed Isobelle's hand, a comforting gesture.

If Bertin's story were true, surely someone at the castle would have known of such a tragedy. Their descendants would remember. And they'd have spoken of it, wouldn't they?

"There we were," Bertin said, his gaze distant. "Only three of us left. Me, Elgrin, and Old Gregor pinned beneath a log, his leg broken clean in two."

A child's voice piped up, asking exactly what Isobelle was thinking. "What did you do, Bertin?"

The old man came back to himself and nodded gravely at the little girl who'd spoken. "We shared a long look, Elgrin and I. We always knew each other's minds, and I knew what he planned to do. He took off toward the river, spraying arrows all the while, to turn the beast his way. At first, I thought he'd failed. Its great gaze held me, froze me in place—I couldn't remember who I was or why I was there. I can still remember those great golden eyes, full of malice."

His voice was dying away now, and Isobelle was leaning forward with everyone else, clutching Gwen's hand tightly.

"And then one of Elgrin's arrows pierced its eye, and the spell was broken. I could move, and as it roared and turned to find him with the eye that could still see, I charged at it with my axe. The beast's hide was so thick I barely scratched its neck with my first swing. The great head started back toward me as I swung again. And as I swung a third time, liquid agony spilled down on my head."

He turned his face again, allowing the firelight to land on the scarred flesh there, and Isobelle lifted her own hand, touching the smooth skin of her cheek.

"But the dragon was already dying as he poured the last of his foul flame upon me. My Elgrin dragged me to the river and submerged my wounds, and it was three days before I could raise my face from the cool water without screaming in pain. When I could finally move again, we dragged Gregor back on a stretcher. The only three to return at all.

"No dragon has been seen in these parts between that day and this. Perhaps the one we slew was the last. But I cannot say for sure what might still be hiding in the forests or mountains or caves, waiting for the day it will attack once more."

The silence stretched after his words ended, broken only by the crackling of the bonfire before him. And then the old man straightened up with a clap of his hands.

Released from the spell, the crowd broke into murmurs and shifted where they sat, and Gwen used her hold on Isobelle's hand to pull her to her feet. "Come on," she said. "He doesn't mind questions, as long as he's not thirsty."

Isobelle followed, still dizzy with the spell of the story as Gwen hurried over to the barrel and tap, filled a mug of ale, and pressed it into Isobelle's hands. She let Gwen spin her around and point her at Bertin.

"Ah, Gwen, my thanks, girl. I see you've found a friend." The man's eyes were kind, moving between Gwen's face and Isobelle's, and Isobelle found her cheeks warming in response.

"This is Izzie," Gwen said, nudging her to hand over the mug. "She's a maid up at the castle. Izzie, this is Bertin, our expert on all things dragon."

Isobelle bobbed a curtsy automatically, which Bertin accepted with a quirk of his mouth, and offered him the ale. "They don't have stories like yours up at the castle," she ventured.

"I should say not, young lady. There haven't been any dragons attacking castles for a hundred years or more. Safe you are, in a castle."

"But we don't even hear of them," she replied. "Surely the knights would be pleased to have even a small one to hunt down."

If they were real. Which of course they're not, not anymore.

Except that woman up at the castle bonfire, tonight . . . Isobelle could still hear the ragged edge to her voice as she shouted the words, like a witch spitting a curse, *Remember us when they come for you* . . .

Bertin took a long swallow of ale before he replied. "Knights? Yes, well. Knights indeed. They came into existence to protect people, that's for sure. But then dragonslaying became less about fighting a single glorious battle on a field outside a castle, and more about weeks of slogging through marsh and wood and cold and wet, for creatures with the upper hand in their own element."

"So they left you to it," Isobelle concluded, wishing the explanation didn't make quite so much sense. "And wished you best of luck with the small ones, who probably didn't need a knight to kill them anyway."

"Well, I couldn't say," he replied. "But I do know that a whole race of creatures doesn't die out because you kill the ones making a ruckus. It just means only the clever ones persist."

Beside her, Gwen spoke gravely. "Some women came to the castle bonfire tonight to petition Lord Whimsitt for aid, claiming a dragon attacked their village. Nobody believed them."

Bertin's brows went up, but he looked far more thoughtful than disbelieving.

"I'm forced to admit that I didn't believe them either," Isobelle murmured.

"I'm used to people not believing," Bertin replied. "All I can do is tell what I know. I have my axe, half melted from dragonsfire, but a skeptic could tell me I inherited it from my grandsire who lived when dragons were everywhere. I have my burned face, but perhaps that was a forest fire, or a mishap over the stove."

Or perhaps, a small voice was saying more and more insistently in Isobelle's head, *it happened exactly the way you say it did.*

"My father's father made weapons for dragonslayers," Gwen said quietly. "You'd have to go generations back at the castle to find someone who could say the same."

"You think they really could have been out there all this time?" Isobelle heard herself ask. "And we just never knew? Nobody ever saw one?"

Gwen shrugged. "If I watched all my friends attacking castles and getting killed by guys in metal clothes, I'd find somewhere else to be."

"The question," said Bertin, "is where."

Others moved in to talk to the old man, and Gwen stayed close as the two of them stepped back. Isobelle had never needed somewhere quiet to sit down with a strong cup of tea quite so badly in her life.

Between the spell the old man's tales had cast, the hedge witch's knowing gaze—which raised questions that she mentally consigned to her pile of problems for another day—and her startling realizations about Gwen, she was dangerously close to reaching capacity. Not to mention the fate of the women who'd been arrested up at the castle.

Gently, Gwen's hand closed around hers once more, and Isobelle let the other girl lead her away. A soft squeeze told her Gwen understood and was taking her somewhere quiet. Of course Gwen understood. She always did.

Chapter Twenty-Six

A WILD HORSE OF FEELING AND EMOTION

Gwen led Isobelle away from the village center and between the fields of Lambton and his neighbor, out to where the trees began. The transition was stark, for the farmers kept the land clear right up to the line of the forest. One moment they were walking through knee-high grass, and the next, they were beneath the ancient canopy of oak and blackthorn and ash. The weight of their age had given Gwen a strange, shivery feeling as a child—as if she were stepping back in time, able to glimpse the ghosts of what these trees might have witnessed centuries ago.

Like dragons.

Isobelle was being uncharacteristically quiet, her eyes focused on where she put her feet. Ahead of them was the creek whose groundwaters fed the village well half a league away, and its whispering chatter rose as they approached, filling the silence between them.

Gwen had grown up listening to Bertin's stories. She'd always known dragons weren't far lost to history—when she'd play in these very woods as a child, her parents would warn her to keep one eye on the branches and the other on the undergrowth, just in case. A village doesn't lose its memories that quickly.

Isobelle, however, had just learned that dragons were *real*. Not a creature found only in ancient histories, but a flesh and blood monster that had nearly cost old Bertin his life.

They came up on the edge of the creek at one of Gwen's favorite spots, where a crop of boulders interrupted its flow in a series of babbling, rushing rapids and tiny waterfalls. She began to climb them automatically, but stopped after the first boulder when she realized Isobelle was lagging behind.

Gwen turned, then dropped into a crouch, wishing the moon were not quite so fickle about hiding behind the clouds. Just now, it was difficult to see Isobelle's face in the darkness.

Then Isobelle spoke. "No one is going to help those women," she said quietly.

Gwen paused. She'd expected her to burst out with some comment about Bertin's story, or the difference between the memories kept by castle and village.

Instead, Isobelle met Gwen's gaze through the gloom. "No one in power is going to listen to those villagers who came asking for help. No one will believe them. *I'm* still struggling to believe them, and I just met a man whose face was disfigured by dragonsfire."

The treetops began to whisper against each other, though the air below was still. The clouds over the moon shifted, allowing a wash of pale light to filter through the leaves, casting swaying spirits of silver across Isobelle's face.

Gwen glanced down and saw Isobelle's hands balled into fists at her sides, and before she could register the impulse, she sat down on the stone, slid forward, and reached out. Gwen curled her fingers over Isobelle's, her thumbs settling against the backs of her hands. They felt chilled compared to Gwen's—she longed to lend Isobelle some of her warmth. Gwen let the pad of one thumb slide across the dips and swells of Isobelle's knuckles, and with some astonishment, watched the tension ease away under her touch.

In a rush, Isobelle said, "We have to do something. If no one else is going to do something about it, then we should."

Gwen allowed herself the briefest look at Isobelle's face, and immediately wished she hadn't. The sight of her—lit by shifting moonlight, anguish flooding her gaze, rosebud lips in a thin, determined line—almost robbed her of speech and sense entirely. Gwen imagined pulling her closer, flush up against the rock where Gwen sat, so she could lean forward and soften the clench of Isobelle's lips the way she'd done her hands.

"We will," Gwen managed faintly, having put so much effort into staying still that she had none left over for words. "You and me. We'll do something about it."

Gwen must have moved after all, because Isobelle answered her summons and shifted closer against the rock, her hips between Gwen's knees where they dangled over the edge of the stone.

"Olivia will tell us in the morning where they're being held, and on what grounds." Isobelle blinked, gaze shifting from a place of future plans and deliberation to refocus on Gwen's face. "This whole white knight thing," she said with a laugh. "I can see why you like it."

Gwen swallowed, so moved she couldn't answer. Isobelle could simply have dismissed Bertin's story and the women who'd come seeking help. It would have been easier for her to let it all be a mere blip of unpleasantness marring an otherwise frivolous evening of snacks and bonfire festivities.

But here she was, rewriting her entire understanding of the world, and making plans to charge into battle to fix it.

"Thank you," Gwen whispered finally, daring no more than to

give one of Isobelle's hands a tiny squeeze. "For coming here tonight with me."

"I'm more glad you brought me than you'll ever know." Isobelle's face was earnest—Gwen could feel the blue stare fixing on her again in that unnerving way it had of trying to see through her carefully constructed barriers. Isobelle drew breath to speak, but then stopped, that breath hitching.

Gwen's eyes snapped up, automatically wary. Isobelle, hesitating? She'd have been less surprised if a dragon had charged out of the undergrowth.

"That girl from before," Isobelle said finally, her words somewhat rushed. "The dancer, at the village bonfire?"

Gwen's heart thudded, and her alarm narrowed down to a single focus. "Fiora," she provided. "What about her?"

Isobelle was looking down at the stone between them. When Gwen dropped her gaze, she saw their skirts pooled together on the rock, the moonlight blending them into one.

"You said you used to have a crush on her," Isobelle said, evenly enough. "What made you stop?"

You.

The mental response was so quick that Gwen had to bite her lip furiously to stop the word from coming out. In actuality, it wouldn't have been true anyway. She'd given up pursuing Fiora a year ago, long before she ever met Isobelle.

Not that you're pursuing Isobelle now, her mind told her, biting back that moonlit pathway of thought just as furiously as she was biting her lip.

For one glaring moment, Gwen considered making something up.

Then Isobelle's fingers shifted slightly. The balled-up fists were gone—her slender hands had turned to cup Gwen's in hers. Isobelle's skin was warmer now, warmer in fact than her own. And it was Isobelle offering her that warmth.

Gwen kept her eyes on those hands, not sure she could tell Isobelle the truth if she had to watch each shift of her expression while she did. This was not a story you told to someone you wanted to . . . someone you wanted to respect you.

"The girls at the tea party," Gwen managed finally. "When they asked if I'd ever kissed anyone? When I said no, I was giving them Céline's answer. Not mine."

Isobelle just waited, while the wind and the trees and the moon formed patterns on her skin for Gwen to focus on.

"She was only interested in me when she was fighting with her boyfriends. I knew she was only trying to make them jealous, but I kept thinking . . . every time she came to me, I thought maybe it was different." Gwen shook her head, as much to buy herself time to breathe as to comment on her own foolishness. "It worked every time. She'd always make sure to let them see her kiss me. And they'd come sprinting back."

Isobelle's hands had gone still under hers. "And where did that leave you?"

"Waiting for their next fight, I suppose. I should've been stronger and stopped letting it happen, but . . ." Gwen lifted a shoulder, a trickle of shame coursing through her, making it hard to speak. "I did overhear her explaining it to one of them, though, and that's what ended things between us once and for all. Just a bit of fun, I heard her tell him. A little show." Gwen paused, snatches of that ill-fated tea party with Isobelle's friends flashing through her mind.

Then, softly, she added, "She called it practice."

Isobelle uttered a soft sound, shades of feeling in it too numerous for Gwen to unpack. When Gwen raised her eyes, finally, Isobelle was studying her, her own eyes widened with sudden understanding, scanning Gwen's features as if seeing her anew.

"You were right," Isobelle said finally, her normally smooth and well-practiced voice low and a little rough. "What you said, after the tea party—you were right. When someone kisses you, it should be because they want to. Need to. Because they can't take another second wondering, dreaming, about what it would be like."

Gwen held very still—Isobelle had remembered every word she'd said that night. Fear told her to drop her eyes, to pull away, lest Isobelle see the truth of what she wondered and dreamed about—see how easily and deeply she could hurt Gwen if this fragile dance of theirs fell apart. Fear told her to end it herself, one way or another, before Isobelle could.

Instead Gwen sat, unmoving, watching Isobelle's eyes, turned pale silver in the moonlight, the flutter of the pulse at her throat, the tiny sound her lips made when they parted. She saw Isobelle's gaze dip, saw her breath quicken as she watched Gwen's mouth.

The realization came, not like a bolt of lightning, but like the slow unclenching of tense muscles at the end of a long day—the soft and subtle remembering of home and safety, and of being *enough*. Gwen felt something come free in her chest, a band of tightness she hadn't noticed until suddenly she could exhale again with her full lungs, with her whole body.

It left her full and aching, the realization that Isobelle was longing to kiss her, too.

Isobelle's hands were shaking a little, where they rested against

Gwen's. Her breathing was uneven. Uncertainty and confusion clouded the silver moonlit gaze.

She was scared. Her Isobelle, frightened. Or if not *frightened*, at least . . . unsure. Caught up in something moving far too quickly for her, a wild horse of feeling and emotion, galloping out of control with no ravine to direct its course.

Gwen closed her fingers around Isobelle's hands again, waiting until they calmed. She let out a long, slow, audible breath, until she felt Isobelle do the same, mirroring her body language automatically. Another breath, letting the tension singing between them drain, letting them both step back from the precipice.

When Isobelle's eyes finally met hers, Gwen raised her eyebrows and gave her a smile. "It's getting late," she murmured. "I guess we should start making our way back before anyone notices you're not there?"

Gwen had meant to make it a suggestion—to show Isobelle they could walk up to this cliff's edge as many times as they needed to before she was ready to leap. Instead it was a question. Instead, it left room for Isobelle to make her own choice.

Isobelle took a tiny step back. When Gwen slid forward, she could feel a place on the stone where Isobelle's thighs had pressed, warming the rock even through her skirts.

"It *is* getting late." Isobelle turned to look back the way they'd come. The distant glow of the village bonfire was hidden by the trees, though it wouldn't take long to retrace their steps back toward their abandoned finery.

"We'll have to go back and get our dresses from the smithy," Isobelle went on with a sigh. "And think of a reason why we took so long. And . . ." Her voice petered out.

Even though Gwen had made that choice to step back with Isobelle, and leave that cliff behind them for a while, her heart was still sinking. Despite her noblest intentions, she longed to stay in this place for a little while longer, where they were both free of their masks. To walk along the cliff's edge, at least, even if they weren't ready yet to leap.

Isobelle's gaze swung back toward the creek, and then sidelong up to Gwen's face. "Or . . . we could just keep walking?"

Gwen managed, with great difficulty, to answer in an even tone despite the thudding of her heart. "Or we could just keep walking."

Isobelle tucked her arm through Gwen's, and they kept walking. The silence between them hung like a warm, woolen wrap, comfortable and easy. Summer was coming to an end, and though the air was still balmy, there was the slightest hint of a sharper chill behind it, like an actor just offstage waiting to make her dramatic entrance.

By the time they reached the point where the creek joined up with its neighbor to form a wider stream, the breeze above the treetops had finished chasing the patchy clouds away from the full moon and had begun to sweep down into the forest, whistling through the trees. Isobelle gave a little shiver, and Gwen felt it as if her own body were chilled. Automatically, she turned her steps east, a path that would eventually bring them back to the road connecting the castle with the surrounding villages.

Isobelle glanced at her and then back at the stream, her steps slowing.

"You're not cold?" Gwen said, and then cleared her throat, surprised to realize how long it had been since either of them had spoken.

Isobelle quirked a smile. "I am, a little, but . . ." She glanced back down the course of the stream, which joined with the river not too far away. The trees thinned out ahead, and with the full moon the meadows and more solitary trees beyond the thicker woods were visible. "Can we go see that massive tree? What kind of tree is that?"

Gwen already knew which tree she meant—the most ancient one in this part of the forest, standing alone in a field that bloomed furiously with wildflowers in spring. "It's an oak," she supplied as Isobelle tugged her onward.

Before they'd gone too far, though, Gwen's steps slowed. She could hear something through the trees: voices, many of them, raised in some sort of song or chant. A prickle of concern made the hairs on the back of her neck stand on end, questioning the wisdom of venturing through a moonlit forest toward ethereal eldritch voices luring you onward. Not that she believed in faerie stories, of course, but plenty of people didn't believe in stories about dragons, either.

But where her steps tried to drag, Isobelle's quickened. The other girl had a firm hold of Gwen's arm, though she was wise enough to keep hidden under the trees by the river.

They came to a dense blackberry thicket still bearing a few of the season's last fruits at the edge of the wood, and without hesitation, Isobelle dropped down to wriggle forward through the brambles, leaving Gwen little choice but to follow. When she reached the edge of the thicket, Isobelle put a hand on Gwen's, and together they gazed out through the thin, concealing layer of blackberry thorns.

The massive old oak had been struck by lightning once, leaving a section of its branches skeletal and brittle—a tiny forked slice of white, stark in the moonlight, amid the joyous green of its living foliage.

But Gwen had never been here at night. And never on the night of a full moon.

A dozen figures stood in a semicircle not far from the trunk of the tree, where a stone bench had been erected—no, an altar of sorts, with stones and feathers and other objects scattered upon its surface. There were candles, too—when the wind gusted just right, Gwen caught the faintest aroma of beeswax over the heady, sweet tang of crushed blackberries all around them.

The figures were all in white, and all women, Gwen realized—they'd shucked their dresses and stood in their shifts, which billowed in the wind. Their voices were raised in a rhythmic chanting that called to something deep in Gwen's bones.

She turned her hand to twine her fingers through Isobelle's and squeezed. "Witches," she breathed, half dizzy with the spectacle and the idea that she might be about to witness true, real magic. Hedge witches tended to be cagey and secretive about their powers—never quite showing someone if they were real, or just a clever combination of mind games and herbalism. Delia would be there among them, though at this distance Gwen couldn't distinguish her. And hedge witches from all across the county must have come here tonight to greet the moon.

One of the women was led into the center of the circle. Though Gwen could not see her face, she could see the way the woman's steps were slow, her shoulders bowed—the specter of grief weighed on her, something heavy and hopeless. Awe gave way to uneasiness, and Gwen shifted her weight.

"Maybe we shouldn't be watching," she whispered.

Isobelle turned away long enough to meet Gwen's gaze. "I . . . I think I was invited. I don't think they would mind."

There was a faint question in Isobelle's eyes, one that left room for Gwen to object. She would go if Gwen wanted to—though something in her just as clearly wanted to stay.

Gwen hesitated, and then shifted so she could sit, rather than kneel, on the loamy earth beneath her. Isobelle flashed her a smile, and then they both ducked their heads to peer back out of the thicket.

The circle of witches drew closer, enclosing the one they'd singled out within their protection. The chant died away to make room for a single voice—perhaps it was Delia's, though Gwen could not be sure across the distance. The wind shifted this way and that, bringing fragments of the witch's voice to the blackberry thicket.

Then the circle all spoke together, the very trees ringing with the words: "We who look upon her are filled with love."

Gwen could not tell if they meant the moon, or the woman enclosed by the circle, or both.

The witches, voices rising in unison, began to chant a name—that of the woman in the circle, perhaps. *Rheda*, they called. *Rheda, we hear you. Rheda, we see you.*

Together they lifted their arms, concealing the woman who stood in their midst, and as if in answer, the wind rose to such a pitch that it began to howl through the trees. Isobelle drew close against Gwen and she leaned back, their bodies conserving their warmth together as the gale threatened to snatch it away.

On the altar beneath the tree, the candle flames vanished into the wind, objects tumbling over and crashing from the stone—the witches' white shifts were flattened against them, their hair flying, their bodies and arms bending like saplings in a storm. The very air seemed to shimmer—Gwen's eyes grew dim and teary in the wind as she strained to see—

And then the gale subsided. The chant, which had grown to a screaming pitch, eased. The name *Rheda* faded away again as the witches lowered their arms. Rheda stood, her chest heaving, her face tilted up toward the moon. As she stepped out of the circle again, the weight she'd carried had shifted. Not banished, but . . . made bearable, somehow. As if, when she walked into the circle, she had been more pain than anything else.

Now, she remembered who she was.

Another chant began, another name, another woman stepping forward. Gwen shifted her weight again and Isobelle responded at her side—they leaned together, getting comfortable, deciding without words that they would watch every moment of this ritual. That they would listen as the names and the voices of women carried on the wind across the moonlit forest enfolded them, too, inside the circle beneath the oak tree.

As one by one, they were made whole.

AH, DEAR READER, DID I catch you sighing or smiling just now? I suppose I can't blame you. The word "chemistry" won't exist for another few centuries, but I assure you, when it does, the dictionary will feature a lovely little engraving of these two as an example of its less scientific meaning.

I feel I must caution you, though: you may wish to wipe that grin off your face. If you're one of those who likes to put down the book when everyone is happy, this is your chance.

But, Unnamed Narrator, you cry, *surely you are wrong! There are no misunderstandings, no convenient obstacles, no sign of the devices storytellers often use to keep star-crossed couples apart. And no mixed love languages or clashing attachment styles to drive a wedge between them. All is well, no?*

All is not well. After all, Gwen has not let herself think about what will happen when—not if—she fails to win the tournament. And Isobelle can't imagine a future in which Gwen does not succeed.

Reality is a far harsher mistress than either of them expects.

I can see you considering turning the page anyway. Fine, keep reading and ignore my caution—you readers are all alike.

Don't say I didn't warn you.

Chapter Twenty-Seven

I THOUGHT WE'D HAVE MORE TIME

Jsobelle woke slowly from the most delightful dream. Light flickered across her closed eyelids, and something brushed her cheek—her questing fingers retrieved a small twig. She blinked her eyes open and forced them to focus as she realized she was not in her own bed. Thorny branches and tight green leaves crisscrossed her vision. Her head rested on something soft and warm, a surface that shifted under her—

Gwen.

Her head was pillowed against Gwen's hip—the other girl had draped one arm over her shoulders, and was sleeping quite soundly, to judge from the quiet rhythm of her breathing.

And then it all came flooding back. The tale of the dragon. The women at the castle. The witches beneath the stars. And the glorious moment last night when she and Gwen had stood together, knowing that if either one of them had moved by even a hair's breadth, they'd have broken the last of their restraint. That the thing shimmering between them, the thing sending her blood surging through her veins, would have sprung to life with a dragon's roar.

In that moment, she could have kissed Gwen. She had *wanted* to kiss Gwen. But the act of wanting had been so surprising, so staggering in its implications, that she had found herself holding still.

She'd seen understanding dawn in Gwen's eyes. Watched as Gwen, without any impatience, any blame at all, had simply made space for Isobelle to face those feelings. To take her time.

While the knights at the castle fought to possess her, Gwen offered her the chance to take ownership of herself, of her own choices.

Gwen worried, sometimes, that she was nothing like them.

Isobelle thought it was her finest quality.

"Gwen," she whispered. "Are you awake?"

"Mmm?" Gwen stretched languorously, then stopped as she registered Isobelle's head in her lap. She went still, and then: "Oh, shit! We stayed out all night—we've got to get back!"

"It's morning now," Isobelle pointed out.

"I know, that's why we have to get—"

"We will," Isobelle replied, hauling herself up to a sitting position and suppressing an unladylike groan. "But that bird has flown the coop, Gwen. The sun's up, and a scramble won't make a difference. Olivia will cover for us if Whimsitt comes round."

Gwen's hair was mussed where she'd been leaning against the tree, and Isobelle had the most compelling urge to lean over to stroke it smooth. Except then it would be all too easy to let her hand slowly curve around the back of Gwen's neck, and . . .

"Fair point," Gwen conceded. "But we still have to get back, Whimsitt or no Whimsitt. We have to submit Sir Gawain's papers this morning."

That was enough to put some of the morning's chill back into the air, and reluctantly—wishing she'd given herself a few more minutes to lie in the sun and listen to Gwen's soft breathing—Isobelle set about extricating herself from the blackberry thicket. It was as though the thorny branches had curled around them as they slept, snaring their thick wool skirts to hold them in place. Isobelle couldn't help thinking of the charms the hedge witch sold at the market—the bracelets made from blackberry brambles.

Love charms.

She peeped through the edge of the thicket, out toward the field. The oak stood, leaves green now where the night before they'd been silver in the moonlight. There was no sign of the witches' circle, or the altar, or the magic they'd summoned.

By the time she and Gwen were free, their hair was tangled and their clothes were torn, but they were both laughing helplessly. They paused to gather a few handfuls of the late summer blackberries for the walk back to the castle.

And as they made their way up the road, Isobelle slipped her hand into Gwen's.

Olivia didn't ask why the two of them were in plain, unfamiliar dresses, why those dresses were torn all over, or where the blackberry stains had come from.

Instead, she bundled her yawning charges into new clothes, scrubbed their faces like a mother cat cleaning a pair of kittens, and promised she had already taken steps to find out what the deal was with the women who'd shown up at the bonfire the night before.

Isobelle worked to keep her head still as Olivia yanked tangles out of her hair—most of her attention was on the way Gwen's cheeks were still becomingly pink after Olivia had scoured the blackberry juice off. She felt caught halfway between the world she had come from—the world of beating hearts and anticipation, of moonlight shimmering with possibility—and this ordinary, sunlit world of the castle, where there were practicalities waiting, and routine around every corner. Just as one hugged the pillow come morning after a particularly delicious sleep, Isobelle wanted to cling to the last strands of the place she had been.

When Gwen slid a small smile in her direction, she lost her focus entirely, and stumbled back into Olivia. Her maid gave a soft, knowing *hmph* and set her back on her feet, salvaging the braid and tying it off with a ribbon. Then she picked up a package and held it out to Gwen, and suddenly the glorious color of the morning dimmed.

It was Gwen's—or rather Sir Gawain's—patents of nobility and credentials.

"They'll be fine," Olivia said firmly, correctly interpreting Isobelle's lip-nibble. "Just slide them in when the herald is busy, so he hasn't time to wonder why it's Céline doing it."

Gwen closed her hands around the packet Archer had prepared and pulled it in against her chest like a shield. "Best get it over with."

"You mean best get on with the next step of our glorious plan," Isobelle replied. She could feel Gwen's nerves, but the world was new, and they were invincible, and Isobelle didn't have the slightest doubt their forged papers would be accepted without a second glance. "I don't suppose you have any snacks we can eat on the hoof, Olivia?"

The bonfires of the night before seemed to have signaled the turning of the season—there was a new crispness to the midmorning air as they made their way down to the tourney grounds, nibbling on croissants.

The crowd was moving slowly, and there were plenty of pale faces and quite a few fairgoers attempting to treat last night's hangovers with a scale of the dragon that singed them, tankards already in hand. The minor competitions—foot races, archery, wrestling—were underway, but none of them were holding much of anyone's attention.

The tent for Lord Whimsitt's steward stood at the edge of the lists, and with so many bleary-eyed people milling about, Gwen simply slipped Sir Gawan's patents of nobility into the pile that had formed. After they'd sidled away again, Isobelle whispered, "Huzzah! Easy as can be."

"That wasn't the part I was worried about." Gwen had found a loose thread at her sleeve and kept worrying the thread back and forth between her fingers, tugging it further undone every time. "When will we know if they've been accepted as authentic?"

"When the herald pins up the opening draw," Isobelle replied. "If all's gone well, Sir Gawain will be on it. It'll be okay, Gwen, I can feel it."

Gwen cast her a sidelong glance, her brow furrowed. "I just—I can't help but feel like something's about to go wrong." Her eyes lingered on Isobelle's face, then fell, a faint flush rising to her freckled cheeks.

Isobelle's throat tightened, realization dawning. Gwen was so used to responding to happiness with a sense of dread. Isobelle had to suppress the urge to go find that Fiora girl and give her a stern lecture about only kissing blacksmith's daughters if she was serious about it.

Instead, she reached for Gwen's hand and squeezed it. "Come on. The herald will take his sweet time. Let's take a turn and kill an hour or so."

"I think I'm going to throw up," Gwen muttered. Under her

freckles, she was white with nerves, but she did crack a tiny smile as her fingers curled around Isobelle's in response.

"I believe that ditch over there is the traditional spot," Isobelle replied, marveling at the way she chirped, despite her own churning stomach. "Though that's mostly for hangovers."

They took a turn around the grounds, and Isobelle listened to herself with no small admiration as she managed to point out far too many sights, produce opinions on the archery she had never known she held, and generally fill the air with chatter. Given the hurricane underway inside her own head, everything she had been sure of tossed hither and yon, she really thought she was doing quite well.

Neither of them spoke about that moment under the moonlit trees, when either one of them could have leaned forward and changed the nature of their friendship forever. Not yet.

It wasn't until well after noon that the head herald, dressed in tournament livery, emerged from the steward's tent with a scroll in his hands. A ripple passed through the milling crowds, the air of bored idleness instantly sharpening to breathless anticipation.

Like a pack of wolves waiting for the kill, rows of squires—and even a few knights, judging by their clothes—were standing in a barely restrained semicircle around the herald, who walked to the list barricade and began nailing his parchment to the post.

Some unspoken agreement seemed to hold them all back, but when the man stepped away, all bets were off. The mass of bodies descended on where he had been, presenting the girls with a solid wall of backs.

"Stay here," murmured Gwen, turning and squaring her jaw. Then, after a pause, she added, "Though if I'm not out in five minutes, send help."

Isobelle was so busy watching Gwen disappear into the seething crowd that she startled when a voice came from behind her.

"So keen, my lady, to find out who your new husband will be?"

She whirled around and found Sir Ralph, well—she didn't like to use the word, even in her head, but there was no avoiding it: he was *leering* down at her. She took a step back before she could stop herself.

"I suppose it's natural for you to speculate," he continued. "But daydreaming won't hurry the day along. You must be patient."

The silence that followed as Isobelle searched in vain for a reply was disrupted by a familiar, but most unladylike, shout from near the pillar itself, and a ripple went through the group of men. Then the mass of bodies spat out Gwen.

She emerged between a pair of squires and nearly ricocheted off the barrier erected to keep the crowd of spectators away from the joust. But where she ought to have lifted her head to search for her companion, instead she just gripped the fence with both hands, head bowed as she tried to catch her breath. Or recover from some deeply damaging blow.

Isobelle simply turned her back on Sir Ralph, hurrying over to push her way in beside Gwen, ducking her head to get a look at the other girl's face. Every line of Gwen had become familiar to her these last days, but she had never seen her look like this before. There was a blankness to her expression, as though she weren't Gwen at all, but a statue of her, the spark of life simply gone from her face.

"It's over," Gwen said softly. "It's over, before I've ever had a chance to try. We're done, Isobelle."

Ice slithered down Isobelle's spine. Archer's papers had looked perfect; how could this be? Olivia had said they would work, and Olivia was never wrong.

How much danger was Gwen in? Were they looking for Sir Gawain even now?

Her body took over. She took Gwen's arm and led her, unresisting, away from the scrum around the newly announced tournament brackets. This was clearly a conversation best had without witnesses, and given she was the prize these men were fighting for, the odds of someone blundering up for another obnoxious chat in the next minute or two were high.

Neither of them spoke until they'd left the crowd behind and reached the stables. Then Isobelle released Gwen and whirled around to face her. "What's happened? Sir Gawain's name wasn't there?"

Gwen leaned back against the stable wall, pressing the heels of her hands into her eyes. "It was. The papers went through, no one's questioning Sir Gawain."

"Then what? Gwen, talk to me!"

Gwen lowered her hands, and Isobelle gazed at her eyes. Forest green, hints of oak, hints of golden sunlight. Shadows beneath. "They put the old hands against the unknowns," she said. "So nobody big goes down in the first round. But I thought at least . . ."

"Gwen!" Isobelle resisted the urge to shake her. "Tell me what's happened! Who did you get?"

"I'm to face Sir Ralph."

"Oh, fuck."

After that, neither of them spoke. Everything was quiet and still, the peace broken only by a horse whinnying an opinion from inside the stable. Isobelle felt as though she were watching herself from the outside, a kind of calm numbness seeping through her veins, until she could barely feel her body.

"Well," she heard herself say, the strain audible through her usual polish. "He'll have his guard down, won't he? That's to your advantage."

Gwen shot her a look that said *stop* as clearly as any words could have done. "Isobelle, don't," she said hoarsely. "Don't try to make it— I was starting to think that maybe, *maybe* . . . I'd at least get a few rounds in. Keep them off you for a couple of weeks. Stay with—" She cut herself off, pressing her lips together hard, closing her eyes tightly.

"Stay with me," Isobelle finished for her, the words barely a breath. She gazed at Gwen, memorizing the details of her face, the placement of every freckle, the swoop of her thick lashes, the firm lines of her brows. She gazed at her as if she might be gone tomorrow.

"I thought we'd have more time," Gwen said.

"Listen," said Isobelle desperately, grabbing for her last shreds of optimism. It couldn't be over. It couldn't just end. "You don't know what's going to happen. Everyone makes mistakes. He's going to assume the same thing as everyone else—that he'll sail through. He won't even give a thought to this first-round match with some unknown knight from nowhere. And that'll give you a chance. You'll be focused, be ready. He'll be daydreaming."

"What are you talking about?" Gwen burst out, the pent-up words exploding. "There's daydreaming—which he won't be—and then there's delusional. I've been trying not to think about it, trying not to let reality poison this . . . this *fantasy* you have that I could somehow win this thing. But I was never going to beat him, even if I made it all the way to the final before meeting him. I was never going to *win*."

"Delusional," Isobelle echoed, her whole body sickening at Gwen's words. "So what was this, then? I thought you were in it with me, as much as I was. I thought . . ." But she couldn't finish that sentence. She couldn't speak her moonlight dream out loud when it was dying here in the sun.

I thought you'd wait for me. I thought you promised that last night. I thought when I was ready, you'd be here. I thought . . .

"You thought what?" Gwen asked bitterly.

Isobelle wanted to wail, to demand that Gwen acknowledge aloud the change that had taken place between them—instead, she reached for something, anything, to convince Gwen to stay. "I thought you wanted to show them all that you deserve to be here. A knight, in armor you made, with a weapon that's yours. *They* just show up and put on the costume."

"So do I!" Gwen snapped, letting herself sag back against the stable wall, wrapping her arms tightly around her middle. "I practiced in an orchard, Isobelle. If you thought that was going to get me through this, then you live in a fantasy world." Gwen's voice was heated and sharp, like a red-hot blade, whipping at Isobelle's last shreds of optimism.

"Why are you doing this?" Isobelle could feel her cheeks flushing, and to her horror, her voice broke. "You're just giving up?"

"You want me to do something impossible," Gwen replied, her snap gone, her fire going out. "You want me to be this white knight, to ride out and save you from the monster, but . . ." There was a flash of helplessness in her face. "It doesn't matter how much I wish I could, Isobelle. We always knew what would happen."

"*I* don't know what will happen," Isobelle replied, trying to ignore the ache behind her eyes. "But I know that if you don't face him, then you lose in every way. You lose . . ." *You lose us,* said the voice that had discovered itself by moonlight. "If you go out there, and you hit the ground in your armor, then you were still a knight. I want that for you—for you to *know* that you are a knight." She gulped a breath. "That's—that's why you were doing this, wasn't it?"

Say no, said the moonlight voice. *Say you were doing it for me.*

"It doesn't matter why I was doing it," Gwen said, not looking at Isobelle. "The end was always going to be the same." She shoved away from the stable wall.

Isobelle reached out a hand to catch her arm, but Gwen deftly twisted away, her reflexes razor-sharp. Isobelle fought the wild urge to sprint after Gwen and catch her, hold her still, *make* her believe again—and then the reality of the tournament, Gwen's heartbreak and disappointment, and her own impending doom all crashed in on her and she could only stand there, arms wrapped across her middle, holding herself together after a terrible, mortal wound.

Chapter Twenty-Eight

YOU ARE NOT THE FIRST TO ASK WHETHER A WOMAN COULD HOLD A SWORD

Lord Whimsitt threw a grand feast that night, celebrating the eve of the first round of the tournament. Gwen knew she should have gone in her guise as Céline to sell the fiction of Sir Gawain before he made his big debut against Sir Ralph the next day.

But Gwen could not bring herself to put on that mask. Layers upon layers of deceit, her head spinning with what role she was meant to be playing and when... Her only consolation and refuge was that at least she hadn't had to pick a persona to play in front of Isobelle.

And now... now she did.

It had seemed so easy last night, under the moonlit canopy of trees, to give Isobelle as much time as she needed to understand her own mind and heart. But today, doused in the icy cold torrent of realization that their charade would be coming to an end not at some hazy, undefined future moment, but *tomorrow*, Gwen had felt an unfamiliar panic reach up and grip her by the throat. They didn't have that time. They would never have that time.

Gwen couldn't wear that mask again in front of Isobelle, not without shouting at her the way she'd done that afternoon.

Ever since she'd agreed to Isobelle's plan, she'd been trying not to think about the stark reality of riding against seasoned knights and counting on her passion to mean more than their birthrights. She'd been trying not to look at the likelihood that she'd end up in jail—or worse—if she were found out. She'd been trying not to imagine Isobelle's despair when Gwen failed her, as she would certainly do eventually, no matter how hard she tried.

Instead, every fear and worry Gwen had been ignoring, like some child covering her eyes against the monster-infested night, had come spilling out in one searing, wrenching explosion. Instead, she'd done exactly what she'd been trying so hard to avoid: she'd crushed Isobelle.

Gwen had told Olivia to inform Isobelle that she was feeling poorly and needed to rest before the tournament. Later, she'd listened to Isobelle's footsteps, unmistakable in their light, graceful patter, pause for a long, breathless moment outside Gwen's door—and then move away again, down to join the feast.

She ought to sleep. But her whole body buzzed and ached for action, to fight this enemy that tormented her—her body didn't know that the enemy was time, and situation, and hopelessness, and longing.

Secure in the knowledge that anyone who would recognize "Céline" would be at the feast, Gwen donned her old riding dress, slipped out to fetch her gear, and made her way to the ballroom where she'd first begun practicing her footwork at the castle.

The room was cavernous and still, illuminated by the moonlight streaming through the diaphanous, sheer curtains. The ballroom's golds and creams and peaches were muted, transformed into silvers and lilacs and deep, secretive rose. The very air quivered with unfulfilled purpose, with the echoes of the thousands of dances and balls that had been held in this space—whispers of memory that made Gwen feel like an intruder, someone who had crept uninvited into someplace sacred.

Which, in fact, she had done. She didn't belong here. Isobelle seemed content to ignore the insanity of her scheme, counting on pure optimism to win the day and forcing Gwen to be the voice of reason. In her mind's eye, she saw Isobelle's face again as it had looked that afternoon, all beseeching eyes and quivering lips as she implored Gwen to remember how she longed to prove herself among the other knights. *That's why you were doing this, wasn't it?* Isobelle had whispered.

Gwen had felt two paths open up in front of her. To leap off the cliff, or turn away and walk back the way they'd come. To say, *No, I was doing it for you*, or . . . or do as Gwen had done, and flee.

Gwen gave herself a shake and pulled her sword from its sheath, the scrape of steel echoing loudly in the expectant air. After a few experimental swings of the blade, she launched into one of Madame Dupont's exercises, an unlikely combination of delicate dancing footwork and deadly swings and blows from her sword. She could almost hear Isobelle playing the organ in the background, the remembered notes hanging ghostlike in the air; could almost see her form at the shadowed instrument.

She shook off that image and tried to focus instead on visualizing the man she'd be fighting tomorrow. To visualize winning, beating him, taking him by surprise. Those piercing, hawklike eyes wide with shock, looking up at her from the ground.

The way those eyes had looked as they scanned over Isobelle at the castle bonfire, like he was an acquisitive collector inspecting his latest purchase.

Gwen stumbled, dropped the sword, caught its hilt on the rebound, and swore as she staggered. She whirled and kicked at the floor and let loose an absolute flurry of invective, using every word she'd been trying not to use in her guise as Céline.

A voice came from the shadows on the far side of the ballroom. "I thought you would be here earlier than this, Mademoiselle le Chevalier."

Gwen let out a bleat of alarm and confusion, even as her brain identified the voice from its rasp and its French accent. Her eyes searched the other end of the room until she saw the dark form perched on a window seat, barely distinguishable from the piles of cushions adorning the benches.

A lantern flared to life, illuminating Madame Dupont's features and striking her silver hair to white gold.

"I knew you would not be so foolish as to try to sleep the night before battle," the Frenchwoman continued, her eyes gleaming with amusement.

Gwen, still trying to swallow her heart back down into her chest where it belonged, gulped for a breath. "I'm beginning to think you have a secret love of the dramatic."

Dupont gave a light bark of laughter. "Secret? Ma chérie, it is not a secret at all. You are here to practice, non? I will light the fire so we can see." She rose from the window seat and crossed toward the large fireplace at the end of the hall, her stick tapping a decorous rhythm with her steps.

Gwen sighed and sliced her sword down and to one side with a muted hiss of wounded air. "Practice? I'd settle for venting some of this energy. I feel like crawling out of my skin."

"Then we shall vent," Dupont replied. She knelt down before

the hearth, where the beginnings of a fire had already been laid, and struck the flints together. Sparks shot from her fingers like magic. "Your lady is at the feast, I take it? Dazzling them all with her wit?"

Gwen forced herself to shrug, fighting the urge to rise to that bait and fire off a retort about how Isobelle wasn't *her* anything. "I think so. I decided I'd be better off resting, or at least not letting her get me wound up."

"Isobelle *is* an enlivening presence," Dupont agreed with a dry chuckle as the sparks settled against the kindling.

Gwen muttered an agreement. "People think that she's shallow," she murmured. "But really, she just . . . throws herself wholeheartedly into whatever lies before her. Whether it's choosing a dress or, you know, recruiting a village girl to ride in a tournament for her."

"Not all who meet her see enough to realize that." Dupont leaned in to blow gently on the infant flame, encouraging it to move across the kindling and onto the larger sticks behind it. "Or the power she wields. After all, here we both find ourselves, practicing for an adventure of her design."

Gwen sheathed her sword and crouched beside Madame Dupont so she could help sort through the split logs. Tearing at them for kindling was a good vent for her turbulent thoughts, and as the silence stretched, she had the unsettling feeling that Dupont had somehow read her mind—had somehow known that when Gwen had said she needed to vent her energy, what she really needed was to speak.

The pile of ready kindling next to Dupont had grown to somewhat ridiculous proportions before a splinter jabbed its way into Gwen's thumb. She hissed an epithet and tore the offending shard of wood out and threw it into the flames.

Closing her eyes, she summoned her courage and blurted, "I'm not so sure I should do this thing tomorrow."

Dupont drew a slow breath, though there was no break in the minute sounds of her tending the fledgling fire. "I think if you were not nervous, it would mean that you did not understand the magnitude of what you intend to do. But you must not mistake nerves for knowledge of what is to come."

"If I lose," Gwen whispered, "then I'm consigning her to a fate I can't prevent. *I'm* the one who lets her down. Who feeds her to the dragon." She dropped her head, gazing down at the marble floor as it flickered and glowed with reflected firelight. "And even if I win, at best I'm only postponing her fate. Maybe she should just run, get out of this castle, out of this county—maybe by offering her this hope, I'm putting her in harm's way. Even if I win, I can't save her."

"You can save her from *this* marriage, *this* moment," Dupont replied. "It is not for you to save her from all things that may come—that isn't what she has asked you to do."

"But it's what I *want* to do," Gwen burst out, dropping her hands to the floor to keep from losing her balance. Her gaze lifted to rest on the massive dragonslaying spear hung over the fireplace, wishing for something so simple as a monster to fight. She bit her lip against the rest of what she desperately wished to say, certain that Madame Dupont, of all people, would chastise her for letting her heart become tangled up in her mission.

But Madame Dupont only smiled a quick, dry smile, and shifted her gaze from the fire to Gwen. "If you lose tomorrow, will you care for her any less than you do now?"

Gwen blinked at her. "Of course not."

"Then why do you assume her feelings will change?"

Gwen could feel the heat of the fire building as it spread to the logs Dupont was painstakingly stacking atop the blaze. "I . . . I don't know."

The silence spread, punctuated by the little cracks and hisses and pops of the fire, creating an expectant space that pulled at Gwen's need to speak far more skillfully than any interrogator could have done.

Finally, unbuckling her sword belt and tossing it aside, Gwen sat down and braced herself, palms flat against the stone floor. She kept her eyes on the reflection of the fire in the marble. "I . . . I'm not so sure losing is what I'm afraid of."

"Hmm." Dupont's voice lacked even the tiniest hint of surprise. "Go on."

Gwen swallowed, the slight sound nearly drowned out by the crackling fire. "What happens if I *don't* lose?" she whispered, finally raising her gaze to look at Madame Dupont, watching the image of her waver slightly as moisture stung her eyes. "If I prove I *am* just as good as any of them, as good as *all* of them . . . if I win, how do I go back to my old, obedient little life when it's over? How do I close this door again and go back to being who I was?"

The words crystallized in the air, surfacing a far deeper fear, one Gwen had not dared even to name.

Madame Dupont turned her head, looking away from the fire and inspecting Gwen's features in the flickering light. Then she shifted her weight, easing down to sit cross-legged, gazing at the fire. "I shall tell you a story, Gwen. I was older than you, twenty-three years of age, and I was . . . well. You are not the first to ask whether a woman could hold a sword."

Gwen felt herself moving, shifting to match Dupont's body language. Even Isobelle didn't know much about Dupont's life before she came to the castle as a dancing instructor.

"How I practiced," Dupont murmured. "Day and night, ignoring everything else. When the tournament came and I presented myself, as I am, as a woman, I was ready to fight them all. But they did not arrest me, or forbid me to fight, or tell me a woman may not enter. They did something far worse." The older woman shifted her gaze from the fire and met Gwen's eyes. In them Gwen could see a decades-old pain, as fresh and sharp as it must have been the day the wound was inflicted. "They laughed at me."

Gwen felt a pain jolt her hands—she'd curled them into fists so tight her fingernails were digging into her palms. Somewhere within her flickered that same fury that had swept through her the day she defeated Sir Evonwald and earned her way past the qualifiers, the day she'd overheard the knights talking about Isobelle like she was nothing more than a thing they could own and use as they wished. "Did they stop laughing when they saw what you could do?"

"They never did." Dupont's words came quick and hard, like blows. "I ran. I let them take my defiance and my joy and replace it with shame, and when I ran away in the night, that shame is the only thing I took with me."

Gwen could feel her eyes burning. A day ago, she would have driven her sword through her own foot rather than let Madame Dupont see tears in her eyes. But now, the moisture wetting her lashes and turning the firelight into a glittering kaleidoscope was all she had to offer in exchange for this story Dupont was giving her. A part of her refused to imagine the invincible woman she'd come to know since arriving at the castle as a broken-hearted girl, running away in the dark of night.

Another, deeper part of her could feel the truth of the tale. Could see how someone could have emerged from that crucible as some harder, stronger substance.

"That was when I made my way here," Madame Dupont went on, glancing out at the moonlit shadows beyond the ring of firelight where they sat together. "I work here to strengthen the wills and spines of these young women—not necessarily to carry a sword, but to hold up under the blows and cuts the world wishes to inflict upon them."

Her eyes swung back again to meet Gwen's. "But I still carry that shame they gave me, because once you accept a thing as yours, it is difficult to cast off again. It is hard, once you have opened a door, to close it once more."

Gwen found herself gulping for a breath, fighting to get the air past the tight knots in her chest. "You're saying that I have to fight," she whispered. "That it is already too late to turn back—whether I run or fight, I will be opening a door and inviting something in."

Dupont nodded, and then took one of Gwen's hands in her own. The gesture was so startling that Gwen looked down, staring at the woman's strong, callused fingers, the back of her hand marked with the same black-on-brown freckles that dotted her cheeks. Her skin was dry and warm, her grip tight.

"Go on," Dupont said. "Say the words again."

"I have to fight." Gwen's vision swam with tears, and she felt one spill down onto her cheek. She could feel that fury in her belly shifting, changing, like lead being transmuted by an alchemist into something far stronger and far more precious than mere gold. "I *want* to fight."

She blinked away her tears and refocused, meeting Dupont's gaze, finding in it a glimpse of that same alloy of anger and pain and courage and love and the *wanting* of something more. The hand gripping hers squeezed.

"Whatever happens," said Madame Dupont, "you will know that you chose to fight. You will know that Isobelle is watching, and that so am I. Even if by no one else but us, you will be seen. You will remember who you are."

Chapter Twenty-Nine

DO YOU YIELD?

Isobelle woke early after a restless night, pulling a robe around herself and padding out to the main room. She didn't know what she was going to do—knock on Gwen's door? To say what?

But Gwen wasn't there.

Instead, she found Gwen's bedroom door open, her bed neatly made, not even an echo of her presence. Her mouth dry, she stood there frozen, wondering if Gwen had simply left her quarters already, or if Gwen had . . . *left*.

At a soft noise behind her, she whirled, only to find Olivia in one of the armchairs, calmly mending the gray dress Isobelle had borrowed from Gwen in the village. Somehow the blackberry stains were gone, and her maid was on to the rips and tears the thorns had left.

"She went to start getting ready," Olivia said, answering the unspoken question. "There's a while yet before it's time to go watch her ride. Come over here, and you can get started on this mess you've made of the hem."

By midmorning, Isobelle had helped Olivia mend both the ruined dresses, stress-cleaned the living room, heartlessly culled her wardrobe—the perfect time to get rid of dresses you'd been hanging on to was when nothing seemed to matter—and choked down a croissant that only made her think of Gwen. What *had* that girl done to her? Isobelle couldn't even enjoy a good stress-eat anymore.

Her stomach churned, tying itself in knots as Olivia laced her into her dress and smoothed down the folds of rich emerald-green fabric with gentle hands. Isobelle bowed her head so her maid could tuck sprigs of lavender in around her temples and across the crown of her head. It felt as though she were about to walk to the gallows, and all she had left was her dignity.

Then came a knock at the door, and her heart leapt, a flood of . . . of *something* running through her, sending a thrill of anticipation through her limbs. She pulled away from Olivia and, fingers fumbling to finish tying the ribbon at her bodice herself, she hurried—*ran*, if she was being entirely honest—to fling open the door.

Orson was waiting on the other side, blinking in surprise at the drama of her greeting. "Good morning," he ventured. "That's a nice dress."

"I . . . oh." Isobelle felt numb, wishing she could simply ask him to leave, but she couldn't remember how to do it nicely. "Come in."

With an expression that said he wanted to ask who she'd been expecting, he followed her inside and took a seat. Olivia poured them each a cup of tea and then disappeared into Isobelle's room to make the bed, or—more likely—listen at the door.

"I wanted to see how you're feeling, with the tourney proper kicking off," Orson said, watching Olivia go. "You've got a brave face on, but I know you better than that."

And he did, the dear thing. Orson had been there since Isobelle was small, like a friendly piece of furniture. She'd seen him cry when he'd fallen off his first pony, a beast of a creature called Snowflake, who had frequently tried to bite him. He'd been there during the awkward phase when she'd tried to dye her hair the deep red of a traveling actress she'd admired.

Isobelle studied his profile. He was classically handsome: square jaw, blond hair that tousled nicely, even a fetching scar on his eyebrow—though it was less roguish when you knew it had come courtesy of an evil-minded pony.

He should have been enough. She wished he were.

"I'm all right," she said when she realized he was still waiting for a reply. "Just . . . for the first time in my life, I'm finding it hard to have to *watch* as things unfold."

"I'll do my best," he said. "You know that."

"Of course," she murmured, her eyes on her skirts as she sat and smoothed them out around her. The note in her voice was all wrong, too dull, and she knew he'd heard it.

"I know I'm not what you dreamed of," he said, giving her the most uncomfortable feeling he'd read her mind.

"Any girl would be lucky to have you," she said firmly.

"But you wanted a love story," he returned, his smile gentle, remembering conversations long past in their childhood.

Isobelle looked down at the cup of tea in her hands. She couldn't remember having picked it up. "That was a silly thing to want," she whispered.

"I think we could be happy," he ventured. "If I won. I don't . . . desire you, as the others do. That's not a part of me. But there are worse things than a marriage of friends, don't you think? Once we'd got it over with, had an heir and a spare, well. Your dowry would make us comfortable. And you'd have my respect, and my friendship, and a great deal more freedom than most women."

Isobelle's chest felt tight, and she couldn't find the words to reply. Or rather, the words she couldn't speak tried to force their way up her throat, past her lips. It was a better option than any of the others she was facing, and a better offer than most women in her position could hope to find.

But how could I want such a gray and cloudy day of a life now I've seen a rainbow?

The silence went on too long, and Orson's eyebrows drew in. "I shouldn't speak so plainly," he murmured.

"No, no," Isobelle replied, glancing up at his honest face with a pang. He was her friend. In his own way, he must dread a marriage too, and she must seem like his best option as well. She searched for the right lie, and when she found it, she let it spill out. "It's just too soon to think about it. I can't let myself want anything. Not yet."

"I understand," he said. "Will you be watching today?"

"Yes," she managed, the numb dread surging back in. "My friend's brother is riding. Sir Gawain." She tried to speak the name without any emphasis, but she saw Orson's gaze sharpen on her curiously.

"Right, against Sir Ralph." He winced. "Well, at least it will probably be over quickly enough. Let us hope so, at any rate. The early rounds in particular, with the less experienced chaps, can be brutal."

Isobelle started, unable to conceal the pang that ran through her. "Brutal?" she echoed.

Orson's brow furrowed. "Well . . . yes. More knights are maimed or killed in the opening rounds than any other time."

An involuntary tremor went through Isobelle, and her cup fell from her lifeless fingers—she sprang to her feet to keep it from soaking her skirts.

Orson pushed his chair back, brushing a couple of stray drops from his shin. "All right, Izzie?"

But now, she truly couldn't speak. The early rounds could be *brutal.*

She had been sitting here worrying about her marriage, when she should have been worrying about Gwen's *life.*

"Will you look out for him?" she heard herself say. "For Gawain? If you get a chance? I'd—I'd hate to see his sister upset."

"Of course," Orson said slowly, his keen eyes thoughtful and curious. He looked at her, head tilting slightly, and his lips parted to speak—and then the door to Isobelle's suite banged open to admit the girls, Sylvie stalking in, Jane and Hilde in her wake.

Orson rose to his feet, bowing politely. "Good day, ladies. Isobelle . . . I'll do as you asked." And then, in the face of four female stares, he took his leave.

"What did Awesome want?" Sylvie asked, walking over to inspect the remaining croissants.

"Seeing if I needed company for the tourney," Isobelle replied, her voice sounding strange to her own ears. "I should have asked him if he knew any hedge witches who could curse Sir Ralph."

"There's still time," Sylvie replied. "Where's Céline?"

"Gone to wish her brother good luck."

"I do hope she's not avoiding us," Jane said, brow creasing as she walked over to carefully pick up the broken pieces of Isobelle's teacup, setting them on the tray. "I was sorry she missed Lord Whimsitt's feast last night."

"And we lost both of you at the bonfire the night before," Sylvie pointed out, her eyes narrowing a touch, every bit as thoughtful and penetrating as Orson's. "I came by here to look for you, but you were nowhere to be found."

"Are you all right?" Hilde asked, marching up to inspect Isobelle, then reaching out to carefully pinch her cheeks and bring some color to them.

"I'm fine," Isobelle managed, which was so great a lie it nearly lodged in her throat—but one which at least spared her from answering Sylvie's question. "It's just . . . very real now. No more games. Now they're playing to win."

And whoever won would have Isobelle as his prize. No matter who it was—even Orson—she found she couldn't bear the thought.

"Chin up, shoulders back," said Jane, reaching out to give her arm a squeeze. "We'll go out and face it together."

They fell in behind her as she made her way through the castle. As though the whole place knew something had changed, people gave way to her, stepping aside like figures in a dream.

Or a nightmare.

A ripple went through the crowd as Isobelle and her companions appeared in her viewing box, and she took her place with Sylvie on one side and Jane on the other, Hilde firmly closing the door behind them and setting down the plate of cakes she'd somehow acquired on the way.

There was no opportunity for reverie out here—though Isobelle was holding on to her skirts with a white-knuckled grip, all around them were laughs and shouts, bodies crammed in on the benches to watch the tournament favorite kick off the proceedings. There were merchants selling snacks and toy dragons, bookmakers trying in vain to interest anyone in betting against Sir Ralph, and the cheerleaders were out in front of the grandstands, waving their streamers and urging the crowd to louder cheers.

Below her and to the right, Isobelle spotted Madame Dupont. The woman's head lifted, as if sensing eyes on her, then tilted so she could meet Isobelle's gaze. She allowed herself the tiniest of nods—the most acknowledgment they could share under such public scrutiny—and then Dupont was looking away again. But even from here, Isobelle could see the tension in her shoulders.

"Is Lord Whimsitt coming?" Jane asked, startling Isobelle. Jane accepted a small cake from Hilde with a pleased sound.

"Too hungover this morning," Sylvie predicted. "He'll probably show up for the afternoon rounds."

Isobelle could barely hear them. The wild urge had seized her to gather up her skirts and vault over the front of his lordship's box, to run straight across the grounds to the little tent on the far side, where Gwen must be getting ready. To grab her, to let her words come pouring out, to stop time until she'd told Gwen . . .

. . . *told her what?*

Isobelle could admit to herself that she'd never really thought about how this would end. She'd never yet met a situation that wouldn't bend to her sheer force of personality, and so she'd tripped into this like it was some sort of lark. A game they could play and win.

And now Gwen would pay the price.

Gwen, who had held her hand as they walked through the dark. Who had looked at her with those green, oak-touched eyes. Gwen, who wanted to kiss her, but was willing to wait as long as Isobelle needed, for the earth-shattering reverberations to settle from the realization that *she wanted to kiss Gwen back.*

Gwen, who had come to the castle, pretended to be someone else, run the gauntlet of her friends, and risked imprisonment or worse, all for Isobelle.

Gwen, who now had to ride out and face Sir Ralph alone.

The opening rounds can be brutal.

The herald was finishing announcing Sir Ralph's pedigree in ringing tones. He shuffled his papers to squint at Gawain's, then once more raised the metal cone amplifying his voice. "And our challenger!" he cried. "Sir Gawain of Toussaint! Sir Gawain, son of Armand, son of André, son of Guillaume of Toussaint!"

The two knights were emerging from their tents, taking the reins of their horses from the attendants. Isobelle's gaze was locked on Gwen's form as she swung up into the saddle. It was only when Sylvie shoved a sharp elbow into Isobelle's side that she realized the other girls were applauding enthusiastically, and remembered to make herself clap.

"I know Céline likes to maintain some mystery, but is she really not going to watch her brother fight?" Sylvie asked, raising her voice above the cheering.

Jane snorted. "Against Sir Ralph? I wouldn't want to see my brother get destroyed, either."

"Hush," said Hilde, squeezing in beside Jane. "There are leeches and surgeons at the edge of the field, all will be well. And I'm sure there's a hedge witch in the stands if we need someone really useful."

"What I wouldn't give for him to knock Sir Ralph clean out of that saddle." Jane sighed, then broke off as Hilde elbowed her.

Achilles was prancing as the two knights rode up to Isobelle's box, trying to dance sideways as Gwen gripped the reins to keep him in line. At least someone was having a good time.

Isobelle rose to her feet, keeping her back ramrod straight and her chin lifted.

The world around her seemed to fade away as the two knights came to a halt and bowed in their saddles, the cheering muffled, the colors of the grandstands and the lists muted.

If only she could see Gwen behind that visor. If only . . .

"Sir Knight!" Both heads snapped up, and Isobelle realized she'd spoken. "Sir Gawain," she managed, her voice firming as she knew what she had to do.

She would *not* let Gwen ride out to face Sir Ralph alone.

Gwen went still on Achilles's back, the bay sidestepping uncertainly. Then her helmet turned slightly to look across at Sir Ralph—but the favorite sat just as still as Gawain, save that his horse was even more restive, responding to the tension in his rider's body.

Gwen pressed her heels into Achilles's sides, and they walked forward a few steps to halt in front of the stands. "Uh . . ." She was keeping her voice low, but that didn't stop everyone around them from leaning in to hear. "Yes, Lady?"

"A little closer, please," Isobelle called, before lowering her voice and addressing her friends. "Girls, if you let me fall over the railing, I shall start rumors even more horrifying about you to divert the attention."

Three pairs of hands gripped her around the waist and the skirts, as she leaned down, fishing in her bodice for her crumpled—but clean—handkerchief. She shook the wrinkles free as Gwen eased Achilles around to stand side-on, so she could reach up with one armored fist to grip the barrier. Only the smallest tilt of her head conveyed a hint of *What the hell are you doing, Isobelle?*

And Isobelle so badly wanted to reply. To say, *Run away, be safe* and *I'm sorry I dragged you into this* and *I'm so afraid this will be brutal, and I would rather marry Sir Ralph himself than let harm come to you.*

But she couldn't say any of that, because Gwen would never turn tail and run, and putting doubt in her mind would only make the danger even greater.

"A favor," Isobelle said instead, and though only her companions could hear, everyone in the stands could see what she was doing. "For you have mine, Sir Knight." Then, lowering her voice to a whisper, her eyes on Gwen's visor: "Today, you are a knight. And today, you are *my* knight."

Gwen was still as a statue—Isobelle thought she wasn't even breathing, visored helmet tilted up to look at her. Then she curled her fingers around the handkerchief and tucked it behind the breastplate of her armor, pushing it through the small gap until it was safely in place over her heart.

Her champion raised her head, and Isobelle saw the faintest glimmer of her eyes behind the visor. Then Gwen lifted one armored hand, turning it so that the gloved fingertips beneath the hard metal mail were what touched Isobelle's palm.

"Yours, my lady," came Gwen's voice, soft and fervent.

And so they remained as murmurs raced along the grandstand, the story of what had happened traveling as fast as words could carry it.

Then one of the girls kicked Isobelle on the ankle to break the tableau, and she startled, and Gwen wheeled her horse away, riding for the far end of the lists.

Sir Ralph remained in place, the protruding jaw of his helmet swinging from where Isobelle stood in the stands, lavender tucked in her hair, to the receding forms of Gwen and Achilles and back again. Finally he too turned away, stiff in his saddle as he trotted toward his starting point.

"That was truly stupid," Sylvie whispered as Isobelle eased back down into her seat. "What are you going to do ten minutes from now, when Sir Ralph is still in the hunt and Sir Gawain is a heap of scrap metal on the ground?"

Hilde sighed. "I think it was romantic."

"And I think . . ." Jane's whisper cracked as she took in Isobelle's white face. "Oh, Isobelle. You care for him." She took hold of Isobelle's hand, her own warm against Isobelle's freezing cold fingers. "And we've been teasing you. Do you love him? I'm sorry. We're here. We'll stay by your side."

Isobelle, for once, said nothing at all.

The two knights took up their places at either end of the lists. Isobelle could feel the pulse at her temples, could feel how shallow her breath was. A hush fell over the crowd, and all Isobelle could hear was the ringing in her own ears.

And then the flags fell, and the two horses started forward, shifting to a rolling trot and finally to a gallop. The knights rose from their saddles, and Isobelle's heart thundered in time with the pounding of their hooves on the dusty ground.

Jane cried out as they reached each other, and Isobelle was distantly aware she was squeezing her friend's hand, and then the lances were shattering as they crashed against the shields, splinters exploding in every direction.

Gwen went flying.

Isobelle shot to her feet, tracking her path as she arced through the air in Achilles's wake, then crashed to the ground with a deafening clatter, landing flat on her back with her arms outflung.

The crowd were on their feet, roaring, and the cheerleaders were waving their streamers, and the stands were breaking into chaos all around Isobelle.

And she was on her feet too, whispering the words like a prayer, every muscle of her body locked in place. "Get up. Get up. *Move*. Get up."

And then, after a handful of heartbeats and a lifetime had passed, Gwen began to move. She rolled over onto her side, and for a heart-stopping moment she grabbed at her head, as though she'd forgotten where she was and was going to pull her helmet off.

"He's not moving," Jane gasped, grabbing at Isobelle's arm.

"What?" She tried in vain to shake her friend off, eyes locked on Gwen, who had managed to get to her hands and knees, clearly winded, and was contemplating the long journey to standing upright once more.

"Is he dead?" Sylvie asked, a sharp note entering her voice—that was what got Isobelle's attention. She blinked and tore her gaze away from Gwen to see what her friends were looking at.

It was Sir Ralph. He lay motionless in the dust, where he had fallen, too.

All four girls stood in a perfect tableau, staring down at the field below in frozen amazement as Gwen staggered to her feet and braced her hands against her knees.

And then she drew her sword.

With slow, painful steps, she made her way to her opponent, coming to a swaying halt above him, the tip of the blade at his throat. The grandstands were perfectly quiet, and the hoarse rasp of her voice was audible when she spoke.

"Do you yield?"

Sir Ralph didn't move.

"Do you *yield?*" Gwen shouted, taking an unsteady step back, but keeping her feet.

A doctor broke from his place on the sidelines, scurrying in and dropping to one knee beside Sir Ralph to raise his visor and peer at his face. He sliced his hand through the air, giving the signal for a knockout, then leaned over the knight to slam his palm against the dusty ground.

The crowd went *wild*.

Hilde threw her arms up in the air, screaming. "He did it! He did it! Gawain of Toussaint!"

"Boom!" shouted Jane, performing a dance of her own invention, whirling in a circle and shaking her hips. "And that was just with a handkerchief! Wait until you see what magic my girl can work with a scarf!"

"Well," said Sylvie, who was clapping slowly, "this is going to make things *very* interesting."

Isobelle couldn't stop staring. Sir Ralph was being loaded onto a stretcher, so heavy in his armor that the attendants had to pick up one end and drag him along like a cart with no wheels toward the waiting medical team.

Gwen had won.

Gwen had *won.*

"Isobelle, what are you—" Sylvie's voice rang out behind her, but the rest of her words were lost to the roar of the crowd.

Isobelle had shoved open the gate to their viewing box and was elbowing her way through the crowd outside. Isobelle was *running*.

Chapter Thirty

THIS GOES A LOT MORE SMOOTHLY IN THE BALLADS

Gwen's head was ringing so badly she could barely see, her dizzy gaze swinging from the doubled vision of her opponent being dragged away in a stretcher, to the box where Isobelle was watching. She could only see a blurry haze of color there, all the girls blending together.

There was a roaring in her ears—sick and confused, she had the electrifying realization that she might be about to pass out. If she did, the physicians would examine her. And the second they removed her helmet...

Gwen clenched her fist around her sword, firming her feet against the ground and sucking in a deep, bracing breath, willing herself to stand firm.

Then she realized... the roaring in her ears was not the rush of imminent unconsciousness. It was the crowd. They were cheering, screaming, undulating all around her like a single living thing.

Cheering... for *her*.

Gwen staggered one step back, turning in a slow half circle—then thrust her sword skyward, her blood singing.

The crowd went *insane*.

Dimly, she could hear her own name—or a version of it, the masculine version of it—being chanted, rising over the more indistinct roar of applause and cheers.

Ralph was gone, eliminated from the tournament. He had no claim over Isobelle, not anymore. Elated, her heart pounding, Gwen swung her gaze over toward Isobelle's box.

She was gone.

Instantly, her elation drained. She let her sword fall, searching again for Isobelle's green-clad form among her friends. But she could see the others clearly now: Sylvie watching with an air of stony confusion, Jane cheering wildly, Hilde with her hands clasped, leaning out over the rim of the box to get a better look at the knight who had taken the crowd by storm.

Isobelle wasn't there.

Slowly, mechanically, Gwen raised her arm to slide her sword back into her sheath—and nearly dropped to her knees as a sickening jolt ran up her arm.

Now that her initial explosion of shock and elation was fading, the pain was starting to creep in.

No, not creep in . . . surge at her, sweep over her, as unstoppable and overwhelming as a force of nature.

Oh, holy hells . . . Gwen thought, turning to look at the far end of the lists and her tent beyond. The exit seemed to draw farther and farther away from her even as she watched. How was she ever going to walk that far?

She felt Achilles nuzzle gently at her elbow, and she grabbed for his reins with one hand and at his saddle with the other. She hoped, as she began to make her way back to the tents, that it looked like she was only maintaining control over an excitable and restive horse . . . and not like she was clinging to him for dear life.

By the time she reached her tent, leaving behind her the still-roaring crowd, she'd managed to get on top of her pain, cataloging the worst of her injuries. She'd certainly hit her head when she landed, and probably had a minor concussion. Her back was bruised in a few places, and the shoulder of the arm that had held her lance was burning something fierce, making her wonder if she had broken a rib or two when she struck Sir Ralph. Her knee stung with each step, something she must've done while trying to stagger back to her feet under the weight of her armor. Her ears were ringing, and her whole body was still shaking in the aftermath of the adrenaline.

She felt bloody amazing.

She left Achilles tethered outside with a whisper of gratitude and limped into her tent. It contained a rough-hewn table, the stand on which her armor had rested, and a bag in which she'd hidden her dress. She staggered to the table and planted both hands upon it, panting for breath, too overwhelmed to even contemplate the long and arduous process of removing her armor.

She'd *won*.

Had Isobelle seen? Had Madame Dupont? The older woman's words were echoing in her ears: *You will remember who you are.*

Despite the pain, despite the dizziness sweeping through her in waves . . . she could feel it. That change. Like stepping into a familiar house or pulling on a favorite cloak or blanket. Certainty tingled through her body, telling her over and over that she was exactly where she was meant to be, exactly *who* she was meant to be.

A rustle of fabric and a faint, exhaled epithet toward the back of the tent made Gwen twist abruptly, then let out a hiss as the movement sent pain shooting down from her shoulder and ribs. Someone had pulled up a couple of tent pegs and was pushing at the fabric of the wall itself. Then the back of the tent lifted enough to admit a slight emerald-clad form that popped into the space.

Isobelle looked up, her cheeks flushed, her breathing harsh—she'd been running. Her eyes were shining.

Her eyes...

Gwen's breath caught, all her newfound certainty crystalizing into one single, ringing truth as she gazed at the other girl. Hands shaking, she reached up, fumbling with her helmet.

"Help me, will you?" Gwen managed hoarsely, a breathless sound of laughter and frustration escaping her.

Isobelle sprang forward, her hands nearly as clumsy as Gwen's—finally, they managed to get the thing off, and Isobelle tossed it aside to land on the grass with a thump without taking her eyes from Gwen's face.

They stood that way, both gazes searching, both panting for breath. Isobelle was leaning against her, one of her hands curled around the top edge of Gwen's armor, keeping hold of her. Gwen bit her lip, feeling blood rush to the spot; she saw Isobelle's gaze flick down, dwell on her mouth, flick back up again.

There was a question in those blue, blue eyes—or, perhaps, the answer to a question.

Isobelle's grip on her armor tightened, pulling Gwen down, or levering herself up, and she tilted her face to Gwen's.

Isobelle's lips were soft and tentative, but Gwen found herself paralyzed. She was so used to holding back around Isobelle that her dizzy mind could barely understand what was happening, how to let go again. She was holding her breath, afraid to move, to wake up from this dream—then Isobelle's lips moved on hers, caressing, parting slightly.

Gwen gasped for breath with an audible half-swallowed sound and leaned into the kiss, her own mouth parting, falling into Isobelle like some poor, foolish creature walking into a faerie spell. Isobelle raised her other hand and cupped Gwen's cheek, her fingers warm and possessive on her skin.

Gwen stepped into her, or tried to, realizing with a jolt that she was still wearing her armor, a cold metal barrier between them. Isobelle, reading her mind, had begun to scrabble helplessly at the straps, her breathing coming in quick, sharp pants.

"This one," Gwen gasped, reaching for the buckle at her side, realizing she still had her gauntlets on, and then trying to remove them without any space between her and Isobelle.

By the time she had the cursed things off, Isobelle had gotten the buckle at her side free and was trying to pull the armor off over Gwen's head. Gwen, with a gasp of laughter and frustration, slid one arm through the chest piece—Isobelle, realizing she was tugging in the wrong direction, let go so Gwen could manage it and burst into breathless laughter.

"This," Isobelle giggled, panting, "goes a lot more smoothly in the ballads."

Gwen, gritting her teeth against the pain shooting through her shoulder, shrugged the chest piece off and let it fall to the ground beside them. "That's because the ballads draw a nice, socially acceptable veil across this portion of the story."

Isobelle was already back up against her, and Gwen slid her good arm around her waist—but then she paused, biting her lip, looking down at the flushed features, the reddened lips. She felt her own heart pounding in her chest as hard as it had when she faced down her opponent in the joust.

"Isobelle . . ." Gwen managed, but there she stopped, words failing her. There were so many things she wanted to say, and they all rushed her at once, leaving her breathlessly trying to separate one thought from another.

Isobelle's eyes had gone to her mouth when Gwen bit her lip, but now they slid back up again, meeting her gaze. "Don't change your mind now," she whispered, eyes flicking back and forth as she searched Gwen's. "I . . . I'm sorry it took me so long to make up my own."

Gwen curled her fingers against Isobelle's lower back, noticing with wonder the way Isobelle responded to that touch, leaning harder against her. "You have nothing to be sorry for," she managed, grateful to have one thread to follow through the knotted tangle of things she wanted to tell the girl in front of her. "I've always known who I liked, who I wanted, and . . . it's still scary for me."

The truth of that admission tightened her throat, making it impossible for her to say more.

Isobelle brushed her thumb along Gwen's cheekbone, her gaze understanding, for she knew about Gwen's past, had seen it at the village bonfire. Gwen lifted her other hand, now free of its metal gauntlet, and slid her fingers into Isobelle's hair. Isobelle drew in a quaking breath, her eyes darkening. Gwen could feel the tension building in Isobelle's body, a tiny shiver up her spine that ended in a soft, muffled sound of longing.

They broke their stillness together, at the same time, meeting for a kiss that held no uncertainty this time, only a silent agreement to set their fears aside for as long as they could make this moment last.

Chapter Thirty-One

DID THAT REALLY JUST HAPPEN?

None of Isobelle's practice had ever prepared her for how truly glorious proper kissing was.

A thrill zinged straight down her spine, and the whole world receded as she focused on Gwen. Outside were distant bangs and clatters and shouts, but the inside of this tent was their fortress, and nobody would dare breach its walls.

Her whole world was the soft touch of Gwen's lips, and the noise Gwen made when Isobelle curved a hand around the nape of her neck, finding the place where smooth skin met her silky hair. She ran her hand along Gwen's collarbone, fingertips curling around her shoulder—until Gwen gave a muffled yelp of pain, making Isobelle drop her hands and break away with a gasp.

She was opening her mouth to apologize—of course Gwen would be sore after getting knocked off her horse—when Gwen's arms went round her and pulled her back in, mumbling something about this being worth it. Isobelle abandoned her concerns . . . though she avoided Gwen's poor shoulder as best she could.

Everything that Isobelle cared for, she threw her whole self into. It was what made her unstoppable—the ability to choose something and run toward it at full tilt. And now, her hesitation gone, she was running as fast as she knew how toward *this*. This moment, this girl, this kiss.

When they finally drew apart long enough to breathe, Isobelle gave herself over to a foolish grin, her arms looped around the other girl's neck. "You did it," she whispered, needing to hear the words aloud to truly believe them. "He was out cold." She shouldn't delight in any sort of violence, she knew that. But truly, Sir Ralph had started it.

"I know," Gwen whispered, her own disbelief and joy spilling over, her eyes wide. "I don't even—but I *did*. Did that really just happen?"

"It really happened," Isobelle confirmed. "And now this is really happening." She laid a hand over Gwen's heart, marveling at the way it beat against her ribs. Watched Gwen match her giddy smile.

And then, because she could, and because she very much wanted to, she kissed her again.

It was at that moment that the tent flap whipped aside.

"Bro," Orson called cheerfully. "Just checking you're not stuck in your . . ." He slowed to a halt, staring open-mouthed at the two girls. ". . . armor," he finished weakly, letting the tent flap fall closed behind him.

Gwen was frozen in place, her muscles tensed, her arms locked around Isobelle.

Isobelle paused to reflect and concluded that the opportunity to leap hastily away from Gwen had passed—and that at any rate, she did not wish to do so.

"Hello, Orson," she offered, sounding almost like herself. "Ah. I see how this has happened. I asked you to keep an eye on—and here you are. So, as you may see—"

"I certainly do," he muttered, gaze swinging between them.

Gwen came back to life. "We weren't doing anything!" she

blurted. "And . . ." Looking down, she seemed to notice she was still wearing the bottom half of Sir Gawain's armor. She looked at it, looked at the girl in her arms, and sagged, letting go of Isobelle. "I don't think there's any way to walk this back, actually," she mumbled.

Isobelle wrapped an arm around Gwen's waist and watched her old friend, waiting to see which way he'd take this.

"This is just . . . I mean, there's a lot to unpack here," Orson said slowly. "This is . . ."

"It's a lot," Isobelle agreed soothingly.

"Is Gawain . . ." Bewildered, he turned to study Gwen. "You're a *girl?*" His voice rose in a way that suggested he very much knew the answer to his question but needed someone to say it out loud.

Gwen lifted her chin, meeting his eyes. "I am."

"Huh." He nodded slowly, then nodded again, and Isobelle wondered how many times he'd do it if he weren't interrupted.

"Orson," she said slowly. "We're—"

"You were kissing her," he said, just now catching up with this fact. Orson *never* interrupted her, but he didn't even register that she'd spoken.

"I—"

He whipped back to Gwen. "Where did you learn to joust?"

Gwen blinked at him. This was presumably not the follow-up question she'd anticipated. "Um," she said. "A little by watching. A little by practicing in the woods near my village. But mostly, I learned in the last couple of weeks."

"So—" Isobelle tried again.

"And she's got armor," Orson said to her plaintively. "Girls don't wear armor."

"Demonstrably not true," Isobelle countered.

"It's better than mine," he protested. "I've been thinking about the articulated joints since I saw him take on Sir Evonwald. Her, I mean. How did . . ." But his momentum, having carried him this far, ran out. His voice trailed away, and he rubbed at the back of his neck.

Gwen's gaze shifted carefully from Orson to Isobelle, and then back again. "I could make some for you," she said. And then, after a short pause, in exactly the same tone—as if she could overwrite what she'd just said: "I could have some made for you."

It wasn't a bribe—that wasn't Gwen's way—but it wasn't *not* a bribe.

Orson silently mouthed the words, but—though Isobelle suspected he wished with his whole heart that he could—he didn't quite manage to erase the first version of the sentence. "Izzie," he said plaintively. "Gawain is a girl. Who knows how to joust. And makes her own armor. And who was kissing you just now."

"All true," she conceded. "It's a *lot*, I see that. Orson, you and I have known each other a long time, and—"

Once more he cut her off, holding up one hand, palm out. "If you're about to invoke Lady Shelham's orchard, or the incident with Emma's scones, you stop right now. Covering for me when we were children does not even remotely begin to—" Finally mastering himself, he squared his shoulders.

Isobelle's heart—or possibly her stomach—did a jig of nervous anticipation. Now they'd see where he was going to come down on this.

"Why?" he asked Gwen, calm now. "Is it because of this"—and a wave of his hand took in the pair of them—"this . . . kissing? Or did you start out with the armor and the insane idea that you could get away with impersonating a man, and tack on Isobelle as a bonus later? Just out of interest."

"I have no interest in being a man," Gwen replied, her conciliatory tone going out the window. "What I want is to be a knight."

"And the rest of it?" he demanded, turning on Isobelle. "Don't tell me you had to kiss her to get her to protect you from Ralph, Isobelle. You've never needed to kiss anybody to get them to do what you want."

"The rest of it was a surprise," said Isobelle quietly, slipping her hand into Gwen's and squeezing hard.

Gwen let out a slow breath, already recovering her temper. "Sir Orson," she tried. "Please. If you care about Isobelle, please wait a few days before you turn me in. If you do it now, they'll let Sir Ralph back in for the next round of the tourney, and then . . ."

"And then," he agreed grimly, lifting one hand to pinch the bridge of his nose. "Look, I'm not going to tell anyone. You won the match fair and square. And Isobelle is my oldest friend. I couldn't—"

Isobelle threw herself at him, wrapping her arms around his neck—which took a bit of a run-up and a jump—and squeezing tighter than was good for him. "Thank you," she whispered fiercely, as he tried to unwrap her.

"Isobelle," he murmured, patting her back gently when the unwrapping failed. "This is improp . . ." He trailed away into helpless laughter.

"That ship has sailed," she agreed, though she let him go.

"And is far over the horizon, probably turned pirate and raiding the nearest village," he muttered. "But listen, both of you. You're going to get caught."

"Tomorrow, maybe," Isobelle said softly. "But today, Gwen just defeated Sir Ralph."

"That she did," he agreed vehemently. "And for that, Lady Knight, I salute you."

"Thank you, Orson," Gwen whispered.

But he simply shook his head and closed his eyes, as though he could unsee everything that had just happened. And then he turned away, pushing his way out through the tent flap and leaving them in silence.

Chapter Thirty-Two

DON'T TELL ME YOU'RE SCARED, SIR KNIGHT

By the time Gwen and Isobelle got back to their suite of rooms, Isobelle's friends were waiting for her. They swarmed Isobelle the moment she opened the door—even Sylvie seemed to have abandoned her suspicions of "Céline" in favor of spouting questions and speculations about the new sensation that was Sir Gawain.

Isobelle met Gwen's gaze over Hilde's shoulder, and an electrifying instant of wordless communication passed between them. Isobelle's eyes gave a flash of anguish—even she didn't want her friends right now—and then she was leading them toward her room, promising to tell them everything that had happened between her and Sir Gawain.

"What?" she was squealing—giving a good imitation of her usual mood—as they disappeared. "Of course he had his shirt on, they have to wear padding under all that armor!"

This left Gwen to slip quietly away, shutting the door to her own room with a sigh of relief. Her head was still spinning, though she could no longer tell how much was from being knocked off Achilles, and how much was from the utter shocking bliss of feeling Isobelle throw herself into her arms.

She carefully sank down onto the edge of the bed, and then lay down just as cautiously. She was beginning to figure out which movements hurt the most—anything that shifted her shoulder, or compressed her ribs, or curved her spine beyond a few degrees, or . . .

Yesterday, the catalog of injuries would have had her face down on the floor, despairing about her ability to get back up and do this again in four days, urging Isobelle to just run and try her luck at avoiding marriage in some other country.

But today, the adrenaline of victory was still fresh in her veins. She had actually won the unwinnable—beaten the tournament favorite, saved Isobelle from the worst of the fates awaiting her. All her fears and worries had been for nothing.

For the first time, Gwen could see the rest of the tournament opening up before her, the possibility of winning it all, of proving herself, of showing the world who she really was. After all, even Sir Awesome, the absolute epitome of what a knight should be and look like, had accepted her.

Sort of.

She decided not to tug at that particular thread. Isobelle was content with his word that he would not betray Sir Gawain's secret and expose Gwen. If he betrayed them both . . . well, that would be a problem for the future.

Because today, Gwen was a goddamn knight.

At some point, Gwen must have fallen asleep, the cheers of the crowd echoing in her ears, and the memory of Isobelle's lips on hers making her skin tingle—for the next thing she knew, her door was opening with a soft click.

She tried to jerk upright and got halfway there before pain knocked her flat again, a groan wrenching its way out of her. Every torn muscle and abused joint had stiffened while she slept, and now . . .

Oh, dear god.

Olivia's face came into view above her, the woman's expression as unreadable as ever. She peered down at Gwen, scanning her features and then raising an eyebrow. "Best let me tend to your injuries, Sir Gawain. Or else your first big win will be your last."

Gwen managed to roll onto the side opposite the sore ribs, get an elbow under her, and lever herself up into a sitting position. Olivia had a nondescript leather satchel with her, along with a basin of water.

"It's just bruises," Gwen said, starting to shrug and thinking better of it.

Olivia ignored this attempt to forestall her, setting the basin down on Gwen's bedside table and then gesturing to Gwen herself. "Strip," she commanded.

Gwen felt her cheeks reddening. "Really, I don't think—"

Olivia's eyes narrowed. "Do you truly want to fight me on this? As of today, you're undefeated. Do you want to ruin your record?"

Gwen swallowed and began pulling off her dress.

Once she was down to her undergarments, Olivia had her pull the back of her shift over her head and sit down. Gwen sat, clutching the fabric to her front, and let the other woman examine her. Olivia gave only a soft intake of breath, but from her the sound might as well have been a shout of dismay.

Gwen felt herself stiffen. "Is it that bad?"

Olivia ran expert fingers over Gwen's shoulder, then slid them down along the shoulder blade to the ribs. Gwen hissed, instinctively twitching away, muscles tightening in reaction.

Olivia let her hands fall away. "The shoulder's been partially dislocated. You're going to have to let me pop it back into place, and we're going to have to strap it up well next time you ride, and cross our fingers you can avoid getting hit. The ribs are bruised, but not broken, I think, and once your shoulder's right, they shouldn't hurt so much."

Gwen eyed the woman apprehensively. "Pop it back into place?" she echoed.

Olivia's eyes narrowed again, and this time, Gwen spied a hint of humor in them. "Don't tell me you're scared, Sir Knight."

Gwen rolled her eyes upward, gathered the fabric of the shift against her chest, and nodded at Olivia to get it over with. Olivia waited until there was a particularly loud round of laughter and exclamations from the suite of rooms beyond Gwen's door, braced her knee against Gwen's body, and *wrenched* at her arm.

Gwen had to sink her teeth into her lip until she tasted blood, but she managed to turn what would've been a shriek of pain into a low groan. She wasn't aware of passing out, but she did have to pause and breathe, waiting for the stars sparking in her eyes to fade. By the time she could properly see again, Olivia had pulled a number of things out of the satchel and spread them on the bed, and was dipping a linen cloth into the basin of water.

The cloth was icy cold on Gwen's skin, somehow far more shocking than the pain of popping her shoulder back into place.

"Don't be such a baby," Olivia commanded severely as Gwen tried to flinch away. "The cold will help with the swelling." She ran the cloth in a precise pattern around Gwen's shoulder joint and down her arm, rinsing and wringing it out every few seconds to keep the fabric cold.

Gwen was watching Olivia's arm move for quite a while before she realized her eyes had fixed on a faint, oddly shaped scar running down the edge of Olivia's forearm and curving a few inches above her wrist.

"How long have you been Isobelle's maid?" Gwen asked, keeping her voice light.

Olivia's eyes stayed on her task. "Three years, give or take."

"And before that? What did you do?"

Olivia's eyes flicked toward hers. There was nothing in them to hint at surprise, or even discomfort. She merely smiled a little, turned her gaze back to her task, and murmured, "Why, are you thinking of hiring me yourself?"

Gwen ground her teeth. Every conversation she'd ever had with Olivia went the same way. Anything that had happened since she came to be Isobelle's maid, she was perfectly willing to discuss. Anything prior to that... well, Olivia was as slippery as the last bit of soap on wash day.

"You must have had some experience working for a physician," Gwen said, trying another tactic. "To know how to do what you just did with my shoulder."

Olivia dropped the cloth into the basin, wrung it out, and slapped it back onto Gwen's skin.

Gwen chewed at her lip. "Was that when you worked with Archer? When you devised some system of communication involving that owl token you gave Isobelle to show him?" Olivia did not flinch so much as take hold of Gwen's shoulder and squeeze, sending a sharp stab of pain down her arm and causing Gwen to blurt, "Ow, son of a bitch!"

Olivia instantly released her and smoothed the palm of her hand across Gwen's shoulder. "Keep your attention where it's meant to be, Sir Gawain. I am a mystery for another time. Get Isobelle out of this mess, and then, if you are so desperate to find dragons to fight, you can keep searching for them in my past."

Gwen clenched her jaw, feeling oddly petulant, as she hadn't done since she was a child. "I was only asking," she muttered. Olivia's bedside manner left something to be desired. Gwen found herself missing her father quite fiercely all of a sudden—and then felt a deep, wrenching ache. She couldn't go visit him now, not with all these bruises and injuries. He'd see how stiffly she was moving and know something was up. Gwen swallowed, fending off the sadness that came with that realization.

Olivia tossed the wet cloth back into the basin and stooped to fetch a little glass tub from where she'd unpacked it on Gwen's bedspread. She pulled off the lid, which bore a word Gwen didn't recognize, or possibly a name: Kadija's.

The tub itself contained a vivid green ointment, the pungency of which made Gwen's eyes begin to water as Olivia crossed back over toward her.

"Oh, what the hell is that?" she asked, leaning away from Olivia and trying to breathe through her mouth. The strength of the herbal concoction was enough that even the back of her throat could smell green.

"Healing ointment. Imported from the land of the pharaohs. Good heavens, you're almost as squeamish as a real knight. Hold still." Olivia dipped her fingers into the ointment and began applying it all across Gwen's shoulder.

Gwen braced herself, but it seemed that Olivia did know what she was doing—the cool cloths had calmed the burning in her shoulder. She drew an experimental breath, keeping it shallow so as not to aggravate her ribs.

"So, if you won't tell me about Archer... will you tell me what you learned about the women who came to the dragon bonfire, who were arrested?"

"Isobelle should hear this, too. I think the others have left, to judge from the quiet out there." Olivia drew a deeper breath, and just as Gwen realized what she meant to do, she called, "Lady Isobelle? Will you join us?"

Gwen jerked and grasped at Olivia's arm, hissing at her to stop, but she was too late. She had the impression of grim amusement in Olivia's gaze before she heard Isobelle's footsteps sweeping toward her door. Gwen didn't want Isobelle seeing her half naked just now, but she *really* didn't want Isobelle seeing her covered in bruises.

Right now, Isobelle thought she was some invincible hero. Was it too much to ask for to let that pleasant fantasy linger a little while longer?

Chapter Thirty-Three

THEY'LL KILL ANYONE WHO TRIES TO UPSET THE ORDER OF THINGS

"Oh my!" Isobelle's eyes started watering as she opened the door, the unmistakable—and eternally objectionable—scent of the green ointment wafting toward her. "Oh dear, I see she's got at you with the Kadija's. Your skin will be green for a month, you know."

The last few words arrived under their own steam, her voice already beginning to fade out as the sight of Gwen sank in properly.

Gwen looked *dreadful*. It wasn't just the vivid smears of green against her skin—there were ugly red marks along her collarbone that would soon be black, lurking beneath the green of the ointment like rocks beneath the surface of a lake. And she was holding herself so carefully, sitting so rigidly, that it was clear even the smallest movement would be agony.

All Isobelle could do was stare, lips slightly parted, her breath stolen by shock.

But Gwen was avoiding her eyes, two spots of color bright on her cheeks, the blush overtaking the freckles Isobelle so loved to admire. Gwen didn't want Isobelle to look at her, and so, with a herculean effort, Isobelle tore her gaze away, fixing it on Olivia.

"You called?" she managed, sounding strangely singsong to herself.

"I found out what happened to the women from the village." Olivia began packing away her medical kit, her mouth pressed into a thin line. "I beg you each let me finish my sentence before you start shouting, because yes, we're going to do something about it."

Isobelle knew she had to focus. Knew this was serious. But suddenly she was seeing Gwen fly through the air again, the arc taking a lifetime on the way to the ground. But this time, she was imagining the fragile, precious body inside the armor. She was seeing the shock ripple through Gwen as she landed.

If she'd lost consciousness, the tournament physicians would have examined her and revealed her secret. If she had cried out in pain, and someone had heard her higher, more feminine voice... If anyone other than Orson had come into her tent afterward... And none of that was the worst that could have happened.

Gwen could have *died*.

"Isobelle?" Olivia's patient gaze was waiting for her.

"What? Oh yes. Yes." She made herself sink down onto the room's single chair, folding her hands carefully in her lap. "Go on."

"They're in jail," Olivia said, forging on over Gwen's noise of dismay. "The good news is that they'll be there until the tourney's done."

"That's *good* news?" Gwen demanded. "What could the bad news be?"

Isobelle could read the truth on Olivia's grim face, a numb feeling spreading through her body. "The bad news is that they're going to execute them. On what charge, Olivia?"

"Spreading false rumors that undermine the security of the kingdom," Olivia replied. "Treason."

"That's bull— Ohmygod!" Gwen tried to surge to her feet, then half screamed her curse, falling back down onto the bed.

"Sit still." Isobelle and Olivia spoke in unison, twin pictures of consternation.

"I told you," Olivia continued, "we'll do something about it."

"Do you have a plan yet?" Isobelle asked, making her voice calm.

Olivia shot her a look. "I'm only an hour into this news," she replied. "And a cell is a cell—thick walls, iron bars. Not easy. But we've got time. Hanging half a dozen women during the tourney would spoil the festive mood. So we're going to pause, think, and then proceed *carefully*."

"They must be terrified," Gwen whispered.

"We'll get them out, Gwen," Isobelle promised, and now, finally, Gwen did meet her eyes, the oak-tinted moss that Isobelle loved so much brimming with fear, with worry. "I can't believe they'd kill them over a warning."

Olivia sighed and allowed herself one slow shake of her head. "They'll kill anyone who tries to upset the order of things."

Her words fell into a hole that was forming deep inside Isobelle.

Gwen was muttering curses, still clutching her shift against herself, holding her body so gingerly that she managed to vibrate with fury without moving a muscle.

But Isobelle was hearing those words again and again.

They'll kill anyone who tries to upset the order of things.

Gwen could die if she came off Achilles the wrong way. Gwen could be impaled by a lance, or break her neck, or get knocked out, never to wake again.

But if she survived all that, and they found out who she was— *what* she was . . .

They'll kill anyone who tries to upset the order of things.

Isobelle's own chest felt tight, as if it were her ribs that were compressed, as she met Olivia's eyes. The knowledge was there waiting for her—this was what her maid had wanted her to understand.

Just as Gwen had truly become a knight, Isobelle was realizing that she'd led this girl she cared for into terrible danger.

And in four days, she would face it all over again.

Chapter Thirty-Four

A GIRL WHO KNOWS EXACTLY WHO SHE IS

Gwen opened her door a crack, then eased it a crack wider. Her eyes fell on Isobelle's door, across the large sitting room at the center of her suite. She'd not seen much of the other girl for the last four days, and to Gwen's dismay, that lack ached worse than her healing bruises.

"Stop fidgeting," Olivia commanded, tightening the strips of cloth she was binding around Gwen's shoulder. "Unless you want your arm to fall off for real this time."

Gwen abandoned her efforts to catch a glimpse of Isobelle and obediently held still. She ought to let Olivia's warning guide her thoughts back to the present, and the next joust. But every time she tried—today's opponent was named Sir Makarios, a heavyset man from the Mediterranean coast—she just thought of Isobelle's face, stricken with horror as she saw the extent of Gwen's injuries.

Gwen could walk from her door to Isobelle's in a few long strides. And yet she'd seen so little of her. How was that possible, unless Isobelle was avoiding her? She gritted her teeth as Olivia wound another strip around her shoulder, and resolutely turned her eyes away from the door.

That wasn't entirely fair. She'd *seen* Isobelle, sat with her, laughed with her, chatted amiably... but only with the other girls around. Gwen had come to enjoy Hilde's cheeriness and Jane's sly jokes, and even to understand why the others appreciated Sylvie's needle-sharp wit. But now . . . now she would quite happily have dropped them off the balcony to get a moment alone with Isobelle. Instead, Gwen had to sit there demurely sipping her tea—*actual* tea, this time—while Isobelle and her friends gossiped and giggled about the charming, handsome, alluring mystery that was Sir Gawain.

And as much as Gwen thrilled at the sidelong looks and occasional sly winks from Isobelle when she'd wax eloquent about Gawain's charms, a part of her chafed at the secrecy. Her friends were all so delighted to see Isobelle crushing on someone—evidently it was a rare enough thing, limited to traveling poets and famous knights.

Just never, apparently, a girl. Maybe Isobelle had simply been carried away by the romance of the tournament, of being rescued by a literal knight in shining armor. Maybe she was rethinking what she'd chosen, the leap she'd made. Maybe . . .

The only time she stopped thinking about Isobelle every ten seconds was during her training sessions with Dupont. They'd been focusing on stretching and protecting her shoulder, while learning to dodge. And then there was an awkward afternoon with Sir Orson, where he swung wildly between the easy camaraderie he would've offered another knight, and the confused distant courtesy he would've offered a lady. And an interminable feast at Lord Whimsitt's table, offering Gwen one of her first good looks at Isobelle's guardian, after which she was forced to agree with Isobelle's eyerolls regarding him. And more training, and more tea, and dodging questions as Céline about her brother, and . . . and . . . and . . .

"Ow, easy!" Gwen flinched away as Olivia yanked the strap tight.

Olivia flashed her a look of satisfaction. "That's what you get when you daydream," she said sharply. "Keep your focus here, Sir Gawain."

When Olivia had finished strapping her shoulder, Gwen carefully dressed herself in Céline's clothes and slipped out while Isobelle and the girls bustled about in the room off the lounge area that served as Isobelle's closet—though it was large enough to have fit the village smithy inside. She felt Isobelle's eyes on her, begging her to look up, but Gwen hurried through the door.

She was halfway down the spiral stone stairs when she heard a rush of footsteps, and she turned in time to catch the flurry of blond hair and magenta skirts that came flying at her.

Gwen staggered, but tightened her arms as she felt Isobelle's go round her neck.

"You were going down without me?" Isobelle gasped, coming to rest a step above Gwen, and looking down now instead of looking up a couple inches, as she usually did. "The absolute nerve!"

Gwen tried to cling to some form of dismay at being caught, but it was impossible to lie to herself when Isobelle was gazing at her with those ridiculously blue eyes. "I . . . I should have done a better job sneaking. But . . . I'm glad you came after me. I think I wanted you to come after me," she admitted in a quieter voice.

Isobelle's eyes lowered. "I should have come sooner. I just didn't know what to say, or how to . . ." She swallowed audibly, an uncharacteristic tension tightening her features. "Gwen . . . are you sure this is a good idea?"

Gwen felt a sickening jolt of dismay clench inside her, silencing her. Perhaps that first kiss had just been adrenaline, joy at escaping Ralph, elation at a plan well executed . . . and now she didn't know how to tell Gwen she didn't want what she'd started. Perhaps that was the *real* reason Isobelle had been avoiding her. She'd decided one kiss was enough. Gwen's mind seemed to shatter into an infinite number of possibilities, each of them razor-sharp, more cutting than the last.

Isobelle, seeing some echo of this on her face, widened her eyes. She touched Gwen's cheek, apologetic. "The joust, I mean! Not the kissing. You don't get to be unsure about the kissing."

Gwen started breathing again. "Oh. Good." She paused, the rest of Isobelle's words catching up to her. "Wait, what do you mean? Of course I want to joust."

"But you've beaten Sir Ralph. You've already saved me from him. Maybe . . . maybe it's better if Sir Gawain vanishes into the mystery whence he came." Isobelle's hand slid lightly to her shoulder, her palm moving slowly, caressing the place where, beneath the fabric of Gwen's dress and the strapping Olivia had done, the bruises were darkest.

Gwen swallowed hard, aware she had a limited window of time to get to Sir Gawain's changing tent and lay low to avoid anyone making the connection between Lady Céline's arrival and Sir Gawain's emergence. But . . . it felt like it had been weeks, rather than days, since she'd felt Isobelle lean into her this way.

"I want to do this." Gwen caught Isobelle's eyes and held them. "Ralph might have been the worst of them, but do you want to marry Makarios instead? Belmar? *Orson?*" Gwen let her breath out shakily. "I could throttle Olivia for letting you see my bruises."

"I'm glad she did!" Isobelle burst out. "Gwen, you could've been killed."

"That's what jousting is!" Gwen shot back, then swallowed and touched Isobelle's cheek, trying to be reassuring. "I promise you, the other knights are as bruised as I am. And I've been training with Dupont, I know more about evasion now. Isobelle... you can't have it both ways." Gwen brushed Isobelle's quivering lips with her thumb. "I'm either your knight, or I'm not. Either I stand between you and all of them, or I'm not really standing at all."

Isobelle drew a long breath. "Just... just don't get knocked off again," she whispered. "That was the longest second of my life, before you hit the ground."

"You and me both," Gwen replied with a soft hum of laughter. "I'll be okay, Isobelle. I will. This mad dream of yours... it's actually working. I can do this."

Isobelle bit her lip, her expressive face betraying how badly she wanted to keep arguing the point. Her gaze searched Gwen's, fingers moving across the bandages under Gwen's dress. Then she leaned in again, and captured Gwen's lips in a kiss that was far briefer, but just as fierce as their first.

"I know you will," Isobelle said, and let her go.

Dupont was waiting for Gwen when she ducked into Sir Gawain's tent. If she noticed Gwen's flushed cheeks and somewhat reddened lips, she said nothing—instead, she gestured to the armor she'd fetched and arrayed on the stand. They'd agreed it'd probably be better if Lady Céline wasn't spotted carrying her fictitious brother's armor, and this way, Gwen had someone to help her into it without having to wrench her shoulder.

"Remember what we practiced," Dupont said, as she tightened the buckles at waist and wrist, and reached for Gwen's helmet. "The lance is narrow. Dodging it takes the tiniest movement, the barest of twists—all you need to do is turn a full strike into a glancing blow to stay on your horse. It's about timing, not strength."

"I remember," Gwen replied, giving an experimental twist in

her armor. Olivia had been right about her ribs being bruised, not broken—with her shoulder back in place, and strapped to boot, she could move and twist with very little pain now.

Dupont stood before her, scanning Gwen's features thoughtfully. She stood there long enough that Gwen began to fidget, shifting her weight from one booted foot to the other.

"What?" she said finally.

Dupont merely shook her head and handed Gwen the helmet. "Just enjoying what I see," the woman said with a faint smile. "A girl who knows exactly who she is."

Gwen's shoulders relaxed—had she been anticipating Dupont would echo the same worries as Isobelle?—and she flashed her mentor a grin. "I'll see you out there."

The crowd was restless, the background din louder than usual as Gwen mounted Achilles and urged him toward the lists. She caught a glimpse of the stands, craning her neck—the entire place was packed, the crush of bodies so complete as to form an absolute wall of faces.

She gathered Achilles's reins in one hand as the announcer stepped up—then halted as she heard the man shout, instead of her own name: "Sir Makarios of Rhodes!"

Gwen fought to catch her breath and not dwell upon the significance. They always introduced the favorite last.

"And now, the debutant from Toussaint, the knight who's blown up overnight . . . Sir Gawain of . . ."

The crowd had begun to roar as the announcer began Gwen's introduction, and now they were screaming so loud she couldn't hear the rest of what the announcer was saying. Someone gestured at her, though, and she touched her heels to Achilles's flanks, and he jolted forward.

The sheer volume of bodies and voices was like a physical force, and Gwen rode to her place in a daze—she could not quite focus on Isobelle's box, but she saluted the ladies there with her sword, held on for dear life as Achilles reared picturesquely, enjoying the attention, and accepted the lance from one of the lance boys as she reached her spot.

The flag went down, and Achilles leapt into a run without Gwen even having to tell him to start. She lowered her lance, her first good glimpse of her opponent revealing an absolute mountain of metal thundering her way. Her grip slipped for a vital moment, and Gwen focused instead on twisting the way she'd learned from Dupont, and heard the tiny tinging scrape as the barest edge of Makarios's lance sheared past her breastplate.

She wheeled Achilles around, catching her breath and shifting her grip on her lance. Makarios was easily twice her size, and he rode an absolute juggernaut of a warhorse. Gwen could simply try to dodge enough times to send the match to a sword fight, but she wasn't sure how well she'd get away with that twisting maneuver a second time.

If she could knock him off balance, just the tiniest bit . . . his bulk would pull him right off his horse.

The flag went down a second time, and Achilles, snorting gleefully, burst into a run again. This time Gwen concentrated on the positioning of her lance, keeping it up a few inches, as if planning the same thing as last time.

At the last minute, she swung the lance down and braced herself. An absolute explosion of ringing metal and shattering wood assaulted her ears, the force of the impact of her lance sending blinding agony searing through her shoulder—but her legs hung on.

She twisted, half turning Achilles in time to see Makarios riding at a forty-five-degree angle, scrambling madly to try to pull himself up, and sliding ever lower. When he finally hit the ground, his foot still tangled in the stirrup, his massive horse dragged him some considerable distance before the beast managed to slow to a halt.

Makarios disentangled his foot and fell in a clanking heap, then sat up, yanked his helmet off, and threw it down in frustration. But then he laughed, the sound half lost in the wild screaming of the crowd, and waved a broad, exaggerated salute toward Gwen.

She drew her sword, raising it—and raising the mad shrieking of the crowd around her yet higher—and letting Achilles vent his energy by riding in a pretty half circuit of the lists.

Something pattered down on Gwen's shoulder, then slid into her lap—it was a veil of some kind. She looked up and noticed an absolute rain of random objects—largely handkerchiefs, scarfs, veils, even a few full-on hats and headdresses—flying down onto the lists from the ladies comprising well over half the audience. Then a tangle of bodice lacings landed on Achilles's saddle, and Gwen hastily sheathed her sword and moved forward far enough to look up into Isobelle's box.

She found Isobelle's face immediately, the blue eyes gleaming with relief and elation—beside her, Jane shrieked something incoherent and hurled her own favor, a heavily embroidered handkerchief. Isobelle shot her a look, and Jane giggled and said something that was inaudible over the roar of the crowd.

Gwen stole one last look at Isobelle before wheeling Achilles and galloping back off the lists again.

Chapter Thirty-five

MEDITATIONS HE LEARNED ON AN ANCIENT MOUNTAINTOP

Gwen dismounted by her tent, her legs as shaky as they'd been after her first ride. Her thoughts were racing, as unsteady as her legs, and she stumbled through the tent flap with her mind awhirl. She yanked off her helmet, sucking in lungfuls of fresh air, and let out a quavering laugh of released tension and relief.

Only then did she register several distinct sets of footsteps squelching across the much-abused field toward her tent, and the boisterous male voices hailing Sir Gawain.

Reality reasserted itself like a torrent of icy water, and she scrambled for her helmet, trying to pull it back over her sweaty face and hair before the other knights entered.

Then a familiar voice called, "Hey, now, that's far enough!" Orson's tone was jovial but firm. "I told you, Sir Gawain sees no one before or after his jousts. He devotes his pregame and postgame rituals to meditations he learned on an ancient mountaintop."

One of the other knights got out half a protest, but Orson cut him off.

"You'll have to see him in the lists, like everyone else."

The other footsteps sounded again, thudding away from the tent, and then Orson himself ducked inside.

Gwen had gotten halfway stuck inside her helmet. "Thanks, Awesome," she murmured, abandoning her attempt to hide her face. "Er, Orson."

Orson laughed and came over to take her helmet from her. "No worries. Isobelle would have my hide if I stood by and did nothing while you got found out. Need some help?" he added, gesturing to her armor. "I promise not to kiss you like your last squire did."

Gwen gave an uneasy chuckle and nodded, turning so Orson could get to the straps keeping her chest piece in place. "Thanks. I'm used to doing it myself, but . . ."

"But it's much harder when your muscles are screaming in agony?" Orson finished for her, working the buckle free and prying the pieces apart so Gwen could squeeze out of them. "Really, this armor is ingenious." He squinted, inspecting the shoulder articulation more closely.

"Thanks." Gwen pulled her hands out of her gauntlets and began unbuckling her vambraces one by one. "I meant what I said before. When all this is done, I can show you how I make it. Make some for you too, if you want."

Orson cast a sideways glance at her, hesitating, his expression saying clearly, *When all this is done, you're probably not going to be in a position to do anything.* But what he said was, "That'd be awesome, thanks."

Once the rest of Gwen's armor was on the stand, Orson turned his back so Gwen could change out of her padding and into her costume as Céline.

"Look, I appreciate you covering for me with the other knights," Gwen said, reaching out tentatively to touch Orson on the shoulder and let him know she was fully clothed again. "But, uh, you might not want to make me sound so very mysterious."

Orson turned and raised both blond eyebrows at her. "Seriously? A brand-new knight who comes out of nowhere, who no one's seen at any of the feasts or salons, who absolutely demolishes the competition and vanishes again as soon as he's done so?" Orson shook his head, rolling his eyes skyward. "Sir Gawain *is* a mystery, you can't avoid it. All I'm doing is muddying the waters with more mysteries, in the hope that no one spots which mysteries are the important ones to focus on."

Gwen had to admit it wasn't the worst idea. "Just ... maybe stop short of implying I'm half dragon or King of the Fae or that I turn into a bat and go flying around by night."

"Oh man, those are great ideas. Hang on, let me find something to write those down . . ." Orson burst into laughter when he saw Gwen's stricken face, and then held out his arm with perfect chivalry. "Come on, Lady Céline. Let's go find Isobelle."

But they didn't find Isobelle. Her friends had already swept her off—Olivia told Gwen, when she reached Isobelle's suite, that they'd gone on a mission to try to find where in the castle Sir Gawain was staying, and lie in wait for him.

That night, as Gwen soaked and resoaked a cloth to bring the swelling down in her shoulder, she could not help but visualize the moonlit living quarters stretching between her bedroom and Isobelle's. Gwen closed her eyes and tried to focus on the wet cloth cooling her skin.

Instead, she could only think of her disappointment that Awesome was the one who came to celebrate with her afterward, and not Isobelle.

With a sigh, Gwen tossed the rag back into the water basin and sat up. She reached for the dressing gown slung across the foot of her bed and shrugged into it before easing silently out of her room.

She got two-thirds of the way across the sitting room before she stopped, heart pounding, ears straining for any telltale sound from beyond Isobelle's door.

There was only silence.

Gwen drew a long, slow breath, trying to calm her nerves. Just because she couldn't sleep knowing Isobelle was so near, didn't mean she had the right to wake her.

Still, she waited there for a long time, far too long, *embarrassingly* long, a single thought playing on repeat: *Isobelle, are you there? I'm right outside....*

Eventually, swallowing her disappointment and feeling entirely too cowardly for someone who'd just won her second official joust in a row, Gwen crept back into her room and shut the door.

Chapter Thirty-Six

RIDE OFF INTO THE SUNSET WITH NOTHING BUT A CHANGE OF UNDERWEAR

Isobelle lay on her bed, tossing and turning as if she were trying to shake off some invisible foe. She kept punching her fancy French pillow to no avail, and her impractical nightclothes were so twisted around her nether limbs that when she yanked them straight, she heard one of the sweet pink bows rip free of the lacy fabric.

Finally, her willpower giving out, she vaulted off the bed and scurried over to the door. She eased it open slowly, avoiding the creak it always gave, and peered out across the moonlit living room.

Gwen's door was firmly shut. She must be in bed, fast asleep.

Her voice was still echoing around Isobelle's head.

I can do this, Gwen had said. And after watching her joust, Isobelle had no doubt those words were true. But what then? What next?

Isobelle had always made up her schemes and plans as she went, counting on sheer charm and force of personality to see her through. But though she'd had a sweeping, romantic vision of Gwen riding to victory in the tournament, she'd never thought much beyond the moment she knocked the last knight off his horse. She was realizing that her childhood memories of the tournaments she'd seen didn't include what happened after the victory was won.

Would they really let Gwen just ride off with her prize money, helmet still on, identity still concealed, no one the wiser as to what she and Isobelle had done?

And if Gwen does escape then . . . what happens to us?

Isobelle stomped back into her room to retrieve her silk robe, pulling it on and yanking the tie around the waist tight before moving into the living room to examine the tea things. Olivia had anticipated her needs and left a carefully wrapped bottle of hot water for tea to help her sleep.

She settled in one of the chairs, carefully spooning out the herbs and inhaling the sweet, smokey scent rising toward her as she poured the hot water into the pot.

She detested herself for letting Gwen continue taking such deadly risks. And alone, in the moonlight, with her cup of slowly steeping tea, Isobelle could admit the truth to herself.

She wasn't letting Gwen continue this insanity because she couldn't bear to marry any of the other knights. She still didn't want to marry any of them—she'd rather climb down from the balcony, using the rings Olivia had carefully hammered into place, and ride off into the sunset with nothing but a change of underwear.

But that wasn't why she'd sat there today, her heart in her throat as she watched Gwen ride out. It wasn't why she'd fought to keep back tears of relief as Sir Makarios had saluted Gwen and conceded the match.

Isobelle was too afraid to ask Gwen to stop. Afraid that if she did, Gwen would leave. Or think Isobelle was no different from the world full of men telling her not to do what she was obviously born to do. Isobelle was letting this charade continue because she didn't want to lose Gwen's esteem.

And what kind of person did that make her?

The tea continued to steep as Isobelle rose to her feet and padded silently across to Gwen's doorway. There she stood, suspended helplessly in place. Not brave enough to go to the girl on the other side. And not brave enough to tell her to leave.

Reaching out, she rested her fingertips against the smooth wood of the door. Then she turned away, walking across to snatch up her cup and return to her room, leaving only the soft scent of tea behind her.

YOU ARE FAMILIAR WITH A montage, surely. Yes? Yes.

The mood will be best conveyed with some backing music—go on, take a moment, and put on something with a strong beat. The latest hit from your favorite bard, or perhaps an old classic often repeated by traveling minstrels. Bonus points if it involves themes of rising up to the top, not stopping believing, or even a final countdown to victory.

Go on. One of the best things about a book is that it's always willing to wait until you return.

As the opening notes of your anthem roll out, picture a town utterly devastated by the worst kind of plague imaginable: absolute, unstoppable Sir Gawain fandom. The women want to give him their favors, and the men want to be in his shoes—well, let's be honest, quite a few of the men want to give him favors, too.

It's mad enough that he bumped one of the local regulars completely out of the tournament in his qualifier, but then he sent the tournament favorite to the physicians, and then knocked "Mountain Man Makarios" on his ass a few days later. With that kind of track record, the rumors that follow—ridiculous under any other circumstance—take on a life of their own.

Did you know, for example, that Sir Gawain fought a troll in

Luxembourg? That he singlehandedly routed an invading army from the north? That that army was actually made of trolls? That those trolls were actually twice the size of the trolls you're thinking of, and that he did it with his bare hands, while hungover, without breaking a sweat?

Oh, and I heard he was once the model for a bodice ad in Paris, but the images were so inflammatory to the ladies and their delicate passions that the modistes had to take the posters down for fear of causing mass hysteria, and a mass burning of said bodices.

Whatever else may be true, by the time Sir Gawain rides into the arena for his third joust—fourth, if you include the qualifier—the entire county knows his name. The stands are so packed that it's standing room only, on the benches and on the floor. More than a few people are toting blankets and pillows, having slept in the stands to reserve their places. The noise is so deafening that, were there any people left in the nearby villages instead of attending the joust, they'd be able to hear it in their cottages.

When Sir Gawain lifts his sword to salute the crowd, one of the stands collapses under the double weight of spectators, spilling a hundred shrieking, bruised, indignant fans onto the ground.

And when Sir Gawain handily knocks Sir Belmar off his horse in one try, without even shattering his lance, it takes the physicians well over twenty minutes to fight through the crowds to get to the lists and help the downed knight limp away. Half of them never make it at all, too busy tending to the fans who, having succumbed to the intense weight of their adoration, fainted before Gawain ever made it onto the field.

The weavers' guild makes a fortune milling the cheapest garments they can manage with Sir Gawain's pennant painted on the front. They call them tournament shirts, though the fans tend to shorten the name to something quicker to say.

The local portrait artist is busier than he's ever been, knocking out card-sized paintings of ladies with Sir Gawain in his armor, their hands juuuuust about to lift his visor and reveal his face.

And a local blacksmith, emerging out of relative anonymity, displays a sudden talent for crafting tiny, beautifully detailed figurines of this new star—his smithy is completely overrun.

Our principal players now find themselves stuck under a rather crushing weight of deception in the face of intense, unrelenting scrutiny.

Sir Orson, cruising through his matches as well, was originally delighted to spread as many mad rumors about Sir Gawain as he could imagine. Now, however, he's left to sit in stunned silence as his friends take turns sharing the wildest rumors they've managed to overhear or invent. He's all: "Um, guys . . . I mean, it probably wasn't the troll *king*, and he probably couldn't shoot fire out of his eyes. . . ." Or: "Well, no, I've never seen him levitate during his pregame ritual, and I'm pretty sure he can't control the other knights' horses with his mind, either. . . ."

Olivia, doing her level best to keep Gwen in one piece—largely through the expert application of tight bandages and lurid green ointment—avoids the worst of the hubbub by lurking around the castle dungeons. She can't get access to the imprisoned villagers yet, but she's become quite the hit with the local lads employed as guards, because she always comes bearing snacks. Thus far, they've all been perfectly harmless. Who would drug a cupcake, after all? Certainly not Olivia. Certainly not yet, anyway.

Sylvie's suspicions of Céline only seem to deepen, her mistrust of the other half of the mystery—Sir Gawain himself—slightly mollified by the obvious, undeniable happiness of her friend Isobelle. Jane modifies one of the T-shirts, sewing fluttering ribbons to the sleeves and tying the baggy hem into a knot around her midriff, showing a scandalous few inches of the curve of her stomach. Hilde begs Isobelle endlessly for her latest account of her "alone time" with Sir Gawain.

Isobelle herself, unable to hide the change in her heart from her friends, has to censor herself every time she opens her mouth. She can't confess that when she and Lady Céline went to visit Sir Gawain, they actually went and made out in Isobelle's hat cupboard. Or that when they left to take a bracing ride around the castle grounds, they never made it out of the stables, and had to spend a good twenty minutes picking straw out of each other's hair.

Most of all, she can't confess that underneath her undeniable happiness, worry seethes like a subterranean river eating away at the foundations of a castle. After Sir Belmar was Sir Lorenzo, who got in such a good hit before Gwen retaliated and unhorsed him that Gwen couldn't breathe for almost a full minute. The skin on her chest was so black and blue that Olivia had had to alter several dresses to include a high-necked collar.

The victory against Lorenzo secured Gwen's place in the final round, to face Sir Orson for the ultimate victory, but Isobelle can't confess to her friends that she'd stop Sir Gawain riding in it if she could.

She can't even confess it to Gwen.

And Gwen . . . well, even for Gwen, *especially* for Gwen, there's no escaping Gawain Fever. Even as Céline, she's mobbed by people seeking her acquaintance now, hoping to learn more about her brother by cozying up to her. Gifts show up at Isobelle's suite multiple times a day, and Olivia occasionally has to serve as bouncer to prevent eager ladies from trying to infiltrate Isobelle's inner circle. The moments Gwen sneaks with Isobelle are the only moments of peace she gets.

If we've timed this right, we should be in the bridge of your anthem now. Perhaps it strikes a minor key—perhaps the beat fades out, a symbolic evocation of the dark night of the soul that looms over our heroes.

Each knight Gwen takes down is another step closer to victory, to saving Isobelle.

But ... then what?

Gwen is now the most famous man in Darkhaven. What would happen to all that fervor and fanaticism if they learned that Sir Gawain was no knight, that he was not a noble, not even a man at all?

She sleeps at night by visualizing her next joust. The next opponent, the next strategy. She looks ahead, but she stops herself before she looks too far, because that hazy mist of uncertainty that follows victory in the upcoming final is too terrifying to face. The tiniest glimmer of something elusive and fragile and beautiful lurks there, a hope she can't name even to herself for fear of shattering it. There comes a moment, in her imagination, after the victory: a blinding release as she pulls off her helmet in front of the world.

But even she cannot see further than that instant, and she drags herself back to the parts of her path she knows. The next joust. The next opponent. The next strategy. She stops herself from stepping beyond the borders of the map she can see, because there ... well. There be dragons.

She knows, as Isobelle knows, as everyone in on the secret knows, that this run can't last forever.

This is, after all, a story ... and what good is a story where the heroes can't seem to stop winning?

Chapter Thirty-Seven

YOU'D BE VERY SURPRISED BY WHAT A FANCY LADY CAN GET DONE

Two days before the final joust was to occur, Olivia summoned Isobelle and Gwen for a council of war. Not to discuss what would happen after the tournament ended—even Olivia could not see that far ahead—but to lay out her plan for helping the villagers who had come the night of the dragon bonfire, who had been arrested for making a scene.

Olivia herself was far from thrilled with the plan she'd made, but time had run out, with the tournament final looming up ahead. She'd drilled both Gwen and Isobelle on every step, until they could repeat it back to her word for word—and now they were making their way down, down into the twisting corridors beneath the castle.

Under any other circumstances, a secret mission of this sort would have been quite thrilling.

Isobelle was, however—despite carefully cultivated popular opinion—capable of taking things seriously. And just now, she was taking the safety of the women imprisoned beneath the castle very seriously indeed.

"Are we clear?" Olivia whispered, as they paused at the midpoint of the servants' staircase.

"We stay put, and don't speak to the guards," Gwen whispered.

"And I, especially, do not try to help you chat them up," Isobelle added. "Unless you need my help, that is."

"No," Olivia snapped. "No unless. You stay here until they're down. We'll get to the cell and try to locate the key. No heroics, remember?" Olivia sighed, then muttered, "It will be a miracle if this works. I don't like bringing you two into it."

"Well, a miracle is required," Isobelle said. "And anyway, we're all you've got."

"Rarely have I so sorely felt the lack," Olivia replied glumly. She was dressed in a simple gray servant's dress, her hair braided back neatly, and she held a small basket of freshly baked custard tarts.

Gwen was dressed in the simple black clothes she wore beneath her armor, with small patches of mail at her elbows and knees. The trousers clung both alarmingly and delightfully to her legs, and to her . . . above her legs . . .

Isobelle had given careful thought to her own outfit. Something dark, to blend in with the shadows, but she might only assist on one jailbreak in her lifetime—she wanted her look to be memorable.

She had settled on a black mourning dress with minimal ruffles. She had left off the underskirts, which interfered with the drape a touch, but meant she was able to move more freely, and as they prepared to descend the stairs, she pulled her black veil down over her face.

"What are you doing?" Olivia whispered, her eyes widening in disbelief.

"I glow in the dark," Isobelle pointed out, carefully twitching the netting into place. "Behind this, I am one with the shadows."

Olivia surrendered and lifted the basket of tarts. "I will feed these to the guards," she whispered. "Once I give the signal, Gwen, you take a look at the lock and search for a key, and Isobelle, you speak to the women. You have two minutes, and then we're leaving."

The pair of them followed the maid as she continued down the stairs, halting at her hand signal and letting her walk on alone.

"Who goes?" called a rough male voice.

"Just me again, boys. Anyone for dessert?" Olivia's singsongy tones paused, and then there was a giggle. "Not *that* kind of dessert, Alaric! Cheeky. Look, the cook's just pulled these out of the oven. Gather round."

She'd been down here every night for a week, and, like the ravens one of the stableboys trained to join him for breakfast, the guards had learned to arrive promptly for their treat.

There was a short silence as they ate, and Isobelle risked a peek around the corner, spotting Olivia chatting in a low voice with a group of four men in castle guard uniforms. As she watched, one of them stepped back, leaning against the wall with a bewildered expression. Then he looked down in surprise as his knees gave way, and he slithered down until he was seated.

"What—" one of them began, and then went silent.

Gwen grabbed Isobelle by the waist, pulling her back out of sight. The touch of her hands created a flutter of sparks that ran all the way down to Isobelle's toes, via several interesting stops along the way. Isobelle caught her breath, but forced herself to keep her mind on their mission, and not on how viscerally Gwen's touch had affected her.

Then Olivia appeared, her basket now almost empty. "They're out," she whispered. "They won't remember anything about tonight, much less the tarts. But none of them have the keys on them. Go on, I'll keep watch here."

Silently, Isobelle and Gwen went on. The passages below the castle itself were hewn out of solid rock, and the builders seemed to have gone out of their way to make the place miserable. Jagged edges were waiting to snag the unsuspecting passerby, and drops of something cold and too slimy to be water fell from the ceiling at unpredictable intervals. Their footsteps sounded far too loud, echoing off the walls as they made their way past the first few empty cells, the doorways thrown open like big, black mouths waiting to swallow you up.

Then they found a doorway blocked by a huge metal grate, and Isobelle slowed to a halt, squinting through the bars for a glimpse of anyone inside.

Gwen took a torch from its sconce and handed it to Isobelle. "Hold this," she murmured. "I need light to work with."

Isobelle angled it obligingly, and Gwen dropped to a crouch to inspect the lock on the doorway—made of metal, it was well within her wheelhouse. And making new friends was within Isobelle's, so she began her appointed task.

"Ladies?" she whispered carefully. "Are you in there?"

A form appeared from the shadows—a woman all in black, or else so filthy she might as well have been—shielding her eyes from the flame. "Who the hell are you?" she asked, wise enough to keep to a whisper as well.

"Friends," Isobelle said simply. "The guards are asleep, for now. Have any of you seen which guard holds the key, or where they keep it?"

"You've got to be kidding me," someone muttered from farther back in the cell. "Rescue finally arrives, and it's fancy ladies playing at being spies."

Gwen looked up from her work. "You would be very surprised by what a fancy lady can get done," she murmured, amusement warming her voice. "There's steel under all that gilt."

"Oh, that's a lovely thing to say," Isobelle whispered, flushing. "You know, so many people think—"

Gwen cut her off gently by taking hold of her hand and giving it a squeeze that said *let's focus on the task at hand, shall we?* and Isobelle gave her a squeeze back to convey that she quite understood, but very much appreciated the compliment. Gwen then redirected Isobelle's hand so the torchlight fell back on the door, which she continued to examine.

"Right," Isobelle said. "Keys?"

But the women just shook their heads numbly.

"Can you tell us what happened?" Isobelle asked gently of the woman closest to the bars. "To you, to your village? Where did you say you were from?"

"Aberfarthing," came the soft reply. "Just outside the village proper, most of us, to the south, toward the new mines. I didn't see much, myself—but I heard it." She gave a bone-deep shudder. "The roaring, the screams."

"I saw it," piped up another voice, farther back in the shadows. "A great black monster flying over the village just before the headman's house exploded in flames."

Another woman stepped forward. "Not black," she argued. "Sort of brownish green, an awful color, like nothing I've ever seen."

Gwen glanced at Isobelle, brow furrowed, obviously thinking the same thing she was: no wonder no one had believed these women and their tales of dragon attacks. No two of them were telling the same story.

Isobelle stepped back, leaving Gwen to continue her examination of the cell door, and glanced at Olivia, who was still within sight up the passageway. "What do you make of this?" she called, keeping her voice low, as the women in the cell debated the sequence of events that had driven them out of their homes.

Olivia was listening with half an ear, her attention partly directed back the way they'd come. "Eyewitnesses are unreliable at best," she said, though her voice was slow and troubled. "The more traumatic the event, the harder it can be to recall exactly what you saw. It doesn't necessarily make them liars."

Isobelle sighed. "You could have just said 'I don't know,' Olivia."

Olivia raised an eyebrow and glanced at her, lips quirking the tiniest bit. "Come now, Isobelle. You know I know everything. Keep working here, I'm going to check on our sleeping beauties."

Isobelle turned her attention back to the women, infusing her voice with the kind of calm confidence she imagined was helpful when leading armies, and undertaking other great deeds requiring courage and confidence. "We're going to get you out of here," she told them. "We'll keep searching for the key, as long as it takes to—"

"Actually," Gwen said, interrupting her and lifting her head. "We don't need the key."

"You can pick the lock?" Isobelle asked, leaning in, heart pounding. "Or break it?"

"I don't need to. Look at these hinges—simple pegs, relying on the weight of the door to keep it closed. Everyone focuses on the locks." Gwen gave a disgusted shake of her head. "Amateur hour over here."

Isobelle had to hide a smile. "Well, why don't we go find whoever's in charge, and let them know what they're doing wrong?

Really make sure no one can get out of this place next time."

Gwen looked up at her and blinked in the torchlight, before a breath of laughter escaped her. "Point taken. The bottom line is that these hinges are atrocious. I can get the door off, with a little help—is Olivia still back there?"

Isobelle handed Gwen the torch and went scurrying up the disgusting corridor as quickly as she dared, regretting her choice of slippers. She found her maid going through the guards' pockets, but at a glance from Isobelle, she straightened up.

"Just checking again for a key," Olivia protested archly. "I wasn't going to steal anything, they're just lads."

Isobelle hid a smile and beckoned for Olivia to follow her back down the corridor.

When they returned, Gwen was instructing the women on the other side of the gate. "If we can lift it enough, we'll raise it off the pegs that form the hinges."

Isobelle and Olivia took their places on the outside, Isobelle's fingers pressed up against the hand of one of the women holding the inside of the door. Her knuckles were swollen, and her skin was dreadfully cold.

Isobelle squeezed the cold hand, then tightened her hold on the iron bar and lifted with everything she had, straining to drag the door up from the ground, a pain shooting through her jaw as she clenched it harder than she'd known she could.

The door lifted off its hinges, giving way, threatening to swing by its new hinge—the lock on the other side of the door—into the cell, pinning the women who were trying to brace it without the help of the hinges. Isobelle kept tight hold of it, throwing her weight backward with the effort, but all she could do was slow its fall.

Then Gwen was there, stepping around her to take hold of it beside her, and with a groan of effort, dragging it back toward them once more. And for all Isobelle had understood how hard it must be to move in armor, to lift a lance, to stay in the saddle, she hadn't realized until this moment just how strong Gwen was.

The gate made a horrible screeching sound as they dragged it out of the way, but there was nothing to be done about that. Half a dozen women quickly made their way out, one of them supported between two others, her feet dragging as she stumbled, trying to keep herself from going down altogether.

"Let's get it back in place," Gwen hissed shortly. "Let them think they just walked out of a locked cell. They'll call it fae or witches and won't go looking for conveniently disguised blacksmith's daughters."

Isobelle caught her breath in a laugh and nodded to the other women, a few of whom joined the efforts to drag the screeching door back onto the open peg hinges, until there was very little sign they'd ever been there at all.

"This way. I know a place where you'll be safe, at least for now." Olivia hurried up the hallway, and the women followed without question—there was an air of competence about Olivia that commanded it, and it was a quality Isobelle was determined to master herself one day. She and Gwen brought up the rear, and Gwen reached out to squeeze her hand again.

I can't believe we've done it.

And then she nearly ran into the back of one of the village women, who'd all stopped.

There was a fifth man in a guard's uniform, standing at the base of the stairs, his gaze snapping up from the four men unconscious by the wall to rest on the group of women standing at the entrance to the cells.

"Ambrose," said Olivia, her tone neutral. "You're not due on duty for an hour. What are you doing here?"

Ambrose stared at her, his mouth slightly open. He gave his head a shake, as though trying to wake himself from a dream, but not succeeding. "I thought I'd come down and see Harlan," he said, pausing to swallow hard. "Is he dead?"

"Dead?" Olivia sounded mildly insulted. "Only amateurs resort to murder at the first hurdle." She nodded to the basket she'd left by the foot of the stairs. "I truly wish you'd eaten a tart too, though."

"Dairy's no good for my insides," he said absently, looking back at the man he'd come to distract from his duties.

Olivia's hand started to move slowly behind her back, to the place where Isobelle knew from experience there was a knife secreted in the folds of her dress at the waist.

Reaching across, she closed her hand over Olivia's wrist in silent instruction. The woman's eyes slid sideways, but with a long-suffering expression, she gave a little nod that invited Isobelle to try her luck.

"Ambrose, was it?" Isobelle asked, lifting her veil and stepping forward to unleash her very best smile on the man. Though it was probably wasted, if he'd been here to visit Harlan.

"Y-yes, my lady—Ambrose Miller," the man stammered, trying to both bow and keep his eyes on Olivia at the same time, shuffling back and nearly tripping on the bottom step. Olivia snorted, none too softly, but Isobelle pressed on.

"I'm sure you're surprised to see us here. May I commend you on your excellent manners? It's such a delight to—"

To her surprise, he held up a hand to cut her off, straightening his posture. "My lady, I know you're about to ask me to let you all by, and you have to know I can't do that. These women are in the custody of Lord Whimsitt, and I am his sworn man."

This was going to be difficult. Not impossible, certainly—Isobelle saw initial refusals as more of an opening gambit than a final position—but time wasn't on their side. As she was trying to choose her best line of attack, a voice came from behind her. Gwen's voice.

"Where are you from?"

He blinked, craning his neck to see who was speaking from the back of the group. "What?"

"Where are you *from*?" Gwen repeated, keeping to the back of the group of women. The rest of them remained silent—too tired or too fearful to speak. Or perhaps willing to trust the ones who'd got them this far.

"Nether Foxholm," Ambrose said slowly.

"Then you're a village boy," Gwen said.

"Aye."

"And you know what it will mean to these women's families to lose them. What it will mean to their children to be motherless. What it will mean to their husbands to find themselves alone."

"I . . ." Ambrose trailed off. He had no answer for that.

"You grew up around bonfires," Gwen continued, her voice still low, her face still hidden. "I won't ask you to believe the story these women told, though I know you must have heard plenty like it. I won't ask you to imagine a dragon sent them running here, knowing they'd be called mad. Just imagine what their homes will be like without them."

Ambrose closed his eyes for a minute, lifting one hand to pinch the bridge of his nose.

Carefully, softly, Isobelle tried her luck. "Harlan will be well. He's just taking a nap. I'm told the dreams are delightful. Couldn't you take a nap too, Ambrose?"

"I'm not eating one of them tarts," he muttered. "I'll destroy the privy. I'll just pretend."

"And when it's time to wake up . . ." Isobelle said delicately.

He didn't look at them as he walked over to sit himself down beside his man, folding his arms across his chest as he prepared to pretend to sleep. "I'll say nothing," he muttered. "Go, get somewhere safe."

And so they did, without risking another word. Quietly the group of them filed up the stairs, and when they reached ground level, Olivia signaled to the village women to follow her. They paused, though, and the gaunt leader who'd come first to the cell door turned to look at Isobelle and Gwen.

"Thank you," she said simply, and Isobelle, finding her throat had an unexpectedly large lump in it, nodded.

"I'm sorry it took so long," said Gwen softly.

The woman managed a tired smile for that. "All we can offer you by way of thanks is our warning," she said, in her dry, tired voice. "Our words were true. Be ready." And then she turned away.

Isobelle waited until they'd gone before she threw her arms around Gwen. The other girl staggered back into the wall of the staircase, putting her hands on Isobelle's hips to steady her, and Isobelle surged up onto her toes to claim a triumphant kiss.

"We did it," she whispered, pressing her forehead to Gwen's when they finally broke apart. "Gwen, you were brilliant! Lifting the door off those hinges like a goddess! Talking round that village boy like—"

"Like you," Gwen said, her pink cheeks visible even in the flickering torchlight.

"It was you that did it, though," Isobelle pointed out, positively bubbling with pride.

Gwen smiled. "So it was a little bit of you, and a little bit of me." Isobelle kissed her for quite a long time after that.

"Gwen," she said eventually, as they turned to hurry up the servants' stairs toward their apartments. "I can't wait to see you take on Orson in the final. You and I are going to be absolutely unstoppable."

And in that moment, floating up the stairs on the wings of their victory, dizzy with kisses and schemes gone right and doing her best to ignore every misgiving she'd been shoving aside for the past week, she very nearly believed it.

That feeling dissolved when Isobelle opened the door to her rooms.

"Isobelle!" Hilde leapt to her feet, wringing her hands. "There you are!"

"Hilde? What . . ." Isobelle paused, as she took in the room. "What are all three of you doing here?" Her mind was scrambling, trying to think of any excuse to explain Gwen's attire, to redirect their attention, to stop the revelations she felt sure were on the verge of exploding. But her thoughts felt like molasses, after so much else happening in such a short period of time, and she could only stand there in confusion.

Sylvie slowly unfolded herself from a chair, crossing her arms and looking Isobelle and Gwen up and down. Something about her wasn't right—it was hard to tell with the lamps so low, but Isobelle could have sworn Sylvie's eyes were red. Suddenly, she felt colder. But before she had a chance to ask, Sylvie spoke.

"Who died, Isobelle?"

"What?"

"Your dress," Sylvie replied, like a patient tutor with a forgetful student.

Isobelle looked down. "Ah," she said. "Yes."

"Forget the dress," Jane cut in. "Why is Céline wearing *trousers*?"

"They are very fetching," Hilde said. "I like the silver highlights at the knees. But Céline, I am not sure you should wear them about the castle."

That dreadful coldness spread through Isobelle as she stood, rooted to the spot, watching Sylvie walk over to Gwen. They were of a height, the two of them, and Gwen met her eye with a steady gaze.

"Sylvie," Jane began. "We must—"

Sylvie cut her off with a raised hand, not turning her head to look across at their friend. "I would like to look at these clothes first. Are they your brother's, Céline?"

Gwen's lips parted to respond. Then, slowly, she closed them again and simply lifted her chin, as if daring Sylvie to land a blow. She knew what was coming.

Sylvie dropped to a crouch in a fluid movement to inspect the patches of mail armor at Gwen's knees. "They fit you very well," Sylvie murmured.

Hilde tried to break the tension, her brow creased in confusion. "Perhaps they will become a fashion," she said. "Sylvie . . ."

Sylvie was still looking up at Gwen, and though she was down on one knee, in the position of a supplicant, there was anything but surrender in her posture.

Isobelle tried to find calm, but the fingers of cold had got a grip on her ribs now, and they were squeezing.

Then Gwen let out a slow breath. "Well, shit," she muttered.

"Sylvie—" Isobelle croaked, but she got no further.

Sylvie let out a dark, bitter laugh, bringing her hands together in slow applause as she rose to her feet. "I can't believe I didn't see it," she said. "A man of mystery, Sir Gawain. He never appears without his armor."

"I don't understand," Jane said, her gaze flicking from Sylvie to Isobelle, brow wrinkled.

"Jane," Isobelle tried, but she was swallowed up by the sensation that something inside her was falling. This was the moment it all came undone. Gwen was looking at her, white beneath her beautiful freckles.

Sylvie whirled around to face Jane and Hilde, her hand sweeping down Gwen like she was some kind of tourney prize. "You don't see it, girls?"

"What?" Jane blinked.

"But how . . . ?" Hilde managed, one beat ahead of her friend.

Gwen closed her eyes. It hurt to watch her, to see the instant it was all stripped away.

Gwen, I'm sorry. I thought we had longer. I still have things to say.

"Ohhhhhh," said Jane slowly, her eyes widening as comprehension wormed its way into her brain and made itself at home. "Oh, no *wonder* Céline never came to the jousts!"

"Well, I for one don't blame us for not seeing it sooner," Hilde said firmly, hands on her hips. "Whoever would have guessed it?"

Sylvie tilted a glance at Isobelle. "I assume this was your idea?"

"Be fair," Hilde chided. "Céline could already joust. Isobelle just recruited her to this particular cause. Have you jousted secretly in Europe, Céline?"

Gwen puffed out her cheeks, then let out a slow breath. "No," she said simply, before making things considerably more complicated: "And my name's not Céline. It's Gwen. I come from Ellsdale. My father's Amos, the village blacksmith."

Ah, thought Isobelle. *So we're divesting ourselves of the lies completely. May as well, I suppose.*

"Oh!" Jane lit up. "Your father's the one who made the delightful horseshoes!"

"I think," said Hilde slowly, "that it was Gwen who made them."

"Wait . . . so your whole romance with Gawain was a lie, Isobelle?" Jane asked, far more distressed by that than by the revelation of Gwen's identity.

Gwen's gaze fell on Isobelle, waiting. Even now, she was giving Isobelle the space she needed to make her decision. Permission to keep this much, at least, a secret—to stay in the comfortable familiarity of her friends without challenging the way they saw her.

To hell with that, Isobelle thought, lifting her chin. "No," she said. "No . . . it wasn't a lie."

Jane's eyes widened and shifted toward Gwen, and then slid back to Isobelle, searching for signs of this new concept on her friend's familiar features.

Hilde's lips curved into a smile, her rosy cheeks going pinker with pleasure, and she stepped forward to take Isobelle's hand and squeeze it. "And here I thought you had not noticed the way you were looking at your champion's sister."

Isobelle gulped for breath, not having realized she'd been holding it. She glanced over at Gwen, her shoulders dropping with relief—only to realize Gwen wasn't looking at her. She was looking at Sylvie, biting her lip, eyes full of sympathy.

Isobelle blinked. Did Gwen think Sylvie was jealous? True, Sylvie had been more suspicious of "Lady Céline" than the others, but... Isobelle inspected her friend, taking in the set of her jaw, the thin line of her mouth. Sylvie's arms weren't crossed, she realized—she was hunched in on herself.

"Sylvie..." Isobelle said, ignoring the cold that had reached her fingertips now. "What's going on? Why were you all gathered in my room, before Gwen and I got here?"

Jane and Hilde both looked to Sylvie.

Sylvie lifted her chin, eyes remote and calm. "My father has arranged my betrothal."

Isobelle pressed her hand to her mouth. "What?" she managed, from behind it.

"He had an offer he couldn't refuse," Sylvie continued. "An unexpected offer, from a man who found himself in the market for a wife."

Isobelle wanted to stop time. She wanted to take two quick steps back and bolt through the door. Back to the staircase, where she'd kissed Gwen, and had been invincible. Back to Hilde squeezing her hand, understanding her and Gwen, together. But the cold dread inside her rooted her to the spot.

"Sylvie..." she whispered.

Sylvie's mouth tremored, just for an instant, before it firmed again. But that small hint was like watching the castle itself crumble, great stones falling to the ground as the walls collapsed. "I am to marry Sir Ralph."

A sound emerged from Gwen like she'd received a physical blow—and Isobelle felt her own body go rigid all over. She could not take her eyes from Sylvie's face, though, seeking something, anything, that would undo what she had said.

This is your fault.

The words forced themselves into Isobelle's mind. She didn't know if they came from herself, or from Sylvie, but they were true. If she hadn't found a way to dodge Sir Ralph—if she hadn't humiliated and infuriated him in doing it—he never would have looked for a way to bring her down a peg. For that was exactly what this was.

And now Sylvie—sharp, clever, dangerous Sylvie—was going to lose her claws. She was going to diminish slowly on some country estate, far from everyone who loved her, for there was no way she'd be allowed to stay with her friends, the only people who would support her, help her keep her strength.

"Oh, Sylvie," Isobelle whispered.

"Don't say anything," Sylvie replied tightly.

So Isobelle didn't. Instead, she flung herself at her friend and wrapped her arms around her neck, wishing she could shield her from all the harm in the world.

With a wordless sound, Sylvie's arms went around her in return.

Chapter Thirty-Eight

I CAN SHOW YOU A THING OR TWO

Gwen slipped out of Isobelle's suite the next morning as quietly as she could. Jane had apparently passed out on one of the chaise longues, and was snoring tiny, delicate snores. Gwen suspected that Hilde and Sylvie had slept over too, but were in Isobelle's room with her.

Sylvie. Gwen's stomach churned just thinking the girl's name, much less remembering the remote, pale look on her face as she stared Isobelle down while she delivered her news, each sentence slamming home for Isobelle like a direct hit from a lance. Gwen had never seen Isobelle look so suddenly stricken, not even when she'd gotten a glimpse of Gwen's bruises after her joust against Ralph.

A soft sound alerted Gwen to another presence in the room. Olivia had returned from seeing the freed villagers to safety, and sat by the window, re-feathering a pink-and-teal confection of a hat. Her fingers moved automatically at their work, her eyes on Gwen.

Gwen hesitated, raising her eyebrows. Her instincts told her it would be wise not to let Sylvie see her here when she woke, that Isobelle could better handle her friend's despair about her fate if the instrument of that fate wasn't sitting nearby, wearing Sylvie's modified dresses and eating cake.

But maybe her "instincts" were just telling her what would be easier for Gwen.

Olivia let Gwen hang there for some time, expression inscrutable. Though she'd seemed pleased with Gwen's abilities the night before, Olivia still gave off a faint air of disapproval, as if she knew what Isobelle and Gwen were trying to ignore: that this plan, all of it, was ultimately a fool's game.

When Olivia finally spoke, her voice was barely audible, a practiced thing that carried far less than a whisper. "The villagers are safe," she said, securing a neatly trimmed peacock plume to the hat with a careful half hitch. Her needle glinted in the morning sunlight.

Gwen eased closer, eyeing the sleeping Jane and lowering her voice. "Where did you take them?"

Olivia's eyes betrayed something, fleeting and easily missed—a gleam of amusement. "Ellsdale."

Gwen's breath caught, and she frantically swallowed to try to stop herself from launching into a fit of noisy coughing. "My village? Why?"

Olivia's needle dipped back into the fabric, circled the calamus of the peacock plume again, and pulled tight. "I needed a place that wasn't too far for them to walk. And they seemed like nice people there. I felt certain they'd find places for those women and their families."

Gwen eyed her askance, confusion having supplanted her unease about Sylvie and her fate. "You've been to my village?"

Olivia eyed her flatly. "If you think I didn't learn everything there was to learn about you the day you showed up here to take part in my lady's ridiculous plan, you're a fool." The needle dipped again calmly. "Your father had things well in hand when I left."

Gwen tried to imagine her father having anything at all well in hand. But Olivia had a way of speaking that brooked no opposition—even Isobelle responded to that note when Olivia employed it.

A muffled thump and rustle from behind Isobelle's closed doors made both Olivia and Gwen glance toward them. Olivia reacted first, looking up at Gwen and tilting her head. "I believe you were sneaking out to avoid the aftermath, yes? Might want to see that through."

Gwen shot her a grateful look and slipped out.

The morning had dawned clear, with the faintest of crisp tangs in the air that warned of the turning of the seasons. The sun would banish that warning within the hour, but Gwen inhaled deeply as she walked across the courtyard toward the stables, allowing her mind to summon the smells of fallen leaves and apples, of long-roasted meats and winter stews.

They were the smells of her village in autumn. Would Gwen be there this year to enjoy them?

Gwen's throat tightened and her stomach roiled. Each time she pushed those thoughts away, each time she made herself focus on the final tomorrow instead of what would come after, the fear gripped her all the harder next time. The tangle of thoughts was like a flaw in a blade; she could hammer it smooth through sheer brute force as many times as she wanted, but the fault was still there, and once she finished the forging, the metal would shatter when it cooled.

And now, she had one more thread to add to the awful tangle of worry and confusion. She couldn't have known it would happen, but the simple truth was that her involvement in this scheme had ruined Sylvie's life.

Achilles greeted her with cheerful enthusiasm, snuffling at her clothes as she saddled him, searching for treats she hadn't brought. She belted her sword to the saddle, swung a leg over—it was early enough no one would be around to see "Lady Céline" riding astride—and galloped away toward the practice fields.

Gwen was so lost in her thoughts—or rather, in trying to push them away—that she didn't notice someone had beaten her to her destination.

"I see you deal with your nerves through action, too," called Sir Orson as he strode toward her, sheathing his sword and offering Gwen a wave. "You know, Isobelle just eats hers. Sometimes I wonder if that isn't the smarter thing."

Gwen blinked down at him in confusion. "Nerves?"

Sir Orson raised one blond eyebrow. "It's just us, you can admit you're worried about the final, too. C'mon, join me. It'll be a better workout with both of us."

Gwen dismounted. "Why are you so worried? It's not like you want to marry Isobelle."

Orson watched Gwen as she unbuckled her sheath from Achilles's saddle and belted it around her waist. "So weird to see you wearing that in a dress," he muttered, brow furrowing. "Hmm? Oh—well, no. I'll do my best to make her happy, but I admit it's not just the chance to marry the dragon sacrifice. There's all the gold, for one thing. That money would go a long way on an estate like mine. I'm not rich like Isobelle. It would solve . . . many problems." His gaze was lowered, thoughtful. Then he looked up with a grin. "And reputation is important for a knight, you know."

For a real knight, anyway. He didn't say it—he was too congenial, offering Gwen a sheepish smile and shrugging. But Gwen could hear the words ringing in her ears.

Orson's smile faded. "You okay?"

"Isobelle's friend Sylvie is to marry Sir Ralph," Gwen found herself saying before she could think to stop herself. "I can't get it out of my head. Sylvie's never been my biggest fan, but no woman deserves a man like that. And it could have been Isobelle. It *will* be Isobelle, eventually."

Orson was quiet, Gwen's heartbeats stretching into the quiet—and, miraculously, slowing gradually. Just speaking about it made the weight of the news easier to bear.

"It wasn't Isobelle this time," Orson said finally, and then added with a shudder, "and if I win, I'll be nothing like Ralph. I wouldn't mind if you . . ." He hesitated, glancing at Gwen and then reaching up to pat Achilles experimentally on the neck. "You know. If you wanted to visit her now and then. So long as you were discreet."

Gwen bit back her reply—that Isobelle no more wanted to wind up with Sir Awesome than she did Sir Ralph. Maybe it was the best solution in a sea of grim outcomes, even if it did consign Gwen to being nothing more than a well-kept secret, sneaking in and out of Isobelle's life whenever no one was around to see. It wasn't as if Gwen could offer her anything more, even if she won the tournament, even if she showed the world who she was, even if they accepted her skill. . . .

Could she?

Orson, unaware of Gwen's roiling thoughts, patted Achilles one more time and then broke the silence. "Come on, let's have a round." He strode away from Gwen's horse, who had dipped his head to lip at the ground experimentally.

The morning sun swept low across the canopy bordering the field, casting each dip and rise in the branches in stark relief. The long, swaying grasses reached to Gwen's thigh, their elongated shadows bobbing and dancing in the slight breeze, providing a whispering backdrop to the thudding and crunching of Orson's footsteps.

Gwen drew her sword automatically when Orson turned and drew his—he gave his a few swings, and Gwen could see he held it well, his grip confident and movements well practiced.

Orson glanced at her and nodded encouragement. "You haven't had to use that yet in the tournament, have you?" He grinned. "I can show you a thing or two if you want. Just so if our match comes down to swordplay in the end, you'll . . . well, you'll look like you know what you're doing."

Gwen felt a tiny smile curve her lips, the ridiculousness of the situation momentarily supplanting the press of worries crowded inside her mind. Here she was, about to have a friendly bout with the man she'd be facing in deadly combat tomorrow, as he nobly offered to give *her* tips on swordplay.

Gwen flashed him a sweet little smile, letting her eyelashes lower demurely, and absently wondered if the guy would recognize Isobelle's very look reflected in Gwen's features. "I'm ready. Bring it, Awesome."

Orson shrugged, bounced on the balls of his feet, and then lifted his blade for a slow, experimental swing. Gwen easily knocked it aside. Orson tried another attack, still ginger, with so little of his weight behind the swing that when Gwen stepped neatly out of the way, he didn't even stagger.

Orson laughed. "All right, all right. For real this time."

Gwen shifted her grip on the hilt. "As you wish."

He met her attack with an automatic parry, his eyes widening in surprise—he stepped back, turned, swung. Gwen parried, sidestepped, pressed in harder. The clanging of blades punctuated the soft susurration of the grasses, along with Awesome's increasingly loud grunts of effort and panting breaths.

He staggered back from one particularly well-placed blow, buying enough space for him to meet Gwen's eyes, his own flashing with shock, and something else, moving so quickly Gwen wasn't sure she'd seen it.

Anger?

Gwen felt a prickling along the back of her neck as she politely waited for him to recover his balance. It was a sense that had sharpened over these last weeks with Isobelle, dodging discovery and facing down well-armed knights every few days—a sense that warned her of the nearness of danger.

Instinct flung up a solution into her mind. She could pretend to lose. Now, before Orson realized what Gwen had known from Orson's first swing of the sword: that she could beat him. When she was a child, she'd fenced once with one of the boys in the village. After she'd knocked him flat, he stopped speaking to her. They had been thick as thieves, and after that day, his eyes slid past her as if she were no more substantial than smoke. That had been nearly ten years ago, and still, the most acknowledgment he ever offered was a distant nod when his wife stopped to chat with Gwen in the square.

If she just pretended to lose to Orson here, now, then all would be well for a little bit longer.

I am so goddamned tired of pretending.

The thought blazed through Gwen's mind as Orson came at her again. All her thoughts fled, and she abandoned caution, losing herself in the rhythm of attack and counterattack, the notes of Isobelle playing at the organ echoing in her head as her feet danced through the long grass.

Another lunge, a parry, a twist of her arm . . . and Orson's sword thudded heavily into the dirt a few feet away, followed not much later by Orson himself, staggering backward with too much momentum to avoid crashing to the ground with a thud and a whoop of expelled breath.

Gwen's heart pounded so loudly she barely heard the scrape of her sword as she slid it back into its sheath. She took a few steps toward Orson, who sat like a crab with his hands braced behind him and his bent knees slightly akimbo, blinking up at her. She saw that flash again, searing and unlikely on Orson's friendly face. Her heart sank, but she held out her hand anyway in a silent offer to help him up.

Orson stared at her a moment longer—and then he burst out laughing, running one hand through his sweaty, disheveled hair and then clapping the other against Gwen's palm. "Well, damn," he said cheerfully, eyes dancing. "I guess I'd better hope I knock you off your horse tomorrow, huh?"

Relief washed through Gwen like a gust of fresh air after a lifetime of being stuck underground. "Want me to show *you* a few things?" she offered with a grin as she hauled him to his feet.

Orson rolled his eyes, shook his head, and went off to locate his sword in the tall grass. "Give me a sec to catch my breath, and then we're going again."

Chapter Thirty-Nine

IF I TAUGHT YOU TO DREAM, THEN I WAS WRONG

Isobelle pressed a coin into the man's hand, unleashing the full force of her blue eyes. "Remember," she said. "I'm relying on you."

"We won't fail you, my lady," he assured her. Then he turned away to lift his fiddle and tuck it under his chin, launching into another tune that set the dance floor swirling.

Under any other circumstances, Isobelle would have been buzzing about the ball for weeks in advance, planning her gown and accessories, discussing dancing and partnering strategy with the girls, and perhaps, just *perhaps*, allowing herself the tiniest little fantasy about some dashing, mysterious stranger showing up to sweep her off her feet.

Instead, she had found herself that evening looking blankly at a crimson dress Olivia had picked out for her, trying to summon some enthusiasm for something so frivolous as a dance, when her mind was on Gwen, on Sylvie, on the fate awaiting Isobelle herself, if—when—all their plans unraveled.

Now she found herself bribing the musicians to play the one song she knew where women partnered each other for sections of the dance, so that she could look Gwen in the eye for just a moment.

She paused at the edge of the dance floor, letting her gaze sweep over the room with practiced ease, absorbing the social intricacies of the scene before her without conscious effort.

There was Jane, chatting in a corner with a boy who looked suspiciously like the squire she fancied. She'd stuffed him into noble's clothes, and he was somewhere between thrilled and terrified, his eyes huge.

Once upon a time, Isobelle would have laughed with delight at the deception. Now, it made something knot with anger inside her. Why shouldn't the two of them be together? Why should the boy have to hide himself, just because he wasn't born to the right parents? Why shouldn't Jane be allowed to choose him if she wanted?

Next she found Sylvie. Her friend looked like a perfect glass figurine, whirling around the dance floor in Sir Ralph's possessive arms. Sylvie's form was flawless, but her gaze distant, as though she was barely aware he was touching her at all.

I'm sorry, Sylvie. I should have seen it coming.

It had been unbearable, the night before, when Sylvie had finally wept. It had felt impossible to be the cause of her pain and somehow try to comfort her. Clever, sharp-tongued Sylvie had always been her most dangerous friend, but also her dearest.

Sylvie's gaze was tracking something, and when Isobelle turned her head slightly, she saw that Sylvie was watching Gwen.

Gwen had found herself dancing with Sir Makarios of Rhodes, the man who had laughed and congratulated Sir Gawain for defeating him. He laughed again now as Gwen said something to entertain him. And when Gwen smiled, Sylvie's expression flickered in something akin to a flinch.

Olivia had outdone herself with Gwen's gown—it gathered in at her trim waist, using fabric in a warm gold that brought out the same shade in her green eyes. It seemed to fold around her body as though she were emerging from a bright, golden flame, accentuating the high neckline necessary to hide her bruises. The underskirts had been thinned out so Gwen could move as she preferred, and Olivia had even got her to sit still long enough to carefully paint shimmering gold around her eyes, giving her the look of a magical creature who'd wandered into Lord Whimsitt's ball.

Gwen was *beautiful*, and smiling at Sir Makarios as he peppered her with questions and comments about Sir Gawain, but Isobelle could see the strain in her face. *She* was the one who had bested him. The compliments on his lips were for *her*, not her imaginary brother. But Gwen would never—could never—see that admiration directed at her.

All around her, Isobelle's gaze took in the same story, over and over.

Jane, Sylvie, Gwen, and Isobelle herself, all trapped in different cells of the same jail, with the men of the court holding the keys.

The musicians drew to a close with a flourish, and her heart leapt as she stepped forward—it was time to claim Gwen, time to take her hand, even if only for a few seconds, and—

"May I have the honor?"

Orson took her arm gently, and she nearly threw him off, nearly whirled away, her breath catching with the effort of it as she restrained herself to a single twitch.

"Izzie?" His eyes widened, his hand falling away. "Are you . . . ?"

"Orson, I'm sorry." She made her mouth smile, made her eyes focus on him.

"It's the saltarello," he pointed out cautiously. "Very few opportunities for me to step on your toes."

The musicians' notes rose above the sound of the crowd, and with them came the sinking realization that this wasn't the song she'd asked for. No Gwen, not yet.

Raise your hand, she coached herself. *Put it in his.*

Scream, said another voice inside her head. *Fight your jailers. Set something on fire.*

She raised her hand and placed it in Orson's, and he led her out to join the dancers.

"Tomorrow," she said, and though it was only one word, there were whole ballads in it, questions and answers, hopes and fears.

"I don't know," he replied, understanding as easily as he'd spotted her twitch. He'd had years of practice. "None of us knows what will happen, Izzie."

"If it's Gwen," she said, her fingers tightening around his—why were her hands so cold?—"what will we do? How will we ever get them to accept . . ."

Her? That a girl dared step outside the cage they've made for her, and . . . The words wanted to push their way up her throat, to spill out, and so she almost missed the flicker in her old friend's gaze: something very like hurt.

"Orson, you know you have as good a chance," she began. "Better, even. I'm just saying—"

"Izzie." He cut her off with a look, and she fell silent, holding still as he danced a circle around her, each of the women on the floor pinned in place as the men moved. Orson didn't speak again until they'd joined hands once more. "I don't think we can," he said quietly. "I don't think there's a way anyone will accept . . . You need to be ready for that."

The buzz of thoughts in her head was rising to a roar, her dress was suddenly too tight, squeezing the breath from her. *You accepted her,* she wanted to scream. *Why can't you make anyone else do it?*

When the music stopped, she stumbled from him without a word, propping up against a table at the edge of the room where drinks were being served.

"That's what I heard," the man beside her was saying as she closed her cold hand around a flagon. "Vanished right out of their cell, lock still intact. Makes the sentencing easy, though."

"They'll have to catch them first," another pointed out.

"Please. Bunch of housewives on the run? Castle guard'll have them back here in no time. And there's always a slump after something big's over, like the tourney. Some executions will pick the mood up."

The women from Aberfarthing.

And come tomorrow, Gwen might face the same fate.

From somewhere nearby came Lord Whimsitt's laugh, and she spun around to search for him. He was the one who would hold Gwen's life in his hands tomorrow. He was the one who would see who she really was, and have a choice to make.

Isobelle had to say something, she had to *do* something. But her mind was blank. Always, she had thrown herself into a conversation, trusting that the right words would come. But now she couldn't make herself take even a step toward him. Couldn't begin to form the first sentence. What she was up against was simply too great.

For the first time in her life, she was speechless.

There was nothing she could do, except watch tomorrow bear down on her like a knight with a lance. No words were coming. No grand idea arriving. Gazing at Whimsitt's smug, satisfied face across the ballroom, Isobelle knew this was a man who would accept nothing less than absolute control.

He held the key to her cell, and he would never let her out. Tomorrow, he would discover Gwen belonged in one, too. And when he did, he wouldn't simply lock her up.

He would have her killed.

Those were the stakes they were playing for.

She felt trapped inside a nightmare—everyone around her laughing and dancing and gossiping, and not a single one of them hearing her scream.

Every noise around her was too loud, every light too bright. All this time, she had thought she and the other ladies were like brightly colored birds, flitting about a beautiful aviary together, not locked in, but rather gorgeously on show. The envy of all.

Now, the gilded edges of the windows, the broad beams across the ceiling, resembled nothing so much as the bars of a cage. All the bright colors were only to distract her from the fact that she was trapped in here, beating her wings helplessly, with no hope of escape.

Tomorrow, whispered Isobelle's heart. *Tomorrow the world ends. And there is nothing you can do to stop it.*

And as the musicians struck up the song she'd requested, she turned to find Gwen there in her magical dress, the gold around her lashes glittering like the bars of their cage.

To her horror, Isobelle saw her vision flood with tears. Gwen's eyes widened, but before she could speak, Isobelle turned and fled. For once not caring if anyone saw her break, she didn't stop until she'd pushed behind the musicians' dais and burst through the thick curtains blocking off the balcony.

The cool night air greeted her, the rowdy noise of the ball muted by the thick curtains, and she gripped the railing of the balcony, leaning out over it as far as she could. She dragged in a slow breath, making herself focus on the moonlit land below. The dark outlines of the grandstands around the lists were visible, and beyond them the hills extending all the way to the woods.

"Isobelle?"

Isobelle squawked and nearly fell over the balcony railing—then Gwen's arms were around her, pulling her back. She turned into that warm embrace, and she let herself sob all over Gwen's beautiful dress, clinging to the other girl as though she might still fall at any moment.

"Isobelle," Gwen repeated, more softly. Comfort, now—no longer a question.

"I can't do it," Isobelle finally let herself whisper. "I can't do it tomorrow."

"Time won't stop because we want it to," Gwen murmured, pressing a kiss to her temple.

Isobelle leaned back enough to look up at her, and she couldn't stop the words spilling out. "We can't stop time. But we could get more of it."

"What?" Gwen frowned. "You mean reschedule the joust? I don't think . . ."

"No!" Wild hope was flickering to life inside Isobelle, jumping from one part of her brain to another, like a fire coming to life and sending sparks to each new piece of kindling. "We *can* get more time, Gwen. All we have to do is take it. We could go. We could run. Olivia could make it happen, you know she could. We could go tonight."

"What?" Gwen drew back to stare at her. "Run? Where?"

"Anywhere! I don't care where it is, as long as we're both there."

But Gwen was shaking her head, and icy rain was starting to patter down on Isobelle's wild flame of hope. "Isobelle, I . . . I can't just *run away*."

"Yes, you can!" She found Gwen's hands, took hold of them, squeezed them to try to make her see. "Why would you stay here?"

"To fight!" Gwen shot back. "To win. To earn your freedom, and prove myself. That was always the plan, that was why we did all of this. I can do it, Isobelle—I can win this thing."

"I don't doubt it. But then what?" Isobelle pressed. "*After* you win?"

"We'll deal with that when we get there," Gwen said quietly. "I can't keep pretending I'm something other than who I am. Once they see me win, once they see who I am—"

"You're dreaming, Gwen," Isobelle snapped. "You must know that. When you win, they'll force you to show your face. And when they see you're not a man, they'll kill you for it. *That's* what will happen."

"But maybe not!" Gwen protested. "They'll have seen what I can do—what *we* can do, working together. Maybe . . . maybe . . ." Gwen faltered, reaching for something impossible and failing to find it. Frustrated, she blurted, "Why bring me here, do all this, only to give up? This isn't just your dream, Isobelle—it's mine now, too. And I think it always *was* mine, you just showed me how to let myself want it."

"I was wrong." And though she tried to stop them, Isobelle's tears began to fall all over again as despair washed over her. "If I taught you to dream, then I was wrong."

Chapter Forty

NO BETTER THAN THEY ARE

Gwen stared at Isobelle's tear-streaked face, part of her mind screaming at her to reach out, pull her close, wipe those tears away. But the rest of her felt so frozen that she found she could not move.

Ever since the night Isobelle had appeared under Gwen's window in the village, calling for her to waltz off into an adventure, Isobelle's sheer force of will had pushed Gwen through her own hesitations. Practical matters like "who could possibly be willing to train me?" and "but someone's going to notice I'm not a man" melted away under that intense blue stare.

Gwen would never have ridden out as Sir Gawain again after that first joust if not for Isobelle. She'd come to rely on Isobelle's nearly magical ability to imagine the world different, and simply *make it* so. Somehow, Gwen had started to believe, in her heart of hearts, that there was no limit to what Isobelle could make happen.

So how had she not noticed the point when Isobelle had stopped being the one pushing her forward?

Gwen's breath felt shallow and harsh, her footing unsteady with fear at finding herself out on a precipice without Isobelle's unconditional belief firming the ground beneath her. Isobelle had never raised her voice that way to her, and she battled the instinct to shout back. "We can't stop now," she said finally. "We have no other choice but to see this through."

"We *do* have a choice," Isobelle retorted. "I told you, we can run—"

"Run where?" Gwen swallowed. "Live where? On what funds, with what support? No one would welcome a woman blacksmith into their village—we couldn't stay at mine, your people would find us there. We'd have nothing—no money, no titles, no safety net. Do you know what it's like to live that way, Isobelle?"

Isobelle's lips tightened, but she leaned forward, shaking her head. "I don't care. If I were with you, I wouldn't care."

"You would." Gwen felt her own eyes stinging, unable to stop the helpless tears prickling them. "You think you wouldn't, but you would."

"You can't know—"

"I can, because it's what happened to my mother!" Gwen snapped, breathing quicker, regretting the sharpness in her voice the moment she heard it cutting through the background din of the ball beyond the balcony doors.

Isobelle stared at her, one tear still rolling slowly down her perfect cheek, confusion muddying the distress in her eyes.

Gwen turned away, bracing her arms on the balustrade, relishing the cool stone against her palms. "My mother really was from Toussaint. Lady Céline of Toussaint is a real person—or was. She fell in love with my father when he was studying under a master blacksmith at the château where she lived, and when his apprenticeship was over, she gave up everything to return with him."

Isobelle's breath caught. "You had all those names ready when we went to see Archer for Gawain's papers," she murmured, her quick intelligence settling the pieces into place, more pieces than

Gwen had realized she'd found. "And the way you spoke French so easily to Sylvie—that you own a horse like Achilles..."

"I think it killed her." Gwen kept her gaze on the landscape below, stroking her thumbs along the top of the balustrade to ground herself. "I mean, I know it doesn't work like that—I know my mother didn't die because she was homesick. But as much as she loved my father, as much as she loved me... all she did was tell me stories of knights, and chivalry, and noble sacrifice. She just... faded away, Isobelle. While my father and I watched."

A soft hand touched Gwen's elbow, and Gwen fought the urge to turn into the comfort Isobelle was offering her. "I never met your mother," Isobelle murmured. "But her story isn't mine."

Gwen shook her head tightly. "I can't do that to you. My parents, with my father's place in the village, with a good house and a community that accepted him—they had more than you and I could ever hope to have. And it still wasn't enough. You don't know my father—he's the strongest man I know and watching her die nearly killed him, too. I don't think I'm strong enough for that."

The hand at her elbow fell away. Isobelle was quiet for a long time, though Gwen could hear her breathing, could feel the tension building in her, like steam under pressure.

Finally, Isobelle burst. "Gwen, you say you don't want to do that to me—but you don't get to make my choices *for* me. Yes, I asked you to be my knight. But I never wanted you to be like the others."

Gwen turned back to her, feeling her own temper rising beyond her ability to control it. "Proving my worth, and yours, that's the only way forward for us!"

"And I'm telling you that's impossible, that the world won't change so easily." Isobelle's voice rose, her appeal in her luminous eyes. "Gwen, you're telling me I'm too weak to leave luxury behind, making decisions to try to protect me—god, you're no better than they are!"

Gwen felt herself take a single, staggering step back. Her vision swam and her head rang the way it did after an opponent got in a good hit, only there was no stiff armor supporting her, no horse beneath her to keep her upright. And when her vision cleared, it was no enemy's visor in front of her eyes, but Isobelle's face.

Isobelle drew a breath, stricken and pale, remorse writ clearly in her expression.

Gwen spoke first. "You're wrong," she managed in a low, even voice. "I am better than they are. And tomorrow I'm going to prove it."

She slipped past Isobelle, twisting to avoid the hand that reached out to her, and threw herself back into the hot, loud chaos of the ballroom, heading for the doors. She thought she felt a pair of intense blue eyes tracking her as she lost herself in the crowd, but she didn't look back. Perhaps she had only dreamed it.

LET'S PAUSE FOR A MOMENT here.

Lift your head and flip through the pages—there are still eighty to go. We're still ten chapters from the end, and yet this is the eve of the great battle, isn't it? This, right here, is the grand showdown that will determine whether likeable but not-for-her Sir Orson will take Isobelle as his prize, or whether Gwen will save Isobelle from a fate worse than . . . well, worse than a lot of things, anyway.

Surely there are only two ways the story could proceed from here: Gwen wins and Isobelle is saved. Or Gwen loses, Sir Orson sweeps the tournament, and both Gwen's and Isobelle's dreams are shattered.

There is, perhaps, a third option, where Gwen and Isobelle both swallow their pride and somehow flee together before the tournament even begins, but that feels a little unrealistic given the style with which they both just imploded.

Anyone who has ever loved a good story knows to be wary when it seems like the climax is approaching but the storyteller is just getting settled in. It suggests that the storyteller is about to pull the metaphorical rug out from under your metaphorical feet—a terrible, unfair manipulation by all accounts. Unforgiveable, really, what said storyteller's about to do. For all intents and purposes: she is about to lie to you.

So, as the sun peeps over the forest bordering Darkhaven town and dawn begins to trickle across the hills and dales and picturesque thatched roofs, down to the tournament grounds already beginning to fill with fans, let us ponder a single question:

Given a choice between winning, losing, or running away . . . what could possibly happen that would be worse than all three of those fates?

Chapter Forty-One

THE CROWD WENT WILD

The morning of the tournament dawned clear and bright, as though the weather knew the importance of the day and did not dare bring rain or fog to mar it. The air was thick with buzzing anticipation, more people crowded into the tournament grounds than Isobelle had ever seen. Children ran about, laughing and fighting each other with wooden swords and lances, people stood waiting in lines a hundred strong for snacks, and musicians were stationed at intervals around the grounds, entertaining those waiting to find their place to watch.

Merriment was everywhere—and all Isobelle could do was paste a smile onto her face.

If she hadn't already been wrestling with the guilt and unhappiness threatening to swallow her, she would have had to acknowledge the seriousness of the situation when Olivia showed up to watch the final joust.

Usually her maid preferred to lurk on the edges of major events, but she must have shared Isobelle's concern that things might move quickly today. Olivia was sitting in the back of his lordship's box, behind Isobelle, Jane, and Hilde, but Isobelle couldn't see how even Olivia, with her nerves of steel, could handle the horrible thickness of anticipation in the air.

"Where's Sylvie?" Jane whispered, leaning in close.

"I wish I knew," Isobelle muttered, twisting to glance back at the gate keeping the crowd at bay.

"Perhaps she is with Sir Ralph," Hilde suggested, wrinkling her nose as if trying to speak the man's name without letting it touch her lips.

"No," Jane replied, tilting her chin. "He's over there with some of the visiting nobles."

Then where *was* Sylvie? Why had she stayed away? There was an uneasiness knotted inside Isobelle's chest no matter how she tried to tell herself that there was some explanation for it—that the apprehension winding its way through her veins was guilt, that Sylvie had simply chosen not to come, having bigger things to worry about. But even facing down her doom, Sylvie was a master at the twisted game that was life in this castle. If she wasn't here, there was some *reason* behind it. Isobelle just didn't know what.

"Is that meant to be Gawain?" Hilde murmured, pointing at a sort of giant scarecrow a group of spectators were trying to hoist above their section of the grandstand.

Isobelle knew it was an attempt at distraction, but she barely heard her friend. Her own words from the night before kept ringing in her head, far too loudly for anything else to stand a chance.

You don't get to make my choices for me.

But hadn't she been trying to do the same for Gwen?

You're no better than they are.

It had been the last thing she'd said to Gwen.

Please, *please* let it not be the last thing she *ever* said to Gwen.

She should be in Sir Gawain's tent right now, apologizing, arguing all over again, trying to make Gwen see she was right, that it *was* horribly unfair, but that nobody who mattered would see it, and nobody would save her just because she deserved it.

Isobelle would rather fade away into nothing than lose Gwen—she ought to be down there now, convincing Gwen to see it.

"Isobelle." It was Jane, leaning in with a worried expression. "Does Gw—Gawain truly plan to try to win today?"

"Yes," Isobelle managed, shaping the words with her lips.

"But then what will—"

"I don't know," Isobelle snapped, her hands squeezing together so tightly her fingers ached.

You're no better than they are.

She would have given anything for one more minute to speak to Gwen, but the last of Gwen's minutes were trickling away through her fingers, vanishing no matter how Isobelle grasped at them.

The audience was starting to stir, rippling with that special knowledge crowds have when the moment they've waited for is imminent. In the grandstand on the other side of the open jousting field, a huge banner read GAWAYN in uneven letters, and most of the crowd had sprigs of lavender pinned to their coats—there couldn't have been a flower left on a plant for leagues in any direction.

In the center of it all, in the middle of the lists—it would have to be carried to one side for the match to begin—was the prize pot. Isobelle's own dowry, converted to glimmering gold and glittering gems, piled into chests until they spilled out and tumbled to the ground. The effect was extremely dramatic. And the sight of the wealth that had put her in this situation in the first place made her feel sick.

The herald took his place, raising the metal cone that allowed him to speak so loudly to his lips, puffing out his chest, and bellowing to be heard over the hubbub.

"Lords and laymen, this is the moment you've all been waiting for... the culmination of a month-long tournament of champions, the must-see finale of the year. Never before has there been a Tournament of Dragonslayers with so many upsets, so many surprises, such mystery..."

The crowd knew exactly which knight the herald was referring to, the background noise rising to a roar that drowned out the herald's amplified voice for some time. The herald stopped trying to be heard and finally waved his arms in silent agreement with the energy of the crowd.

When they finally started to calm down again, he lifted the cone back to his lips. "Now, it is my great honor to present the gent from Kent, the Englishman with a winning plan, it's Darkhaven's very own... Sir Orson the Awesome!"

Orson came cantering out onto the lists, past the chests of gold and jewels, raising a hand to the crowd's somewhat perfunctory cheers, one hand grasping his reins as his horse sidestepped nervously at the hubbub all around them.

Isobelle gazed down at him, picturing his familiar face behind the helmet. He wouldn't have been a bad husband. He wouldn't have loved her and brought her to life, as Gwen did. But Isobelle wouldn't have put him in danger, either.

"And now, lords and laymen, one and all, prepare yourselves!" A hush fell over the crowd, like the heavy, tense silence before a gale strikes. "Mysterious and charming, he's taken Darkhaven by storm.... Can he go the distance and claim his prize? He's the one that you want: The knight from Toussaint! The newcomer from France who's here to take his chance, it's Sirrrrrr Gawain!"

Gwen rode out, and the crowd went *wild*.

Achilles half reared, and Isobelle found she was on her feet. It was too late to choose her last words to Gwen again, but she wanted with all her heart for Gwen to see her, to know that she was there. That she was ready to walk this path with her, whatever happened next.

There was an official speaking hurriedly to the herald, and after a moment the man lifted his loudspeaker for one more announcement: "Will the competitors please approach his lordship!"

Isobelle's head snapped around to look at Lord Whimsitt, who was coming slowly to his feet. Perhaps the knights were to salute him?

Then she saw Olivia's face. Her maid's jaw was clenched, and when she caught Isobelle's eye, she flicked her gaze toward the far side of the lists.

There were two columns of guards making their way out onto the field, breaking into groups and taking their place by each of the exits.

Isobelle went cold all over, sinking down to her bench as her legs went weak.

Something was wrong. Very wrong.

Chapter Forty-Two

THE TERRIBLE SOUND OF A THOUSAND PEOPLE NOT KNOWING WHAT TO SAY

Gwen's eyes were on Isobelle, drinking her in. She tried to calm her heart, which was thudding in a ragged, lurching rhythm of relief at the sight of her. A part of Gwen had been sure Isobelle wouldn't be there after the things they'd said to each other the night before.

You're no better than they are. Isobelle's words, sharp as daggers, still hurt.

Gwen had awakened still angry and left before Isobelle that morning. But once she met up with Dupont at Sir Gawain's changing tent, the anger had shattered into a tangle of fear and longing and despair and hope that made her hands shake as she tried to put on her armor.

Madame Dupont had curled her freckled hands over Gwen's, meeting her eye, squeezing her fingers until they stopped shaking. "Show them who you are," the woman said, solemn, nodding. "Let everything else fall away."

Now, Gwen longed to lift her visor so she could meet Isobelle's eyes properly. Let her see in Gwen's face that it wasn't about beating the other knights, or showing that she was the best, or even changing the hearts and minds of the spectators. It was about proving something to *herself*. Something that had been inside Gwen as long as she could remember, long before she ever met Isobelle.

She may have started on this path to save Isobelle—but she had to finish it for herself. Isobelle had seen her, the real her, when no one else had . . . not even Gwen herself.

She would ride and finish this tournament. And when she'd won, she would salute Isobelle, and then run. Achilles could clear the rails that blocked off the end of the lists, and Gwen could be away before anyone realized her headlong flight was anything other than a display of victorious adrenaline. She could lie low while the dust cleared, and as the rest of the county was trying to figure out where Sir Gawain had gone, she would come back for Isobelle.

And if Isobelle still wanted to go . . . Gwen would go with her.

Gwen's eyes burned as she gazed intently at Isobelle's face, willing the other girl to somehow see past her visor, to see her heart in her eyes.

But Isobelle wasn't even looking at her. Her head was turned, gaze lifted to fix on something more distant, and she . . . she'd gone white.

Gwen twisted to see a column of guards marching down past the spectators. The cheers and chanting of the crowd had changed to a confused, wild susurration of conversation and speculation.

Something was wrong.

Achilles, sensing his rider's uncertainty, danced back a few paces, half turning toward the exit. The end of the lists was covered by guards, too. There would be no escaping that way, unless the guards left before the joust began. An anxious whinny made her glance to her right, where Orson's horse was becoming restless too, reacting to the tension in his rider's body.

"Dismount, Sir Gawain." The voice came from Lord Whimsitt,

standing in his box with both hands braced against the barrier.

Gwen looked up at him, not moving yet, her head spinning as it tried to catch up. Whimsitt's voice was even, but she was close enough to see his face as he looked down on them—on her. She was close enough to see the anger transforming his ordinarily placid countenance into something aggressive and full of fury.

She knew that look. She'd been getting it all her life—whenever a man realized she had made the weapon he'd commissioned from her father. When she'd beaten her childhood friend play-fighting with sticks. Every time she'd ever been stronger or smarter or cleverer than they expected her to be, every time she'd dared to step out of line without softening the surprise with a smile or a lowering of her eyes. She'd seen it just yesterday, on the face of the nicest man she'd met these past weeks, when she'd beaten him at swordplay.

It was the same look now that turned Whimsitt's face into such a threatening, furious mask.

He knows.

That certainty washed through her like a cool, calm stream, carrying with it the last traces of her confusion. Her exits were blocked. She was surrounded by guards. Even if she was willing to hurt or even kill perfectly innocent men who were just following their lord's orders, there were too many of them for her to fight.

She ran a hand over Achilles's neck to calm him, and then dismounted. One of the guards came up to snatch at Achilles's reins, leading him away with some difficulty as Achilles reared and attempted to get back to his mistress's side.

"Lift your visor," Whimsitt's voice came again, low and cold.

Gwen lifted her chin, her hands at her sides. "If you would let me finish the tournament, my lord, I will—"

"Lift your visor and show them who you are!" Whimsitt's calm evaporated, this repetition of the command sounding out in a higher, more penetrating shout. This time, he did not wait for Gwen to comply, but rather gestured to one of the guards, who leapt forward and seized Gwen's helmet. The metal scraped at Gwen's ear, leaving behind a searing line of pain as the man wrenched the helmet from her, half knocking her down in the process.

Gwen caught herself as she staggered, and went still, listening as reaction swept across the stands. Those farther away could not see what was happening, but ripples of gasps and cries of shock and alarm scattered back from those closest to Whimsitt's box, murmurs and explanations spreading across the stands before dropping into an unnatural hush.

Gwen stood, the breeze ruffling her hair and tugging at the loose strands that had fallen from her bun, a trickle of blood dripping from the spot where her helmet had scraped a layer of skin off her ear . . . and listened to the terrible sound of a thousand people not knowing what to say.

Her gaze swung across the hushed crowd, seeing not individual faces so much as a bewildering composite of wide eyes and open mouths, of shock and confusion and disgust. Now and then she thought she saw something else—hope or admiration—but she lost sight of it whenever she tried to focus on those few faces, seeing only more anger and betrayal wherever she looked.

Finally, her eyes found Isobelle again. Her cheeks were glinting with tears, her hands white-knuckled where they clutched at the barrier. Gwen's own heart wrenched, seeing her heartbreak—she bit her lip, then mouthed the words: *I'm sorry.*

It would probably be the last chance she had to tell Isobelle anything at all.

Isobelle's face crumpled, just before Whimsitt—seeing this exchange—stepped between them, face purpling with fury.

"As you see, this . . . this *woman* has made a mockery of our oldest, most sacred traditions!" His face twisted around the word "woman" as if it had tasted nasty on his tongue. "She has stripped her opponents of their right to face their peers in noble combat, she has robbed you of your final, and tainted this ancient rite."

Gwen felt that heated, metallic something deep inside her stir, rising in a way it hadn't since that first qualifying joust, after she'd heard the way the other knights talked about Isobelle.

"No, *you* are robbing them of their final!" she burst out, tearing her arm away from the guard's grip and striding toward Whimsitt's box. "If you let me ride, if you let me show you what I've *been* showing you, all this time—"

The guard had scrambled to catch at Gwen again, joined by one of his comrades, so that the two of them wrestled Gwen back. Whimsitt was gesturing, indicating something violent by the curse words spilling from his tongue—but the guards, uncertain about punching a woman in the mouth the way they'd apparently happily do a man, simply dragged Gwen down onto her knees.

"*You will not speak!*" shrieked Whimsitt, slamming his hands down on the railing hard enough to make the stands reverberate with the blow. Murmurs scattered through the crowd as they whispered and shifted nervously, uncertain how to react. Whimsitt stood panting, regaining some measure of his composure before he continued. "I was informed last night of this *woman's* vile treachery and deceit. She will be taken into custody and held until we have finished the tournament festivities. And then ... then she will pay for her crimes."

The words fell into the silence of the crowd like the incantation of a spell. Having been told what to think, how to react, a handful of spectators began jeering, calling out a few of the more vile obscenities Whimsitt was too well-bred to speak. The jeers spread, not as fast as the chanting and cheering had done when Sir Gawain first rode out onto the field, but fast enough. Gwen turned in time to see them pull a giant straw effigy of Sir Gawain down off the post they'd been using to wave it around. The crowd milled about and then cast the effigy down onto the ground before the stands.

They'd tied a rope around its neck.

Gwen's vision and hearing went strange after that—the scene played itself out in bits and pieces, some mental scribe inside Gwen's head struggling to record everything and noting only a few random moments.

She felt rough hands tear at her straps, and then a blade slicing through the leather to pry the pieces of her armor away.

You're ruining it, she wailed, her voice stuck inside her own mind, as they pushed and pulled at her. She knew she ought not to care about such a small thing now, in the midst of all that was happening, but she'd made that armor herself, piece by piece over the years, modifying and perfecting it with an attention to detail that she hadn't even understood herself until she wore it on the jousting field.

They tossed the pieces of her armor into the dust.

She felt cold metal around her wrists as they jerked her arms behind her back, the loud, heavy sound of a lock closing, the weighty clink of chains. She saw Isobelle, her mouth moving soundlessly, the words lost in the hubbub as she tried to climb over the railing of the box to get to Gwen. Olivia was holding her back, her expression as stoic and unchanging as ever.

Hilde was there, crying quietly and holding on to Jane, who stood watching with a faint, confused frown, as if she'd never fully understood the revelation of Sir Gawain's identity to begin with, and was only now grappling with the implications.

And Sylvie . . . wasn't there.

Gwen felt a stab of sorrow, searching for anger and finding none. She couldn't even blame Sylvie for betraying her to Whimsitt, for it must have been she—the truth of Gawain's identity was the only dagger Sylvie had. Could Gwen blame her for using it, even if the target it found was her own heart?

The guards hauled Gwen roughly to her feet, wrenching her bad shoulder hard enough to tear a cry of pain from her lips.

"Hey!" Orson's voice snapped as he pulled off his helmet, his eyes flashing. "You're to detain her. Not hurt her."

Gwen glanced over at him, grateful to have an ally in all the chaos—and then froze.

His eyes met hers and slid away immediately, his lips tightening. Then he drew himself up, lifting his chin, and looked back at her.

Gwen stared at him, a strange numbness spreading through her as her body understood what she had seen before her mind caught up.

"It was you," she murmured, wishing the guards had left her on her knees, for her legs were struggling to hold her up. "*You* told him who I was."

Orson tucked his helmet under his arm and met her gaze. His

eyes held sorrow—but not regret. "You would have won if you'd been allowed to ride," he said, under the din of the crowd as Whimsitt stood, barking orders. Orson took a breath and let it out slowly. "You would've beaten me."

Gwen was still staring at his features, so perfectly sculpted, his blond hair stirring in the breeze, his blue eyes straight out of every ballad of perfect knighthood she'd ever heard, when a shadow passed over the sun.

She shivered, grateful to the shifting clouds for breaking the tableau.

But then the sun blinked back in again, faster than any cloud could move.

A cry of confusion rippled through the crowd as something swept past them, above them, impossibly huge.

Gwen looked up in time to see a sinuous forked tail vanish across the sky.

For a long, long moment, no one moved. No one so much as glanced at their neighbors to see if they'd imagined the sight—no one wanted to know if what they'd seen was real.

And then, with a roar that shook the very ground beneath Gwen's feet, the creature swept up the hill, behind the stands, and launched itself into the sky with a ribbon of searing, spraying flames that engulfed the tents at the far end of the lists.

A single voice, high and piercing with terror, screamed: *"DRAGON!"*

The crowd erupted into screams, turning from a quiet, meek pool of humanity into a seething, vicious, storming sea. Everyone tried to flee, and with the stands at twice their normal capacity, there was nowhere for anyone to go. Screams of fear turned to screams of agony as many were trampled, and people spilled out over the barriers onto the lists in an attempt to find escape and shelter.

Whimsitt vanished immediately, though his voice was still shouting orders, demanding the guards do something. "It's after the gold in the prize pot!" he screamed from a crowd of other nobles also fleeing the scene. "Stop it!"

A few halfhearted crossbow bolts went whizzing up into the sky, nowhere near the dragon, which was half a league away, gleefully setting fire to the town encircling the base of the hill where the castle sat. Only when every one of the thatch-roofed buildings was surging with flames did the great beast, its scales gleaming a burnished bronze in the sun, turn back toward the tournament grounds.

The guards holding Gwen burst back into action, instinctively holding her as they ran away toward safety, dragging her toward the castle. She fought them, trying in vain to break free. "I can help!" she cried, digging in her heels, carving twin grooves in the mud. "Let me go, I can fight!"

Then one of them, too terrified to obey his compunctions about hitting girls, drove his fist with expert accuracy into her bad shoulder. Gwen felt her muscles go limp, her vision spinning as pain flooded her senses. The last thing she saw, as dizziness swept through her and robbed her of the last of her sight, was a blond-haired, blue-eyed girl standing absolutely still, clutching the railing and staring after her.

Chapter Forty-Three

SOMEONE GET THIS HYSTERICAL GIRL OUT OF HERE!

An eerie chill had taken over Isobelle's body. She wanted to scream, and cry, and fight off Olivia's iron grip to go running after Gwen, but the part of her that had taken control knew she didn't have a moment to waste—that to scream would be an indulgence she couldn't afford.

The huge beast took a long, leisurely pass down the length of the jousting field, sending the crowd below darting this way and that like a frightened school of fish. It was playing with them.

"Fight it," Isobelle shouted to Lord Whimsitt, who was like a statue, staring up at the great beast. "Why are you just standing there?"

He whirled around to gape at her, eyes bulging. "It's a *dragon*, you stupid girl!"

"And this place is full of knights!" she shot back. "This is the Tournament of *Dragonslayers*! What were they competing for, if not the chance to do this?"

He stared at her, and she stared back, steel in her gaze. They both knew the answer: the knights had never volunteered for something so dangerous. All the dragons had been presumed dead long before these knights were born—not one of them had signed up to face one down.

"This *is* the Tournament of Dragonslayers." It was Sir Ralph, standing in the adjoining box among the other nobles scrambling for cover. "And our prize is named for what the dragon really wants—what the dragon used to be given, in times gone by." He found his feet and raised one hand to point directly at Isobelle. "The dragon sacrifice."

"I'm sorry, WHAT?" Isobelle shrieked, giving up on all her resolutions about not screaming. "Are you out of your mind?"

"The beast must be ancient to be so large," Sir Ralph shouted over the noise of the crowd. "Ancient and far too dangerous to take head on. But if we give it what it wants . . ."

Olivia finally let go of Isobelle, moving to push past her, and now it was Isobelle's turn to grab her maid by the arm. The last thing she needed was Olivia in jail too, and that was what would happen if she got anywhere near Sir Ralph.

"Sir Ralph," Isobelle gritted out, eyes narrowed, spine straight, skewering the man in place with her gaze. "If you think for one moment I'm going to let you—"

"Someone get this hysterical girl out of here," Lord Whimsitt demanded.

He wasn't siding with Sir Ralph—but Isobelle noted he wasn't naysaying him, either.

"Isobelle," Olivia said quietly in her ear, composed once more. "Let's go now."

The words were like cold water flowing through her veins, washing away all the fire that had held her upright. Olivia was right. They had Gwen. There was a dragon in the skies. The town below was on fire. Everything was horribly, disastrously wrong, and she had no idea what to do next.

This was always how it was going to end. They had been careening toward catastrophe for weeks, and now it was here. And Isobelle's world was going up in flames.

After several hours—or perhaps an eternity, who was she to say—Isobelle lay on Gwen's bed, crying. Olivia had shoved her into Jane's and Hilde's hands with orders to get her back to the suite, and then vanished. When she returned from her mysterious errand, pink-cheeked and smelling somewhat of horse, she'd taken one look at Isobelle sobbing on the bed and then started packing.

Isobelle could not summon enough interest to ask Olivia where she'd been. The wind had gone out of Isobelle's sails, the fire had gone out of her veins, and the unshakable certainty that had carried Isobelle through life so far was in ashes.

Gwen was locked up below the castle. Olivia had heard from the servants' gossip channels that the dragon had flown away out of sight, and most of the castle's forces were focused on fighting the fires in the town below.

"There's no point in packing," Isobelle called to Olivia, hugging the pillow harder. It smelled like whatever Gwen used to wash her hair, and a little just like Gwen. A warm smell that was part leather, part Achilles, and part linen. Isobelle had always liked it, and now she breathed it in again, wrapping it around her heart.

"No?" Olivia called back, visible through the doorway as she carefully pushed a set of knives into pockets on a long strip of canvas, and then rolled the whole thing up to shove it in a bag.

"No. I'm not going anywhere."

Olivia looked up from her work, let out a sigh, and walked

across to brace her hands against the doorframe. "And what's your plan, my lady?"

"I'm going to lie here until I grow moss," Isobelle replied, allowing herself a sniffle.

"Is that what Gwen would tell you to do?" Olivia asked, raising one eyebrow.

Isobelle buried her face in the pillow, muffling a genuine sob, and most of her words. "No. She'd tell me to run. But she'd be wrong." Another sob pushed its way up from her gut, shaking her body. "That's what I told her, last night. That she was *wrong*."

"Isobelle," Olivia said, clearly reaching for patience. "My job is to keep you safe. And once those men have put out the fires and had time to think, they're going to work out that you knew what Gwen was doing. That you were wrapped up in all this, handing Gawain your favor in front of everyone. This is going to go badly. I hammered those rings outside the balcony for a reason, and this was it. You and I are going to head down that rope with our emergency supplies. I'll have you in Londonne by tomorrow morning, and on a boat to Europe by tomorrow night."

"You'll have to drag me," Isobelle shot back.

"We both know I can, if that's what it takes. Listen, I'm only *mostly* sure they're not going to stake you out for a dragon to take you. That the conversation even took place tells me we're done here."

Isobelle squeezed her eyes shut. The same image of Gwen kept welling up in her mind—blood trickling down her face, pale beneath her freckles, green eyes fixed on Isobelle. *I'm sorry*, she'd mouthed.

Sobs took over again. She couldn't—*wouldn't*—leave. She had to tell Gwen that *she* was the one who was sorry. But Gwen was under guard, and nobody was taking another drugged custard tart, and her head was throbbing, the urgent beat of her heart drumming through it as her thoughts ran in circles.

But... wait. The loud pounding was someone thumping at the door.

Isobelle lifted her tearstained face. Olivia shot her a look warning her to stay put, then threw open the door to reveal... Sylvie.

"I've just heard," Sylvie said by way of greeting, heaving for breath as though she'd been running.

"I was beginning to wonder if I'd have to go out and find you," Olivia said, stepping out of her way and tilting her head to send Sylvie through to Isobelle's—or rather Gwen's—room. "I've been trying to provoke her into doing something—see if you have better luck."

Isobelle gazed up at her as she filled the doorway. "Where were you?" she whispered, hoarse. "You didn't show up to the final."

"I was—never mind." Sylvie squinted at her, then strode over to throw open the curtains. "What are you doing just lying there, hugging Céline's—Gwen's—pillow? Isobelle, what's wrong with you?"

But when Sylvie dismissed the question about where she had been, Isobelle felt a horrible certainty click into place. There was *always* a reason that Sylvie was anywhere, and she hadn't been at the joust.

"You told," she gasped, sitting up straight.

"What?" Sylvie took a step back.

"You told them about Gwen," Isobelle whispered, horror creeping over her. "Because if Gwen hadn't ridden, Sir Ralph would have made it through, and you never would have— I know you blame her. And me."

Sylvie stood perfectly still, her expression made of stone. When she spoke, she shaped each word carefully, as though if she didn't, one of them might drop to the floor and shatter. "Isobelle, you are an idiot in love—it would be obvious even if you hadn't told us, you should have kept a straighter face around her if you didn't want to give it away—so I'm going to pretend you didn't just accuse me of betraying our friendship."

Isobelle had to remember to draw in a breath, her chest so tight she thought the air wouldn't come. Then with a hiccup and a sniffle, she managed it. "You didn't?"

"I would *never*," Sylvie replied, her voice rising as she continued. "Listen, if I'd had the right gossip to destroy her when I thought she was lying to you about who she was, perhaps I would have done it to keep her from hurting you. But I would never—not for anything—betray her to *them*."

Her words echoed between the pair of them, and Isobelle felt them settle into her bones with the weight of truth, followed by a hot flush of shame—her own guilt had planted the idea that Sylvie had betrayed them.

"I don't know how Whimsitt found out, but Ralph told me this morning, just to watch my face when I realized what it meant." Sylvie lifted a hand to brush her hair out of her eyes, and Isobelle saw her nails were torn, her fingertips bloodied. "And then he locked me in my room, to keep me from you. I tried to fight my way out. I tried to warn you."

"Sylvie!" Isobelle threw aside the pillow, scrambling across the bed. "I'm sorry, I should have known. You deserve so much better than for me to think . . ."

"I do deserve better," Sylvie agreed, taking a step back in alarm as she realized there was a very real prospect of a hug unless she took evasive action. "But we have far bigger issues. They're all going to be shouting at each other and putting out fires for a while yet, so we have time to think. Let's do that very carefully and get this right."

"Get what right?"

Sylvie blinked at her. "Rescuing Gwen, of course."

Chapter forty-four

A FOOLISH, RECKLESS IDIOT WITH HER HEAD IN THE CLOUDS

Gwen wedged herself into the corner of the cell and tried not to shiver.

We should've gotten those villagers out of here the moment they were taken, she thought guiltily. She'd never been in a jail cell before, but between the unrelenting chill, the constant steady dripping sounds from the ceiling, and the sporadic, not-so-distant rustlings of rodents, Gwen realized she'd never fully imagined quite how awful it was.

At least she could lean her shoulder against the stone wall and let the chill soothe the pain for her. It was even better than Olivia's basin of cool water. She'd tried, when she'd first been tossed in here, to haul the heavy door up off its hinges again—but the other night, it had taken her efforts combined with Isobelle's and Olivia's, plus the help of a few of the villagers. On her own, she could barely shift the door at all.

The distant screams and foundation-shaking roars from the dragon had long since faded. If any of the lore about them was right, though, it would be back. The gold mines had been closed long ago because the precious metal attracted the monsters. Now, a fortune in gold and gems would be under guard at the heart of Darkhaven castle, and the beast had gotten quite a good look at it while it flew about the tournament.

Gwen closed her eyes and her mind filled instantly with a memory of the dragon as it had flown over the tournament grounds. Its wingspan was wide enough to block out the sun across the entire stands, and with one casual breath it had razed half the festival.

And yet her blood *sang* when she saw it. Some terrifying instinct, buried deep within her, had burst out in one piercing rush, and she had actually *fought* the guards dragging her toward safety in order to stay where the dragon was. In order to stand, to fight.

Gwen shuddered and buried her face in her hands. When had she turned from a sensible, practical village girl into a foolish, reckless idiot with her head in the clouds?

Isobelle, she thought, heart aching. *That's when.*

The faint illumination in her cell came from a torch some distance down the corridor and around the bend. Her first indication that someone was coming was a sudden, massive shadow on the wall, and then a mad flickering of the light as whoever it was tugged the torch out of its sconce.

She recognized the heavy, clinking steps of the mail-enhanced boots worn by the castle guard and braced herself. She thought she'd have more time before they decided what to do with her. But perhaps it was better this way, without an eternity in these cells, replaying the choices she could have made differently.

The torchlight bobbed and weaved, illuminating a large, burly form, and came to a halt before the bars of her cell.

"Gwen?"

Gwen's head snapped up. She knew that voice. Knew it better than any other in the whole world.

"D-dad?"

Her father tossed the torch down onto the stone, pulled off his helmet, and pressed in against the bars. "Gwen!"

Gwen scrambled to her feet, biting back a sob as she rushed for the bars, reaching through them so Amos could wrap her hands up in his own big, scarred ones. "Dad, how . . . I don't . . ."

Her father gave a soft, strained laugh, and squeezed her hands hard enough to make her bones ache. She didn't protest. "I came as soon as I heard. It took me a while to get everything together, but as soon as that lady showed up to tell me what had happened—"

"Lady?" Gwen interrupted, her heart staggering.

"Well, I don't know what she was. She was dressed like a servant, so I suppose . . ."

"Olivia?" Gwen gasped, hands going somewhat limp now under her father's. "Was she the same woman who brought a bunch of refugees to the village?"

Her father nodded. "The very same. She brought me your armor, all messed up, straps cut and everything. Gwen, who the hell is she? She's not any kind of servant, that much I know."

Gwen fought the somewhat hysterical urge to laugh. "I have no idea. She's supposed to be Isobelle's maid, but . . . well, we don't ask how or why she knows and does the things she does. The villagers from Aberfarthing—they did get to you?"

Her father nodded. "They're all well, by the way—we've sent a few of them on to other villages, and we're all making sure they're well cared for." He let out a sigh, a faint smile on his face. "I forgot how much easier it is to take care of someone else than it is yourself."

Gwen swallowed, scanning her father's torchlit features. "Dad . . . how did you get in here? The whole place is guarded. How . . ." Now that her shock had worn off, she could scan his attire, trying to wrestle with the confusion of seeing her father, who in her entire life Gwen had only seen wear a total of three shirts, all in the same style, dressed as a castle guard.

Amos laughed and released his grip on her hands enough to pat one of them gently. "Gwen, my darling—we *make* the armor for the castle guard." He rapped his knuckles against the breastplate with a lopsided smile.

Gwen felt herself losing her grip on her own emotions, an uneven sob of laughter escaping her. Then she looked up, meeting her father's eyes, and swallowed hard. "Dad... there was no blacksmithing internship."

Amos's expression softened, and he patted her hand again. "I know, Gwen. I've known since the first day you came back, glowing like a miniature sun, and tried to tell me you didn't know if you'd gotten your internship."

Gwen's legs, already unsteady, gave way and she sat down rather heavily on the floor of her cell. "What? You knew? Why... why didn't you tell me you knew? *How* did you know?"

Her father grinned at her, then groaned as he braced a palm on the stone and sat down on the other side of the bars. "I'd love to blow your mind and just say 'A father knows, dearest.' But the truth is, everyone was talking about this mysterious new Sir Gawain, who'd rolled up out of nowhere and earned a spot in the tournament by unseating Sir Evonwald."

Gwen stared at him, still trying to process that her father had known what she was doing *all this time* and had said nothing.

Her father raised his eyebrows, eyeing her. "Gwen, how thick do you think I am? You're not the only one with ears who was around to hear your mum's stories. Sir Gawain this, Sir Gawain that...

and, mon chou, you even said your alter ego was from Toussaint, where your mum was born." He reached through the bars, fitting his larger hands with some difficulty, and patted Gwen's knee. "I didn't say anything because you didn't want me to."

Gwen's eyes were burning as she scanned her father's features, her muscles tensing under a weight she hadn't realized she was carrying. "But . . . you weren't worried? Why didn't you stop me?"

"I'm gratified you think I could've stopped you. Of course I was worried. But my daughter is strong and clever, and a damn sight better at fighting than most of those puffed-up nobles in shiny armor. She can take care of herself. She's been taking care of me for years." His smile vanished as his eyes met hers. "Oh, Gwen . . . what kind of dad would I be if I tried to stop you from being who you were born to be?"

Gwen felt that weight on her shoulders collapse, slipping away, and she leaned forward with a sob to press her forehead against her father's hands. She could not remember the last time she had wept that way—possibly not since the day her mother had died. But she couldn't have stopped herself now if the dragon itself had knocked the prison down around them.

The storm was intense, but brief. After, she lifted her head, tears making her father's visage waver and dance in the torchlight. "Dad, it's all gone so wrong. I've messed everything up so badly."

Amos's eyes were damp, and he sniffed loudly before saying briskly, "I don't see how. You're talking about that girl, I presume—the one you brought home the night of the dragon bonfire?"

Gwen choked, having thought her father had run out of terrifying surprises to spring on her. "Wh— You know about Isobelle, too?"

"Is that her name?" Amos's eyes twinkled. "Listen, as far as she's concerned, I don't think you have to worry. If you don't get yourself out of here soon, I imagine she'll be storming the place to get you out."

Gwen swallowed hard. "But everything else—the tournament, the nobles... they all know. I never got to show them who I *really* am, never got to finish what I started. And now... now I can't be a knight anymore."

Her father's eyebrows drew together. "Gwen, that has to be one of the silliest things I've ever heard you say. Why do you care what those people think of you?"

Gwen blinked at him. "I don't, I just..."

"You want to be a knight?" her father pressed. "Then be a damned knight. It'll take a little while to fix your armor, but..."

Gwen gaped at him in confusion.

Amos gave a noise of frustration and dug in his pocket. When he lifted his hand again, he held a tiny, perfect figurine of a knight, the twin of the one still left in Gwen's room in Isobelle's suite, with Gawain's pennant flying in an imaginary breeze.

Then she looked closer and recognized the articulation in the joints that she'd invented, replicated there to the last detail.

This figurine wasn't Sir Gawain... it was *her*.

"You may be surprised to learn that we are quite a bit richer now than we used to be," her father said, offering the figurine for her to take. "They've been selling faster than cheesecake on a stick."

"But... but now they all know that I'm not Sir Gawain."

Amos gave a wave of his hand. "You think that's stopped them? I left Theo dealing with a crowd outside the smithy a dozen strong, waiting for a new batch of figurines to drop. Yes, Lord Whimsitt is an idiot, and yes, I'm sure he managed to tell a bunch of other idiots what they should think about the idea of a woman in armor. But not everyone is listening to him, Gwen."

Gwen inspected the little figurine resting in the palm of her hand. He'd even captured Achilles, down to the cowlick in his mane that insisted on standing up, no matter how she tried to comb it down. Her horse. Her armor. *Her.*

Her father reached through the bars, took her hand, and gently curled her fingers closed over the figurine in her palm. "Look at me, Gwen."

Gwen swallowed around the lump in her throat and lifted her face toward her father.

"All those stories your mum used to tell you, about chivalry and slaying monsters and defending the helpless . . . none of those stories were about being a knight." He squeezed her hand, his voice rough with emotion. "They were about being a *hero*."

Gwen bit her lip, reaching for breath and finding she could inhale longer and deeper than she'd been able to do in a long time. She blinked back her tears and tightened her fingers around the figurine in her hand.

"Right," she said, in a voice that was miraculously steady. "Dad—have you gotten a look at the cell door yet?"

Amos let out a derisive snort. "Peg hinges. I mean, what kind of shortsighted idiot would take such a stupid shortcut when designing a jail? Whoever they hired as their ironworker for this dungeon ought to be—"

"Yes, Dad," Gwen interrupted, fighting back a grin. "When all this is over perhaps you can go tell them how wrong they are and offer to do it right. Do you think we can . . . ?"

Amos chuckled. "Girl, please. Your dad's a blacksmith." He stretched his broad shoulders, cracked his knuckles, and then turned to set his back against the grill. Waiting for Gwen to take her place on the other side, he curled his hands around the crossbar and took a deep breath. "On my count? One . . . two . . ."

Chapter forty-five

. . . OR IT'S TRICKY TO PUT BACK TOGETHER AGAIN

There were two guards on duty, and Jane dealt easily with the first. Isobelle and Hilde had watched with fascination on the servants' stairwell as their friend tightened her bodice to straining point, pinched her cheeks until they were red, ran a hand through her hair, and then went racing down the stairs.

"Oh, quickly!" she cried. "Oh, sir, please help me!"

Moments later she'd come hurrying up the stairs, towing a guard by the hand, straight past the alcove where Hilde and Isobelle were hiding. Sylvie had stayed behind at Olivia's insistence, in case Sir Ralph came looking for her.

"That's one down," Isobelle murmured. "I can't imagine he'll get a chance to ask where they're going for quite some time."

"The other is yours," Hilde said softly. "Go to her, Isobelle."

But Isobelle—despite every part of her pulling toward Gwen—hesitated. Her mouth was dry, and her stomach was attempting to twist itself into impossible knots, and her feet weren't sure they wanted to take a step.

"Hilde," she whispered, reaching for the other girl's hand. "What if she tells me to go?"

I'm sorry, Gwen had mouthed. But she'd had plenty of time to think since then, all of it in a cold, frightening jail cell.

"Isobelle." Hilde—who looked like the most wholesome of milkmaids, with her crown of blond braids and her round cheeks—managed to frown properly for once.

"I—"

"No," Hilde said, raising a finger to silence her. "Isobelle, no. Take it from me, you must go. I know what everyone thinks of me . . . foolish Hilde. Look at her, waiting for Sir Arnau, a ghost to her for six years. Look at how she clings to this romantic dream, the poor thing."

"Hilde," Isobelle protested immediately. "I never—"

"I am not so foolish, Isobelle," Hilde continued. "I know he has forgotten me. But what other joy does a life like ours hold, except to dream of romance? Look at Sylvie, whose choices have been stolen. One day, my turn will come. For now, I choose to be happy with a dream, rather than empty without one."

Isobelle simply stared at her, held by the force of Hilde's eyes.

"I must be content with a dream," Hilde whispered. "But your knight is real. Go to her."

Taking Isobelle by the shoulders, she turned her to face down the stairs, and with a gentle push, sent her on her way.

Isobelle still hadn't collected herself when she reached the bottom of the staircase and found herself face-to-face with a boy who was fourteen at most, and in possession of a worried expression and a too-large suit of armor.

"Halt?" he tried. "Who goes there."

Isobelle let out a slow breath and invited her instincts to take over. As if they'd been waiting for permission, they surged through her, straightening her spine, lifting her chin, and tugging up one corner of her mouth into a self-assured smile. "What a silly question," she replied, sweeping toward him. "You know exactly who I am."

"Lady Isobelle," he replied, proving he was not entirely beyond redemption. "Um, stop please."

She took a few more steps to prove she could, and then halted to look him up and down. "You are not the usual guard," she supposed. "What's your name?"

"Brian, my lady. Everyone else is in the war room."

She tilted her head. "We don't have a war room."

"Well, they've taken over the ballroom, so all the visiting knights and people can fit...."

She sighed, put upon. The part of her that was still dreadfully worried about Gwen was watching the rest of her, and couldn't help admiring how calm she sounded. "Then you stay here on guard, Brian, and I'll just head through on my own."

"My lady, you can't..."

Isobelle exited the conversation by means of walking straight toward Brian, who—faced with the terrifying prospect of making physical contact with her—jumped out of the way. She paused to wrestle one of the torches out of a sconce with only a minor loss of dignity, and then strode down the dank corridor to where she supposed Gwen would be. Brian made no attempt to stop her or to ask how she knew her way around so well, and contented himself with scuttling after her, making little chirps and gurgles of protest.

Isobelle reached the end of the corridor and raised the torch high, her heart trying to force its way up into her throat, preparing her for the sight of Gwen slumped on the floor, Gwen bleeding, Gwen white and cold.

What nothing had prepared her for was the total absence of Gwen in any form.

Isobelle and Brian stood side by side, staring at the empty cell with two very different kinds of horror, the silence broken by the sound of water dripping somewhere in the distance.

"Shit," Brian whispered. "I'm so dead."

"Where is she?" Isobelle demanded, calm evaporating as she whirled around to face him. "What have you done with her?"

"I thought she was right here!" Brian squealed, backing away from her until he hit the wall. "She's supposed to be right here. Maybe they brought her up to sentence her and didn't tell me? I'm not even meant to be on duty here, I can't—you have to tell someone I didn't—"

Isobelle didn't hear anything else he said.

She was already gone.

The tapestries in the ballroom had been covered in war banners, the coats of arms of the great houses of the county of Darkhaven, and those of all the visiting knights and nobles, strung up on display. The center of the room was dominated by a table that must have been brought through the doorway in pieces, and which was now covered in maps of the region. The grand organ was hidden behind a crowd of bodies; every knight, squire, and nobleman who could find a place had crammed into the room, craning their necks to see what was under discussion.

Isobelle stormed past the man at the door, who belatedly shouted her name after her, though it was unclear whether he was trying to stop her or announce her.

"Lady Isobelle of Avington!"

Lord Whimsitt looked up from the head of the table. "Ah, Lady Isobelle," he said genially, though there was a note of steel beneath his purr that she couldn't miss. "There you are. Excellent timing, we can cross another thing off our list."

Isobelle ignored that, wasting only a moment to catch her breath. "What has happened to Gwen?" she asked, once she knew her voice wouldn't shake.

"Gwen?"

"Sir Gawain."

A sound traveled around the room when she said *Sir Gawain*. A whisper of anger from those Gwen had unseated. From those who *felt* she'd unseated them, just by existing.

"The girl is in jail," said Whimsitt, with a flick of his fingers.

"She's not," Isobelle shot back.

"She's escaped? Then she will be in the jail again, as soon as we have recaptured her," he snapped.

It was at that moment—as though her brain had been waiting for the chance to present what it had noticed when she had first scanned the room—that Isobelle's gaze lifted from Lord Whimsitt's red face to the wall behind him.

To the place where the dragonslayer's spear had once been, and was no more.

Like snow slowly drifting down to settle on her, turning her skin cold and dousing that internal fire with a slow chill, the knowledge came to Isobelle.

Gwen had not *run away*. Gwen had *run toward*.

"She's gone after the dragon," she breathed.

This time, the sound rippling through the room wasn't anger, but laughter. Snickers, the low buzz of soft remarks the speakers thought were witty.

"Why are you laughing?" Isobelle snapped. "Why aren't you chasing down the dragon yourselves?"

It was Sir Ralph who replied. "Because there is no need. It has seen the castle, it has assessed the threat we pose, and it will not likely return. This is not the same place it knew centuries ago, and it is old enough and wise enough to understand that. It would not have come at all, save that the reopening of the mine awakened it."

"Indeed," Lord Whimsitt agreed. "We will abandon the mine again, which has served its purpose, and the dragon may simply go back to sleep."

"Are you insane?" Isobelle felt like she was standing outside her own body, watching herself stare at them all in disbelief. "All these knights, here for the Tournament of *Dragonslayers*, and there's a girl you won't even allow among you out there, heading for the dragon on her own, to stand between it and your people?"

Sir Ralph rolled his eyes. "She has saved us an execution, is all."

Whimsitt nodded in agreement. "We will declare the tourney in Sir Orson's favor and try to forget any of this happened." A wave of his hand indicated Orson sitting a couple of spots along the table from Whimsitt himself.

Her friend gazed at the map in front of him and didn't look up. The tips of his ears were red, though, a sure sign she'd learned to read when they were small.

Guilt.

"Sir Orson," she repeated slowly. Everything had happened so quickly after Sylvie had come to shake her into action that she had not stopped to think about who else could have betrayed Gwen to Lord Whimsitt.

"He has conducted himself admirably," Lord Whimsitt went on. "And it is very much apparent that the sooner you are safely married and out of trouble, the better."

Isobelle scarcely heard him, her eyes still on Orson, a flush of rage rising up her throat, across her cheeks, a burning fire she could barely contain within her. "You," she said, her voice a thin, taut wire. "It was *you*."

Orson finally lifted his head, the chiseled jaw squared, the blond hair as charmingly tousled as ever, his eyes meeting hers. "Yes." His voice was soft, but there was no apology in it.

With a wordless sound of fury, Isobelle's control broke and she lunged for him.

He caught her, gripping her arms tightly and bringing his mouth to her ear. "Izzie, stop it. I had to. Last night at the ball, what you said . . . if he found out in front of the whole county, he might've had her killed on the spot. I did it for you—I did what was best for *you*."

Isobelle went still, panting for breath. "How convenient that deciding what was best for *me* earned *you* the money in my dowry."

Orson's hold slackened, and she staggered free of his grip.

There was a tale Isobelle once heard as a child. It was about a great ruler who claimed to be dressed in the finest of clothes—silks and furs that only the worthiest could see. None of his subjects wanted to admit they couldn't see them, so they all pretended he wasn't naked. Until a child called out the truth, and nobody could pretend anymore.

She felt like she was living in that story now, looking around at the knights in their war room. Suddenly she was seeing all their finery and pageantry for what it really was, and she couldn't unsee it.

"Little boys playing knights," she murmured distantly, a memory overtaking her. "Afraid to be undone . . ."

She was back in Ellsdale, upstairs at Gwen's house on the night of the dragon bonfire.

Gwen's fingers had worked the lacings on her dress free, and they'd talked softly, to keep from noticing how close they stood. They'd been talking, joking—but also not joking—about the work that the world required of women so that men could ride out into adventure and become heroes.

The more I think on it, the more questions I have about that system, Isobelle had said. And then, as Gwen kept pulling on her lacings: *Don't bring it all the way undone, or it's tricky to put back together again.*

The system, or the laces? Gwen had laughed.

Both, Isobelle had whispered.

But it *was* undone. Isobelle had tugged too hard at the laces, and now she knew she'd never be able to put the world back together the same way.

Now, as Isobelle scanned the gathered men—Orson's reddened but resolute face, Whimsitt's darkly angry countenance, Ralph's predatory, possessive eyes—she realized one more thing: she didn't *want* to put it back together.

Last night she had begged Gwen to run away with her, thinking it was the only way to escape their cage—that they had to bend its bars and somehow slither out between them, flee beyond the reach of their jailers.

But the cage wasn't the ballroom, or the castle, or even the county of Darkhaven—the cage was a *part* of her, something driven into her by every word and glance and deed of those around her, by every breath she took while accepting she was theirs to keep.

"We live inside cages of your design." Isobelle's voice summoned every gaze in the room to fix on her face. "Little boys with wooden swords, and cages that hold us as long as we think we belong inside them. Even when I tried to rebel, I did it within the confines of those bars. I went looking for a champion to keep your knights from claiming me, and in doing so, I agreed you had the right to give me away."

"I have *every* right," Whimsitt snarled. "You think these swords at our belts are toys, girl? That your privilege protects you if you defy your lord?"

"Why does that scare you so much?" Isobelle shot back. "If one of us dares to test the bars of our prison, you threaten her— *kill her*—as you planned for the women of Aberfarthing, and for Gwen. Why? Why are you so frightened when we go searching for the edges of the cage you put us in?"

The room was perfectly silent, filled with a tension as profound as the one that hushed the crowds when the guards ripped Gwen's helmet away.

"I'll tell you why you're so afraid," Isobelle said slowly, gathering her dignity about her like a queen. "Gwen was right. Gwen realized long before I did, this truth you're all so frightened we'll uncover."

Isobelle's heart was pounding, her blood singing in her veins as she drew one more breath.

"The truth is, *there is no cage.*"

She turned on her heel, vibrating with both fury and a strange, ferocious joy as she stalked toward the door, half certain she'd feel rough hands grab her at any moment.

But no one touched her.

I'm coming, Gwen.

Chapter Forty-Six

IT CAME UP FROM THE MINE

Gwen closed her eyes and let Achilles carry her through the forest toward the dragon's lair. The thudding of her horse's hooves was rhythmic to the point of being hypnotic, and after several rounds of trying to gather her thoughts and corral them, she finally let them go, to run alongside Achilles in his joyous sprint.

Her father had stripped off the armor pieces of his disguise and given them to her, allowing her to sneak out of the dungeons, with his assurance that he could make his own way out. After all, nobody had been told to guard *him*. The armor had even allowed her to sneak into the ballroom as several dozen servants scrambled around, trying to reassemble a massive oak table. The diagram the castle staff were following was clearly a poor one, with half the servant battalion waving bits of metal and various pegs while the other half turned the pieces of the table round and round, arguing which way was up.

They never even looked up as Gwen slowly, silently took the ancient dragonslaying spear from its spot over the grand fireplace.

She had retrieved her horse from the stables and had beaten her father back to Ellsdale, galloping straight to the smithy and leaving Achilles stamping and pawing at the ground as she hurried inside.

Olivia had brought Gwen's armor to her father, and if there were any pieces the guards hadn't ruined, they would be better than the guard's armor she still wore.

She'd walked in expecting an empty smithy—only to find a broad-shouldered figure standing in the middle of the room, staring at her with wide eyes.

"Theo!" she gasped, trying to catch her breath from her headlong ride and her surprise.

His eyes lit as he saw her. "Gwen! Oh, Gwen, I saw part of your joust last time against Lorenzo, and it was *brilliant*—of course, I didn't know it was you, but I would've just thought it was even more brilliant if I had, and obviously now I—"

"Theo," Gwen had cut in, aware the boy would go on talking until someone stopped him, like a runaway horse with an infinite amount of road. "I can't stay. Do you know where my dad put my armor?"

Theo's face had glowed even more. "Oh, I have it! I fixed the leather straps—they're a little stiff, definitely not as good as the ones you made, but they'll work in a pinch, because I figured if they end up letting you finish the tournament and all that, you'd want—" He had turned, retrieving a pile of gleaming metal as he'd spoken.

Gwen's breath seized in her lungs at the sight of her armor, and when she'd looked up to Theo's shiny-cheeked face, every misgiving she'd ever had about the boy went flying out the window. "Theo, you're amazing!" she cried, and leaned up to kiss him on the cheek.

She'd left Theo behind, staring at her red-faced as he watched her ride away. She'd paused only to ask a question of a woman who'd emerged, yawning, from their neighbor's cottage—Gwen had recognized her from the jail cell, the night they'd freed the villagers from Aberfarthing.

The gold mine, the woman had said in response to Gwen's urgent question, her eyes wide as she gazed up at the woman in armor. *It came up from the mine.*

Achilles's long, loping gait ate up the distance with ease, despite the added weight of Gwen's armor and the dragonslaying spear lashed to his saddle.

The moon was gibbous, its light filtering through the thinner trees that arched over the road, casting monstrous shadows onto the silvered dirt. The air streaming past Gwen's cheeks was cool, growing colder as the day's warmth slipped away into the night. Before her rose mountains beyond the woods, looming higher every minute she rode, blocking out the stars.

Without warning, Achilles burst out of the trees and onto a village path. Gwen reined him back into a trot, catching her breath... and then he stopped as her grip on the reins went lax.

It wasn't a village anymore.

Aberfarthing.

Not a single structure was still standing. Charred, blackened beams and pillars stretched up against the stars like the ribs of some long dead monster, piles of ash and partially burned thatch strewn about like decaying patches of flesh and scraps of hair. The stones of the well at the village center were black with soot, and sunken on one side where the fire had been hot enough to melt the stone and send it weeping down toward the water below.

Achilles's skin twitched and rippled, trying to shake off the invisible weight of the destruction around them, and he walked with slow, nervous steps through the ruins. The air smelled of old, rank smoke and something else, something far more disturbing that made Gwen's stomach roil with nausea. Not everyone had made it out of the village alive. If she lingered here long enough to sift through the rubble, how many charred bodies would she find buried beneath the layers of ash and ruin?

Fury rose within her, so quick and fierce Gwen's eyes watered with the intensity of it. If Whimsitt had spared even one man to go check on the women's claims that a dragon had attacked their home, the truth would have been undeniable. No one who witnessed this scene could have concluded that bandits were responsible, or some careless youngster mishandling a torch. Not even the lord of Darkhaven could dismiss this attack as simply imagined by a group of women, lying for attention and hysterical with superstition.

At the far end of the village, the path ended in a wide clearing at the foot of the mountains. The entrance to the mines was no more than a squat, black, rectangular hole at the edge of the clearing.

Gwen swung a leg over Achilles's saddle and slid to the ground, keeping her palm against his shoulder. Her big bay stallion gave a nervous whicker, his eyes rolling and nostrils flaring as he sniffed and snorted. His senses told him there was danger here—he could smell the dragon that had made this place its home centuries ago.

Gwen ran her hand over her horse's cheek and then stroked his neck, running her fingers through his mane until his breath calmed. "Stay here," she whispered to him as his ears flicked and swiveled toward the sound of her voice. "Unless something comes—then run."

She left him untied, wanting him to have the option to flee if the mine was empty and the dragon came flying over while she was inside. Her mouth had gone dry, and it went drier every time she glanced at the squat little opening into which she had resolved to go. The miasma of death and sour smoke hung in the air, and Gwen's every instinct screamed at her to turn and ride away again as fast as Achilles would take her.

Eventually, Lord Whimsitt and the knights would do something. They would have to, for the dragon was not likely to stop again so soon after being woken from its sleep—at some point the dragon would attack the castle again.

But it would attack more villages first. Aberfarthing was the closest settlement to its lair, but the destruction would spread, and the beast would visit its wrath upon countless people unable to fight back. Any who survived would be like those women who had come to the dragon bonfire seeking aid—penniless, terrified, with no means or homes to return to.

Gwen found a torch among the mining supplies strewn about the clearing, and after a few too many tries with her flint, got the thing lit despite her shaking hands. The light of the flame against the mountainside flickered and wavered far too much.

Gwen retrieved her helmet from Achilles's saddle, but she left the spear. It was a weapon for use on horseback, far too long and heavy for Gwen to use in the tight confines of the mines. If she could find the beast and catch it unawares, inside the tunnels, she had a chance—if the dragon managed to get outside, the odds slid wildly in its favor.

Gwen pulled the helmet down onto her head, drew her sword, and stepped into the darkness.

Her breath was harsh and metallic against her visor, too loud to her own ears in the heavy silence of the underground. The tunnel sloped sharply downward and bent back on itself, so that the exit was swiftly out of sight, leaving Gwen wrapped entirely in stone and the meager, wavering glow from her torch. Twin ruts in the rocky floor marked the tracks of the mine carts, so she followed those down, ignoring the occasional side passages that opened up in favor of moving deeper into the earth.

Something dry and leathery whispered above and just behind her. Gwen jumped and nearly dropped the torch, even as she shut her eyes and told herself, *Bats. It's bats. It's only bats, stop cowering!*

The sharp pounding in her chest made her stop, turn, and lean back against the wall, trying to catch her breath. Despite having seen the beast flying overhead at the tournament, Gwen was not entirely prepared for how desperately afraid she felt. The fear was like a monster in itself, infecting her moment by moment, replacing her strong limbs with ones that shook and weakening the fingers clutched round the hilt of her sword.

What the hell am I doing here? she thought desperately, closing her eyes and focusing on the air moving in and out of her lungs. Dupont had taught her a pattern of breathing that forced the body to relax as a way to combat her nerves before jousting. Gwen wasn't sure she'd ever really mastered it, though, relying instead on her fury at her opponents, at the tournament itself that reduced a human being to a prize. Now, the anger she'd felt at seeing the destruction outside paled in comparison with her fear.

Still, Dupont's breathing exercises worked, even though the air she inhaled was acrid with sour smoke. Her heartbeat was slowing, quieting. Each inhale felt easier, her lungs less tight. The hand holding the torch steadied enough for the flames to stop quivering.

And as her mind quieted, Gwen became aware of a soft sound.

At first it seemed to her that she was hearing some distant underground ocean, tides still stirred by the moon invisible beyond the top of the mountain—she heard the rise and fall of the surf, a soft, rhythmic susurration. The sound was so incongruous, there in the depths of the earth, that Gwen could only stand still in confusion, staring into the darkness beyond her ring of torchlight.

And then a section of shadow beyond the light moved, and all at once the meaning of the sound, the moving shadow, and the faint rumble that now echoed through the tunnel clicked together into a single, awful truth.

The dragon was there.

It lay just beyond the light of her torch, chest rising and falling in a rhythm like an ancient sea. Gwen's body moved of its own accord, even as her mind froze like a mouse before a deadly serpent—she took one step, and then another, moving as silently as she could in her heavy armor. Sweat gathered damply against the padding at her lower back, and dripped, itching, between her breasts.

The torchlight fell upon a flow of thick scales—an outstretched leg, the foot alone as large as Achilles, each scaled toe tipped with a black claw as long as Gwen's leg. She stepped closer, still strangely distant from her own movements, like an observer watching some foolish ant about to be annihilated by a booted foot.

Gwen lifted the torch higher.

The dragon lay on its side, its back half out of sight around a curve in the tunnel. Its body was covered in scales the color of decaying bronze, with shades ranging from deep brown to copper to the pale, putrid green of corrosion. Its front legs were grotesquely, disproportionately long, forming the arch of the wings, which were currently folded in close against its thick body. The neck was long and serpentine, and its head rested on the ground, pointed squarely at Gwen. One of its eyes was a mess of scar tissue, the marks of ancient blades etched into the ridge of scales forming the upper edge of its eye socket.

The other eye was closed.

Slowly, Gwen backed up, moving along the wall until she found a place to wedge the torch. Then she gripped her sword, breathing in the bitter scent of latent dragonsfire, and moved in.

Carefully, she stepped between the taloned toes of the monster. Her armor scraped the tiniest bit, the articulated plates at hip and knee whispering against each other, and her boots tapped a soft, irregular patter against the stone. She was close enough now to feel heat radiating from the creature, not from its body, but from the base of its long, curled neck—the place from which it brought forth its flames, a burning forge above its heart.

The scales there were long and thicker than Gwen's arm, impenetrable, but they overlapped much like the articulation on the joints of Gwen's armor. If the beast stretched its neck back far enough, it might be possible to thrust a sword or a spear between them. But not while it lay curled up this way.

Gwen crept instead toward the head, approaching the closed eye. Even these scales on the dragon's eyelids were thick, but if she struck at the seam and managed to drive her blade deep enough, she might reach the creature's brain before it could react.

Gwen caught her breath, wrapped both hands around the hilt of her sword, and raised it over her head.

The eyelids parted. They were followed by the wet slide of a second cloudy membrane sweeping back from the outer corner of the eye. A gaping hole of a pupil rolled down from the top of the eye socket, wandered a moment, and then narrowed into a wicked slit, pointed directly at Gwen.

Neither of them moved. Gwen could see her armored reflection, sword raised, in the huge eye. Its irises were the color of molten gold and seethed like cauldrons of liquid fire. The slitted pupil trembled, adjusting its focus as the creature clawed its way out of sleep.

Then Gwen drove the sword down, throwing her entire body weight behind the thrust, a scream of effort bursting from her—and suddenly she was flying, breathless, suspended for two heartbeats in the air until she hit the wall with a horrible metallic clatter and dropped to the ground. She'd managed to keep hold of her sword, and she scrambled up, head spinning, to see the dragon shaking its own head where it had knocked her aside.

It was climbing stutteringly to its feet, though the confines of the tunnel prevented it from standing fully—Gwen would have thought it ridiculous or pathetic, a dragon crawling on its belly through a tunnel barely large enough to fit its body, if she'd heard it described to her. But as its head swung toward her and it lunged into effortless motion, flowing sinuously along the cavern far quicker than she could move, all hints of the ridiculous vanished.

Gwen threw herself to the side, down one of the excavated tunnels. Though she could see the light of her torch glinting off bronze around the corner back the way she came, it didn't reach far enough to illuminate the darkness ahead of her.

From behind her came a sound that would almost certainly haunt her dreams for the rest of her life: an awful, keening, bubbling roar, like that of a beast with blood in its throat. She had only an instant to realize what the sound betokened, and saw a brief tableau blossoming into illumination before her—she threw herself down behind a cart loaded with stone as a gout of flame filled the tunnel.

She held her breath as long as she could, and when she finally gasped for air, it scorched her lungs, her eyes watering with smoke and the acrid stench of the thing. Her armor was warmer to the touch now than her skin, the air as dry and hot as that of an oven, hotter than the air above her father's forge. She might have passed out if she hadn't spent so many hours laboring in those conditions. Tears streamed from her eyes, and she blinked furiously, blinded by the sudden darkness as the flames died away. She focused on trying not to sob, on staying as quiet as she could.

The creature was still waking up. Gwen didn't have much time before it was fully alert—and she had only one idea.

She waited, listening to the awful scrape of the scales lining its belly dragging along the stone, each one screeching like a blade on ceramic. The thing snuffled and grunted as it searched for her blindly in the dark, seeking the stench of burning flesh. Gwen closed her eyes, though it made no difference to what she could see. She listened, waiting.

The scrape of scales on stone was nearly beside her now, and her mind constructed an image of the beast creeping past the cart at her back. She moved slowly, silently, easing out of concealment—she imagined the head was there, just before her, weaving back and forth as it sought her in the pitch blackness.

A faint glow blossomed to her right, and a wave of dread slid down Gwen's spine to rest like lead in her belly. She turned and saw twin orbs of sullen red emerge from the darkness, a low, rumbling growl cutting through the quiet. The glow brightened and became two trickles of molten flame that spilled forth, dripping from the beast's flared nostrils inches from where she stood before the tip of its snout. The flames slid onto the floor of the cave, creating puddles of fire that illuminated the dragon's head as it turned, the light pooling in its one good eye as it fixed on Gwen.

Gwen knew that this was her last chance, that the dragon's fire had given her exactly what she needed, enough light to find her target. She raised her sword, shifted her weight, and struck—

Except she didn't. She hadn't moved. She was still standing there, motionless, helpless, so close to the dragon she could have put a hand on its scaled lip if she could move. Its arms were curled on either side of her, the wings folded so she was very nearly encased by the creature. She could not so much as tear her gaze from the seething gold of its one furious eye, now fully awake. It held her, even as the pupil scanned side to side, trying to see past the slit in her visor.

Unbidden, old Bertin's story swept through her mind, his tales of being frozen by the dragon's gaze. She remembered the traditional target of practicing knights everywhere: a suspended ring called a dragonseye. The fact that the knights of old, centuries ago, who had died fighting this creature, had taken out the monster's right eye before succumbing.

She should have known not to look into its eye.

Despair swept through Gwen, but she found she could not so much as tremble, her paralysis was so complete. Her own eyes began to water from lack of blinking, and even her ribs refused to shift, her lungs becoming as still as stone.

The dragon's eye narrowed a touch, and from its throat came a hideous, growling rumble. The frequency was so low and the sound so raspy that it rippled, a shuddering sound that hit Gwen's ears like some terrible, mocking chuckle of laughter.

She knew, in that moment, that she was going to die.

But through the despair, rising like a breath of soft, cool air in the parched heat of the tunnels, came a single thought: *Isobelle.*

If Gwen was going to die, she would do it thinking of Isobelle's laugh, not the mockery of this monster. She would die picturing her blond hair and blue eyes and her particular way of wrinkling her nose when Gwen said something unexpected. She would die thinking of the look on Isobelle's face when she came to Gwen's tent after her defeat of Sir Ralph—the sudden lifting of all her reservations, the joy and yearning and release in those glorious eyes.

Gwen dragged in a breath, chasing away the spots swimming in her vision. She thought of Isobelle's arms around her neck, of waking in the blackberry thicket with Isobelle's head on her lap, of the way Isobelle's fists had uncurled and softened as Gwen held them in hers.

Gwen found she could shift her weight, moving onto the balls of her feet, clawing her way back toward some kind of agency.

She could imagine Isobelle so vividly it was like having her there, standing at Gwen's side. Gwen could picture her, hands on her hips, eyes wide with alarm. *What are you doing?* she would cry. *Go on—MOVE!*

Gwen felt a groan rise up inside her, a sound that burst into an agonized cry by the time it reached her lips and wrenched her body into movement. The dragon blinked once in surprise, and that was all the reprieve Gwen needed to lunge forward, stepping up onto its clawed foot and launching herself upward to swing her sword in a glittering arc toward the only vulnerable part of the dragon she could reach.

The wing membrane tore with a long, satisfying rip like that of a canvas tent, spattering the stone with a fine mist of blood from the delicate capillaries branching out from the creature's elongated arm. The dragon let out a scream of fury and pain so loud Gwen lost all sense, coming back to herself lying flat on her back. The beast had flung her aside, knocking her helmet loose—Gwen gulped in a breath of air, dizzy. A sluglike wave of liquid flame dribbled from the dragon's mouth, illuminating the scene in time for Gwen to see its foot come down on her helmet, flattening it as if it were no more substantial than a costume piece of paper and paste.

Roaring again, the dragon crouched, its muscles bunching—Gwen realized what it was going to do an instant before it launched itself into the ceiling of the tunnel and erupted through the stone like a whale breaching the surface of the ocean.

Gwen caught the briefest glimpse of the sky overhead as the dragon burst up through the edge of the mountainside in a shower of house-sized boulders, saw the creature silhouetted for an instant against the pearly white of the waxing moon as it spread its wings—one whole, one torn—before the rocks and stones came showering down again, bringing the darkness with them.

Chapter Forty-Seven

LIKE SHE'D RIDDEN STRAIGHT OUT OF LEGEND

Isobelle's horse burst out of the edge of the forest in time for her to see the side of the mountain explode, a massive shadow launching itself into the sky. Her horse squealed, rearing so abruptly that it fell, knocking the breath out of Isobelle as she tumbled from the saddle. Isobelle scrambled back to her feet as its hoofbeats disappeared back through the forest.

Then Achilles was behind her, whickering and prancing, pawing at the stones and sending up clouds of dirt and dust. Instead of running away from the destruction, he had run *toward* it, his warhorse breeding holding true.

Isobelle stared at him, at his empty saddle. "Where's Gwen?" she cried, her voice hoarse. "Achilles, where . . ."

The horse ignored her, half rearing and driving his hooves against a splintered beam from the mine entrance. For one long moment Isobelle stood motionless as the terrible truth wrapped itself around her heart and *squeezed*.

Gwen was in there.

Isobelle threw herself down amid the rubble, grabbing at a chunk of rock and trying to toss it to one side, but the damned thing was so heavy she nearly went flying instead.

With a cry of frustration, she tried again, every muscle straining as she turned it end over end, gasping for breath. The rock tumbled down the slope and she began digging at the rubble with her bare hands, working frantically by moonlight. Achilles paced and snorted beside her, whinnying his agitation.

"Gwen!" Isobelle shouted, shoving aside chunks of rock and broken timbers, then pausing to listen as she called again. "Gwen, can you hear me?"

Silence.

The moonlight had turned the green skirts of her dress a silvery white, and as she grabbed a handful of fabric to shove it out of the way, her bleeding fingers left a black handprint behind, color stolen by the darkness.

"Gwen," she whispered, letting the tears stream down her cheeks now, grabbing another rock and tossing it clear. "Gwen, don't you dare. Gwen, *please*. This isn't how stories end."

And then suddenly, gasping for air, her pale face smeared with dirt, there was Gwen. Beautifully, brilliantly *alive* Gwen, who was reaching up with one gauntleted hand to shove the splintered remains of a timber beam to one side.

"Isobelle?" she croaked hoarsely, squinting at her as though she was quite sure Isobelle would dissolve into a beam of moonlight, even as she began to haul herself up through the hole that Isobelle had so painstakingly made. "Really?"

"Really," Isobelle managed, somewhat laughing and mostly crying, grabbing Gwen under the arms when her hips got stuck, and *pulling*. Gwen scrambled and kicked, and then came free. They collapsed, clinging to each other.

"Isobelle," Gwen whispered, as Isobelle tried to wrap herself around the other girl, only to find that armor was extremely effective at preventing embraces. "Isobelle, I'm sorry. You were right. We absolutely should have run away to France."

Isobelle's tears began all over again, a sob shaking her body. "No, Gwen, I was wrong. I'm so sorry. I tried to stop you being who you are, I tried to make you fit into their mold, and I—"

Gwen's lips found hers, and though the kiss tasted like earth and salt, Isobelle wanted it to last forever. But far too soon, Gwen was drawing back. "There's no time," she gasped. "I don't know if you saw, but . . ."

Isobelle's eyes widened. "The dragon!" She let go of Gwen instantly, and they both rolled away from each other, coming up on all fours and rising to their knees to look for the great beast. It had flown out over the forest in a wide circle, but it was clawing its way through the air back toward them now, one wing shredded.

And it was making a noise that made Isobelle freeze inside—that made her want to flatten herself to the ground or run away to hide in the nearest hole. It was bellowing its fury, the low, rough roar of its voice overlaid with a high screech that made her hair stand on end.

"Gwen, I'm back where I started," Isobelle managed. "We should run away."

Gwen gently took her hand. "I can't," she said softly.

"I know," Isobelle said, and her tears were falling again, but she made no effort to stop them. Some things deserved to be cried over. "I know."

"I think I could kill it, if only I could get near it without looking it in the eye," Gwen said, tracking the creature as it came closer. "It has some sort of hypnotic power, an ability to paralyze—I broke through it before, but I don't know if I can do it again, especially while I'm trying to fight the thing. I just need one clear moment to strike."

Isobelle wrenched her gaze away from the dragon and settled it on Gwen. "One moment?"

Gwen nodded slowly.

Isobelle gathered her courage around her like her own suit of armor. "I can make that happen."

Gwen's gaze snapped across to her. "You can distract it?"

"I can give you your moment."

"You're sure?" There was such a tangle in Gwen's familiar gaze—hope, worry, a dazed understanding that they were talking about fighting a *dragon*.

"I promise," said Isobelle.

Gwen hesitated, her fear obvious in her eyes—and then nodded. "All right."

Isobelle knew time was of the essence, but she couldn't help kissing Gwen again quickly. The men back at the castle would have sent her on her way. They would have insisted she hide somewhere safe. It never would have occurred to them—they never could have *imagined*—that she could help.

But Gwen simply took her at her word. With her life on the line, Gwen trusted her to be there.

The dragon landed in the woods that stood between the village and the fields beyond, thudding down with a great cracking of smashed and splintered trees and another scream of rage.

Isobelle and Gwen broke apart. Gwen sheathed her sword with a scrape of steel, reached for Achilles's reins, and swung up into the saddle in one fluid movement. "Isobelle . . ."

"Go!" Isobelle shouted. "When the moment comes, I'll be there!"

Gwen gazed down at her from atop her warhorse, the words that hung between them shimmering like a skyful of stars. All the things they wanted to say but hadn't time for. All the things they didn't need to say at all.

For an instant, Isobelle pictured the smith's daughter she'd first seen at the market, their eyes meeting across a table full of horseshoes.

How had they ended up here?

And then Gwen twitched Achilles's reins, turning him toward the great beast. She leaned down to pull the spear from his saddle, touched her heels to his flanks, and, as brave as his rider, he launched himself forward.

Her spear at the ready, her black hair streaming behind her, the moonlight gleaming off her armor, she looked like she'd ridden straight out of legend. She was *magnificent*.

And she was so much more than a knight.

She was a hero.

Chapter Forty-Eight

TWO WOUNDED CREATURES, FACING EACH OTHER ACROSS THE EMPTY BATTLEFIELD

The dragon had carved a ragged corridor through the strip of trees dividing the town from the fields on the other side, and it was along this path of devastation that Gwen guided Achilles. He was snorting with bloodlust, and she offered up a silent thanks to her mother for bringing her horse with her when she ran away with Gwen's father. Any normal horse would have been halfway back to Darkhaven Castle by now, but Achilles was ready for a fight.

She guided him in an arc, sticking to the edge of the trees. She kept an eye on the dragon as it crouched, mantling its wings and curving its long head around to inspect the wound she'd dealt it inside the mine. The ancient dragonslaying spear was heavier than the lances she'd jousted with, requiring a tight grip to keep it planted against the stirrup platform.

Somewhere out there, hidden in the darkness, was Isobelle. Gwen could have cursed the dragon for coming back around before she got the details of Isobelle's plan, but Isobelle was so much smarter and cleverer than anyone in Darkhaven Castle knew, and Gwen would not deny her her right to fight. Even though Gwen's body was icy cold with the knowledge that, should the dragon get past her, Isobelle could be its next target.

Her mind tried to throw out reassurances. Mounted on Achilles, she could move much faster out in the open than she could in the mines. The spear had a much greater reach than her sword. The dragon was wounded, and surely slower and clumsier now.

But as the massive head swung toward her, weaving back and forth low enough to part the long grasses in huge, whispering furrows, Gwen knew the truth, deep in her heart. Even wounded, the dragon was far more dangerous than a single girl on horseback.

She shifted her weight, and Achilles, utterly responsive in his heightened state, broke into a trot, and then a run, gathering speed. The dragon let out a sullen roar, sparks flying up against the stars, and began clawing its way across the ground toward Gwen. The joints of the elongated front legs thrust upward, ungainly but undeniably powerful, the sheer size of the creature allowing it to eat up the distance between them in a few ground-shaking stomps.

The dragon lifted its head with a snarl, preparing to make a lunge for Gwen, and she leaned hard as she tugged at Achilles's reins—the horse veered to the right in a perfect arc as the dragon's jaws slammed home on empty air.

Gwen lifted the spear and felt a stab of pain shoot through her bad shoulder, the one the guards had worsened with their blows as they dragged her from the tournament grounds. She banished that pain, locking it away in some remote corner of her mind, and focused on leveling the spear and tucking it under her arm.

But before she could get the tip of the heavy weapon lowered toward a viable target—the neck, if it lifted its head again, or the eye if she could manage it—the dragon threw one of its arms out, forcing Achilles to leap over an outflung wing tip and land, snorting and staggering.

Together, they wheeled around. Gwen saw a massive black shape swinging at her through the darkness and threw herself flat against Achilles's neck. The dragon's tail whistled over her, so close she felt her hair billow in the disturbance of air that followed. Achilles was already lining himself up for another pass, and Gwen let him, focusing this time on the spear's tip rather than directing her horse.

They dodged another snap of the dragon's jaws, and this time Gwen got the spear leveled at the dragon's chest. The tip struck with a screech that made Achilles's gait falter, and slid until it stuck with an impact that nearly threw Gwen from her saddle. Her knees held on with the instinct of long practice, but she had to let go of the spear or be torn from her horse's back.

As she and Achilles galloped away again, Gwen looked back over her shoulder and saw the spear wedged between two of the dragon's armored plates. There was no blood—she hadn't so much as scratched it.

Gwen swore and turned Achilles again. They paused there, each of them catching their breaths. The dragon reared back, spreading its wings and beating them down, turning the grasses beneath it into a surging, roiling storm—but it only lifted a few yards off the ground before thudding down again with a snarl of rage, tucking its injured wing against its body.

Gwen felt an answering throb of pain in her own shoulder—it was the same arm as the one she'd injured on the dragon. That much they had in common—two wounded creatures, facing each other across the empty battlefield. For a moment, Gwen could almost feel a grim sympathy for it—until it swung its head in her direction, the cruel intensity of its gaze forcing her to wrench her eyes away before it could snuff out her life as it had done to so many of the villagers of Aberfarthing.

Achilles leapt into movement again, ending the brief respite. Gwen thought, wildly, about drawing her sword—but it would be of no use, for if she was close enough to use the blade, she would probably already be dead. She needed the spear back.

Achilles charged directly at the dragon, which dropped its head low and began clawing its way across the field toward them, snarling a challenge and gathering speed. Again, Gwen tugged Achilles's reins to the right—but then, abruptly, threw her weight left. Her horse responded instantly, with a whicker of effort, and dodged past the dragon's snapping jaws close enough that Gwen heard a drop of its saliva land wetly on the shoulder of her armor. She leaned low as Achilles raced beneath the neck of the monster, and stretched out her arm as they neared the spot where the spear was wedged.

The jolt through her arm, up into her shoulder, as she grabbed the shaft of the weapon and tore it loose ripped a ragged cry of pain from Gwen's throat—but she kept hold of the spear as, once again, Achilles raced away to a safe distance.

She was armed again. They would turn in a moment, regroup, think of some new way to run at it that might allow a better thrust of the spear between those armored plates. . . .

A rush of air and a keening roar made Gwen look over her shoulder, confusion and dread sweeping in. The dragon was gone. But where— How . . . ?

The ground shook with a heavy impact, and Achilles reared with a shriek of effort and fear. Gwen nearly dropped the spear, her view blocked by her horse—and then, as he regained his feet, she saw that the dragon had leapt into the air to land on their other side, cutting off Achilles's charge. Her horse had reared to a stop just a few feet away.

And there, so large she could see herself distorted in the curved, glittering arc, was the dragon's eye.

Gwen and Achilles both froze in the same heartbeat. She felt her horse's body grow rigid beneath her, felt her own body stiffen, the spear only half raised, the weight of it still an agony on the injured tissues of her shoulder—and she could not lower it or drop it.

Isobelle, she thought frantically, reaching for the glimmer of light and hope that had saved her last time. *Think about Isobelle.*

But the instant the thought crossed her mind, a cold and irrevocable dread swept through Gwen.

Something was wrong.

In the depths of the mine, she had been able to see the dragon's eye through the slit in her visor, had watched as its pupil searched in vain for her eyes in the darkness of her helmet. She had been able to see the dragon's eye clearly enough, enough to be paralyzed by the horrid power of the monster. But now, she had no helmet, nothing standing between her and it.

Now, it could see *her.*

The huge golden eye fixated on her, seeming to swell until it eclipsed all else, blocking out the moon and the sky and the grasses all around, until all Gwen knew, all Gwen *was* or ever would be, was that eye.

Before, her body had gone still, but she had felt her mind thrashing wildly inside like a bird in a cage.

Now, even her soul was frozen. She could feel the dragon's thoughts, sliding into her like some ancient, unspeakable curse. Its mind was vast and complex and alien, and filled with a cruelty as cold as iron in midwinter and as unyielding. Its eye burned, and its mind froze.

She could feel it examining her, pulling apart her soul as easily as its teeth and claws would pull apart her body. Crushing each flicker of hope or rage as easily as it had crushed her helmet. Devouring everything—everything except her fear.

She tried again to summon a thought of Isobelle—not to save herself, for she knew now that she was beyond saving, that the dragon was right to rip her hope from her. But Gwen just wanted to think of her, one more time.

The dragon gave that low, cruel growl from the mine, the one that had chuckled and gone through Gwen like the echo of everyone who had ever laughed at the idea of a woman in armor—now, it laughed at her for thinking of love.

Then it ripped that away, too.

She felt as though she were dangling from a cliff over an infinite pit, and that to fall into it would consign her to an eternity of madness—that if she fell, she would be abandoning all that was ever good and bright, abandoning even the memory of ever having lived some other life.

The only thing she had left was a distant, wavering memory. Isobelle's face, her voice. *I'll be there, when the moment comes.*

Gwen gasped and wrenched her mind away. She would not let the dragon take that from her too—and somewhere, in the last flickering recesses of her thoughts, she knew that to think of that last hope now, to use it to cling one breath longer to the edge of the cliff, might warn the dragon of whatever Isobelle meant to do.

So Gwen turned her mind away from hope with one last, wrenching effort, let go of the edge of the cliff, and fell.

IMAGINE A SHIP.

A single vessel, silver in the moonlight. An undulating sea of grass stretches all around it, in every direction. The little boat is entirely alone, drifting at the mercy of the currents.

Before it is a sea monster, wounded and full of rage and all the more dangerous for both these things. It moves, sinuous, toward the boat, as we watch from above.

That's going to be the best vantage point for what comes next.

Gwen is our silver ship, clad in armor made of ingenuity and courage. The dragon is our sea monster, centuries old, its history littered with the knights it has killed. And as Gwen abandons the last of herself on that moonlit sea of grass, it's clear there's only one way this ends.

... *Or is there?*

Lady Isobelle of Avington is still at large, after all.

Her torch flares to life, a tiny spark—a single guiding star in this great black sea of night, beckoning Gwen back home, to hope.

Nothing happens. Gwen is no more than a crumbling statue, her mind lost in the darkest of dreams. The great dragon slides toward her, with a low growl calling for her blood.

Isobelle's torch waves wildly, but still she draws no attention from either of them, even as she begins to run toward the girl she loves, a single shooting star, seen from above.

Is she too late? Is it too little? Will she be forced to watch, the way one does in a dream, running as fast as she can but never coming closer, too late to throw herself between Gwen and that great dark maw?

Perhaps not.

For oh, reader—you didn't think she came alone, did you?

One by one, they come from beneath the trees, women bearing torches of their own. One by one they kneel, hearts thumping and skin crawling, to jam their torches into the hard earth and strike their flints. The sparks fly, catching and blazing to life in bursts of orange and gold—distant lighthouses marking the shoreline in a great ring around the two combatants.

There is Hilde, fierce as the Viking warriors that lurk deep in her blood, screaming her defiance as she grabs for her flaming brand, and there is Jane, white with fear but never wavering, raising her torch before her like a shield, trembling but holding fast.

There is Sylvie, her own anger burning as bright as her flame, thrusting it up toward the sky. Braver than the man trying to claim her for his own, and made of stronger stuff.

Olivia is there, deadly and determined, nothing of the demure maid about her now as she lifts her torch skyward and faces the creature that would kill the ones she is here to protect.

There is Madame Dupont, her face set, her torch in one hand and her sword in the other, striding toward the danger from which she once ran. Watch as she reclaims the part of herself she thought it was too late to find again.

And they are not the only ones who have come.

Now we see Delia the hedge witch, her coven arrayed to either side, curving around the arc of the great circle the women have formed. With them stand the women of Aberfarthing, returned to their burned and broken home, pushing past their terror to stand in support of the one champion who rode out for them. Some weep as they raise their torches. Some are gaunt with grief, or diamond-hard with anger. None of them waver.

And there is Isobelle, their general, who has placed each of them just so. Who has rallied them and brought them together, and who raises her voice now, bellowing with a roar equal to the dragon's. "Forward!"

This is the oldest and the wiliest of the dragons—the one that has outlived all its fellows. The beast that has seen off the knights who went before, who took one of its deadly eyes, but fell before its baleful stare.

This creature could not be defeated with bravery alone.

But perhaps with *unity* . . .

As one, the women walk toward it, their hearts trying to leap free of their chests, their hands trembling, their faces set.

This is what it will take to defeat this last, great dragon. This is why it has never been done, until now.

This, reader, is women's work.

Now, see as the beast begins to turn its head, imagining itself challenged by a dozen other, smaller dragons. Hear the low rumble of momentary confusion as it tries to size up this new threat, instinct driving it to protect its territory against these interlopers.

Watch as the statue of a knight shakes her head, like she's coming out of a dream.

Hold your breath, as Gwen realizes that this is her moment. . . .

Chapter Forty-Nine

YOU WERE NEVER ALONE

Isobelle had half blinded herself with her own torch, waving it in desperate arcs that left white stripes dancing in her night vision, but she saw Gwen adjust her grip on her spear. Saw Achilles snort and paw at the ground—saw Gwen's weight shift.

I only need a moment, Gwen had said. But she could see the unsteadiness in Gwen's movements, the uneven balance of her seat in Achilles's saddle as she tried to recover from whatever the dragon's gaze had done to her. Isobelle's heart caught, sank, stuttered—and then leapt into hope once more.

Take your moment, she silently urged Gwen.

Gwen sat up and touched her heels to Achilles's flanks, her body weight shifting back as she raised the spear and hurled the ancient weapon with a cry of rage and effort that rang across the field.

An earth-shaking scream of fury and pain nearly knocked Isobelle flat, but as she fell to her knees, she looked up to see the spear drive deep into the creature's eye, the molten gold bursting and shrinking in around the metal shaft. Isobelle wanted to look away from the gruesome sight, but she could not stop staring until her eyes began to water—not until a ragged cry of triumph went up around the ring of torchbearers did Isobelle dare believe what she'd seen.

The creature was blind—the power of its paralytic eyes was gone.

Achilles blew hard, prancing backward, then wheeling away to canter across the field as the dragon thrashed, flailing with its long forearms and spraying a gout of raging flame into the sky. Gwen clung to Achilles's saddle, still staggered, gathering her wits—and the dragon turned blindly toward the sound of Achilles's hooves.

Isobelle dragged herself back to her feet, her torch no use as a distraction now the creature could no longer see. "Over here!" she cried, as the dragon threatened to turn toward Gwen.

"To me, you wicked thing!" called Jane, making up for her lack of conviction with sheer volume.

"We will rip your head off!" Hilde screeched, truly caught up in the blood of her ancestors now, on the verge of looking for a country to invade.

Gwen drew her sword, shifting her grip and letting the tip of the blade fall, her arm lax at her side. Isobelle's heart squeezed. Gwen's bad shoulder was in some kind of terrible pain, Isobelle could see that much. But before Isobelle could draw another breath, Gwen swung the sword, tightened her grip, and touched her heels to Achilles's sides. Then came the drum of Achilles's hooves as he pushed from a trot to a canter and up to a gallop.

"Fall back!" Isobelle cried, and as one the women began to retreat, the circle around the dragon growing once more.

Gwen had nearly won the Tournament of Dragonslayers, but even the best of knights only hit the other rider's shield sometimes. Achilles had charged endlessly through that orchard under Madame Dupont's eye, Gwen aiming for that dragonseye ring, missing more often than she hit.

Now, she had one chance, and one chance only, to finish the beast. For Gwen would have to ride close enough to the dragon to use her sword, and in doing so, she would give the dragon its opening to finish her with a single sweep of head or claw.

Gwen was lit by the moonlight, the pinpricks of the flaming torches reflected in her gleaming armor as though she were made of stars. She seemed to become part of the night sky itself, nature's answer to this unnatural beast from beneath the earth that spewed fire and killed for the love of it.

She came flying across the open field, her black hair streaming like a banner, white skin smeared with blood and dirt, steel luminous in the silver light.

Facing her was the dragon itself, all browns and bronzes and lurking flame, the color of dried blood and darkness. It had heard the thunder of Achilles's hooves and spread its wings wide, its head snaking toward her, swinging this way and that to pinpoint the origin of the sound.

Isobelle was vaguely aware she had stopped breathing—that she had lowered her torch until the tip rested on the cold earth at her feet. That she was whispering something, mouthing the words, her body rocking forward as if she were riding Achilles, too.

"Go, Gwen. *Go*."

She whispered the words again and again, like a prayer—like a spell she was casting, one she knew the others were casting, too.

And then Gwen was there, and she was rising up in her saddle, perfectly balanced in her stirrups and moving with the rhythm of Achilles's gait, both hands wrapped around the hilt of her sword.

The dragon roared and threw its head up, swiping at her with one great forefoot, tattered wing trailing as it raked its claws toward Achilles's rump. The horse dodged with a breathtaking leap, and Gwen braced one foot against his saddle and then *threw* herself at the dragon's throat.

For a moment she seemed to hang there, suspended in the darkness, her silver form lit by the moonlight as she flew at the great beast, its head thrown back to roar its fury to the sky.

And then she struck, the crash of her armor hitting scales thunderous even over the dragon's roar. Her sword wedged between two of the armor plates protecting the dragon's neck. The beast staggered in surprise, one of its arms crumpling beneath it and sending it crashing to the ground. Gwen threw her entire body weight onto the sword, and with a terrible, screeching crunch of blade on bone, the sword thrust home.

The dragon gave an awful, keening, bubbling roar as it thrashed once, wildly, threatening to toss Gwen aside—but she hung on, clinging grimly to the hilt of her sword, the blade buried in the armored throat. Then, with a terrible, gurgling spray of molten flame from the place where Gwen had driven her sword, the beast went still.

There was no sound at all except Isobelle's heart slamming in her rib cage. Her vision swam, but she found she could not so much as breathe, as paralyzed as Gwen had been when the beast's eye had found her.

Then a scream of pain rang out across the field, and before Isobelle's mind had even registered that it was Gwen's agony she was hearing, she broke into a run.

The burst of rolling liquid fire that had come from the dragon's mortal wound had lit several patches of grass ablaze, but Isobelle could see something else, a reddish-orange glow on the crumpled form by the dragon's body. Gwen wasn't clutching her sword anymore—she was rolling, crying out in pain, the dragon's death flames clinging like burning leeches to her armor.

Isobelle yanked off her cloak and threw herself down on top of Gwen, smothering the flames with the thick fabric, bunching it up to try to scrub some of the sticky, burning tar-like stuff away. Her fingers fumbled with the buckles of Gwen's armor, tossing piece after piece away, and she was glad she had learned how to do this after so many of Gwen's jousts.

Her fingertips encountered a patch of smoldering padding under the last piece, Gwen's right vambrace. She cried out as the heat burned her skin, though she didn't let go, grabbing the fabric and ripping it away. Some of the flame had gotten inside the joint of Gwen's armor, and a long, reddened, blistered strip of skin along her forearm explained Gwen's pained scream.

Now, shuddering and gasping for breath, Gwen lurched forward to wrap her good arm around Isobelle. Her grip was bruisingly tight, but Isobelle uttered not a word of protest. Instead, she wrapped her arms around Gwen's neck, clinging and mumbling incoherently.

When she pulled back to meet Gwen's eyes, she could see the other girl was half delirious with exhaustion, with pain—and with victory. Her face glowed in the moonlight.

"It's—it's dead, right?" Gwen panted, lips trembling, half trying to twist around to see.

Isobelle's eyes burned with tears and with the smoke rising from the body of the dragon behind them. "Yes, it's dead. You did it. It's over." She stroked Gwen's cheeks, her scorched fingertips stinging.

Isobelle pressed her lips to Gwen's temple. "It's okay, it's over."

Gwen shivered, pulling herself in against Isobelle, entirely unashamed to seek the comfort in her touch. "I couldn't have, without you," she murmured, her lips against Isobelle's collarbone. "We did it together. You, and me, and all of them . . . how . . . ?"

Isobelle stroked Gwen's hair, trying not to look down at the awful burn on Gwen's arm, which seemed redder and more brutally painful by the moment. "I told them where I was going. I don't think anyone could have stopped them all from coming, Gwen. You were never alone."

Gwen mumbled something into her skin. Isobelle caught only a few words, Gwen's voice quaking too badly from pain and adrenaline. ". . . knew you were out there . . ." was one of the phrases Isobelle heard. ". . . wouldn't let me . . . I was falling for so long . . . didn't want to die alone . . ."

Isobelle's heart squeezed, realizing Gwen was barely conscious, succumbing to the agony of her burned arm. Isobelle raised her head, desperate, about to cry out for help—when she realized the others were already coming toward them, a great circle of women who'd come to help defeat the dragon. Olivia was running, pulling her satchel of supplies off her back, Delia and a couple of the hedge witches on her heels.

The others were there, ready to carry them.

Gwen wasn't alone, and neither was Isobelle.

They never had been.

Chapter Fifty

NEVER SENDE A MANNE TO DO A WOMAN'S JOBBE

The sun rose over Darkhaven town, setting the awnings and tents of Market Day ablaze with color against the brilliant blue morning sky. In the fortnight since the dragon attack on the tournament, rebuilding efforts in the town were well underway. More than one resident had chosen to keep their soot-blackened stonework, anticipating being able to point to a spot for generations to come and claim, "See? This is where the dragonsfire struck." The thatch roofs all needed replacing, however, and teams from half a dozen nearby villages had come to assist in the effort before the onset of winter.

The forests around Darkhaven were all dressed in their best autumnal finery, and the crisp breeze brought the smells of fallen leaves to the market to mingle with the smells of frying batter, roasting meats, and spiced apples.

Gwen breathed deeply, struck by a memory. "I wondered, once, back before the tournament final, if I'd even be here to smell the changing of the seasons this year."

Isobelle's arm, linked through hers, tightened. Gwen could *feel* the force of her eyes boring into her. "That's awfully melodramatic, you know."

Gwen let out a snort, glancing down to find that she was,

indeed, being stared at by a pair of narrowed blue eyes. "Well, to be fair, you had just begged me to run away with you because you thought I was going to die, so if I was being melodramatic, I wasn't the only one."

The stare softened. "Hush. I am sensible and practical at all times. Oh, there's your father! Shall we go say hi?"

They were walking down the same well-worn slope where Gwen had first laid eyes on Isobelle, clad in her pinkest, most outrageous gown and flanked on both sides by other girls dressed to the teeth. Just ahead was her father's booth, though if Isobelle had not pointed it out, Gwen might have missed it entirely. Not a single flash of the booth, or of Amos, was visible through the throng of customers clustered about the place.

Gwen snuck a glance at the other side of the path. Her father's main rival, the blacksmith who favored flashy—and noisy—sword demonstrations to attract customers, was leaning against the wall with a thoughtful frown on his face as he glowered at the mob of people clamoring for Amos's figurines.

"He's busy," Gwen said finally, with a smile. "Fortunately, he has help. A couple of the women from Aberfarthing are still staying in Ellsdale, and the one who's been staying in my room has been helping him with sales so he can focus on doing what he loves."

Isobelle gave a dreamy little sigh. "If I were him, I'd rather make Sir Gwen figurines than horseshoes, too."

Gwen drew Isobelle on down the path, flustered by the tangle of emotions that always flickered to life in her when she heard that name and title.

She wasn't a knight. Lord Whimsitt had made that much clear, after Olivia, Sylvie, and the others had gotten Gwen and Isobelle back to Darkhaven just as dawn was breaking, the night of the battle against the dragon.

It had taken some time for the assembled lords and knights to grapple with the truth of what had taken place—that a girl, armed only with an ancient spear and the power of friendship—had done what none of them had dared even attempt. But after Whimsitt had dispatched several men to go investigate the battleground, and they'd come back visibly shaken to report that there was, indeed, the corpse of an *extremely* large dragon exactly where the ladies had said there would be . . . well.

When Whimsitt rather tentatively suggested that Gwen be returned to the jail "where she belonged," the instantaneous uproar from Isobelle, her friends, the Aberfarthing survivors, and more than a few of the knights threatened rather quickly to spill over into violence. Whimsitt had been forced to pardon Gwen for her "trespasses."

But when Isobelle had pointed out that Gwen ought to be hailed as the victor of the Tournament of Dragonslayers—after all, she had slain a *literal* dragon—Whimsitt had dug in his heels.

"She is not nobility," he retorted, face purpling. "And she is a *she*! And leaving all that aside, she entered the tournament under a false name, with false patents of nobility and lineage. She was never truly, properly entered into the tournament, so she cannot be the victor."

He would have gone on to hand Isobelle over to Orson, if Orson hadn't objected. His face set, not daring to look at Gwen at all, he'd simply demanded the tournament be declared a draw, null and void, with no victor at all. The prize money would go back into Isobelle's dowry, and he would lay no claim to her hand in marriage.

Of course, that meant neither Isobelle nor Gwen had any money of their own to spend anymore. Though they hadn't spoken about it, Gwen knew it weighed on Isobelle heavily, the knowledge that her wealth was still locked behind an ironclad gate that only marriage, to a man, would unlock for her.

But, for now, she and Isobelle were untouchable. And the name Sir Gwen seemed to be sticking.

The first few times Gwen had heard it, she'd bristled, annoyed that the world had decided to give her a man's title. But Isobelle had pointed out to her that there weren't any alternatives. There was no title for a knight who also happened to be a woman, and that by using the title of "Sir," the people of Darkhaven were, each of them, insisting on calling Gwen a knight even if the law didn't recognize her as such.

Isobelle gave a little cry of enthusiasm, tugging Gwen's thoughts back to the present. She slid her hand from Gwen's arm, took her hand, and dragged her along to a spot where Jane and Hilde were waving their arms to beckon them over.

Isobelle was careful to tug only on Gwen's left arm. Her right was still in a sling, at Olivia's insistence. The shoulder was certainly injured again—had probably never healed to begin with, Olivia had pointed out severely—but the burn was far worse than they'd realized that night on the field. Even with the aid of that lurid green ointment Olivia insisted on using, it was healing slowly. Gwen knew she would have a nasty scar there for the rest of her life.

But she was alive. She was alive, and so were the others who'd come to aid her. And so was Isobelle.

Hilde greeted them with a shout of pleasure, offering Isobelle the remains of the spiraled fried potato on a stick she was eating. "You must fill your stomach, ja? Jinna is reopening the tavern tonight, and it is important to eat before one drinks!"

The girls regaled them with the bits and pieces of news and gossip they'd gleaned from the market thus far, and Jane showed off a new tournament shirt she'd bought that featured stylized images of a knight and a dragon facing off with one another, and a line of text beneath it that read "Never Sende a Manne to Do a Woman's Jobbe."

Gwen's eyes wandered, searching the crowds. Isobelle, sensing her distraction, gave her hand a squeeze, and Gwen glanced down and asked, "Where is Sylvie?"

Isobelle eyed her sideways, and then flashed a smile at Jane and Hilde. "I'm peckish for a cheesecake on a stick—we'll catch up with you later!"

They hadn't gone far when Isobelle pulled Gwen into a makeshift alley between two stalls. "I'd meant to tell you. I saw her the other day with Olivia, who was taking measurements and cutting some fabric to make her some new dresses. I think that's probably where she is today—with Olivia."

Gwen's brow furrowed in confusion. "New dresses? But... why couldn't you say that in front of Hilde and Jane?"

Isobelle raised one eyebrow, eyes grave but lips quirked with the faintest of knowing smiles. "They were black dresses, Gwen. Mourning dresses."

Gwen bit her lip as the implications of *that* struck her. She'd just seen Sir Ralph the day before, alive and well. "Um..." she said slowly, feeling herself slip back into her old habit of stalling for time when trying to keep up with Isobelle's mercurial conversational talents. "Olivia... she doesn't *really* assassinate people, does she?"

Isobelle opened her eyes until they were very wide, and very innocent. "A lady would never ask such a direct, distasteful question, Gwen. I certainly never have." The eyes began to sparkle, just a little. "But, I mean, you're welcome to go ask her if you want."

Gwen gave a theatrical shudder. "I'd rather fight another dragon, thanks."

Isobelle laughed, but soon her amusement died away, and she gazed up at Gwen's face, her own thoughtful as she raised a hand to trace the shape of Gwen's cheek. The brush of her fingertips made Gwen shiver, and she could feel a flush rising to the spot where Isobelle's skin had touched hers.

"Are you all right?" Isobelle asked softly. "You've been quiet. You're not having nightmares still, are you?"

Gwen shook her head quickly, squeezing Isobelle's hand. She'd woken more than once to find Isobelle's anxious face bending over her in the dark, having come running from her room in response to Gwen's cries as she fought dragons in her dreams. "No, I just . . . I can feel it. The people love us right now because we saved them from the dragon, and Whimsitt has to go with it and pretend he's behind us to avoid them turning on him. He's a politician, and he's not stupid. But it's not going to last forever. I can see the way he looks at me when no one else can see him."

A part of Gwen quailed, weary and bitter, wondering if she would have to see that look on men's faces for the rest of her life, every time she stood up when they wanted her to fall fainting to the ground.

Isobelle's face sobered even more. "I've seen it, too," she admitted. "I guess some men can't forgive a woman who reveals them to be a fool in noble clothing."

"It's only a matter of time," Gwen said. Part of her wished she could just bury her worries, or at least keep them from Isobelle, because she hated seeing that worry reflected in those luminous eyes. But the rest of her knew that was foolish, even if it wasn't also unfair. Of the two of them, Isobelle stood a much better chance of strategizing their way through Lord Whimsitt's machinations. "A matter of time before we're not welcome here anymore. Somehow, I don't think we can rely on having a dragon pop out of the ground every time I need a public relations boost."

Isobelle's lips quirked, and she said, "When I was searching the castle archives for some loophole about my dowry, I did find something interesting." Her expression betrayed the tiniest flicker of sadness about her failure to find the loophole she was looking for. "Did you know that this county was originally called Drakhaven?"

Gwen felt her eyebrows rise. "As in, a haven for dragons?"

Isobelle laughed, lifted one of her shoulders in a shrug, and gazed whimsically up at her. "At some point, someone must have thought it'd be a good idea to do some rebranding. But, well, when it comes to dragons popping up, you never know."

Gwen found herself smiling, though she couldn't quite banish the chill that ran down her spine at the memory of Whimsitt's anger whenever he saw her. "I hate leaving our fate up to chance."

But far from looking afraid, Isobelle just looked thoughtful, her lips pursing slightly. Finally, she said airily, "By the way, I've had a letter from Astreta."

Gwen blinked at her. "The dancer, from the dragon bonfire? The one who danced the part of the knight?"

Isobelle nodded. "She and her troupe are performing in Direcrest, a few hours' ride north of here. People have been vanishing from the woods near the town, and others are telling tales of a large, shadowy creature lurking at the edges of the forest. No one in power there believes them."

Gwen's heart began to beat a little faster. "Another dragon?" she breathed.

Isobelle's eyes searched hers. "Or something else entirely. We thought dragons had been extinct for a hundred years. Who's to say there aren't more impossible things out there . . . people only you can help, battles only you can fight?"

Gwen's mouth had gone dry with a potent mix of anticipation and fear, and she didn't realize that her grip on Isobelle's hand had tightened until the other girl gave a squeak of protest. Gwen let her go with a startled oath and an apology, but Isobelle just laughed.

"I've always wanted to hit the road and travel, like a hero of old," she murmured. Instead of taking Gwen's hand again, Isobelle leaned up against her and slid her arms around Gwen's neck. "Setting up camp, managing provisions, going town to town questing for glory . . ."

Gwen could not resist Isobelle when she leaned in like that, and Isobelle knew it—she was watching Gwen with a smug smile, eyes sparking with amusement and no small amount of eager desire. So Gwen kissed her, and for a moment—quite a long moment, actually—she completely forgot what they had been talking about.

When Isobelle pulled away, fingertips toying with a lock of Gwen's hair, she asked, "What do you think?"

Gwen fought valiantly to recover her breath, and managed to say quite evenly indeed, "I don't know. Do you think they have cheesecake on a stick in Direcrest?"

Isobelle laughed, glanced out of the mouth of the makeshift market alley, and took Gwen's hand again. "We ought to eat our fill now, just in case. Better safe than sorry."

Gwen could not help but give a sharp huff of laughter. "And better free than safe," she added. Isobelle squeezed her hand, raised it to her lips, and then pulled her back out into the colorful chaos of the Darkhaven market.

Acknowledgments

And so we meet one more time, dear reader. Yes, I am still here after *The End*—I am your narrator, after all. My talents are many, and not all have been disclosed just yet.

Alas, our tale ends here for now—but not forever. Sir Gwen and Lady Isobelle have many adventures ahead, and this storyteller hopes you will join her for their next installment soon.

As *this* adventure concludes, however, thanks are due to sundry parties. The relation of any tale, particularly a true one such as this, is never a solitary endeavor.

First, my deepest gratitude to Lord and Lady Adams, and to Lady Christabel, for the use of their carriages in traveling the countryside to track down elements of this tale. They have been the most faithful journeying companions any storyteller could wish, for some ten years or more. One would particularly like to thank Lord Adams for his titular contribution.

This storyteller offers her thanks as well to Countesses Tara and Sarah, and the good folks of the Harpers' Guild for access to their archives, which contained many useful texts relating to dragons and their ilk. One could not be certain of getting this story right without their excellent assistance and faith.

In relation to the incident that took place during research in Lower Flushmire, which was entirely a misunderstanding, the aid of Baroness Liz and her team of diplomats from the Far Shore is deeply appreciated in avoiding a distinctly unpleasant evening in the stocks.

Marchioness Anna of Allunwin Castle and her kinsfolk are due thanks for the loan of particular items of clothing at a time of great need. As Lady Isobelle would be the first to say, the right dress is the key to any important endeavor.

This storyteller must also thank the mysterious Kristen of Pettitshire, of whom little is known, except that she wears a fascinating pin in her lapel, fashioned into the shape of an owl. One day, reader, perhaps you will find out what it signifies, but we have many leagues of story to cover first.

The researchers who have assisted this storyteller and her agents in hunting down specific references are too many to count, but Marquise Catherine is due particular thanks for secret information translated from French on more than one occasion. On this, I can say no more.

One also wishes to thank the many fine purveyors of books in shoppes and libraries for their unfailing support, most especially in the face of the dark magic that would silence them. They are witches all, of the most extraordinary power.

Many and varied scholars—including you, dear reader—have acted as patrons, and provided generous introductions or recommendations to others of their acquaintance. For this, one is eternally in your debt. Without the listener, the storyteller is nothing.

For magic both natural and alchemical, this humble storyteller owes a great debt of gratitude to certain covens in Asheville and Melbourne, as well as outlying agents, whose locations must not be disclosed for the sake of their safety. In particular, one wishes to thank the many brave and compassionate souls who live in or traveled to the misty blue mountains of North Carolina to aid this storyteller, and so many others, in recovering from a most devastating storm of unprecedented destruction.

Finally, this storyteller wishes to thank her tireless scribes and their noble families. These families are the last on the list—but never the least. Their deeds are many. They have smuggled these faithful scribes into stately homes, assisted them in uncovering society secrets, and outfitted them with necessary supplies. On one memorable occasion, they were involved in the payment of a ransom.

King Brendan and Princess Freya dealt with sundry duties and diplomacies, including entertaining the emissaries of the fae court—notoriously difficult to do. Today, and every day, Amie—one of this storyteller's scribes—would like to specify that she would charge a dragon for them.

And now, dear reader, we must part—but as I foreshadowed, we will see each other again. Until we do, my scribes wish you to know they share with my readers a regularly dispatched letter of news—a newsletter, if you will—which can be found by whispering the following passwords to any town crier in the know: amiekaufman.com or meaganspooner.com. In these dispatches, they will advise you of Gwen and Isobelle's latest exploits, and their own adventures in recording them.

So, dear reader, take care, do not mention my name in Lower Flushmire, and the best of luck on your own adventures until next we meet. Our heroes' next adventure will surely cast a spell on you. . . .